FLOWERS IN THE MIRROR

Li Ju-chen was born in 1763 in Ta-hsing in the Hopei province of China. He studied philology and established a reputation as an author on this subject. His varied interests included astrology, medicine, mathematics, music, rhetoric, poetry, calligraphy, painting, gardening and chess.

The Chinese version of this book, which has also been adapted as an opera, runs to more than 400,000 words and it is regarded as one of the most original works in Chinese literature, with no parallel in Western literature.

Lin Tai-yi was born in Peking. She is the author of nine books, including *Kampoon Street* and *The Lilacs Overgrow* which have been translated into ten languages. Miss Lin has lived extensively in Europe and the United States, where she taught Chinese at Yale University. She is married to Lai Ming (author of *A History of Chinese Literature*), and they have a son and a daughter.

D1108652

'The *Ching Hua Yuan* (*Flowers in the Mirror*) stands in a class by itself among the more outstanding Chinese novels. Clothed in the form of a book of travels to strange countries, it offers the author, Li Ju-chen, a chance for displaying his unique, refreshing ideas and satirical comments on human nature. In this sense, it is like *Gulliver's Travels*.'

Lin Yu-tang

Li Ju-chen

FLOWERS IN THE MIRROR

Translated from the Chinese
Ching Hua Yuan
and edited by
Lin Tai-yi

An Arena Book

Published by Arrow Books Limited
62-65 Chandos Place, London WC2N 4NW

An imprint of Century Hutchinson Ltd

London Melbourne Sydney Auckland
Johannesburg and agencies throughout
the world

This translation first published in Great Britain
by Peter Owen Ltd 1965
Arena edition 1985

Translation © Lin Tai-yi 1965

Printed and bound in Great Britain by
Guernsey Press Co. Ltd., Guernsey, C.I.

ISBN 0 09 935980 4

UNESCO COLLECTION OF REPRESENTATIVE WORKS

CHINESE SERIES

This book has been accepted in the Chinese
Translations Series of the United Nations Edu-
cational, Scientific and Cultural Organization
(UNESCO)

Introduction

Li Ju-chen was born in 1763 in Ta-hsing, Hopei province in China and probably died in 1830. At a time when passing the Imperial Civil Service Examinations was the prerequisite for an official career, and an official career was the only way of living open to scholars, Li would not learn how to write *pa ku wen*, a fixed style of composition which was one of the requirements of the Examinations, because he objected to its form. Thus, he failed to pass any but the county level of the Imperial Examinations, and like Tang Ao, the hero of his novel, was only a *hsiu-tsai,* or scholar of the lowest rank. However, if *Flowers in the Mirror* reflects the author's philosophy of life, it is easy to see that he was a man who had too much sense of humour, too much common sense, and who saw through the hypocrisy of society too quickly to have been bothered by it. Certainly, he could have written *pa ku wen* if he had wanted to, as his book demonstrates, and he was a scholar of the lowest rank probably by choice. At one point in his novel, one of his characters cries, 'My feet have enjoyed the kind of freedom which scholars who are not interested in official careers enjoy! How can you think of binding them?' Li was a freedom-loving soul and an individualist, and his book contains many jibes at scholars who had no independent judgment of life, for all their erudition.

Li's brother Ju-huang became an official in the Salt Bureau in Haichow in Kiangsu province in 1782, and Ju-chen, at the age of nineteen and already a widower, went to live with him, and stayed for almost twenty years. Ju-huang supported his younger brother almost all his life, and did not seem to have grudged it. In Haichow, Li Ju-chen became the pupil of one Ling Ting-shen, who first interested him in philology. For one brief period in 1801, Li Ju-chen went to work in the Honan provincial government as an assistant to the magistrate, and there, had a part in building dykes to prevent the flooding of the Yellow River. We do not know how good a dyke-builder he was, but it's a fair chance that while there, he did not try very hard to advance his position in government. When *Li's Phonetics* was published in 1805, it was mentioned in a preface written by a friend that the author was 'about to assume an official post in Chungchow'. But in 1815 when a revised edition was published, there was no mention of the post, perhaps because it failed to materialize after all.

Li's was a very active mind, and that he did not support himself or have an official post did not mean that he was idle. During the Ching Dynasty, China was ruled by the Manchus, who persecuted Chinese scholars. In the reign of Emperor Chien Lung (1736-1795), an innocent remark about history could lead to a scholar and his entire clan being wiped out, if the remark were construed to be a slur upon the sovereign. Scholars took to doing research work as the safest occupation, and at a time when philology and exegetical work on the Confucian classics were the vogue of the *literati*, Li Ju-chen made a name for himself for his scholarship. His keen mind led him to many other fields, and he had expert knowledge of astrology, medicine, mathematics, music, rhetoric, poetry, calligraphy, painting, gardening, chess and parlour games, all of which contributed to the writing of *Flowers in the Mirror*.

The book is essentially a social commentary and a human satire. But it is also an historical romance, a fairy tale, an allegory, and in its original form, a built-in anthology of expertise in the various fields of the author's interest, was linked together by sheer outrageous invention. Certainly, it is one of the most original works in Chinese literature, and there is nothing like it in Western literature either, unless we think of a work which has the combined nature of *Grimm's Fairy Tales, Gulliver's Travels, Aesop's Fables* and the *Odyssey*, with *Alice in Wonderland* thrown in for good measure. Today, *Flowers in the Mirror* takes its place with perhaps a dozen other works in the domain of the classical Chinese novel, although to call it a novel is perhaps a mistake.

The stuff of Popular Taoism forms the background of the story. But unlike other Taoist narrative writers, who presented the supernatural and miraculous in support of their faiths, Li wrote a novel of fantasy to present his own unique vision of life.

The story is set in the reign of the notorious Empress Wu Tse-tien (who reigned from 684-705) in the Tang Dynasty, who usurped the throne from her own son, Emperor Tang Chung-tsung.

Power-mad and extremely conscious of her 'unique destiny' as the first 'Female Emperor' of China, Empress Wu, after several cups of wine too many one evening, orders all the flowers on earth to be in bloom by the next morning. The flower-spirits in heaven, afraid to offend the earthly ruler, obey her. For doing so, the Fairy of a Hundred Flowers and her ninety-nine subordinates are banished to earth to live in the 'bitter sea of transmigration' until they have done their penance, and may go back to heaven again.

The father of the incarnation of the Fairy of a Hundred Flowers is Tang Ao, who is stripped of his scholarly rank by the Empress when he is suspected of having had a part in plotting rebellion against her. Disappointed, Tang Ao decides to 'free himself from the coil of mortal strife' which 'bind the soul to the body', and become an Immortal by 'cultivating Tao'. He sets out with his brother-in-law Merchant Lin by junk for foreign parts after he has been told by a dream-spirit that his destiny lies overseas. In the course of the journey, he finds a dozen of the flower-spirits incarnate, and helps them out of their difficulties. In doing these acts of charity, Tang Ao becomes eligible to become an Immortal, and when the junk arrives at the fairy mountain of Little Penglai, he disappears.

It is the account of this journey, which takes the travellers to places like the Country of Gentlemen, the Country of Women, the Country of Intestineless People, the Country of Sexless People, the Country of Two-faced People and many others, which is the most celebrated part of the book, for here the writing is at its wittiest and most original, and the author gives vent to his aspirations for an ideal society. Among other things, Li Ju-chen was a champion of equal rights for women at a time when feudal society forbade Chinese women to mingle with men or share their activities, and *Flowers in the Mirror* is, indeed, a strong plea for recognition of the equality of men and women. In his day, this was a revolutionary idea.

The second half of the book deals with how Tang Ao's daughter goes to Little Penglai to look for him, and how the young ladies who Tang Ao found overseas, together with the other incarnations of the flower-spirits, took part in the 'Imperial Examinations for Women', and with their husbands and brothers, rose and overthrew Empress Wu's rule, and restored Emperor Tang Chung-tsung to the throne.

I have briefly outlined the story of this novel here with the thought of giving some assurance to the reader, for there are some obvious structural flaws in the work which no editor can overcome. For instance, after introducing the incarnate of the Fairy of a Hundred Flowers, we do not hear about her again until half the book, or Tang Ao's trip overseas, is over.

In preparing this manuscript for Unesco, I have tried to render a version which will appeal to the general Western reader. The original book has some 400,000 words, of which I have deleted most of the passages which have to do with classical texts and discussions of the Chinese language, dissertations on history, poetry, phonetics, etc., which can be of little interest to the non-specialized reader.

Where necessary, I have written linking material (indicated by indentation) which is intended to flow smoothly from and back into the narrative, giving a synopsis of what happened. In other places, I have compressed dialogue into straight narrative where it served only to carry the story forward mechanically in question and answer form, and was therefore cumbersome. Of the thirty-three foreign countries which Tang Ao and his friends visited, however, the author himself devoted only a paragraph or two to some of them.

I have given the material new chapter divisions, and this translation is the extract of the entire original work, which has a hundred chapters.

Li Ju-chen intended to write a sequel to the novel, but never did. At the end of the story he explains that when he had written these hundred chapters, he showed the manuscript to some of his friends 'who were suffering from anxiety and depression'; they burst into fits of laughter after reading it, and regained their good humour. They urged the author to have the book published without waiting for the rest, and Li complied, since he had already been working on the book for fifteen years. Three years after the book was published, he died.

In translating this novel, I have tried to keep to the spirit in which the author wrote it. While much of it was written in deadly satire, there are parts also where the author was simply having a lot of fun. In this novel where history and fantasy take place side by side, I feel that it is the character Merchant Lin, who brooks no nonsense from mortal or Immortal, and takes events natural and supernatural equally in his stride, who gives the book its unique balance. The reader is advised to take what comes in the same spirit, and let the chips fall where they may.

The fastidious reader may like to think that Tang Ao's voyage took him from the South China coast to the Pescadores, the Luzon and Indonesian islands, and perhaps as far as New Zealand, Tahiti and Fiji. We know that sea-going junks are capable of travelling long distances, and all the countries Tang Ao visited were islands, which happen to abound in that geographic area. The fairy mountain Kunlun where the Western Queen Mother resides was traced by some historians to the Hindu Kush, and we know that the rebel Shu Ching-yeh tried to flee to Korea, but was decapitated before he could do so. In this novel, some of his family were found near the waters of the Country of Scholars. However, as far as we know, flowers never all bloomed at the same time, and no such journey was ever made by a man like Tang Ao.

At the end of the book, I have prepared a section of Notes which may be helpful to the reader.

The full title of the book in Chinese is 'The Destinies of the Flowers in the Mirror', the word 'mirror' being meant to convey the idea that life is an illusion.

I would like to thank Dr Chen Yuan, Mr Daniel L. Milton and Dr Cyril Birch for their help in making this translation possible. The edition from which this translation was made was published by the Yatung Library in Shanghai in 1932.

Lin Tai-yi

Hong Kong
1964

A Note on Popular Taoism

The understanding of Taoism given in this novel is the religion of Popular Taoism.

Taoism as a philosophy may be divided roughly into three stages, the original stage, the stage of development, and the stage of Popular Taoism, sometimes called the stage of degeneration. The philosophy originated with Laotse, who was born in 604 B.C., and whose teachings are preserved in the much-translated *Tao Teh Ching*. Condensed into a single phrase, his philosophy of life was 'Follow nature'. He concluded that behind the manifold workings of Nature, there exists an ultimate reality which in its essence is unfathomable, yet manifests itself in laws of unfailing regularity. When one speaks of 'seeking Tao' or 'cultivating Tao', it means following the path of nature, in this purest sense.

Chuangtse and Liehtse (Lieh Yu-kou) were two writers who were largely responsible for developing Laotse's philosophy. Both these writers, who lived in the Chanquo period (403–221 B.C.), or about two hundred years after Laotse, elucidated Laotse's teachings by writing allegorical tales and parables. In Liehtse's book, stories are to be found which hinted at the possibility of transcending natural laws. But he also said, 'That which has life must by the law of its being come to an end, and the end can no more be avoided than the living creature can help being born. So that he who hopes to perpetuate his life and to shut out death is deceived in his calculations.'

In the beginning of Han dynasty (206 B.C.–A.D. 219), Prince Huainan promoted a new eclectic Taoism and was responsible for attracting to it a large following. Taoism's influence became so great that it vied with Confucianism in popularity, and a prime minister, Tsao Tsan, was ready to practise a policy of government based on the concept of 'value quietism and the people will govern themselves', in the manner of the mythical Yellow Emperor, who is described in Liehtse's book. A host of minor writers came into being, who were preoccupied with presenting tales of the supernatural and the miraculous in support of their faith and incorporated a mass of folklore and mythology into the religion. Some of them tried to pass off their work as that of the ancient masters.

11

This was the rise of Popular Taoism. As with Confucianism, the line cannot be drawn exactly where philosophy ends and religion begins. But in the case of Taoism, what started out as allegorical tales and fables to illustrate a philosophy began to be taken for real. By the 4th century A.D. Taoism had developed into a folk religion with all the attendant miracles and superstitions which are pre-requisites of a religion if it is to have popular appeal, and Taoism as a philosophical system had just about run its course. In the 5th century the religion absorbed many features of Mahayana Buddhism.

It is interesting to note that in Taoism as in Buddhism, the division between ordinary mortals and those endowed with super-natural qualities is not clear. While ordinary beings may become Immortals and Spirits, the Spirits on the other hand are endowed with very human qualities indeed, and the idea of holiness is seldom attached to the gods. We do not find the hush and the air of sanctity in temples which we find in cathedrals and churches. Monks and nuns are not held in high regard by society because they are poor. We continue to ply our gods with sacrificial offerings of food and money and the creature comforts of life, although the gods are supposed to have none of the vanities and cravings of mortals.

This is a paradox, and it has perhaps come about because the Chinese are really religious believers only in this human world. It is revealing to note that the highest ideal held out to human beings in Popular Taoism is to become an Immortal; and although a person becomes an Immortal by freeing himself from the selfish cravings which bind the spirit to the body, the Immortal retains all the qualities of the living after illusory symptoms of death appear, when the body is in a pupal state leading to perfection. When the state of perfection has been reached, its occupant can travel at will through the universe, and enjoy the pleasures of the table and all the advantages of perfect health!

The man who was largely responsible for the application of the term 'degenerate Taoism' to the religion was Chang Taoling. Chang rose during the rebellious days which preceded the fall of Han dynasty and proved himself to be a commercial genius who knew how to capitalize on mass psychology. The desire for longevity had always appealed to the Chinese mind, and Chang 'sold' his religion by inventing a written charm to ward off evil spirits and practised alchemy in the search for the philosopher's stone. He was supposed to have received a mystic treatise from Laotse himself by means of which he was able to compound the elixir of life. A vision directed him to a stone in which he found the writing of the Three Perfect Emperors and an ancient book of rites. By dint of self-discipline, he was supposed to have acquired power over the elements. Legend has it that he rode on a tiger and brandished a magic sword with which he vanquished the 'Five Poisonous Animals'. He captured them and put them in the vessel in which he was distilling the elixir of life. The animals yielded their venom, which contributed to form the 'true elixir'. At the age of a hundred and twenty-three, Chang swallowed the elixir and ascended to the heavens and became 'immortal'.

The title 'Master of Heaven', which was granted to Chang Taoling by imperial decree in the year 424, made him the Taoist Pope, with the power to grant titles to Taoist priests. The title was hereditary, and the sixty-third Master of Heaven is the present incumbent. He escaped to Hong Kong from his palace in the Dragon-Tiger Mountains of Kiangsi Province when the Communists took over in 1950. The gentleman, however, had left behind the magic sword of Chang Taoling and other heirlooms and properties for practising magic.

Today, Popular Taoism is a romantic religion which has many adherents in Taiwan and Hong Kong. It is rich in folklore and mythology, and its religious festivals held to celebrate the birthday of this or that god or goddess bring to life legendary characters and myths. The temples are crowded with people strewing orange peel and melon seeds, the young men are on the alert for good-looking girls; roast pig and chicken and wine is offered in sacrifice. A rousing good time is had by all, and one has the unquiet feeling that the Taoists are actually celebrating the enjoyment of the senses instead of the opposite! It would be wrong for the Westerner to think that we take it very seriously.

This form of Taoism is the background for this novel. Thus, when the character Tang Ao speaks of 'acquiring Tao', it is shown that he must first do so many 'acts of charity'. However, Li Ju-chen borrowed the features of Popular Taoism primarily to shed light upon his own vision of life and as a humorist, and perhaps a fatalist, could not have been a believer in Popular Taoism himself. If he was a Taoist, it was in the original sense of the philosophy, and in this novel, anecdotes are to be found in which he illustrates some of the mystic concepts of Taoism in allegorical form, in the fashion of Liehtse, while he demonstrates impatience with the rituals which accompany any form of religion. For further explanation of Taoism, see *Notes*.

L.T.

The Cast

Tang Ao
 his wife Mistress Lin
 their daughter Little Hill (Daughter of Tang)
 their son Little Summit

Tang Min (Tang Ao's brother)
 his wife Mistress Shih

Merchant Lin (Mistress Lin's brother)
 his wife Mistress Lu
 their daughter Pleasant
 his mother-in-law Mistress Chiang

Old Tuo, the helmsman

THOSE WHO WERE FOUND OVERSEAS

Red Lotus (daughter of Lo Pinwang, a leader of the Rebellion)
 her brother Young Lo

Flowering Maple
 her mother Mistress Liang
 her brother Brilliant

Scarlet Dogwood
 her brother Jade
 her father Yin Yuan

Red Rose

Purple Lily
 her mother Mistress Tsu

Purple Cherry
 her brother Warrior
 her mother Mistress Wan

Marsh Orchid

Beautiful Hibiscus
    her cousin Young Shu (son of Shu Ching-yeh, a leader of the
        Rebellion)

Fragrant Angelica

Sweet Asarum (Fragrant Angelica's cousin)
    her brother Select
    her mother Mistress Hsuen

Melody Orchid

Orchid Fragrance

Flowerlike, 'Crown Prince' of the Country of Women

SOME OF THOSE WHO LIVED IN THE KINGDOM ON EARTH

Little Spring
Phoenix-in-Flight } Old Tuo's nieces

Purple Silk, Little Hill's neighbour
    her brother Cliff

Wise Maxim, daughter of the Ninth Prince
    her brother the White Prince
    Ultimate Emptiness (Mistress Chi), who took care of her

Honeybush, eldest son of Governor Wen Yin

Prince's Feather, eldest son of Governor Chang Ken

THE ACTUAL HISTORICAL FIGURES

Empress Wu Tse-tien

Princess Taiping, her daughter

Emperor Chung-tsung, Empress Wu's son

Imperial Concubine Shangkuan Waner

Shu Ching-yeh
Lo Pinwang } leaders of the Rebellion

The above are some of the people who are involved in the
romance of *Flowers in the Mirror*, not to mention the Fairies
who reside at Kunlun and Little Penglai Mountains. For a list of
the young ladies who took part in the Examinations, and the
families of Governors Wen Yin and Chang Ken, please consult
Notes at the back.

Of the great mountains under heaven, apart from the Kunlun, where the Western Queen Mother resides, there are known to be three in the islands overseas; the Penglai, the Fangchang, and the Yingchow. All are mountains of great height, far away and difficult to climb. In the *Historical Record* it is said that these are the gathering places of spirits and fairies, and in both *Shih Yi Chi* and *Po Wu Chih* are passages describing the fabulous scenery and extraordinary treasures to be found there, the flowers which are in bloom all the year round, the grass which is green throughout the seasons, and the magic fruit, divine plants, and precious grain.

It is said that on the Cliff of Hard Luck on Penglai Mountain, in the Cave of Beauty, there lived for a long time the Fairy of a Hundred Flowers, who was in charge of all the flowers on earth.

On the third day of the third month one year, the air was filled with circling clouds and purple mists, all going in the western direction towards Kunlun Mountain. It was the Western Queen Mother's birthday, and the fairies and spirits, flying on clouds, were on their way to her birthday party. The Fairy of a Hundred Flowers, who was taking a gift of hundred-flower nectar, was also on her way with her friends, the Fairy of a Hundred Plants, the Fairy of a Hundred Fruits, and the Fairy of a Hundred Grains.

They had not been on their way for long when there came a blinding flash of red light ten thousand feet high from the Palace of the Big Dipper, and from the middle of it stepped a beautiful girl who was holding a writing brush in her right hand and a dipper in her left. Riding on a rainbow-coloured cloud, she also flew in the direction of Kunlun Mountain.

'That looks like the wife of the Star of Literature,' said the Fairy of a Hundred Grains. 'Isn't it extraordinary that the Star of Literature should have a wife?'

'What's extraordinary about it? These spirits are capable of infinite variety,' said the Fairy of a Hundred Flowers. 'But maybe it isn't his wife, but himself, and something extraordinary is about to take place on earth, so he has for some reason assumed a female human form.'

'Whoever it is, by the way she is turned out, it looks as though something extraordinary were going to happen indeed!'

'Well, the Star of Literature is in charge of literary affairs on earth,' said the Fairy of a Hundred Flowers, 'and the Palace of the Big Dipper has been sending off a lot of red flashes lately, so I suppose some important literary event is going to take place on earth.'

'Ah, even if we are fortunate enough to be present when it happens, what if it turns out to concern the literary destiny of men? What humiliation it will be for the fair sex!' said the Fairy of a Hundred Flowers.

'I wouldn't be too sure of that,' said the Fairy of a Hundred Plants. 'If the Star of Literature has anything to do with it, isn't it significant that he has assumed a female form? It could be that the literary event concerns women, and not men.'

'That may be,' said the Fairy of a Hundred Flowers. 'Still, if it has nothing to do with us, wouldn't it be just like admiring flowers in the mirror, and the moon's reflection in the water?'

'How can you be sure that it has nothing to do with us?' said the Fairy of a Hundred Plants. 'Is it mere chance that we should have an apprehension of what is going to happen now? But anyway, there is no use guessing about something which may not happen for years. We had better be getting along to the party.'

On their way, the Fairies met four spirits. One had a green face, sharp pointed teeth, and green hair with a golden band around it, and wore an onion-green robe. Another had a red face, sharp pointed teeth and red hair with a golden band around it and wore a red robe. The third was all black, and the fourth all yellow. Each bore a rare gift of some sort for the Western Queen Mother.

'I've seen those four at the Western Queen Mother's birthday parties,' said the Fairy of a Hundred Flowers, 'but I cannot think which mountain and which cave they are from.'

The Fairy of a Hundred Plants said, 'The one in green is in charge of the furry animals on earth and is called the Unicorn Spirit, or the Spirit of a Hundred Animals. The one in red is in charge of the feathered animals on earth and is called the Phoenix Spirit, or the Spirit of a Hundred Birds. The one in black is in charge of the shellfish and is called the Spirit of a Hundred Crustaceans, and the one in yellow is in charge of the scaly animals and is called the Spirit of a Hundred Scaly Animals.'

After them came many other fairies and spirits, young and old, such as the Star of Good Fortune, the Star of Happiness, the Star of Longevity, the Star of Wealth, the Star of Prosperity, the Spirit of the Forest, the Scarlet Child, and the Golden Infant. All were heading for the party on winds and clouds.

Soon they arrived at Kunlun and converged upon the Fairy Pond, where they gave their presents to the attendants, and after bowing to the Western Queen Mother, proceeded to their places at the banquet table.

The Western Queen Mother was seated at the very centre, with the Lady Yuan, the Weaving Maid, Maku, and the Lady of the Moon beside her. As the guests seated themselves, they were each given a peach, which was a symbol of longevity and the Western Queen Mother thanked them all for coming.

As succulent dish followed succulent dish, and ambrosia followed nectar, the sound of the fairies and spirits making merry carried far into the clear, windless sky. There was singing and dancing, too, and after a while, the Lady of the Moon said, 'What a wonderful time we are having! But we have all seen fairies and spirits dance and sing before. Now I have long heard that birds can sing and animals dance. I wonder if we could prevail upon the Spirit of a Hundred Birds and the Spirit of a Hundred Animals to show us?'

'We are much honoured by your suggestion,' said the Spirit of a Hundred Birds and a Hundred Animals. 'However, we are afraid that our attendants are clumsy and unrehearsed, and their performance will offend the Western Queen Mother.'

'It is all in fun,' said the Western Queen Mother with a smile. 'What does it matter?'

Whereupon the Spirit of a Hundred Birds told his attendants to follow Scarlet Phoenix and Green Phoenix, and proceed to the Fairy Pond and bow to the Western Queen Mother. The Spirit gave the order, and lo and behold! the Scarlet Phoenix and Green Phoenix and the others all turned around and assumed their earthly forms!

The attendants of the Spirit of a Hundred Animals followed one of their leaders called Unicorn Child to the Fairy Pond, and as each passed before the Western Queen Mother, making his bow, the Spirit of a Hundred Animals gave the order, and each one, too, assumed its earthly form. Tigers, leopards, rhinoceri, elephants and deer began to cavort and dance, and birds of all kinds sang, each vying to do better than the next.

The Western Queen Mother was delighted, and ordered her attendants to serve hundred-flower nectar to everyone.

The Lady of the Moon raised her wine cup to the Fairy of a Hundred Flowers and said, 'Now that birds are singing and animals dancing, why don't you order your flowers to bloom as well? Wouldn't it make the party even merrier?'

Everyone thought that this was a wonderful idea and urged the

Fairy of a Hundred Flowers to do so and make it an unforgettable party.

But the Fairy of a Hundred Flowers was worried, and said, 'What a predicament the Lady of the Moon has put me in! You see my flowers must follow a schedule and cannot simply be ordered to bloom as animals and birds can be ordered to sing and dance. Before every flower blooms on earth it must first receive the approval of the Deity. The Fragrant Jade Maiden has to plan everything to the last detail a month in advance, such as the number of petals and the shade of colouring. She is a genius and thinks of endless original designs. That is why there is so much variety, so that among plum blossoms we have the white blossom with the green calyx and also the vermilion variety, and double or single petalled lotuses and even twin blossoms growing from a single stem, not to mention the different kinds of orchids in the spring and chrysanthemums in the autumn. Every leaf and every blossom is determined in advance, and while in bloom (in heaven) the Supervisor of Flowers checks them and notes the improvements which are to be made. The flowers which blossom according to design are ordered to bloom on earth in private gardens and choice spots, where they are given care and nourishment and clean water, so that poets may sing their praises, and people enjoy them. The flowers which do not blossom the way they should are brought before the Magistrate and punished according to the severity of their offence. The serious offenders are ordered to bloom near official buildings at the harbours (where traffic is heaviest) to be tormented by people and trampled upon by horses' hooves and wheels, and splashed by mud. The less severe offenders are beset by butterflies and bees and rain and frost. The minor offenders are ordered to deep mountains and lonely valleys to burgeon and wilt with no one to admire them. This is the kind of work I am responsible for, and I dare not take liberties with it. How can I suddenly ask all flowers to bloom at the same time?'

After hearing this, the Lady of the Moon did not insist, but Aunt Wind, who was a close friend of the Lady of the Moon, had never been a friend of the Fairy of a Hundred Flowers. Now she felt called upon to express her opinion.

She said: 'According to you, the rules of heaven are never broken. How then do you explain that the plum blossom, that finest of flowers, blooms on Ta Yu Mountain in October, and elsewhere in spring? And for all the fuss and bother which go into tending them, how do you explain that the Taoists can make them blossom at will? Aren't you perhaps taking things a trifle too seriously? And all this talk about the supervision of flowers being so strict! How do you account for the fact that the peony and the green-peach blossom may be induced to bloom in winter if given warmth and special nourishment? I maintain that the matter is in your hands for you to decide at will. Now since the Lady of the Moon has expressed the wish to see all flowers bloom at once, you should not refuse. I shall help by blowing a few gentle breezes. Don't be afraid. The Western Queen Mother is witness, and if there is any trouble later on with the Jade Emperor, I will share the responsibility.'

The Fairy of a Hundred Flowers knew that she was in a dilemma. However she smiled and said, 'Of course you realize that temperature and terrain influence the blossoming of flowers. So it isn't extraordinary that the plum blossom should bloom on Ta Yu Mountain earlier than elsewhere. And how can I answer for Taoist magic? As for forcing flowers to bloom through artificial means, I cannot be held responsible for that, either. But as you yourself must surely know, the seasons must be respected. You would not blow a wintry blizzard in the warm season. And the Lady of the Moon knows that it is impossible for a full moon to shine upon the blue sky and green sea every night and not wax and wane. But would you like me to order the Peach Blossom and the Almond Blossom to show their best blooms and sing and dance for you?'

'Why trouble yourself?' the Lady of the Moon replied sarcastically. 'There are peach and almond blossoms everywhere just now. I only made the suggestion because I wanted the Western Queen Mother to enjoy herself. But since you are so afraid to trouble the spirits in your charge, I won't press the matter any further. Only why assume such airs and make such an issue out of a very simple matter?'

Now the Fairy of a Hundred Flowers could not contain herself. 'I beg you pardon!' she cried. 'Of course I am only a small and cowardly fairy, inferior to you in every way. I do not have a beautiful palace, and I don't possess the nectar of immortality. But since I am so worthless and inferior, how dare I go against the rules of heaven? I would not order all flowers to bloom at once even if the earthly ruler ordered me to do so unless the Deity agreed to it. I have no choice but to refuse your suggestion!'

'Then never mind!' cried the Lady of the Moon angrily, and embarrassed because the Fairy of a Hundred Flowers had implied that she had stolen the nectar of immortality. 'There is no need to become malicious, is there?'

The Weaving Maid tried to make peace between them. 'Now you two have always been friends,' she said. 'Why quarrel like this and spoil the party?' and the Lady Yuan added, 'The Western Queen Mother has already shown great patience, but aren't you being very rude? If this comes to the hearing of the Deity, I am afraid neither of you will be invited to attend any more parties.'

But the Lady of the Moon said, 'The Fairy of a Hundred Flowers said just now that she would not order all flowers to bloom at the same time even if the earthly ruler wished it, unless she had the Deity's permission. What if hundreds of years from now an earthly ruler does command all flowers to bloom at the same time, and flowers do so without the Deity's consent? How should the Fairy of a Hundred Flowers be punished? Let us make it perfectly clear now in the presence of the Western Queen Mother and all the senior spirits and fairies.'

'If that should happen,' said Maku playfully, 'what about making the Fairy of a Hundred Flowers sweep the floor of the Moon Palace for three years?'

'What earthly ruler of the nine continents and four seas who rules on behalf of the Deity would turn the principles of Yin and Yang upside down?' cried the Fairy of a Hundred Flowers, 'unless the Lady of the Moon goes down to earth one day and becomes the ruler! Barring that, I shall willingly go to earth to suffer transmigration in the rimless ocean of births and deaths, if I should ever be so muddle-headed as to order all flowers to bloom at the same time.'

The Fairy of a Hundred Flowers had hardly finished speaking when the Star of Literature raised her writing brush, and made a dot on the Fairy of a Hundred Flowers' forehead, and left the Fairy Pond in a flash of red light.

The Lady of the Moon was going to answer back, but the Weaving Maid said hurriedly, 'Now look, the Star of Literature has already put her mark on the Fairy of a Hundred Flowers, and left in anger. If you keep on quarrelling and spoiling our pleasure, I am afraid the Western Queen Mother will soon be ordering all of us to leave.'

When the party was over, the Western Queen Mother presented the guests with fruit and syrup, and the fairies and spirits thanked her and made their bows and went away.

Soon, the Fairy of a Hundred Flowers and her friends forgot their chagrin, and returned to their caves in Penglai.

Day followed day, and year followed year. When the Fairies were idle, they played chess together. So time passed, no one knew how long.

One day it was winter, and there was little the Fairy of a Hundred Flowers had to do. So she asked the Peony Spirit and the

Orchid Spirit to mind her cave, and went visiting. But the Fairy of a Hundred Plants was not at home, and she could not find the Fairy of a Hundred Fruits or the Fairy of a Hundred Grains either. Just as she was starting back to her own cave, it began to snow, and Maku, whom she had not seen for a long time, came along. So the Fairy of a Hundred Flowers went back with Maku to the latter's cave. Maku ordered her attendants to bring wine and food, and the two began to play chess as the snow fell outside.

It was then that, unknown to the Fairy of a Hundred Flowers, the supreme ruler on earth issued an order for all flowers to bloom at the same time.

If the reader wants to know how this came about, please turn to the next chapter.

In fact, the ruler on earth at this time was no man at all, but a woman, Wu by surname, Chao by name, who called herself Tsetien, mother of Emperor Tang Chung-tsung whom she had deposed, and the spirit of the Heart-Moon Fox incarnate.

It came about this way :

The Emperors Tang Tai-tsu and Tang Tai-tsung were originally ministers in the Suei dynasty (589–617 A.D.) who usurped the throne of Emperor Yang, and established the Tang dynasty (618–905 A.D.) by killing, pillaging, and committing atrocities and debaucheries.

When Emperor Yang arrived at the nether world, he put his case against the House of Tang before the spirits and demanded justice. After considering the evidence, the spirits of the nether world reported to the Jade Emperor, who decided that Emperor Yang must be avenged. However, instead of decreeing that he should be reincarnated on earth to avenge himself, the Jade Emperor decided that an evil spirit should be sent to earth and let loose upon the House of Tang, and let things run their natural course. Thus it came about that the Spirit of the Heart-Moon Fox was ordered to be born on earth, and eventually to become a 'female emperor', thus confounding the principles of Ying and Yang, and settle the score with the Tang family on behalf of Emperor Yang.

When the Heart-Moon Fox received the order, she was delighted, and after deciding on a propitious date for her descent, went to say goodbye to the Lady of the Moon.

The Lady of the Moon remembered the incident of several hundreds of years ago, and had an inspiration. 'Now you are going down to earth to become an Empress,' she whispered to the Fox, 'and all that you desire will be at your command. If you should command all the flowers of the four seasons to bloom at the same time, so that the earth should be covered with a million colours and reflect your might and glory, you will be talked about forever and the unprecedented feat will go down in history.'

The Fox smiled. 'That's easy !' she said. 'When I am Empress, who or what shall dare disobey my commands? I will not only make all the flowers bloom at once, but even the Sago palm which never bears any flowers will burgeon for my sake ! Just wait and see.'

(Wu Tsetien first entered the House of Tang as a palace maid of the sixth rank. After receiving the favours of Emperor Tai-tsung, she entertained his son, Emperor Kao-tsung. She then plotted and had Queen Wang dethroned on the false charge that Queen Wang had perpetrated a crime, and had herself declared Queen. Upon the death of Kao-tsung, whom she had long ago robbed of real power, she became Empress Dowager, whereupon she had all four of Kao-tsung's sons by Empress Wang murdered. The throne then passed on to her own son Chung-tsung.)

Under the mighty aegis of the House of Tang, the reign of Emperor Chung-tsung was a peaceful one. But Empress Wu was determined to establish a dynasty of her own, and bring the Wu family to power, and she hated the descendants of the House of Tang, even her own son. Before he had reigned a year, Wu Tsetien banished him to Fangchow and gave him the title, Prince of Luling. She then declared herself Female Emperor, and changed the dynasty's name from Tang to Chou.

Outraged by her usurpation of the throne, Shu Ching-yeh, the grandson of Archduke Lichi, together with some of the officials whom Empress Wu had ousted from Court, declared war on her, knowing that the whole country was behind him. Unfortunately, the leaders of the Rebellion were all scholars and had no experience of commanding troops. To the rebels' ten thousand men, Empress Wu sent thirty thousand under the command of Li Hsiao-yi, and in two months put down the Rebellion.

When their numbers dwindled to a few thousand men, Shu Ching-yeh and the scholar Lo Pinwang knew that they must go down in defeat, and tried to make their escape. With the Empress's army in hot pursuit, there was no time to lose.

Both Shu and Lo had a son who was not more than ten years old. Both men tore off pieces from their garments, and bit their fingers, and wrote down in blood their declaration of war. Lo tore off another piece of clothing and wrote a letter on it in blood. Pressing this and the declaration of war on his young son, he said, 'Take these to your Uncle Shih Yeh, the Governor of Lung-yu. He is my old friend, a man of integrity and courage, and learned in astronomy. This time because of weakness in numbers, he has not led his men in rebellion against the Empress. But if a man should rise in the future to overthrow her, it must be him. Go to him, and if you do your best to carry out my unfulfilled wishes, I shall be happy in that knowledge when I am in the Nine Streams.'

In the same manner, Shu wrote two letters and gave them to his son together with the declaration of war. 'Take this to your Uncle

Wen Yin, the Governor of Huainan,' he said, 'and this to your Uncle Chang Ken, Governor of Hotung. They are both righteous men who want to see the Emperor return to his throne, but who did not rise in arms this time because of lack of strength. If you can make your way to either Huainan or Hotung, you will be safe.'

As the Empress's men pressed close, fathers and sons parted company. Each boy had two loyal soldiers to go with him.

Before he could make good his escape, Shu Ching-yeh was assassinated by one of his officers who severed his head and, with it in his hand, surrendered to Empress Wu's soldiers. Nothing more was heard of Lo Pinwang, but the families of both the rebels escaped overseas together with some of their supporters.

After the Rebellion, the Empress was afraid that the capital city of Changan was not safe, and in daily consultations with her brothers, decided to encourage building outside the Great Wall. In addition, she ordered that four passes should be built to thwart potential invaders, and put one of her brothers in charge of each pass. As all four Wu brothers possessed magic powers, they could cast magic spells before the passes, so that anyone who wanted to enter the city became spellbound. Thus, they successfully kept away any man who wished to return the Emperor to the throne, and Empress Wu felt secure.

One evening toward the end of winter, there was a heavy snowfall, and Empress Wu, together with her daughter Princess Taiping and the Imperial Concubine Shangkuan Waner, was drinking and admiring the snow scene from the window. As the snow fell harder and harder, the Empress said, 'The ancients say that a heavy snowfall presages a good harvest. This is a good omen! We shall have bountiful crops this year, and there will be peace on earth!'

Tipsy and in high spirits, the Empress suddenly noticed that the winter-sweet in the garden were in bloom. Drifts of their perfume filled the air.

'What inspiration it is of them to bloom in this weather!' she cried. 'It must be because they know I am happy, and want to help me make merry! They must be rewarded for their thoughtfulness!'

She decreed that the award of the golden plaque should be given to the winter-sweet, and ordered her attendants to hang a plaque on the branches of each tree, and to decorate them with swatches of red brocade.

'It would not surprise me if the other flowers, aware of my fondness of them, should be in full bloom, too!' she said, turning her wine-sodden eyes to her attendants. 'Prepare litters. I and the

Princess are going to the Garden of Many Fragrances and the Forest Park to look at them!'

The attendants had no choice but to do as they were told. But the Princess said, 'The winter-sweet are in bloom now because it is their time. No doubt the moisture from the snowfall has helped them to open. But I really doubt if the other flowers can be blooming now, not far from spring though we may be.'

'All flowers are alike!' cried the Empress. 'If the winter-sweet can brave the cold to please me, why can't the others, especially since the ancients say, "Heaven comes to the help of the Divine Ruler". There have been many Emperors, but I alone am Female Emperor. I am unique! Do you think that these wretched flowers and plants would dare disobey me if I were to order them all to bloom at once? Come with me and see! Oh, I wouldn't be surprised if they were preparing to blossom already!'

Princess Taiping again tried to prevent her from going, but Empress Wu would hear nothing of it, and ordered her and the Imperial Concubine to follow.

However, when they arrived at the Garden of Many Fragrances, not a flower or a green leaf was to be seen, except for the winter-sweet, the narcissus and the heavenly bamboo.

The Empress was almost shocked into sobriety when she saw this. A little eunuch came from the Forest Park and reported, 'It is the same in the Forest Park. According to my humble opinion, the flowers are not in bloom because they are not aware of Your Majesty's presence. However, I have already told them of Your Majesty's wishes. If Your Majesty would give them the command personally, I am sure they will all be in bloom by tomorrow.'

'Very well, then,' said the Empress reluctantly. 'It is late, and I shall be generous. Let all flowers be in bloom tomorrow!'

Writing-brush and paper were brought immediately, and Empress Wu, after some thought, wrote the following edict :

Let it be known to spring. I am coming to the Palace gardens in the morning. All flowers are ordered to make preparations at once and to be in bloom before dawn tomorrow.

This she handed to the eunuch, who set upon the edict the Imperial Seal, and posted it in the garden. At the same time, he gave orders for the palace kitchen to prepare a feast for the next day, when the Empress would want to celebrate the occasion.

Princess Taiping and the Imperial Concubine could not refrain from smiling, and returned to the Palace with the drunken Empress.

If the reader wants to know whether all the flowers bloomed, please turn to the next chapter.

◀ *3* ▶

When the Winter-sweet Spirit and the Narcissus Spirit read the edict, they hurried to the cave of the Fairy of a Hundred Flowers to tell her, but their mistress was out. In fact, the Fairy of a Hundred Flowers had not yet returned from Maku's cave because it was still snowing. When the Peony Spirit heard the news, she immediately went out in the snowstorm with the Orchid Spirit to look for her, but they did not find her in any of the caves she often visited.

'What shall we do?' said the Peony Spirit when they came back.

'There are thousands of caves in these seventy thousand *li*s of Little Penglai, and we have no time to lose!' said the Peach Blossom Spirit. 'I think each spirit should be responsible for the flowers in her charge, and obey the earthly ruler's command. Even if we do find the Fairy of a Hundred Flowers, what can she do but obey?'

The Myrtle Spirit nodded in agreement, but the Peony Spirit was not sure if they should.

'I think we should wait for the Fairy of a Hundred Flowers,' said the Orchid Spirit. 'What can the earthly ruler do to us even if we disobey her? Some of us exist not only for aesthetic reasons, but have medicinal properties as well. Dare she liquidate us all for disobedience?' to which the Cassia, Plum Blossom, Chrysanthemum and Lotus Spirits agreed. But the Myrtle, Arundo, Sunflower, Day Lily, Water Caltrop, Wisteria, Smartweed and Apple Blossom Spirits talked it over and said, 'We don't know about you, but as for ourselves, we think it would be best for us to obey the earthly ruler's command. We are low-ranking flowers which have no medicinal properties, and which cannot compete with some of you for fragrance, and we dare not take a chance. And since we have to be in bloom before dawn, we think we had best be getting along. Are you coming with us?'

They were off before the others could answer. And they had scarcely gone when the monitors of the Forest Park came in and demanded to know what was the delay, whereupon many of the other spirits also went.

It had stopped snowing, and was almost dawn.

'What are we going to do!' cried the Peony Spirit worriedly. 'I had better go out and look for the Fairy of a Hundred Flowers again!'

When the monitors came again to hurry them up, neither the Peony Spirit nor the Fairy of a Hundred Flowers had come back. Most of the spirits decided to go to earth, and when the sun came up, only eleven were left in the cave : Cassia, Plum Blossom, Chrysanthemum, Lotus, Bigonia, Peony Albiflora, Narcissus, Magnolia, Rhododendron, Orchid and Winter-sweet, and they decided that they might as well go, too.

When the Peony Spirit came back alone and found only two attendants guarding an empty cave, she hurried to the Park as well.

When the Empress woke up the next morning, she had slept off the effects of the wine. Suddenly she remembered what she had done the evening before, and was filled with disquiet. What if the flowers had not obeyed her? Would she not become the laughing stock of the people?

She got up, and was trying to think how she could conceal her disgrace, when the eunuchs in charge of the Forest Park and Garden of Many Fragrances came and reported that flowers were in bloom everywhere!

The Empress immediately summoned Princess Taiping, and after breakfast, proceeded to the Park. It was a sight to behold. Her eyes were dazzled by the splendid reds, purples and greens which greeted her! It was as if the whole universe were made of satins and brocades! Even the frozen pond had thawed out, and a spring-like warmth filled the air.

Empress Wu's delight was beyond measure. She hurried forward to admire the flowers.

Suddenly, she discovered that the peony alone of all the flowers was not in bloom, and upon inquiries was told that it was not in bloom in the Garden of Many Fragrances either. Fury rose in great flashes in her.

'How dare you not bloom!' she thundered at the peony plants. 'Is this your way of showing your gratitude, when for thirty years since I came to the Palace, I have tended you and given you shelter from frost in the winter and from the heat in the summer, when you have been watered when you were thirsty and given every nourishment you needed! And you know you are my favourite! Is this your way of repaying me?'

She turned to the eunuchs and cried, 'Dig them all up and have them all burnt at once!'

29

Princess Taiping tried to intervene. 'Peonies are large flowers, perhaps it takes them more time to bloom,' she said. 'Give them half a day more, and it will not be too late to punish them if they do not obey you.'

'Very well,' said the Empress. 'I will give them until noon. How many peonies are there altogether?'

'There are more than two thousand bushes here, and the same number in the Garden of Many Fragrances,' replied the eunuchs.

'Prepare a thousand basins of hot ashes, and roast their branches and stalks, but do not harm their roots,' she said. 'That should teach them a lesson! If they show signs of blooming after this treatment, roast the other bushes in the same way. And if they are not in bloom by noon, dig them all up and chop them to pieces and pulverize the pieces. I shall give the order to eliminate peonies from the earth.'

As the eunuchs carried out the Empress's orders, the Imperial Concubine whispered with a smile to Princess Taiping, 'Have you ever smelled or seen anything like it? It would be just as effective if she had told them to beat drums to induce the flowers to bloom!'

But before the eunuchs' work was done, some palace attendants rushed over to report that in the Garden of Many Fragrances, leaves and buds were beginning to appear on the peony bushes.

'So!' cried the Empress. 'They understand the language of force after all!' and ordered the attendants to discontinue the punishment.

Soon, the peonies began to unfold. Even those branches which had been roasted to a crisp began to burgeon with blossoms – which accounts for the variety of peonies called the 'dry twig blossom' we find in Piching, Huainan today, which will burn like kindling as soon as fire is set to its branches.

The Empress was now pacified, but she still felt that the peony had given her a personal affront since it alone had bloomed late. 'Now I will not eliminate peonies from the face of the earth as I intended,' she declared. 'Besides, they do have some medical value. Instead, as punishment for the caprice, they will be banished to Loyang. After I have entertained my ministers, the army will be ordered to escort them to Loyang, where the Governor Chang Ken will be ordered to send back to me every year so much bark for medical purposes.' Which accounts for the profusion of peonies in the city of Loyang today.

Now the Empress ordered the eunuch in charge of flowers to make a list of all the different kinds of flowers which were in bloom, and note which varieties were presented to her by which officials from different parts. She received a list of ninety-nine kinds of flowers, and was very pleased.

The Imperial Concubine said, 'What happened today will never cease to be talked about.'

Princess Taiping said, 'Not only are the rare flowers in bloom, but twin blossoms are growing out of single calyxes from the *loru* and blue-purse, and there are twin stalks, too. This indicates the predominance of the Yin principle. Basking in the reflection of your glory, may I be the first to offer my humble congratulations!'

The others all joined in congratulating the Empress.

Empress Wu was extremely happy, and ordered the attendants to decorate the plants and bushes with red brocade as signs of honour, and awarded the *loru* the title of 'Damsel of Literary Destiny' and the blue-purse the title of 'Damsel of Culture'. Golden plaques were so inscribed and brought at once, and hung upon their branches, whereupon the two kinds of flowers, as if aware of the honour bestowed upon them, began to burgeon anew, and vie with each other in producing more and more splendid blossoms. From the hearts of the double *loru* and blue-purse sprang new blossoms.

The Empress was delirious with joy. 'It is like babies springing from their mothers' wombs!' she cried. 'From now on each double flower which produces a flower from within a flower will be awarded a gold plaque and three cups of wine!' Immediately, she wrote this down and it was posted. And, strangely enough, in a little while, ten kinds of double flowers began to produce flowers from the heart of flowers. Of these, the pomegranate proved to be most proficient (as it is full of seeds).

Then the Empress toured the Garden of Many Fragrances, and prepared to entertain her officials at a feast.

If the reader wants to know what happened next, please turn to the following chapter.

◄ 4 ►

In the cave of Maku, the Fairy of a Hundred Flowers was playing chess with her hostess when an attendant came after sunrise and reported, 'All the flowers on earth are in bloom! Would the two fairies care to step outside and see?'

The Fairy of a Hundred Flowers hurried outside, and, to her consternation, found that indeed, the world was covered with flowers. 'This is terrible!' she cried. 'Remember the agreement I made with the Lady of the Moon so many hundreds of years ago?'

'You had better report your negligence to the Deity right away, and ask for punishment,' counselled Maku. 'And you should go at once and beg the Lady of the Moon's pardon. Otherwise, she and the other spirits will surely not be satisfied until you are officially censured.'

'I could never bring myself to admit my mistake to the Lady of the Moon,' said the Fairy of a Hundred Flowers. 'We have not spoken to each other since we quarrelled hundreds of years ago. How can I go to her now and be humiliated!'

'Would you rather become her floor-sweeper?' said Maku.

'When we quarrelled, I promised that I would go to earth to become a mortal if this should ever happen,' said the Fairy of a Hundred Flowers. 'How can I escape this fate? It must be that destiny had it in store for me to go down to earth, and that is why all the flowers have bloomed at the same time.'

Scarcely had she returned to her own cave and heard from her attendants what happened, than an emissary from the Moon Palace came and said that the Lady of the Moon was waiting for her to go over and sweep the floor.

Her face scarlet with shame, the Fairy of a Hundred Flowers said, 'Go back and tell your mistress that I vowed I would go down to earth if this should ever happen, and I shall not try to get out of it. But let her not be exultant, but wait and see whether I shall let the temptations of the world corrupt me, and whether I shall return to my fairy state after I have done my penance by the Wheel of Karma! Then she will know of what stuff I am made!'

That evening, the Fairies of a Hundred Plants, a Hundred Fruits, and a Hundred Grains came to see the Fairy of a Hundred Flowers in her cave. 'We have just heard that an indictment has been brought against you,' said the Fairy of a Hundred Plants. 'You have been officially charged with negligence of duty and failure to control your subordinates, and they have been charged with disobeying the rules of Heaven in order to please the earthly ruler, who issued the command not for the benefit of the people or any reason of state, but because she was drunk. For this, you are all to go down to earth to undergo the trials and tribulations of human beings. We hear that before you are fifteen years old, you will cross seas and travel to uncivilized parts as a form of punishment, and that you will be ordered to earth any moment now. We came to arrange a farewell party for you.'

'What about Narcissus, Winter-sweet and some of the others?' asked the Fairy of a Hundred Flowers. 'Are they being punished as well?'

'Yes,' said the Fairy of a Hundred Grains, 'because they did not stop the others from blooming, although they themselves were quite in order to bloom at this time. Including yourself, altogether a hundred fairies are being sent to earth within the next three years.'

'We shall be scattered,' sighed the Fairy of a Hundred Flowers. 'Who knows when we shall meet again, and it is all my fault! When we do come back to this mountain, how shall we ever find each other again?'

'If it is any comfort to you,' said the Fairy of a Hundred Plants, 'I heard that all of you will be born within the ten provinces or somewhere in the islands overseas, and that you will all be reunited in the end.'

'Oh, please tell me, what are the ten provinces, and what is meant by the islands overseas?' said the Fairy of a Hundred Flowers.

The Fairy of a Hundred Plants said, 'Now the Kingdom on Earth is divided according to terrain into ten provinces, namely, Kuan-nei, Honan, Hotung, Hopei, Shan-nan, Lungtso, Huainan, Chiangnan, Chien-nan and Lingnan. As for the islands overseas, they are countless, but we gathered that some of your spirits will be born in such places as the Country of Gentlemen, the Country of Black-toothed People, the Country of Virtuous People, the Country of Split-tongued People, the Country of Women, and so forth.'

Now the Lady Yuan, the Weaving Maid, and Maku also came to see the Fairy of a Hundred Flowers, and all said that it was too bad that she failed to admit her guilt and offer herself up for punishment, and was too proud to apologize to the Lady of the Moon, or she might not have been sent to earth.

'If you had held your tongue at the party, or even been willing to show your contrition now, things would not have come to such a pass,' said the Lady Yuan. 'Now there is nothing more we can do!'

'Maybe it was fate that I couldn't help saying the things I did at the party, and cannot beg the Lady of the Moon's pardon now,' said the Fairy of a Hundred Flowers.

'No, that is not fate,' said the Lady Yuan. 'It is not fate when it was within your power to exercise your forebearance then, and to show your humility now. It is only after one has done his best that the rest is left to fate. If you think that you cannot help the things you do, I do not wonder that you are being sent to earth! Surely you know that nothing we desire ever comes to us without our exerting our own efforts?'

So the fairies were busy with many parties, large and small, for the Fairy of a Hundred Flowers. One day, the Scarlet Child, the Golden Infant, the Green Maiden and the Jade Maiden gave a party on the Cave of Mystic Travel on Dream Cliff for her, to which most of her friends as well as the four Spirit Chiefs were invited.

The Fairy of a Hundred Flowers expressed her consternation at the prospect of travelling to foreign parts, perhaps to encounter bandits and evil spirits.

'Do not worry,' said the Scarlet Child. 'If you need help, just call out our names, and we shall come to your side speedily. We would not let you suffer without trying to help.'

'I don't think that will do,' said the Jade Maiden. 'She will be a mortal, remember. How will she know whom to call out for? And if she does remember our names, wouldn't that mean that she possessed fairy powers, and in that case she wouldn't need us to help her get out of human difficulties?'

'Ah, I realize my mistake,' said the Scarlet Child. 'Then this is what we shall do: we shall watch over you all, and tell each other if any one of you is in trouble, and come of our own accord. But it will be no mean task, since there are a hundred of you, and we should be careful, too, lest we get sent to earth as well!'

When they had all toasted the guest of honour, the four Spirit Chiefs said, 'We have a small gift for you. It is a small expression of our sentiments at this time of your departure. It is a plant of long life, which is over two million years old. Therefore it has benefited from the pure essences of heaven and the vigour of the sun and the moon, and whoever takes it will have a very long life.'

Next, the Fairies of a Hundred Plants, Fruits and Grains, the Weaving Maid, the Lady Yuan and Maku presented the Fairy of a Hundred Flowers with a divine plant. 'We have found this divine plant which grew soon after the universe was created, and therefore has the equal of nine-fold magic properties,' they said. 'It will not only bring the dead back to life, but will make the person who takes it immortal. Please accept this humble gift as a small expression of our friendship for you.'

The Fairy of a Hundred Flowers thanked them, and asked the Fairy of a Hundred Plants to keep the gifts for her until her return from earth.

When the party was over, several of the flower spirits' time had come, and they descended to earth without delay to be born.

The Fairy of a Hundred Flowers was born into the family of the scholar Tang in Hoyuan county in Lingnan. If the reader wants to know what happened next, please see the next chapter.

◀ 5 ▶

The *Hsiu-tsai* Tang was called Ao, and had the literary name of Yiting. His ancestors came from Hoyuan county in the district of Haifung in Shunchow, Lingnan. His second wife, whom he married after the death of his first, came from a family called Lin. Tang Ao had a younger brother whose name was Min, also a *Hsiu-tsai* of the local district, whose wife had the maiden name Shih. The brothers and their wives lived together on a few acres of fertile land left to them by their parents.

Tang Min loved to study, but cared nothing for fame and social position, and was content to be a teacher. Tang Ao would not spurn honour and acclaim, but since he loved to travel and spent half of each year doing so, he had failed to pass any but the elementary examinations, and still wore the blue collar of a scholar of the lowest rank.

When Tang Ao's wife Mistress Lin gave birth to a baby girl, it is said that the house was filled with a rare fragrance which was like neither musk nor lavender. For three days, the perfume changed from that of one flower to another, in a hundred varieties. The neighbours marvelled at this, and henceforth called the hamlet where the Tang family lived Hundred Fragrances Crossroads.

It is said that on the eve of the baby's birth, Mistress Lin dreamt of climbing a steep hill of rainbow colours and that when she woke up, the baby was born. So she called the baby Little Hill. Two years later, when the family was further blessed by a son, the Tangs decided they might as well call him Little Summit.

Little Hill became a beautiful little girl, and was extremely talented as well. At four or five years of age, she was already an accomplished reader, and retained the meaning of whatever she read after reading it only once. The family possessed many books, and under the guidance of her father and uncle, Little Hill became, before she was very old, well-versed in the classics and thoroughly at home in literary matters. Her inclinations, however, were not only scholarly, for she had an adventurous spirit, and loved to play with spears and lances, and did so although her parents did not encourage it.

One evening, as her father was preparing to go to the capital to take the Imperial Examinations once more, Little Hill sat under the eaves of the house with her Uncle Min, looking at the brilliant moon and chatting about literary matters.

'My father has gone so many times to take the Imperial Examinations,' she said. 'Why don't you go as well, since you are also a *Hsiu-tsai*?'

'I have never cared for public acclaim,' said Tang Min, 'and I am not sure I would pass even if I did go. So why tire myself out in the effort? I would rather enjoy myself here at home with my books. Besides, if it isn't in one's fate to become prominent in life, there is nothing a person can do about it.'

'There must be Imperial Examinations for women as well as men?' asked Little Hill. 'I wonder how often the Examinations for women are held? I want to work hard and be ready when the time comes.'

Tang Min could not help smiling. 'I have never heard of Imperial Examinations for women,' he said. 'Why, could you be entertaining the idea of having an official career? Truly, you are your father's child!'

'Oh, no, I was not thinking of that,' said Little Hill. 'I was asking because I thought that since we have a Female Emperor, there must be women ministers and advisers at court. Now you tell me there is no such thing. How strange! If that is the case, why don't I spend my time learning to embroider instead of studying?'

She did put away her books for a few days, and take up her needle. But Little Hill found it boring, and soon was back again at her books, and making verses and reciting poetry to pass the time, and even her uncle had to concede that he could do no better.

Before long, Little Hill acquired the reputation of being a girl of rare talent.

This time Tang Ao went to the capital, he won the rank of *Tan-hua* in the Imperial Examinations. Unfortunately, one of the Empress's advisers submitted a report concerning Tang Ao as follows:

'During the reign of Tang Kao-tsung, Tang Ao became the sworn brother of the rebels Shu Ching-yeh, Lo Pinwang, Wei Tsewen, Hsueh Chungchang, etc. Although he did not take part in the Rebellion, his connection with the rebels put him under suspicion. If his name is posted as a successful candidate, and he fills an official post, we cannot be sure of his loyalty. It would be most expedient if he were stripped of all title now, as punishment for being associated with the rebels.'

The Empress, after reading this report, had Tang Ao investigated, but could find nothing to incriminate him. So instead of stripping him of all his titles, allowed him to retain the rank of *Hsiu-tsai* as before.

When Tang Ao learned this, his anger was such that after brooding about it for many days, he decided that there was nothing for him to do but renounce the vanities of the worldly existence, and detach himself from his worldly entanglements.

He decided to take a long journey to forget his disappointment, and since his brother had, upon hearing the news that he had at last passed the Examinations at the capital, sent him a large sum of money, he was well provided for. He dismissed his servant, and carrying his baggage himself, began to travel, crossing rivers when he came to them, and climbing mountains when he found himself on the road to one.

After a year's wandering, he found himself, in the early spring, back in Lingnan, close to his brother-in-law's house, which was not more than twenty or thirty *lis* from his own. But, still reluctant to meet people, Tang Ao could not decide whether to go in and see his relative. He told the boatman to tie up at the bank, and went on shore, trying to decide which road to take.

There was an old temple in the distance with the words 'Dream Spirit Temple' written across its portal. Sighing, Tang Ao said to himself, 'What is life but a dream! Good dream and bad dream, I have dreamt them all during these fifty years of worldly life! But now I am finished with it all! I seek only the way of Tao. Why don't I ask the spirits what my future is to be?'

So thinking, he approached the temple, and prayed silently before the idol. After this was done, he sat down on the ground for a rest.

Suddenly, there came a boy who said, 'Would the scholar please follow me? My master would like to speak to you.'

Tang Ao followed the boy to the back of the temple, where an old man invited him to sit down.

'If I may ask, what is your name?' Tang Ao said. 'I wonder what I may do for you?'

'My name is Meng,' said the old man. 'I live here. I know that you are seeking the way of Tao, so let us discuss the matter. Would you please tell me what foundation you have made for Tao?'

'I have made no foundation,' said Tang Ao. 'But I shall find Tao by renouncing the worldly ties and giving up the seven emotions and six desires. By devoting myself to this, I should be able to find Tao.'

The old man smiled. 'Would it were as easy as that! By renouncing the emotions and desires, you merely prolong your life and save your body from illness. As for Taoist Immortality, I think the Immortal Keh put it best. He said, "The way of Tao lies in loyalty, filial piety, righteousness, kindness, a peaceful and genial nature, and trustworthiness. Before a man may seek Tao, he must first perfect his moral character. Before he can become a perfect mortal, he must do three hundred acts of charity." Now you have not made any moral preparations for Tao. Yet you seek it. Is this not asking the impossible?'

'Please teach me,' said Tang Ao. 'Truly, I am in a dilemma and need your wise counsel. My original intention was to do my best to succeed in the world, in order to restore the Tang Dynasty and bring the Emperor back to the throne. How was I to know that I should encounter such unexpected obstacles in my path?'

'It is a shame that you could not fulfil your wishes,' said the old man. 'Still, who can know whether it is for better or worse? From now on consider yourself as a spirit, with neither ties nor attachments, ready to meet what comes your way. I have heard that the spirits of a hundred flowers are being punished and have come to earth, of which twelve, unfortunately, have drifted overseas, some in foreign mountains and others in alien valleys. They are all destined to be reunited in the end, but if you have the spirit and the determination, travel abroad and find them, help and cultivate them, and bring them back to the Kingdom on Earth. This will be a meritorious service. If you do this, and dispense charity without selfishness, I am sure you will be eligible for a place in the rank of Immortals carved on the tablet in Little Penglai Mountain. This is my advice. If you take it, I am sure you will be rewarded in many unexpected ways. But in any situation, do your best.'

Tang Ao was going to ask another question, but the old man disappeared. He rubbed his eyes, looked around, and found himself sitting in the temple before the idol. He realized that it was a dream, and stood up. Looking at the idol carefully, Tang Ao realized that the idol and the old man had been one. So he made another kowtow, and departed.

After he returned to the boat, he had time to ponder his dream, and thought, 'No doubt some strange destiny is in store for me if I go overseas now. I wonder why the spirits of a hundred flowers are being punished, and where they can be. What a coincidence this is! I love to travel, and was just thinking of journeying abroad. It is a pity I did not have a chance to ask the dream spirit what the twelve flowers are called, and where they may be found. I suppose I shall just have to keep a sharp lookout for them, and if I find any, take care of them the best way I can, and see what mystic destiny will unfold for me. Now I will go and find my wife's brother. He often goes overseas, and if he will go abroad with me, so much the better.'

He instructed the boatman to wait, and went on shore again to find Lin Chih-yang.

Lin Chih-yang, a native of Pingyuan district in Tehchow, Hopei, was a merchant who travelled by junk to far places to sell his goods. His parents were dead, and his wife was a woman who had the surname of Lu. They had a daughter, Pleasant, who was just thirteen years old, and extraordinarily clever and pretty. When the family left on their trips abroad, Lin entrusted his family affairs to the care of his mother-in-law, Mistress Chiang.

When Tang Ao entered the house, he saw bags and merchandise piled up in front. It looked as if Merchant Lin were going to leave for another of his trips.

The family hurried over to greet Tang Ao.

'You have changed since I saw you two years ago,' Tang Ao said to Pleasant. 'No doubt you have abandoned the needle and like Little Hill, acquired a taste for books?'

'It is true, she loves to read and write,' said her father, 'and I have bought her many books. But since I have been so busy, and so often ill these last years, there is no one to instruct her properly.'

'Do you know that talented and learned girls can go further nowadays than boys?' said Tang Ao.

'Why do you say that?' said Merchant Lin.

'The idea started with the Imperial Concubine more than ten years ago,' replied Tang Ao. 'The Imperial Concubine Shangkuan Waner made a great reputation for herself at the time all flowers bloomed at once, when she out-versified all eleven of the Empress's ministers at the celebration party. The Empress was extremely pleased with her, and awarded her the rank of Chao-yi, the highest office a woman can hold, and gave her father an official post as well. In addition, the Empress ordered her ministers to bring to her attention any specially talented girls whom they came to know about, with the view of summoning them to Court and rewarding them according to their merit. When this news spread to the length and breadth of the land, every young girl, be she from a rich family or poor, began to pay greater attention to her studies than to the domestic arts. Although the Empress so far has not summoned any of the young ladies to Court, to be sure, the talented young girl who makes a literary name for herself need have no worries about her future! My niece should make the most of her gifts indeed!'

'We shall rely on you to teach her from now on,' said Mistress Lu. 'Although she has not been taught how to read, she practises her calligraphy by the hour. But she is too shy to let Little Hill help her. We really don't know how good she is.'

'Let me see a specimen of her handwriting,' said Tang Ao. 'What style does she copy?'

'I have been trying to learn how to write blindly, without understanding what the words mean and where to start,' said Pleasant, 'and I have been too embarrassed to show my writing to sister Little Hill, for fear she laughs at me.'

Tang Ao looked at a specimen of her calligraphy, and recognized it as the *li* style of Han dynasty. Upon careful examination, he found that not only had she perfected the style, but some of her characters were actually better formed than the text from which she had copied them.

'Genius!' he cried. 'This is absolute genius! It would be a shame to let such talent go to waste.'

'I was thinking of sending her over to you to instruct her,' said Merchant Lin, 'but you have been so little at home recently. Who could have known that you should have become involved in this misunderstanding over the rebels, after you had won the rank of *Tan-hua*!'

'And now that we have met again, it looks by the preparations that you are about to go off somewhere again. Is this true?'

'I am just about to take a shipload of merchandise overseas,' said Lin. 'I have been ill for some time, and now that I am somewhat better, I must make a living again to support my family.'

'A trip abroad is just what I have been longing for!' cried Tang Ao. 'I have been feeling extremely downhearted since I left the capital, and I want a change of scenery. I have travelled all over this country, and long to see some ocean and island life. If you would take me with you, I shall pay my way, and try not to be a burden to you.'

'How can you talk about paying your way?' said Lin. 'Aren't we all one family?' and to his wife, Lin said, 'Have you ever heard such talk!'

'We have quite a large junk,' said Mistress Lu. 'There is plenty of room, and what can your board amount to? But you must be prepared to do without some of the comforts a scholar like you is used to on land. Water is the first thing. Not only will taking a bath be a hardship, but even water for tea will be limited. I wonder if you can get used to that. And then, for people who are not used to it, the high seas can be quite frightening.'

'You must consider carefully before you decide,' said Lin. 'Once we leave, it may be anywhere from two to three years before we come back, depending on our luck with the wind. I shouldn't like you to miss any important affairs on account of it.'

'What important affairs have I left in the world?' said Tang Ao. 'My only important affair used to be the Imperial Examinations. Now my hopes have been dashed, and there is nothing which requires my presence here. As for water, I have never cared much for tea-drinking, and I can take a bath or leave it. And I have had some experience of sailing, having travelled so much on the lakes and rivers. But I have heard say that sea water is salty, which is why it cannot be drunk, and fresh water must be taken along on the junk.'

'If you feel this way about it, you are welcome to come along,' said Lin. 'But before you set out, aren't you going to tell my sister about it?'

'I have already informed her of my desire to go abroad,' said Tang Ao. 'But if it will make you happier, I shall write another letter to her on the eve of our departure.'

Merchant Lin said nothing more. Tang Ao wrote to his wife, told the boatman fetch his baggage from the boat and dismissed him. He tried to pay Lin for his board on the voyage, but Lin would not hear of it. At last Tang Ao pressed the silver on Pleasant, saying that she could use it to buy paper and writing-brushes.

'How can she ever use up all the paper and brushes she can buy with all this money?' protested Lin. 'But I have been thinking, why don't you take some kind of merchandise along, and who knows but that you might sell it at a profit overseas?'

'I was thinking of the very same thing,' said Tang Ao.

Later, he came back from the market with some sailors from the junk who carried many flowerpots, and several loads of pig-iron.

'Why, what have you bought these for?' said Lin. 'You won't have much demand for flowerpots abroad, and there is pig-iron everywhere overseas.'

'I know the people don't appreciate flowers overseas,' said Tang Ao, 'but I thought that rare flowers and plants must abound in foreign parts, and if I should be able to cultivate a few of them on the voyage, it might be rather amusing. As for the pig-iron, I thought it would help to steady the boat if we should meet with severe weather, and it does not rot. I didn't spend much on them, so don't worry about it.'

Merchant Lin had nothing to say but, 'You are quite right,' since these goods could not be returned.

Soon, everything was ready. A small boat took them to the seaport where the junk was anchored, and the sailors brought the cargo on sampans.

If the reader wants to know what happened next, please turn to the following chapter.

◄ *6* ►

The wind was with them, and after the cargo was loaded, Lin gave the order to sail. It was in the middle of the first month of the year. After several days of fair wind, they were surrounded by the ocean as far as the eye could see.

Tang Ao did not keep track of the distance or of the number of days. After they passed Portage Mountain, he remembered what the dream spirit told him, and asked to go ashore whenever they came to any high mountains. Merchant Lin had great respect for his brother-in-law, and knew that he loved to explore new places, so they tied up, and he saw to it that Tang Ao was provided with food and drink. Tang Ao was extremely pleased. Time meant nothing to him, and he had succeeded in convincing Lin that he no longer sought honour and acclaim.

Thus he toured many strange islands, and when on board, tutored Pleasant in poetry. The girl was extremely clever, so it was no effort to teach her, and it also helped to pass the time.

One day they came to a great mountain, and Tang Ao asked his brother-in-law what it was.

'It is the Mountain of Eastern Opening,' said Lin, 'the first great mountain of the eastern wilderness. The scenery from the top of it is supposed to be breathtaking, although I have never been up there myself. If you like, we could stop, and I shall go up with you.'

'Then the Country of Gentlemen and the Country of Giants must be in the neighbourhood?' said Tang Ao.

'The Country of Gentlemen is to the mountain's east,' said Lin, 'and the Country of Giants as well. But how did you know?'

'I have long heard of the Country of Gentlemen,' said Tang Ao, 'where the people yield to each other's wishes instead of competing for selfish gain. And I have heard that in the Country of Giants, the people do not walk, but float on clouds. Is this true?'

'I have been to the Country of Giants,' said Lin, 'and each man there is supported by his own cloud, which makes walking effortless. As for the Country of Gentlemen, the people there, no matter what

44

their calling, are all refined and cultured. And beyond these two is the Country of Black-toothed People, who are black all over. We will come to the Country of Restless People, the Country of Long-eared People, the Country of Intestineless People, and many others. You will see everything for yourself.'

When the junk dropped anchor, the brothers-in-law disembarked, Merchant Lin carrying a rifle and wick and Tang Ao a precious sword.

They climbed the mountain up a winding road, past magnificent scenery, and when they were standing on the top, they could see as far as the horizon.

Tang Ao thought, 'There must be extraordinary flowers in these majestic mountains. I wonder whether I shall find any.'

He was so thinking, when he saw a weird-looking animal, about six feet long and four feet high, with a pair of large ears and four tusks like those of an elephant, on a far-away summit. It was shaped like a pig.

'What is that?' he asked.

'I don't know,' said Lin, 'but my helmsman would know. He has been sailing on the seas for many years, and knows these foreign parts thoroughly. There isn't a rare flower or plant, bird or animal, that he does not know. We should have asked him to come with us, but we shall do so in the future.'

'What is his name, and is he literate?'

'His surname is Tuo,' said Lin, 'and he is number nine in his family, so we call him old Tuo Number Nine, because of his advanced age. Or, if you like, the sailors call him Know-Nothing Tuo (because he knows everything). In his youth, he also passed the first-level examinations, but abandoned his studies to make sea-trading his career. He did not make a success of it, however, and became a helmsman. He is over eighty years old, but full of vigour and extremely honest. You would have a hard time keeping up with him in walking. We like each other, and besides, he is a distant relative, so I always ask him to help me out on these voyages.'

As Lin was talking, Old Tuo himself came toward them. Lin waved and beckoned him, and Tang Ao went up with his palms together and said, 'I have not had the pleasure of meeting you, although we have seen each other. I only realized now that you are a relative of ours, and my predecessor in the pursuit of learning. I hope you will forgive my lack of courtesy!'

Old Tuo said, 'How dare I presume?'

'Have you come for a walk as well?' said Lin. 'We were just talking about you. I wonder if you can tell us what that animal is over there, with the long teeth?'

'It is called the tang-kang,' said Old Tuo, 'because that is the noise it makes. It never appears unless there is prosperity on the land, so I would say that it signifies peace on earth in our time.'

He had hardly finished speaking when the animal verily cried, 'Tang-kang!' and danced away.

Tang Ao was still watching it when a small stone dropped from the air and hit him on the head. He was startled. 'Where did this come from?'

'Look at those blackbirds over on that mountain there. They have been picking up stones, and dropped one.'

Tang Ao saw that the birds looked like crows, and were as black as ink, with white beaks, red claws and spots on their heads. They were flying back and forth, busily picking up stones.

'Do you know where those birds are carrying the stones to?' Lin asked Old Tuo.

'They are trying to fill up the ocean by dropping them in it,' said Old Tuo. 'In ancient times the Emperor Yen lost a daughter in the Eastern sea. Her spirit became a bird like this one, and took revenge upon the sea by trying to fill it up. In time, the bird multiplied, and now they have become quite a breed.'

'I always thought that "trying to fill up the ocean by dropping stones" was just an expression,' said Tang Ao. 'This bird may be stupid, but the spirit with which it is doing the impossible is indeed to be admired. What couldn't we human beings do if we had its persistence! But we avoid difficult tasks, and do only what comes to us easily, with the result that when we are old, we have not profited from our labours.'

As they walked into the forest, they came to a tree which was fifty feet tall, and which would take the arms of five men to go around. There were no branches, but whiskers grew from it like those found on ears of corn, each bunch being about ten feet long.

'I have heard say that there is a kind of grain which grows on trees,' said Tang Ao. 'Could this be it?'

'Yes, and it is a shame it isn't harvest time, or you could have taken some large-grain back. It is very rare.'

'I suppose the animals consume all the grain which is grown,' said Tang Ao.

'Let us see if I can find some left over from last year on the ground,' said Lin, and began to search. Soon, he said, 'I have found one!'

He was holding a grain of rice three inches wide and five inches long. 'I imagine it will be double that size after it is cooked,' said Tang Ao.

'This is nothing,' said Old Tuo. 'I have eaten a single grain of rice which made me full for one whole year.'

'I don't believe it,' said Lin. 'How big was it, and how did you cook it?'

'The grain was five inches wide and a foot long, and double that when it was cooked,' said Old Tuo. 'It was extremely tasty, and after I had eaten it I felt very strong and refreshed, so much so that I did not think of eating again for a year. This grain used to be one of the local products the people of Pei-yin presented to Court in the reign of Hsuen Ti, and is called "Clear-Intestine Grain".'

'No wonder when an important official shoots with bow and arrow, the subordinates always say, "Missed by a grain of rice!" when the official misses the target by at least a couple of feet!' said Lin. 'They must mean this kind of rice.'

They were laughing, when suddenly, they saw a little man astride a little horse of seven or eight inches long galloping in the distance. Tang Ao took to his heels and ran after them. Old Tuo began to make for them, too, but stumbled on a stone on the winding road.

Tang Ao's legs flew. About half a *li* later, he caught up with the little man and horse, seized them and quickly put them in his mouth and ate them.

When Old Tuo came up, leaning on Merchant Lin, he said, panting, 'It must be destiny! Your destiny must be magical! It was no easy thing to catch up with them!'

'I just heard Old Tuo say that you have caught a little man and a little horse,' said Lin. 'I never saw them, but I saw you put something in your mouth. Did you eat them, man and horse? I don't understand.'

'This little man and horse are called "noble meat",' said Tang Ao. 'I didn't know about them either until I left the capital, and became interested in ancient theories of health and diet. In an old book I found an item which said, "If a person comes across a little man five to seven inches tall astride a little horse in the mountains, he should eat them. They are called 'noble meat'. A man who has eaten noble meat will enjoy longevity, and even become an Immortal." I don't know whether it is true, but since I had caught them, I thought I might as well eat them. Anyway, it could not do any harm.'

Merchant Lin laughed. 'Then you must be on your way to becoming an Immortal! Perhaps you will not ever need to eat again. But I am famished. Would you by any chance have a leg left over?'

'If you are hungry, here's something,' said Old Tuo, plucking a few blades of grass from the ground. 'Eat it, and you will not only cease to feel hungry, but be extremely clear-headed.'

It tasted like a kind of leek. There were a few green flowers attached to the tender stalk. 'It is sweet and quite delicious,' said Lin. 'Hereafter I shall look for it when I am in the mountains.'

'It is called "Blessings to Spare", isn't it?' said Tang Ao. 'I have heard it grows on Blackbird Hill.'

Old Tuo nodded. As they walked on, Lin said, 'Strange! I feel really full! We should find a couple of basketfuls of this and take them back to the boat. Wouldn't it come in handy when we are short of provisions, and much better than trying to become Immortals through starvation!'

'It is a very rare plant, and it loses its efficacy if it is not freshly picked,' said Old Tuo.

Tang Ao found a plant on the ground with needles on it like a pine, but of an extraordinary greenness. There was a seed, about the size of a mustard seed, upon it. He plucked it off and consumed the plant. Then he opened his hand with the seed in it, and blew on it. Another plant of about a foot long immediately sprouted from the seed. He blew on it again, and it grew another foot. When he had blown three times, he ate this new plant, too.

'The way you eat!' said Lin, laughing, 'I am afraid there will be nothing left on these mountains which is green after you are finished! But what is this seed which grows so quickly?'

'This is the walk-on-air plant, also called the seed-on-palm. It will grow to a height of three feet on the palm if it is blown on three times, and he who eats it can walk on air,' said Tang Ao.

'Is that so? Let me have some as well. I'll be able to catch any thief who tries to sneak into my house when we go back!'

They tried to find another plant, but could not.

'Save yourselves the trouble,' said Old Tuo. 'This plant does not grow unless it is blown upon by animal breath. What Brother Tang has just eaten must have been near sparrows which were feeding on the ground, and received some of their breath. That is very unusual. This is the first time I have seen it in all these years I have travelled abroad, and if Brother Tang had not blown on it, I would not have known that it was the walk-on-air plant.'

'Let us see you walk on air,' said Merchant Lin.

'I have only just eaten it,' said Tang Ao uncertainly. 'Oh, well, let's try.' He sprinted, and actually found himself standing in the air, fifty or sixty feet from the ground. He stood firmly, with his body very straight, and did not move.

Lin clapped his hands with joy. 'Isn't he cunning! Try walking about,' he said. 'You will save money on shoes and socks if you can do that.'

Tang Ao took a step forward, and immediately found himself back on the ground.

'Look, there's a date tree with huge dates,' said Lin. 'Go up there and pick a few to quench our thirst.'

But when they approached it, they saw that it was not a date tree at all.

'This is a magic tree which bears a kernel of no definite taste,' explained Old Tuo. 'People who eat the kernel will enjoy a very long life, if not become immortal. However, the kernels grow on top of the tree, and it is hundreds of feet high. I don't know if even you will be able to reach it, Brother Tang.'

'Let him try,' said Lin.

'Remember, I only reached a height of fifty or sixty feet,' said Tang.

But Merchant Lin insisted. 'Why don't you give a leap as before,' he said after some thought, 'and when you are standing in the air, wait a moment, and leap upwards again. This way you will surely reach the top.'

Tang Ao was still reluctant to try it, but Lin would not let him off, so at last he gave another lurch and found himself standing in the air as before. After a moment, he gave himself another push upwards, and found that his body was as light as a pair of cicada's wings, and that he was floating in the air. Slowly, however, he settled to the ground like a kite severed of its string.

'Why didn't you leap upwards?' Lin cried, stamping his foot.

'I don't know,' said Tang. 'It isn't as if I could help it.'

Old Tuo laughed. 'According to Brother Lin, you would have been able to leap straight up to heaven. Of course it cannot be done.'

'But I smell something fragrant,' said Tang Ao. 'Is it the smell of the kernel?'

'No, indeed, I think the fragrance is being wafted to us from that direction. Let us find out what it is.'

Tang Ao followed the scent through the forest toward a precipice, and found a lovely vermilion plant of about two feet high growing from a crack in a rock on the roadside. After scrutinizing it, Tang Ao remembered a passage from an ancient book of nutrition which said, 'The vermilion plant resembles a dwarf mulberry bush. It has a coral coloured stalk with blood-red juice in it. Gold or jade, upon coming into contact with it, will dissolve into paste, called "gold paste" or "jade paste" depending on which is used. He who takes of this paste will leave the worldly existence and enter the region of Immortals.'

'Lucky those two have not yet come, it must be that I am destined to become immortal . . .' Tang Ao thought. He took a very small piece of jade from his head-scarf, and plucked the plant up from its roots. Laying it carefully between his palm and the piece of jade, he rubbed them together. Sure enough, it all melted into a brightly coloured red paste. He put this in his mouth, and immediately felt a fragrance permeate his brain, and was at once extremely invigorated.

'Now I am on my way to becoming an Immortal,' he thought, very pleased with himself. 'I have taken so many kinds of magic plant today. If I succeed in cultivating abstention from food, the rest should be easy. But I wonder whether I have gained any strength from it?'

There was a stone tablet which had fallen over on the roadside, which looked as if it weighed between five to seven hundred catties. Tang Ao bent over, and without any effort picked it up and leaped into the air with it. After a while, he floated down again gently. 'I do not only feel as if my ears were more alert, and my eyes brighter, but as if I could remember all the lessons I studied as a child, without the slightest effort. Even the poems I composed long ago are coming back to me so clearly as to appear to be before my very eyes. I never thought that the vermilion plant could work so many wonders.'

'What is that red stuff you have all over your mouth?' said Lin as he came along with Old Tuo.

'I've just found the vermilion plant and eaten it.'

'What is the good of it?' asked Lin.

'The plant is grown from the essence of heaven and earth,' said Old Tuo. 'Those who have made a proper foundation for Tao will join the ranks of Immortals after taking it. But isn't this remarkable! Your destiny must be magical!'

'Well, you'll soon become an Immortal,' said Lin. 'But why are you looking so miserable? Is it because you cannot bear the thought of leaving your family, or you quaver at the thought of joining the spirits?'

'I have a stomach-ache,' said Tang Ao. 'I don't know why.'

He had hardly finished speaking when there was a rumble in his stomach, a loud explosion, followed by an appalling smell.

Clapping his hand over his nose, Lin cried, 'Good! The vermilion plant has purged the impurities from your system! I wonder what else you have lost!'

Tang Ao kept saying, 'Strange! Strange! Just now, I could

remember even the verses I composed as a child. Now I can remember only a tenth of it.'

'That is strange indeed,' said Old Tuo.

'Doubtless nine-tenths of your learning went out with that break of wind,' said Lin. 'The one-tenth you retain must be the inoffensive part. If you put it down on paper it will all be good. Why don't you take some vermilion plant, too, Old Tuo?'

'I am afraid I should be a vacuum then,' joked Old Tuo. 'My system is full of worthless knowledge. How about you?'

'There is nothing in me to purge,' said Lin. 'I am not learned like you two. But now I don't wonder that you love to travel, Brother Tang. Indeed, it does you a world of good!'

'Speaking of indeed,' said Old Tuo. 'Here comes the indeed itself!'

A strange-looking animal appeared on a hill. It resembled a gibbon, with a white coat with black lines on it, and was about four feet long, with a tail which was almost two feet long after it was wound around the body. Its fur was fine and long, and there were black whiskers under its chin. They saw that it was guarding the dead body of another indeed and crying very hard.

'Is that an indeed?' said Lin.

'It is indeed,' said Old Tuo. 'It is also called the indeed animal. It has a fierce loyalty to its own kind, which is why this indeed is crying. Its coat is used by hunters to make bedding, and very expensive, too. And they are easy to catch, because they do not run away from people. I suppose the dead indeed has been left there as a lure by a hunter. Soon, he'll come along and catch the live one without any trouble, because an indeed will always stop to weep over a dead one.'

Suddenly, a fierce wind came up from the mountains, and the trees shook and the leaves trembled. The three travellers thought it very strange, and hurried for shelter in the woods. When the wind blew over, a very large spotted tiger came swooping down from the opposite peak.

If the reader wants to know what happened next, please turn to the next chapter.

◄ 7 ►

When the large hairy tiger suddenly appeared from out of a high peak, the indeed shuddered with fright, but still did not leave the carcass of its dead companion. The tiger let out a blood-curdling screech, and opened its huge mouth and started to clamp its jaws down on the indeed. But an arrow flew out from the side of the hills, and pierced it precisely in the eye. The tiger dropped to the ground, and after struggling for a little while, turned over and died, with its four feet sticking up in the air.

'Marvellous shot!' cried Old Tuo. 'This is a hunter's poisoned arrow. It clots the blood as soon as it pierces the animal's skin, and causes instant death. But the tiger's skin is tough, and the hunter must shoot for the eye. What a marvellous one this must be! We must meet him!'

Soon, they saw a small tiger come along from the hills, and proceed to unburden itself of its coat. In fact, a young and beautiful maiden stepped out from it, dressed in a white hunter's suit, with a fisherwoman's scarf around her head, and with her bow slung across her shoulder. She came toward the tiger, and took from her waist a sword, and slashed the tiger's chest. She withdrew from its body a large, bloody heart. Then she put her sword away, skinned the animal, and rolling up the tiger skin, started to walk downhill.

'What a courageous young girl!' said Lin. 'Let me see if I can frighten her!' He raised his rifle, lit it, and fired a blank shot at her.

The girl immediately called, 'Please hold your honourable fire! I am not a bandit! Let me talk to you!' She came toward them, and greeted them with her palms pressed together.

'Please, may I inquire who you three elders are, and how you came to be here?'

Tang Ao told her where they came from, and who they were. The girl said, 'There is a Mister Tang, called Yiting, from Lingnan. I wonder if he is related to you?'

'Why, Yiting is my literary name,' said Tang Ao in surprise. 'How come you to know it?'

As soon as the girl heard this, she went down on her knees and cried, 'So it is you, Uncle Tang! Excuse me for not recognizing you at once!'

Tang Ao immediately pulled her to her feet and said, 'May I ask who you are, and why you address me as uncle? And why did you take the heart out of the tiger just now?'

'I come from the Kingdom on Earth myself,' said the girl. 'My surname is Lo, and I am called Red Lotus. My father was official record-keeper of Changan, and later became assistant to the Governor of Linghai. Since he helped Uncle Shu in the Rebellion, I don't know what has become of him. Grandfather, mother and I have been hiding overseas, here in an old temple. However, last year, the temple was wrecked when the tigers assaulted other beasts in this mountain, and my mother was crushed to death in the wreckage. I have pledged to avenge my mother by killing all the tigers in the mountain, and was taking the tiger's heart out of this one to offer up to my mother's spirit, when you came along. I have often heard my grandfather say that my father and you were great friends.'

'So you are the daughter of Lo Pinwang!' said Tang Ao. 'I wonder if you could take me to see your grandfather?'

Red Lotus led them to a temple which was called the Temple of Lotus. Its walls were crumbling, and there were no monks living in it. All that was left of it was the altar of worship, and two rooms in the back, the rest being in ruins. But so much foliage had grown around them that they lent the place a quaint charm.

Red Lotus, with the tiger's heart in her hand, went inside to announce the visitors. Soon, an old man with a white beard came out, whom Tang Ao recognized as Lo Lung. Immediately, they bowed to him. The old man asked them to sit down.

'We have been in exile for fourteen years,' said Lo Lung, 'ever since my son took part in the Rebellion, and I don't know the whereabouts of my grandson, either, who was in the Rebel Army with his father. I escaped with my daughter-in-law, who was expecting Red Lotus, to these foreign parts. Now the child is motherless also, and to avenge her mother, she has abandoned her studies and taken up bow and arrow, and vowed to kill all the tigers in these mountains before she will take off her mourning clothes. Last month she killed one, and today, another. But what chance it is for her to meet you today! I am not able to return to the Kingdom on Earth because of my son, but I am a willing exile, as my time is limited. But Red Lotus is young, and should not spend the rest of her life in this place. There is a nursemaid and a servant, too. If you could adopt her, and take her back with you to Lingnan, and when she is old enough, find a good husband for her, I should be forever grateful to you though my spirit be in the Nine Streams.'

He began to weep.

'I shall take her back with me,' said Tang Ao. 'Pinwang and I were like brothers. You should come back with me too, were it not for the fact that the Empress has orders to kill off the family of all the rebels, and it is not safe, especially since you have a record as an official yourself. And it will not be as easy to hide you as to hide a young girl. As for myself, it was my cherished ambition to do good in the world, and with a few faithful and loyal friends, try and bring the Emperor back to the throne. Now, however, I have severed my ties with the worldly life. But it is the least I can do to take your granddaughter back with me, although I do not know when we shall actually be going back.'

'I don't know how to thank you,' said Lo Lung, 'but I must not detain you. I shall ask Red Lotus to consider herself as your adopted daughter, and tell her and her nursemaid to come with you.'

When Red Lotus heard this, she began to wail, and at the same time, kowtowed eight times to Tang Ao as her godfather. She kowtowed to Merchant Lin and Old Tuo as well, and said, 'I should like to come with you, but I cannot leave my grandfather alone in these remote parts, and also, there are two more tigers in these mountains which I must kill. Please leave your address in Lingnan, and in the future if the Empress proclaims an amnesty, we shall come back and pay our respects to you. But I cannot come with you now.'

They all tried to persuade her, but Red Lotus would not listen, and vowed to take care of her grandfather until the end of his days.

'Why don't we leave her here for now and pick her up later on our way back?' suggested Lin.

'How do I know I shall come this way again?' Tang Ao asked mysteriously.

'Of course you'll come back,' said Lin.

So it was decided, and Lo Lung wrote down their address for them.

Red Lotus said, 'Will you be passing the Country of Witches? I have a sworn sister there, Sweet Asarum. She escaped with her father Hsueh Chungtsang at the same time as grandfather did, and we swore that if one of us had a chance to go back, she would try to take the other along. Last year a silk merchant came through here, and that is how I know she is in the Country of Witches.'

Old Tuo said that the Country of Witches was on their way. While Red Lotus was writing her letter, Tang Ao asked Lin to go back to the junk, and get two packages of silver, which he gave to Lo Lung.

It was already dark when they returned to the junk.

'What a filial child that is,' said Old Tuo. 'It just goes to show that where there's a will, there's a way, and it doesn't matter if one is too young! I'll wager that this mountain will soon have no tigers left in it!'

'Seeing the tiger attack the indeed has made me think,' said Lin. 'I have heard it said that when a man meets a tiger, whether the tiger eats him or not depends upon destiny, and if it isn't in one's destiny to be eaten by a tiger, the tiger will not harm him even though he comes face to face with it. Is that true?'

'No, indeed,' said Old Tuo, shaking his head. 'Actually, tigers don't want to eat people at all. It is best put this way : if a tiger eats a man, it is because it mistakes him for a beast, because the man is like a beast in some way. Actually, tigers and leopards are afraid of human beings. The reason why some people are mistaken for beasts by tigers is this : we men all have a radiance over our heads, and a tiger will shy away from it when it sees it. But if a man's light is dimmed through evil-doing, the tiger will mistake him for a beast, for beasts don't have any radiance. The brightness of a man's light depends on his goodness, and a good bright light will not only keep tigers away, but all kinds of evil spirits as well. That is the difference between human beings and animals. But take the indeed, for instance, who would not abandon its dead friend. Indeed, it may be said to have a beast's face, but a human heart. How are we to know that it does not have a radiance over its head, too, for did not the tiger ignore it, and not harm it? By the same token, when a tiger sees a man with a human face and a beast's heart, why should it not eat him? People hate tigers for injuring people, but they don't know why they do it.'

'This really makes a person want to mend his ways!' Tang Ao said.

'But I had a relative who was extremely devout,' said Lin. 'He was a vegetarian, too, and spent most of his time chanting sutras. One day, he was on his way up a mountain to worship at a temple when he was eaten by a tiger. Can you say that a person like that has no radiance over his head?'

'It is difficult to say,' said Old Tuo. 'He may appear to be a devout Taoist, but had no love for people in his heart. Perhaps he was unfilial, perhaps he coveted another man's wife. Who knows what else he was besides a vegetarian who chanted sutras!'

Lin said, 'According to you, then, if a man has done wrong, no

55

matter how hard he tries to correct himself (by acts of contrition) it is useless?'

'No, one cannot say that either,' said Old Tuo. 'It depends upon the wrong he has done, and the act of contrition. If you are un-filial to your parents, or have coveted another man's wife, abstaining from eating meat and chanting sutras will not be enough to help. These are but outward signs of contrition. Who knows whether the man has changed at heart? In other words, all depends on a man's heart. One cannot judge by the appearance of outward piety alone.'

When they were not far from the junk, they saw a large bird fly from the forest. It was shaped like a human being, with arms and legs, but it had two heads, a pair of wings, and was covered all over with feathers. One head was that of a man, and the other of a woman, and on the forehead of each was inscribed the word 'unfilial'.

'Speak of the devil!' cried Old Tuo. 'Here comes the unfilial bird!'

Upon hearing the word 'unfilial', Lin lit his rifle, and brought the bird to the ground with a shot. It was still struggling on the ground when Lin punched it, and killed it off. They saw that not only was the word 'unfilial' inscribed on their foreheads, but the words 'no charity' on their lips, 'no righteousness' on their arms and 'neglected her parents because of her husband' on the right wing, and 'neglected his parents because of his wife' on the left.

'I have heard of this bird, but I have never thought that I would see it with my own eyes,' sighed Tang Ao. 'Weren't these people whose behaviour during their lifetime was more like animals than human beings, and who were not allowed to be reborn in human form after death, but were changed into this kind of bird by their foul vapours?'

Old Tuo nodded. 'Brother Tang is truly well-informed. I have seen this bird before, but with two men's heads, and it did not have the words "neglected her parents because of her husband" on the wing. There are also birds with two women's heads. They are supposed to be most adapt in cultivating Tao and atoning for their sins. As they approach Tao, the words fade from their bodies, until they disappear altogether. After a further period of cultivation of the soul, the feathers drop off, and they are eligible to go to heaven.'

'It proves that heaven gives everyone a second chance.'

Some sailors who had come ashore to get fresh water crowded around to look at the bird. 'Since it is an unfilial bird,' they said, 'there is no harm in plucking its feathers and making brooms out of them.'

When they finished doing this and were about to return to the junk, there came a spray of glue from the forest, followed by a foul smell. A weird-looking bird flew out, which was shaped like a mouse, about five feet long, with red claws and very long wings.

Lin was going to fire a shot at it, but discovered that his wick had become wet. 'We have seen a great many queer birds, but nothing like this,' said the sailors. 'Does it have Old Tuo stumped?'

'This is a saliva bird,' said Old Tuo. 'It comes from the Country of Dog-faced People. When it is hungry, it drools all over the trees and anything which sets foot on its saliva is stuck in it because of the glue-like consistency. That is how it traps its food. See, the poor unfilial bird has been plucked of its feathers and is now being devoured.'

When they returned to the junk, Merchant Lin showed Mistress Lu and Pleasant the large grain, and they thought that it was remarkable.

After a few days of sailing, Merchant Lin's ship dropped anchor in the waters of the Country of Gentlemen, and Lin went on shore to sell his merchandise. Tang Ao had heard that to the people of this country, others' desires mattered more than one's own selfish interest, and thought that it must be a model country. He went with Old Tuo to explore it, and after walking several *lis*, they came to the city gates on which were inscribed the words, 'Only Kindness is Precious'.

To know what happened next, please see the next chapter.

◄ *8* ►

The streets appeared to Tang Ao and Old Tuo to be much like those in the Kingdom on Earth, and were full of people buying and selling. Going up to an old man, Tang Ao inquired whether it was true that to the people of this country, other people's desires always mattered more than one's own. But the old man could not understand what he was talking about. Tang Ao asked him what was the meaning of 'gentlemen' and again, the old man could not reply. Finally, Old Tuo said, 'You are asking him to judge his people by the standards of other countries, therefore asking him questions he cannot answer. He does not know what being a gentleman means, because he does not know what it is to be anything else.'

When they came to the market, they overheard a soldier talking to a shopkeeper. He was holding something in his hand and saying, 'What a lovely thing this is! But you are charging too little for it! How could I deprive you of it? Please do me the favour of making it more costly, so that I may buy it with an easy conscience. If you refuse, it will only mean that you do not consider me your friend.'

'I suppose this is an example of what is meant by other people's interest mattering more than one's own,' whispered Tang Ao to Old Tuo.

The shopkeeper replied, 'You know that we are not allowed to haggle here. All prices are one! I am afraid I shall have to ask you to shop elsewhere if you insist on paying more than the fixed price, for I cannot oblige.'

'You are putting me in a extremely difficult position by refusing to charge more,' said the soldier. 'I should not be kind if I agreed. How dare I take advantage of you?'

The shopkeeper still would not give in, so the soldier had no choice but to pay him what was asked, but took only half of what he had paid for, and started to go. But the merchant pressed the rest of the goods on him, and would not let him go until he had taken more than his money's worth. The dispute was finally settled by two passersby, a pair of old men, who said that the soldier should take not less than eighty per cent of what he paid for.

Tang Ao and Old Tuo thought that it was just.

After a few steps, they saw another soldier who was trying to buy something. He was telling the merchant, 'I asked you the price of this, and you would not tell me, but kept asking me to name my own price. Now I have done so, you tell me it is much too much, so I have lowered it and still you say the price is too high. What shall I do?'

'Truly, I dare not charge too much for my articles, which are inferior in quality to what they sell in other shops, and none too fresh, either. How can I think of charging you even half of what you want to pay?'

'Really,' thought Tang Ao, 'customer and shopkeeper have changed places. Each is saying what the other would say in other countries.'

'What are you talking about?' said the soldier. 'I recognize the quality of your goods, and they are not inferior at all. How could you think of charging me only half price?'

'I can only charge you half price,' replied the merchant, 'if you insist on paying more, I am afraid you will have to take your custom elsewhere, for I honestly cannot let you pay so much and feel easy about it.'

When the soldier saw that this was the highest price the merchant was willing to charge, he paid it, took only a few items of inferior quality, and started to walk away.

The merchant hurried after him, saying, 'Why are you such a difficult customer? Why do you take so little, do you want me to make a profit from it? I didn't think that you would be so hard to please!'

The soldier said frantically, 'I didn't want to take the best quality. I only took the worst, because I would not feel right about it otherwise, since I had paid so little.'

'But if you only wanted the inferior quality, you should have given me even less money. How can you pay me so much and take so little?'

The soldier did not heed him, and went away. The people on the street thought that he had not given the merchant a fair deal, so he had no course but to come back, and exchange half of what he had taken for goods of the best quality.

Then there was a farmer who had finished his purchases, and was in the act of paying for them. The merchant was weighing the silver and said, 'Please, brother, don't go away. Here in the city we deal in second-grade silver only, and you have given me the best grade. I know you don't mind over-paying, but I don't want to be over-paid, either. Please take some of this back.'

'It is only a small sum,' said the farmer. 'Why don't you keep it, and we shall even up next time I come to do business with you.'

The merchant said, 'No, no. Last year there was a customer who wanted to do the same thing, but he never came back! I owe him to the next incarnation! What shall I do if you don't come back either? Shall I become a horse or donkey in the next life and work for you to repay what you have left me, when I must already be reincarnated once as a horse or donkey to pay back what I owe the other fellow? Please, take what is yours, to save ourselves trouble later on!'

Put this way, the farmer obliged, and took a few things from the shop in place of the silver, and went away, while the merchant continued to complain that it was not fair, that he had taken too little. But the farmer was gone now, and there was nothing he could do.

A beggar happened to come by. The merchant weighed out the silver he thought he owed the farmer, and gave it to him.

'Now I have seen everything,' thought Tang Ao. 'This is truly a country of gentlemen!'

He was so thinking when down the road strutted two gentlemen of style, smiling and bowing. Tang Ao and his friend shied to one side to let them pass, and the two gentlemen asked their names.

Tang Ao learned that these two were brothers, Wu Tseho and Wu Tsehsiang, and after Tang Ao and Old Tuo had identified themselves, the brothers invited them to their home for a chat. Their home was covered with climbing wisteria, and there was a pond full of water caltrop in front.

It was soon evident that the two gentlemen were learned in scholarship and appreciated the fine arts of living, as well as possessing the most original and sensible opinions on the values and customs of society. They spoke eloquently against the custom of choosing propitious burial places for one's parents, and against the killing of fowl and pigs and lamb for feasting to celebrate the birth of a child. For, as Wu Tsehsiang said, 'Is it heaven's will to sacrifice many lives in order to celebrate the birth of one, human though that one may be?'

The brothers were especially against the custom of placing a high value on a comodity simply because it is rare, such as birds' nests, which are considered to be the finest of foods in the Kingdom on Earth, because they are rare, and yet tasteless, without nutritional value, and not unlike wax in substance, and had to be cooked in the best chicken soup to be palatable. Birds' nests abounded in the Country of Gentlemen, but no one would eat them.

In fact, the brothers were against most of the rituals which were attendant upon eating, living, being born and dying, considering them to be senseless and extravagant.

Tang Ao and Old Tuo listened with great appreciation. Then an old servant hurried in and said, 'Begging your pardon, gentlemen, but the King is coming to discuss some urgent matters with you.'

'In our country when we want to get rid of guests, we give the servant a wink, and he comes in to say that someone is calling, or awaits our presence, so that the guests will leave,' thought Old Tuo. 'I wonder if this is the same trick.'

He and Tang Ao both rose, and left, only to find that the road leading to the house was being swept, and that people were keeping clear of it for the King, proof that it was no excuse at all.

'These gentlemen surely have my admiration,' said Old Tuo. 'How vulgar our own officials seem in comparison!'

'They are really worthy to be called "gentlemen" in the truest sense of the word,' said Tang Ao.

When they returned to the junk, they found Merchant Lin had already come back, having failed to make any profit because it seemed that the Country of Gentlemen had plenty of everything. Just as they were about to cast off, messengers came from the Wu family, bearing gifts of fruit and pastry, and for the sailors, ten piculs of melon and ten piculs of bird's nest.

The messengers had just left when Wu Tseho himself came, and after being welcomed on board, said, 'I am sorry my younger brother has not come, but the King is in our house, and he is entertaining him. My brother has informed the King of your presence, and he has sent me especially as emissary to convey his respects. I should wait to see you off, but as the King is waiting for me, I must take my leave now. I hope you will return.' Then he hurried away.

The sailors stowed the melon and the bird's nest in the ship's hold. They sailed soon after, and when evening came, cooked a mess of melon and a mess of bird's nest. The sailors were delighted to taste this food, which they could not afford to eat in ordinary times, but when they put the bird's nest in their mouths, they frowned and cried, 'What is this stuff? It is like glutinous noodles! Have we been tricked?'

At the end of the meal, they had eaten all the melon, but there was still a lot of bird's nest left, and Merchant Lin was delighted, and told Old Tuo to buy what was left in the hold from the sailors at the price of noodles, thinking that he would make a handsome profit when he went back to the Kingdom on Earth.

As they were going to drop anchor for the night, they heard a cry for help.

Tang Ao emerged from the cabin, and found a big fisherman's boat by the bank, and told the sailors to pull alongside it. There was a young girl on board, who was dripping wet, but very pretty, with white teeth and ruby-red lips, and who was wearing a green silk turban, a silvery red vest with a silk sash with a sword stuck in it, and a pair of leather trousers. Around her neck there was a rope, which was tied to the mast. Beside her stood a fisherman and his wife.

Tang Ao stared at them and asked, 'Is this your daughter? Why have you tied her to the mast? Who are you, and what is this place called?'

'You are still in the waters of the Country of Gentlemen,' said the fisherman. 'I come from the Country of Green Mound, I am a fisherman. I know that the people who live here are all gentlemen, and I did not want to come here to fish secretly, but I have not had much luck lately, and I heard that fish abound in these waters, so I cast my net here, and just as I was hauling it up, I discovered this girl in it. I don't know how many coppers I'll get for her when I go back, but at least it won't be nothing. However, this girl keeps wanting me to let her go. How can I do that, when I have caught nothing for so long, and spent so much money to come here? Do you want me to go back empty-handed? Can I live on air?'

Tang Ao asked the girl, 'Who are you, and why are you dressed like this? Did you fall into the water or did you try to drown yourself? Tell me quickly so that I can help you!'

The girl's eyes grew big with tears. 'I come from Narcissus Village in the Country of Gentlemen,' she said. 'I am fourteen years old and have studied since I was a child. My father was Lien Li, an official. Three years ago, he was ordered to a neighbouring country to help fight a battle. The battle was lost, and he was exiled to a remote part of the land where he died, and our property was destroyed. My mother's name is Liang, and she is ill and unable to take ordinary medicine, but depends only upon sea slugs for nourishment. This is a food which we have always purchased from abroad. However, since we have no funds, and I was told that there are sea slugs in the deep waters here, I thought I could dive for them if I understood the nature of water. So I purchased a large urn, and filled it with water, and practised being submerged in it every day in order to know its nature. Eventually, I could remain submerged in it for a whole day. After I acquired this skill, I thought that I was ready to dive for sea slugs in order to save my mother's life. I was on this errand when I was caught in the fisherman's net. Really, my life is worth nothing to anyone but my widowed mother. If you help me, I shall become a horse or dog in the next incarnation to serve you!' She began to cry.

Tang Ao was sceptical of the girl's story. 'You said you have studied since you were small,' he said. 'Then you must know how to write your name.'

The girl nodded. Tang Ao asked a sailor to fetch brush and paper. 'Please write your name for me,' he said.

The girl took the brush in her hand, and after a moment, began to write. When the sailor handed it to Tang Ao, he saw that she had written a poem:

Like a fish floundering in shallow waters,
I am waiting for help;
Open your net and save me.
'Tis a fish which has wandered far from home.
Written in tears by a maiden in distress,
Lien Flowering Maple of Narcissus Village,
Country of Gentlemen.

Tang Ao thought, 'I doubted her story about looking for sea slugs for her mother, but now I believe her.'

'You are not only literate, but a poet! Quite extraordinary!' he said, and turning to the fisherman, said, 'Here, I will let you have ten strings of a thousand cash each, be a good fellow and set this girl free. She comes from a good family, and you will be doing yourself a good turn by letting her go.'

'You'll never have an empty net again, your business will prosper if you let her go,' chimed in Lin.

The fisherman shook his head. 'Mind your own business,' he said. 'How can I let her go for ten strings of cash?'

'What are you talking about?' said Old Tuo. 'Is she for you to dispose of as you please?'

'You may dispose of the fish in your net as you please, but not if your catch is a person,' added Lin. 'What if we say that we don't let *you* go until you let *her* go?'

He leaped over to the fisherman's boat. The fisherman's wife cried, 'Heavens above! Bandits! Well, we will see who wins!' and tried to leap over to Lin's junk, but was prevented by the sailors.

'Fisherman, how much do you want for the release of this young lady?' Tang Ao asked.

'A hundred strings of cash, fair and square.'

Tang Ao went into the cabin and fetched the money and gave it to the fisherman, who untied the girl. Flowering Maple stepped over to Merchant Lin's junk, and after taking off her leather outfit,

thanked her saviours and asked them who they were, as the fisherman's boat made its getaway.

'Where do you live?' asked Tang Ao. 'Is it far from here?'

'No, it is only a few *li*s from here. It is called Narcissus Village
because there are a lot of narcissi there.'

'Then we shall take you home.'

'I wonder if you could wait a little while,' said Flowering Maple.
'All the sea slugs I found today were on that fisherman's boat, and I
would like to go down and get some more before we go back.'

'Take all the time you want,' said Tang Ao.

Flowering Maple put on her leather outfit again and dived into
the sea. When Lin saw this, he cried out in alarm, 'You shouldn't
have let her go! Who knows what will be her fate in this big sea!'

But Old Tuo said, 'Don't worry about her. I think she is used
to it, and will not drown. And she is carrying a sword to protect
herself from man-eating fish and tortoises. She will come up again
in a moment.'

They waited for some time, but still saw no trace of the girl. 'I'll
bet she has been eaten by a shark,' said Lin. 'What are we going
to do?'

'There is a sailor on board who is extremely good at diving,' said
Old Tuo. 'What about it if we send him down?'

The sailor immediately jumped into the sea, and after a moment,
surfaced and said, 'The girl is having a fight with a big oyster. She
has just killed it, and is on her way up.'

Soon, Flowering Maple herself came up. There were traces of
blood on her body, and after she climbed on board and took off her
diving outfit, she showed them a brilliant pearl. Kneeling down in
front of Tang Ao, she said, 'I had no way of thanking you for what
you did for me. When I was in the sea, I saw a very large oyster,
and took this pearl from it. I hope you will take it as an expression
of my gratitude.'

'It is a jewel fit for a king,' said Tang Ao. 'Why give it to me?
Present it to your King, who will surely reward you for it, and help
toward the support of your mother.'

'We place no value on jewels in our country,' said Flowering
Maple. 'That is what is meant by "Only kindness is precious".
Please take it, as we have no use for it in our country.'

Tang Ao had no alternative but to accept the pearl. The sailors
set sail for Narcissus Village, and he took Flowering Maple into the
cabin to meet Mistress Lu and Pleasant, who immediately took the
girl to their hearts.

At Narcissus Village, Tang Ao took some silver and together with
Lin and Old Tuo, accompanied Flowering Maple to her home. An

old woman answered the door when she knocked, and taking Flowering Maple's leather clothes, said, 'Why are you so late? Madam is a little better. Did you find any sea slugs?'

Flowering Maple hurriedly showed her guests inside, and soon came in with her mother, Mistress Liang, on her arm, who thanked Tang Ao and his friends soundly for saving her daughter's life.

After talking a little, Tang Ao discovered that Flowering Maple's ancestors came from Lingnan, and that they came here during the confusion of the South-North Dynasty, and had made their home in the Country of Gentlemen ever since. In fact, Tang Ao's great-grandfather married a daughter of the Lien family, so they were related.

Mistress Liang was delighted. 'We have been here for three generations,' she said. 'Now my husband is dead, I have no brothers, and my son is still young. We are very lonely here. I have always thought of going back to Lingnan, but dared not venture the long journey with no one to protect us. If you could take us on your way back and look after us, we should be eternally grateful to you.'

'We should be glad to,' said Tang Ao, 'but we still have far to travel, and don't know when we shall return. I wonder how old your son is, and whether we might meet him.'

Mistress Liang called the boy, and Brilliant came in, and made his bows to the guests. 'I am thirteen years old,' he said, 'and study with my sister, as the family has no funds to engage a tutor. I have finished the *Nine Classics* and am now studying *Laotse* and *Chuangtse*.'

'Last year, when we leased some of these rooms to a teacher, the boy was able to study with him in lieu of our receiving any money for rent, but now the teacher has left, and there is no one to teach him,' said Mistress Liang.

'Did my cousin not leave any property or money to you?' said Tang Ao. 'How do you maintain yourselves, and does it cost very much to send the boy to school?'

'It only costs ten or twenty pieces of silver a year,' said Mistress Liang. 'I and my daughter have been earning our living with our needle. Luckily the price of rice is not high, and we can just make ends meet.'

Tang Ao gave Brilliant two packages of silver and told his mother, 'What a splendid boy you have here! His studies should not be neglected. If he studies hard, I am sure he will pass the Imperial Examinations when he returns to the Kingdom on Earth, and repay you in happiness many times.'

Mistress Liang thanked him and said in tears, 'I really don't know what to say. My life is like a candle flickering in the wind.

Although my daughter brings me sea slugs, it only prolongs it for a little while, for my illness is incurable. If you would look after my children and see to their marriages when they return to Lingnan, I should be more than grateful.'

'Of course I shall do so,' said Tang Ao. 'Please rest assured.'

When they returned to the junk, Tang Ao expressed his admiration for Flowering Maple, and began to consider her as a possible wife for his son Little Summit.

After a few days of travelling, they arrived at the Country of Giants. If the reader wants to know what happened there, please read the next chapter.

Lin did not want to trade in the Country of Giants, because he knew the people here were very much like those in the Country of Gentlemen which they had just left, and where he had made no profit. But he accompanied Tang Ao on a tour of the country.

Tang Ao said, 'I have heard that the people of this country walk on clouds. I cannot wait to see them!'

'We'll have to walk more than twenty *li*s before we see anybody,' said Old Tuo, 'and it will be late before we come back. The roads are confusing, and it won't be easy to find the peak where the people make their city.'

They walked for some time, and saw a few farms, and a few people living on them, who were taller than most people by two or three feet. Everyone walked on his own cloud, which was about half a foot from the ground, and when the person stood still, the cloud remained under his feet.

The travellers climbed up a hill, crossed two peaks, and found that they were nowhere near where they wanted to go.

'We must be lost,' said Old Tuo. 'Let us go over to that temple there and ask the way.'

They approached the temple, and knocked on the door. But before anyone opened it, an old man came by, holding a pot of wine in one hand, and the roasted head of a pig in the other.

'We beg your pardon, sir,' said Tang Ao. 'Could you tell us the name of this temple, and whether any monks live in it?'

The old man put his wine and roast pig's head down and said, putting his hands together in supplication, 'This is the Kuan-yin Temple, and I'm a monk.'

Merchant Lin could not conceal his surprise. 'Why, how could you be,' he said, 'when you have not shaved your head, and obviously you have been buying meat and wine to enjoy yourself? From the look of things, would I be unreasonable to conclude that monks and nuns live together in this temple?'

'There is indeed a nun, and she is my wife,' said the old man. 'Apart from us two, no one else lives here. We are keepers of the temple, but in our country, we do not know anything about monks and nuns. It is from your illustrious country that we heard that those who live in temples must shave their heads and be called monks and nuns. Accordingly, we follow the custom, but we have not bothered to observe the other requirements. I wonder where you are going and where you came from?'

Old Tuo told him, and the old man said, bowing, 'Oh, I was not aware that I was in such distinguished company! Please come in and have a cup of tea!'

Tang Ao demurred, saying that they were anxious to get across the peak. Merchant Lin said, 'I am wondering what you call a child who has a monk for a father and a nun for a mother?'

The old man laughed. 'We are only keepers of the temple,' he said. 'What would you expect our children to be called? What do you call the children of the keepers of your temples?'

'I hear that in your country, everyone walks on a cloud. Is this cloud born with a person?'

'These clouds are born with us,' said the old man. 'They are not man-made. It is best if one has a rainbow-coloured cloud. Yellow is second, and black is the worst.'

'We have far to travel before returning to our ship,' said Old Tuo. 'If you would be so kind as to point the way, we should be going along.'

The old man told them which way to go, and they took a winding path, and crossed the peak.

When they found the city, they saw that everything looked much the same as in the Country of Gentlemen, except that everyone was walking on clouds of different colours. A beggar went past walking on a rainbow-coloured cloud.

'Isn't that odd,' said Tang Ao, 'since the rainbow-coloured cloud is supposed to be best, and the black cloud the worst.'

'And that old fellow at the temple was obviously a monk who had not kept his vows,' said Lin. 'Yet he, too, had a rainbow-coloured cloud.'

'When I came here before, I was told that the colour of one's cloud depends not on whether he is rich or poor, but on the way he conducts himself,' said Old Tuo. 'If a man is open with people, straightforward and honest, he has a rainbow cloud, but if he is secretive and conniving, he walks on a black cloud. The colour of one's cloud changes with his temper, and so you may find a rich man walking on a black cloud, and a poor man on a rainbow cloud. However, look! Hardly a soul is walking on a black cloud! The people of this country must all be kind-hearted and good-natured – doubtless, because they would be ashamed to be seen with a black cloud under their feet, and are proud when they can show off a good-coloured cloud. This country is called the Country of Giants. People who don't know think that the people are really giants. Actually, it refers to the largeness of their hearts.'

'But I have often heard that there is a country abroad somewhere where the people are very tall,' said Tang Ao. 'Can I be mistaken?'

'Oh, you must mean the Country of Tall People,' said Old Tuo, 'which is different from this one.'

Suddenly, the pedestrians shied to either side of the street, and someone who was obviously an important official swaggered past, wearing a black turban and an elaborate costume. He carried a red umbrella, and had a retinue of subordinates behind and in front of him, who shouted to the people to make way. But the official's cloud was surrounded by a red curtain, so that no one could see it.

'I suppose this official doesn't need a carriage to ride in, since he is already walking on a cloud,' said Tang Ao. 'But I wonder why he has hidden his cloud behind a curtain?'

'Sometimes a man will get an attack of stormy grey cloud,' said Old Tuo, 'because he has done something which conscience tells him is wrong. This man has hidden his grey cloud behind a curtain because he doesn't want people to see it, but of course by hiding it behind a curtain he is only calling attention to it. Luckily, a cloud changes colour when a man changes heart, and a man who persistently walks over a dark cloud is ostracized by everyone in this country, and even punished.'

'Oh, how unfair!' said Lin.

'How unfair?' asked Tang Ao.

'How unfair it is that only the people of this country have clouds under their feet! If everyone in the world had to carry a self-advertisement like this, how wonderful people would be!'

'We may not have clouds under our feet, but when we do something wrong, the smoke which rises from our heads can be seen from far away. Isn't that just as effective?' said Old Tuo.

'What do you mean?'

'Whatever we do, old Father Heaven always knows,' said Old Tuo. 'He knows exactly who has done right and who has done wrong.'

'I suppose heaven is not unjust after all,' said Lin.

After walking about a little more, they returned to the junk before dark.

After a few days, the junk arrived at the Country of Restless People. The people here had black faces, and were so restless that they moved about all the time. Even when they sat down or stopped walking, they could not keep their arms and legs still.

'They look like epileptics,' said Lin. 'I wonder if they keep moving when they are asleep! It's lucky I don't live here, I'd fall apart in a couple of days.'

'Do they live to an old age for all their ceaseless activity?' Tang Ao inquired.

'Yes, they do,' said Old Tuo. 'They all live to a ripe old age, because they exercise their muscles so much, and because, being too restless to farm, they live on fruits and nuts, and being too nervous to cook, fried food never touches their mouths. But I am getting dizzy watching them. I would like to go back.'

Tang Ao thought that he had seen enough, too, and they all went back after Lin had bought a pair of two-headed birds which could make marvellous sounds, which he thought he would sell at the Country of Split-tongued People.

After a few days, they came to the Country of Long-eared People, where the people's ears hung down to their waists, and they walked about holding their earlobes in their hands.

Then Tang Ao and his companions arrived at the Country of Intestineless People, who considered eating a social embarrassment, much as people in other countries considered defecation, and ate only when no one was looking. This was because as soon as they ate something, it passed through their bodies undigested to emerge at the other end.

Next to the Country of Intestineless People was the Country of Dog-headed People, who, on the other hand, spent all their time in the enjoyment of food and drink, and did not know how to do anything else. Tang Ao wanted to go and look at them, but Old Tuo thought that they should not, since the people had no pupils in their eyes and were so greedy that they had lost their sense of judgement, and could not tell a good man from a bad man.

One day, the travellers arrived at the Country of Black-bottomed People. The skin of the people was black from the waist down, although the upper part of their bodies was fair. They were a country of fishermen, and the place was desolate and poor. The sailors, however, wanted to buy some fish, so they tied up, and went up along the seashore. The people wore capes and fish-skin trousers, and were bare-footed. One man was hauling up his net which had a queer fish in it with one head and ten bodies.

'Is this the *Chih* fish from the *Chih* waters which tastes like spice and smells like orchids?' asked Tang Ao.

Before Old Tuo could answer, Merchant Lin crouched down, took a sniff of the fish, wrinkled up his face and retched.

Old Tuo laughed. 'You should not have been so hasty,' he said. 'Give it a kick, and it will bark like a dog.'

Lin did so, and the fish barked.

'This, then, is the other one, the *Holo* fish,' said Tang Ao.

'Yes,' said Old Tuo. 'Both the *Holo* fish and the *Chih* fish have ten bodies to a head, but one smells heavenly, and the other extremely foul. Our brother here should have found out which one this one was first.'

As they were watching the fishermen haul a big net in, an old man with white hair came over and said, 'Brother Tang! Do you remember me?'

He was wearing a fisherman's hat of woven bamboo, with a fish-skin cape around his shoulders, and his legs were as black as the bottom of a kettle. Tang Ao took a good look at him, and got the shock of his life.

In fact it was his old teacher Yin Yuan, the Imperial Censor. 'What are you doing here, Master, and in this garb?' he cried. 'Can I be dreaming?'

'It's a long story,' said Yin Yuan. 'I live not far from here. I'd be happy to tell you all about it if you come to my house.'

It was a very small thatched-roofed house of two rooms, but clean and tidy, although there was no furniture in it. So they sat on the floor.

Yin Yuan explained that when the Emperor was banished from the throne by Empress Wu, he had incurred the displeasure of Her Majesty when he submitted three official memoranda to her, advising her to abdicate and allow the Emperor to come back. He resigned from his post, and had lived a quiet life from then on. However, at the time of the Rebellion, some minister at Court brought up his past record and called it to the Empress's attention. He had no choice, then, but to escape overseas.

The people of this country were poor, and they did not like to have strangers living among them. But luckily, Yin Yuan had a daughter who was skilled at making fishnets, and they sold these for a living. After some time passed, the people came to take pity on them, and told Yin to paint his legs black. When he did this, he passed as a native, and was allowed to fish along with the rest of the people.

In turn, Tang Ao told his story, and then asked his teacher about his family.

Yin Yuan sighed and said that his wife was dead, but he had a son, Jade, and a daughter, Scarlet Dogwood, aged thirteen, whom he called in to meet the guests.

Although the children were shabbily dressed, both seemed extremely intelligent and well-mannered, and the girl was unusually pretty.

'Why don't you take them and go home?' Tang Ao asked. 'It is many years since the Rebellion. The Empress should no longer make any trouble for you.'

'I dare not risk it,' said Yin Yuan. 'And even if I did, where would the money come from? I am having a hard time to find enough money to buy our food and clothes.'

'Then why don't you try to go somewhere else, where the people are more civilized, and will treat you better, for instance the Country of Gentlemen or the Country of Giants?'

'I would like to, but I am weak and old, and much as I hate this place, and hate being a fisherman, I am afraid that I cannot leave,' replied Yin Yuan.

Tang Ao thought of the Lien family in Narcissus Village and said, 'I know a place you can move to. I wonder if you would consider it?'

'What place is that, and how far is it?'

Tang Ao told him about Flowering Maple, and added, 'The mother is worried about the education of her children and she has spare rooms to let. You could move in, take a few pupils, and your daughter could earn something from her needlework. I should think that you could make enough to live on. I'll lend you some money for your passage, and when we return to the village, we can make plans for going home together.'

Yin Yuan was delighted, and extremely grateful. 'Come to think of it,' said Tang Ao, 'the son and daughter of the Lien family are just about the age of your own children. They would be perfect matches for each other. Would you have any objections if I broached the subject to the mother?'

'From what you have told me, what more could I ask for in a daughter-in-law and son-in-law?' said Yin Yuan.

'Then I shall write a letter suggesting it, for you to take along. I am sure they will agree.'

'Why do you say that?'

Tang Ao explained that Mistress Liang had entrusted the marriages of her children to him.

'But from what I hear of Flowering Maple, you should take her for your own daughter-in-law,' said Yin Yuan. 'How can you give her to me?'

'There is no hurry about my son,' said Tang Ao. 'And besides, there is another candidate for him,' and told his teacher about Red Lotus.

'Then after I am in Narcissus Village, I'll go to the Mountain of Eastern Opening, and arrange the match for you,' said Yin Yuan gratefully. 'Leave everything to me!'

Tang Ao returned to the junk, where he fetched a lot of clothing, two envelopes full of silver, and brought these to his teacher with his letter.

Yin Yuan washed the black paint off his legs, put on the shoes and stockings and clothes that Tang Ao gave him, and took his son and daughter to Narcissus Village. Mistress Liang was delighted when she read Tang Ao's letter, and the two families lived harmoniously together. Yin Yuan took a few pupils, and taught them together with his own children, and his prospective son- and daughter-in-law. Scarlet Dogwood made some money with her needle, so the three found that they could live quite comfortably.

After some time, Yin Yuan went to the Mountain of Eastern Opening, and arranged the match between Tang Ao's son Little Summit and Red Lotus with Lo Lung. Narcissus Village was not far from the Mountain of Eastern Opening, and Yin Yuan went there often to visit, because Lo Lung was in failing health.

Not long after, Lo Lung died, and Red Lotus buried him in the old temple. She had already killed the two tigers which remained in the mountain, so she readily consented when Yin Yuan asked her and her nursemaid and servant to come and live in Narcissus Village. Mistress Liang was glad to have her, and treated her like a member of the family for Tang Ao's sake.

When they did not hear from Tang Ao again for two years, the families thought that he must have returned to Lingnan by another route, and began to make plans for going back to the Kingdom on Earth themselves.

When Tang Ao returned to the junk after taking leave of his old teacher, he heard a noise which sounded like many babies crying. In fact, the fishermen had caught a lot of mermaids, who were making all the noise.

'It must be the first time you have seen those,' said Old Tuo. 'You should take a couple back with you on the junk.'

'I cannot bear to hear them crying,' said Tang Ao. 'How can I have the heart to take them away? They should be set free.'

He bought all the mermaids from the fishermen, and set them

free. The mermaids dived into the water quickly, but after they had swum a distance, they surfaced and turned their heads and nodded to Tang Ao to thank him.

When they finally disappeared, Tang Ao and his friends prepared to cast off once again.

After passing several other countries, the travellers arrived at the Country of Sexless People.

Tang Ao said, 'I have heard that the people of this country do not give birth to children. Can that be true?'

'I have heard that it is so,' said Old Tuo, 'because there is no distinction between men and women among them. I have been here before, and, indeed, the people look like neither men nor women.'

'But if they don't give birth to children, shouldn't they have all died out long ago?' asked Tang Ao.

'No, because their bodies do not corrupt after death, but they come back to life again after a hundred and twenty years. Thus, their numbers neither increase nor decrease. They think of death as sleep and life as a dream, for well they know that all mortal strife ends in a long sleep. Therefore, they don't crave fame and power and personal gain. They know that these things don't last, and that if they succeed in winning them in one life, they will only wake up a hundred and twenty years later to find that they have to struggle for them anew. Needless to say, these people also eschew violence.'

'How foolish we must seem to them then,' said Merchant Lin, 'when we don't even come back to life again, and yet struggle so hard for wealth and fame!'

'If you can look at things that way,' said Tang Ao, 'all you need to do is to place a different value on these very things.'

'That's easy to say, and, theoretically, I can see that wealth and fame are of dubious value when we think that life is like a fleeting dream. Yet, when I find myself embroiled in a real situation, it is as though I were crazed, and I cannot help becoming excited and engaging in the struggle and the strife. However, in the future, when I find myself in that state, I should be happy if someone pinched me. Then I would wake up at once and see the futility of it all.'

'Ah, but when you are in that state, I am afraid that you would not listen if I tried to remind you of the futility of it all, but on the other hand, would turn around and blame me for interfering!' said Old Tuo.

'That's true,' said Tang Ao. 'Lust for fame and fortune are like an intoxication. While a man is intoxicated he doesn't realize it. It's only after it is all over that he realizes that everything is like an illusion. If men could realize this all the time, there would be much less trouble on earth, and there would be much happier people, too.'

'But I hear that these people eat the soil, is that true?'

'Yes,' said Old Tuo. 'They don't farm, and they don't like the fruit which grows on trees, but prefer to eat the soil . . . perhaps because by nature they are really an earthy lot.'

When the travellers arrived at the Country of Deep-eyed People, they discovered that the eyes of the people grew on their hands, and that it gave them great freedom when they wanted to look at things high and low, as well as an advantage when they came to a crossroads, and wanted to know which was the right road to take.

'I wonder why their eyes are in their hands?' said Merchant Lin.

'No doubt because they are a cautious people,' said Old Tuo, 'who like to look at things from every different angle before they decide to do anything.'

At the country of Black-toothed People, Merchant Lin sold a lot of cosmetics, and Tang Ao discovered that the people loved scholarship above wealth. There, they met two girls, Lee Red Rose and Lu Purple Lily, who were so learned that they put Tang Ao to shame.

In the Country of Little People, the citizens were only seven or eight inches tall, and the children about four inches. But these were a contrary people, who called everything by their opposites, saying sweet was bitter, and salt had no taste. Crochety, mean, caustic and cunning, they carried rifles wherever they went for fear of big birds pecking at them.

Tang Ao did not like them much. 'I didn't know people could be so small,' he said.

In the Country of Tip-toeing People, the inhabitants, who were eight feet tall and eight feet wide, walked about on tip-toe all the time.

Tang Ao took one look at them and said, 'What squares!' and did not bother to go ashore.

When they arrived at the Country of Tall People, they saw a vast mountain with a city built upon it, and men who were seventy, eighty feet tall. Lin sold a lot of goods here, and after a busy day, they were under-way again, and arrived at the border of the Country of White People.

The steep mountain loomed before them as the junk drew near, which gave off a radiance in the sunlight.

'It is the Unicorn and Phoenix Mountain,' said Old Tuo. 'It is the first big mountain of the Western Sea, and is more than a thousand *li* from one side of it to the other. There are all kinds of fruit and trees here, and birds and animals of all sorts. But only birds are to be found on the western side, and four-legged animals on the eastern side.'

'Why is that?' asked Tang Ao.

'It is because a lion lives on the eastern side, and a buzzard-eagle on the western side, and these two are constantly sending the animals under them to fight with each other.'

'But do the Phoenix and the Unicorn do nothing about it?'

'The lion is king of the four-legged animals, and the buzzard-eagle is the leader of the birds. The Phoenix and the Unicorn try to make them behave, but many battles are waged during the course of which feathers fly and the mountains tremble.'

'I have never seen a phoenix,' said Tang Ao. 'I have always wanted to see one.'

'We shall have to climb over the summit and into the kolanut tree forest,' said Old Tuo. 'The Phoenix lives in it. With luck, we may see him before long.'

After walking several *li*s, the travellers heard an outburst of bird calls which was extremely pleasing to the ear. They thought that it must be cranes or egrets, but as they came nearer and nearer to the sound, they could see no sign of any bird.

'Isn't this strange?' said Old Tuo. 'It is making such a loud noise, and yet we cannot see it.'

'Look over there by the big tree,' said Tang Ao. 'There are so many flies. The sound seems to be coming from there.'

The noise was deafening when they came to the tree. Suddenly, Lin held his head between his hands and jumped violently up and down. I cannot stand it!' he cried.

If the reader wants to know what was the matter, please turn to the next chapter.

When Merchant Lin began to jump up and down and cry, 'I cannot stand it!' his friends asked him what was the matter.

'One of those flies flew into my ear. It gave a piercing scream, like a clap of thunder. It was so loud that I became dizzy. Now I've got it in my hand.'

Before he finished talking, the fly screeched and screamed again in ear-piercing tones. Lin tightened his fist about it, and shook it, saying, 'We'll see how you like that!' The fly stopped screeching, and Tang Ao and Old Tuo bent close to Lin's fist, and heard it making a remarkable sound, like that of a flock of little birds.

'Let's have a look at it,' said Old Tuo.

They made a cone with a piece of paper, and Lin released the insect into it. Upon a closer look, it turned out to be nothing like a fly at all, but was a tiny little parrot, complete with green feathers and a red beak.

'It is the diminutive bird,' said Old Tuo. 'In the time of Emperor Wu of Han dynasty, the people of the Country of Leh-pi used to present them to court by the hundred in jade cages. They may be small, but their voices carry for miles around.'

When they walked on again, a sudden hush fell over the forest. The travellers saw a shepherd boy come toward them, who wore a white outfit and carried a weapon.

'Please, little brother, will you tell us what this place is called?' asked Tang Ao.

'This is the Jade Kolanut Peak, and next to it is the Cliff of Scarlet Cassia, which belongs to the Country of White People,' said the boy. 'You must be careful when you come to it, for there are many wild beasts.'

The kolanut trees grew thicker and thicker. When the travellers were on the summit, they saw, to the west, standing among countless kolanut trees, the Phoenix, which stood six feet high and had a tail several yards long. Its feathers were of rainbow colours, of which the red was like a flaming sunset, and it had a snakelike neck and a hen's beak, and was covered with spots all over. Beside it there stood countless other rare birds, some ten feet tall, green, blue, yellow, red, white and black.

To the east in the cassia forest stood a large bird which resembled a falcon and had a rat's feet. It was green all over, and had a long neck and stood six feet high. It, too, was surrounded by a phalanx of different birds, some of which had three heads, and others with two pairs of wings and two tails.

Tang Ao and his companions were stunned.

'That's the buzzard-eagle,' said Old Tuo, 'who is going to make trouble again. The Phoenix and its followers have gathered together and are going to try and stop him. We are going to see a fight.'

Suddenly, the buzzard-eagle gave two cries, and a large rainbow-coloured bird with a flowing tail of several yards flew from its side to the ridge of the cliff, shaking its feathers and spreading its wings, and danced like a cloud of silk brocade. Beside it, a large piece of talc, which was as smooth as a mirror, reflected its colours and added to its splendour.

'That's the pheasant,' said Old Tuo, 'which is very vain about its looks, and often drowns in the water, dazed from admiring its own reflection. It has all the phoenix's outward appearance, but none of its virtues, and is sometimes called the dumb-phoenix. I suppose the buzzard-eagle is using it to show off to the birds of the Phoenix's camp.'

From the Phoenix's side walked a peacock to the ridge of the Jade Kolanut Peak. It spread its seven-foot tail and its gorgeous wings, and began to dance for the birds in the Cassia Forest, flashing its golden and green plumes with round discs, and shedding radiant lights of red and yellow, with gold and silver glints in it.

The pheasant kept up its dance a little longer. But when it realized that it was outshone by the peacock, it gave way to screeches, and dashed itself against the plate of talc and died.

'It has died of shame from knowing that it is inferior to the peacock,' said Tang Ao. 'Too bad that we people don't often know when we are beaten.'

The peacock returned triumphant to her own forest.

From the Cassia Forest now came another bird with grey feathers and yellow legs and a pointed beak, which began to make all kinds of bird calls.

Simultaneously, a bird of rainbow colours with a short tail and sharp beak walked out of the kolanut forest and turned and spread its wings, and began to vie with the other in making bird calls.

'That's the carolling bird,' explained Old Tuo. 'The grey one is called the bird of a hundred tongues.'

Suddenly from the cassia forest came a goose-like bird which was twenty feet tall, with wings several yards wide, nine tails and ten necks, but only nine heads. When it came to the ridge of the cliff, it spread its wings and from its nine throats began to make sounds.

'That's the nine-headed bird,' cried Old Tuo. 'And it's evil!'

'I wonder what bird the Phoenix will send to match it,' said Tang Ao.

Before Old Tuo could answer, a little jade-green bird with a white neck and red beak walked to the ridge of the mountain and let out a noise which sounded like a dog barking. As soon as the nine-headed bird heard it, it shook with fright and shrank back into the cassia forest like a rat.

'It's the dog-bird,' said Old Tuo, laughing. 'The nine-headed bird is afraid of it because it lost one of its heads to a dog once, and it hasn't stopped bleeding since. It is an unpropitious bird, and when people see it coming, they usually send a dog to chase it away for fear its blood stains their doorsteps.'

From the cassia forest came an ostrich eight feet tall and pitch black, which looked extremely like a camel. It ran screeching to the ridge of the mountain, as from the kolanut forest flew a red-eyed, red-beaked bird with white feathers and a tail twelve feet long with a very large dipper at the end of it.

From the east flew a bald-headed eagle about eight feet tall, with a long neck and green feathers. From the west came another bird, four feet high, with a pig's tail sixteen feet long, hopping on a single long leg. He raised the tail like a whip and lashed across at the bald-headed eagle, which began to bleed and whimper. The bird of a hundred tongues fled. The bald-headed eagle rose up into the air for refuge. The ostrich's wings broke, and it fled into the cassia forest.

The buzzard-eagle began to let out great cries, and with its flock, dashed to the ridge of the mountain. The birds of the kolanut forest came to meet him, and a furious battle began. The bird with the long tail with the dipper at the end scooped up the bird with the pig's tail, but the latter swung around and whipped back. Back and forth the tails flew and snapped and inflicted punishment.

In the heat of the battle, there came a noise from the east which sounded like a thousand horses galloping. The mountain trembled with vibration, and dust flew high into the air.

The birds fled. The Phoenix and buzzard-eagle both disappeared.

The three travellers took to the woods as a herd of wild beasts came at them from the eastern direction. At the head of them was an animal which looked like a tiger, but with blue fur and sickle-like claws, teeth like saws, a snub nose and flat ears and eyes which flashed like lightning.

After them came another pack of strange beasts, also covered with bloodstains, which charged into the cassia forest with a beast in the lead. As it went into the forest it gave two tremendous bellows. This beast had the body of a deer, the tail of an ox, horse's legs and a single horn in the middle of its head. It was a bluish yellow colour.

'That must be the Unicorn,' said Tang Ao. 'Was the other animal a lion?'

'Yes, indeed, and he is doubtless going to make trouble, so the Unicorn has come after him.'

When the lion saw the Unicorn coming, it let out two roars. Immediately, a boar, as though obeying an order, ran up to it, twitching its ears, and extended its head. The lion sniffed at it and roared again, and opening its tremendous mouth, bit off the boar's head and then devoured the whole animal.

'Now I suppose the lion is ready to fight, with a full stomach,' said Merchant Lin. 'I wonder if the boar thought it was just making a polite gesture to its superior, or if it knew that the lion would really devour it?'

He was pointing to the lion with the hand that held the diminutive bird in the paper cone. The bird gave an ear-shattering screech which took Lin by surprise. He began to shake his fist furiously, but the bird would not stop.

The lion raised its head to see where the noise was coming from. Suddenly, it let out a ferocious roar and charged toward Merchant Lin with the other beasts behind him.

The three men ran.

'Dear Brother Lin!' cried Old Tuo. 'Open fire! What are you waiting for?'

Merchant Lin let go of the diminutive bird, and turning around, fired a shot at the pack of animals. He felled two, but the rest continued to come at them as if nothing had happened.

'My dear fellow!' Old Tuo yelled. 'Aren't you going to fire another shot?'

Lin fired another shot. It seemed only to encourage the beasts, who were at their sides as if they had grown wings and flown.

Merchant Lin bawled. 'I hear that scholars are sour by nature, so that their flesh cannot taste sweet. So the lion must be after me! If this lion has no intestines like the people of the Country of Intestineless People, I may pass right through him and still hope to live. Otherwise, what is going to happen to me?'

Tang Ao sprinted into the air with a cry of, 'This is terrible!'

Suddenly, there came a rat-tat-tat like thunder. A cloud of black smoke followed. The lion reared its head, turned this way and that, danced, but could not hide. It fell to the ground and the other beasts surrounded it. There was another rain of shots and another cloud of black smoke. Dust flew into the air and the mountains reverberated with sound. Smoke covered everything like a fog, and the sound of the rat-tat-tat continued like a shower. Some of the beasts fled, others fell down dead. The Unicorn and its followers had disappeared.

Tang Ao came down on earth and Merchant Lin hurried up to him. 'Who is this hunter and what is his splendid rifle?' said Old Tuo. 'We must find him and thank him for saving our lives.'

A young lad of fourteen or fifteen came from the ridge of the mountain, dressed in a blue hunting costume, and carrying a rifle over his shoulder. They rushed up to him and said, bowing, 'Thank you for saving our lives! May we ask your name, and where you come from?'

The lad hurriedly returned the courtesy and said, 'My name is Wei, and I come from the Kingdom on Earth. May I ask your names also?'

When they had told him, Tang Ao said, 'Are you any relation to the Wei Szewen who is famous for his handling of the repeating rifle?'

'He was my father,' said the lad.

'What a coincidence,' said Tang Ao, and told the boy his own story.

The lad fell to his knees after he heard it and said, 'So you are Uncle Tang! Forgive your niece for not recognizing you!'

'Get up,' said Tang Ao. 'Why do you call yourself my "niece"?'

'I am Purple Cherry,' came the reply, 'and I have a brother called Wei Warrior. We fled to this country after the Rebellion. My father was asked by the local people to help them kill the wild beasts in these parts, which often came to harm them. My father killed countless numbers of them, but last year he died, and the commission to kill the beasts fell to my brother. Unfortunately, he is ailing, and unequal to the strenuous job, so I learned how to use the rifle, and masquerading as a boy, took the commission in order to support ourselves and our mother. Just now I was out hunting when I saw the lion hard at Uncle's heels. I dared not open fire until Uncle jumped into the air. Really, your life must be protected by the spirits! But before father died, he left us a letter, saying that we should go to Lingnan and find you, and that you would take care of us. Will you come home with me for a cup of tea?'

'Indeed I will,' said Tang Ao. 'I have not seen Mistress Wan for years, and would like to pay my respects to her. I am very sorry to hear of Szewen's death.'

They followed Purple Cherry across the mountain. Tang Ao thought to himself, 'The dream spirit told me that I would find famous flowers on my trip. Up to this moment, I have not found a single one, but have met many young girls instead.'

The Wei house was decorated with bows and arrows. Purple Cherry took the travellers in and introduced them to her mother, Mistress Wan, and her brother Warrior, who indeed looked poorly, although he was rather handsome. Purple Cherry produced her father's letter and gave it to Tang Ao, who read it and learned that his old friend had entrusted the care of his family to him. Sighing, he put the letter away. Mistress Wan said, 'We were going to return after my husband died, but were afraid to cross the country with so many wild beasts at large. I don't know if they are still looking for rebels at home, and that has kept us away, too. How fortunate it is for us that you have come !'

'It's more than a decade since the Rebellion,' said Tang Ao. 'It should be quite safe now for you to go back. But I shall come here on my way back and take you home.'

He asked about their welfare, and was told that the local people were extremely grateful to the family for killing so many beasts, and that they were therefore well provided for, and even had a little money to spare after they had paid for their food and clothes. So Tang Ao left them only a few pieces of loose silver which he happened to have on him, saying that they were for Purple Cherry to buy cosmetics with, and left, after burning incense and wailing before the spirit-tablet of his old friend.

After a few days' sailing, Lin and Tang were standing on the bridge-tower one day when they saw an apparition ahead which was like neither smoke nor cloud. From its misty outlines, there seemed to be a city. There seemed also something very fragrant.

Old Tuo looked at the compass and the basin of incense (to tell the time) and said, 'I think we have come to the Country of Scholars.'

As they approached it, they saw that thousands of tall plum trees enclosed the city. The travellers went ashore, and walked into the forest of plum trees. Leeks were growing everywhere on the ground.

Soon they saw farmers wearing scholars' costumes. After walking for a long time, the travellers came to a pass. On the city gate was a couplet inscribed in gold which said :

Kindness elevates a family's social position.
Learning makes good sons and daughters.

'The King of this country is supposed to be a descendant of Chuan Hsueh, who is a descendant of the Yellow Emperor,' said Tang Ao.

Before they could enter the city, however, soldiers came forward and asked them who they were and searched them.

When they were allowed to enter the city, Merchant Lin said, 'I suppose they thought we were thieves. We should all have taken some walk-on-air plant and leaped over the wall.'

The people on the streets all wore the scholars' blue or green costume, and the scholars' scarf around their heads. Even the merchants were dressed like this, and the shops were very simple. Apart from books, paper and ink, spectacles and toothpick shops, there were only a few wine and grocery shops which sold mostly green plums and leeks.

The three went into a wine shop and sat down at a table. Soon they saw an old man come in and sit down near them.

'Give me half a pot of light wine, and a dish of salted beans,' the old man said to the proprietor.

Tang Ao asked the old man's name, and was told that it was Ru. He introduced themselves and said, 'Would you have a drink with us?'

'How dare I impose on you when we have just met?' said the old man.

'Then what if we come and drink with you?' said Old Tuo, and told the waiter to move their wine and food to the old man's table. After toasting each other and eating a little, Tang Ao said, 'Could you tell us why the people in your country, no matter what their business, all dress like scholars? Do your officials dress this way, too, so that one cannot distinguish between high and low?'

'We all dress alike, but we make a differentiation in colour and material,' said Ru. 'Yellow is for the man of the highest rank, red is next, then purple. Blue is lower, and green is lowest. He who is not educated is called a "vagrant" in our country, and is ostracised. So even the merchants and farmers are at least scholars of the lowest or second to lowest ranks. It is only after a man qualifies as a scholar that he may pursue his livelihood with any self-respect.'

'But in such a vast country as this, can it be possible that everyone passes?'

'The subjects are various. A man may qualify in any one of the subjects; classics, history, poetry or prose; calligraphy, music, rhyme scheme, law, mathematics, painting or medicine. One needs to pass only one subject to wear the green costume, but to wear the blue, one must pass in one of the literary subjects.'

When it was dark, Tang Ao paid the bill, and as the old man

rose, he took a towel from his person and spread it on the table. He emptied the few salted beans which remained on the plate into it, and wrapped it up. There were two cups of wine remaining in the pot, and he said to the proprietor, 'Keep this for me for tomorrow. If I find one cup less in this pot when I come back, I will make you pay for it ten times.' Then he scraped the left-over sauced bean-curd and wine-cured beancurd into a dish, and gave it to the waiter. 'Keep this for me,' he said.

On his way out, the old man saw a used toothpick lying on one of the tables. He picked it up, wiped it, and slipped it into his sleeve.

When Tang Ao was out on the street, he saw a great crowd of people gathered around a beautiful girl of thirteen or fourteen, who was weeping very hard.

'She has exposed her face and head to the public for days now,' said the old man, sighing, 'it's a shame that no one has come to her aid.'

'Why has she come to this?'

'She's an orphan, who served in the Palace as an attendant,' said Ru. 'She has been in the service of the Royal Son-in-law ever since the Princess was married. Some time ago, she incurred the displeasure of the Royal Son-in-law, who handed her to the official matchmaker to be sold to anyone who wanted her. She is going very cheap, but in our country we cherish money like our very lives, and no one has come forward to buy her. And besides, the Royal Son-in-law is a ruthless man who would not hesitate to kill, and the people want to have as little to do with him as possible. The girl, in despair, has tried to commit suicide many times, but has been foiled each time by the official matchmaker. If you want to do a good deed, you can save her for a few strings of cash.'

'If I free her and give her back to her relatives, that would be a good deed done,' said Tang Ao. 'Has she any relatives?'

'The Royal Son-in-law does not allow her relatives to claim her,' said the old man.

Tang Ao scratched his head. 'In any case, we had better save her first,' he said, and asked Lin to go back to the junk and fetch ten strings of cash. He gave the money to the official matchmaker, who set the girl free, and the old man Ru went on his way.

Tang Ao took the girl back to the junk, and found that her surname was Szetu, and her given name was Marsh Orchid. She said that her father had died in battle abroad, and that she had been in service at the Palace since she was a child.

'Did your father ever promise you to any one, young lady?' said Tang Ao.

84

Marsh Orchid said, 'Please don't call me young lady! I am a mere servant whom you have bought!'

'Regard him as your godfather,' said Merchant Lin. 'We shall have none of this master-and-servant relationship here.'

Marsh Orchid then bowed to Tang Ao as her godfather, and was led inside the cabin to meet Mistress Lin and Pleasant. When Tang Ao asked again whether she was promised to anyone, Marsh Orchid made her bows all around, and burst into tears. 'If it weren't for my ungrateful fiancé, things would not have come to such a state!'

'What is it all about?' Tang Ao asked.

'My fiancé came from the Kingdom on Earth to join the army here,' said Marsh Orchid. 'The Royal Son-in-law took a liking to him because he was very brave, and made him his aide, and promised me to him as his wife; I knew that my fiancé was unhappy to be in this country, and that the Royal Son-in-law was an extremely cruel and difficult man, and my fiancé would be wiser if he did not take the job. So one night, while the Royal Son-in-law was asleep, I stole to my fiancé's room, and told him that he must go back as quickly as possible to the Kingdom on Earth, and find another future for himself. The man, however, reported my words to the Royal Son-in-law, who punished me very severely for it. This was in the spring. A few days ago, the Royal Son-in-law was going to leave for an inspection of the troops, and I was afraid that my fiancé would have to go with him, and waste his time working for that horrible man. So again I crept into his room, and tried to persuade him to escape. I had stolen a banner-of-order and gave it to him. With it he would be allowed to go out of the pass. But the ungrateful fellow again reported me to His Highness, who was furious, and after having me soundly beaten, ordered me to be sold.'

'But how did your fiancé come to the country, if he did not like it?' Tang Ao said. 'And I cannot see that going to inspect the troops with the Royal Son-in-law can necessarily do him any harm. I don't understand. Who is your fiancé, how old is he, and why didn't you marry him?'

'His family name is Shu,' said Marsh Orchid, 'and his given name is Cheng-chih. He is more than twenty years old. I was reluctant to be married to him because I knew something must have happened in his past, or he would not have come so many thousands of *li*s to this place. Last winter, when he was away, I stole into his room and found a letter which was written in blood among his things. When I read it, I realized that he was one of Archduke Lichi's descendants. That's why I thought it so important for him to escape from here, and go back to carry out his father's wish to return the Emperor to the throne. But that ungrateful and unfeeling thing not only would not listen to me, but turned around and betrayed me instead. When I almost died from punishment this spring, the whole household knew about it, but did he care? And now when I have fallen into shame, he behaves as though it were none of his business.'

Marsh Orchid began to cry out loud.

Tang Ao was surprised and excited. 'Then your fiancé must be the son of Shu Ching-yeh! I tried to find out where he had gone, but never succeeded. I never thought that he would be here! But I do not understand his behaviour at all, there must be a reason for it. Now don't worry. I'll go and see him and find out what it is all about.'

Tang Ao told the girl who he was, and how he came to be there, and then left with Merchant Lin and Old Tuo for the residence of the Royal Son-in-law.

After many inquiries, Tang Ao was at last face to face with Young Shu. The young man looked him up and down and said, 'We cannot talk here.'

He took them to a tea shop, and there, in a private room, at last made a bow to Tang Ao and said, 'When did Uncle arrive? I never dreamed that I would meet you here!'

'How do you know who I am?' said Tang Ao.

'You often came to our house when we were at the capital,' said Young Shu. 'I was not more than ten then, but I remember you, and you still look the same after all these years.'

Merchant Lin and Old Tuo also introduced themselves and the waiter brought tea. Young Shu then explained that he had parted from the son of Lo Pinwang during their flight from Empress Wu's troops, and escaped abroad, and earned his living by becoming a servant-boy. When he came to the Country of Scholars, he thought that the life of a soldier would be better than that of a servant, so he joined the army.

'But how did you know I was here?' Young Shu asked, to which Tang Ao said, instead, 'But you are more than twenty years old now. Are you married?'

When Young Shu heard this, tears welled in his eyes.

If the reader wants to know why Young Shu started to cry, please read the next chapter.

'I suppose I shall have to remain a bachelor all my life,' said Young Shu.

When Tang Ao asked him to explain, the young man made sure that no one was listening outside the door, and said, 'It is like this. The Royal Son-in-law has a very suspicious nature. Although he took a liking to me and made me his aide, he was afraid that I might plot against him since I was an alien, so he put me under constant surveillance and even placed guards outside my room at night. I was warned that I must be very careful in order not to get myself into trouble. When he promised me a palace attendant called Szetu Marsh Orchid as wife, the people cautioned me to be on my guard. They thought that he must have a reason for treating me so well, and that I must be careful of my words when I spoke to the palace attendant. So when Marsh Orchid came to me one night in the spring and told me that I must escape from here for my own sake, I lay awake all night wondering what her motive was. The next day, I consulted my friends, who all thought that she must have been sent by the Royal Son-in-law to test my loyalty, and if I didn't report the incident to him, I would get myself into a lot of trouble. When I heard that Marsh Orchid was punished as a result of this, I didn't know whether it was true, as it is not easy to find out what really goes on in the inner apartments. Then a few days ago, she came again to try and persuade me to return to the Kingdom on Earth. I gave this another night's thought, and the next day, after consulting my friends, decided that it was still the wisest course for me to report it. I did not know until the Royal Son-in-law had her flogged and ordered her to be sold that this girl had only my good at heart, and had suffered so much on my account. Therefore I said to myself, "I owe my life to my parents, but my heart belongs to Marsh Orchid." If I cannot find a way to repay her, what use am I on earth? I have made several attempts to escape and return to the Kingdom on Earth to carry out my father's wish and help to bring the Emperor back to the throne. But the pass is heavily guarded, and no one is allowed to leave without permission. Everyone knows me, and it is impossible to slip through. I am more sorry than ever that I gave the banner Marsh Orchid stole for me back to the Royal Son-in-law.'

Tang Ao told Young Shu that Marsh Orchid was in fact safe on Merchant Lin's junk, and Young Shu was extremely grateful and relieved to hear it.

They considered how they should help Young Shu escape, and decided that it would be best to wait until after dark, and let Tang Ao carry him over the city wall.

When they left the tea shop together, the travellers followed Young Shu to a corner of the city wall, which was no more than forty or fifty feet high, and where Young Shu thought that it would be best to make their escape, since it was in a remote part of the city.

'There's no one about,' said Merchant Lin. 'Why don't you practise a little, so that you won't run into difficulties later?'

Young Shu climbed on Tang Ao's back, and the latter effortlessly lifted him up into the air. From the top of the wall, he could only see plum trees outside.

'I say,' said Tang Ao, 'have you anything of importance to take away? If not, why don't we go now?'

'Your nephew has nothing of importance,' said Young Shu. 'I always keep my letter-in-blood on my person for fear of discovery. Let us go, then!'

Tang Ao made a sign to Old Tuo and Lin, and came down on the other side of the city wall with Young Shu. Merchant Lin and Old Tuo walked swiftly out of the city, and it was not long before they arrived at the junk. There, Tang Ao told Marsh Orchid all about what happened, and cleared up the misunderstanding between her and Young Shu.

'You'll have to come with us now,' said Old Tuo. 'When we come across a junk we can trust, it can take you back to the Kingdom on Earth first.'

To this, Young Shu agreed.

When they arrived at the Country of Two-faced People a few days later, Young Shu remained on board, as he was afraid that the Royal Son-in-law might have sent men ahead to catch him.

The three travellers therefore went on shore, but after walking a little, Old Tuo complained of a pain on his leg, and turned back. Tang Ao and his brother-in-law decided to go a little further to look at the people, and it was not until then that Merchant Lin discovered that he had forgotten to change his clothes in his hurry to come ashore, and looked like a poor man next to Tang Ao in his scholar's scarf and silk costume.

Old Tuo returned to the junk, took some medicine, and had a nap. When he woke up, he felt much better, and saw Tang Ao and Merchant Lin coming back.

'Why, you are wearing each other's clothes,' he remarked.

'We walked over ten *li*s after you left us before we met any two-faced people,' said Tang Ao. 'But everyone was wearing a turban at the back of his head, so we could not see both their faces at once. I went up to some of them and had had a nice talk. I asked them about the customs of the country, and they were all smiles and spoke to me most respectfully and in the most cordial manner. I thought they were charming, lovely people, quite different from the people we've met anywhere else.'

'But as soon as I put in a few words, they all looked at me and stopped smiling, and became cold and reserved and were most reluctant to have anything to do with me,' said Lin. 'Afterwards we wondered if it might have had something to do with our clothes, so we changed, and sure enough, they began to treat me with the utmost respect, and to give Brother Tang the cold shoulder.'

'So that is what is meant by being Two-faced,' said Old Tuo.

'Not only that, but when Brother-in-law was talking, I sneaked around the back of one of these people, and stealthily lifted his turban. When I saw what was underneath, I received the shock of my life and screamed. There was an ugly face with rat's eyes, hooked nose and a furious expression on it, and when this face saw me, the bush-like eyebrows gathered in a deep frown. It opened its huge basin of a mouth, and stuck out its long tongue at me. I was overpowered by an extremely vile smell which made me almost faint. When I turned around again, Brother-in-law was on his knees.'

'Why were you doing that?' asked Old Tuo.

'You see, this man was talking to me in a most pleasant manner when Brother Tang lifted his turban and revealed not only his other face, but his true self. Then his good face turned green, too, and stuck out its tongue at me. I was so surprised I didn't know if he was going to kill me next. My knees buckled, I sank to the ground and kowtowed to him repeatedly, and then ran for my life. Have you ever heard of such a thing, Old Tuo?'

'It is not surprising,' said Old Tuo. 'I have met many people of this kind in my long life. The difficulty lies in recognizing them for what they are. But if you are more careful about whom you speak to, you can save yourself many an unpleasant surprise.'

It had begun to rain, so they did not sail. In the evening, just as they were preparing to go to bed, the travellers heard women crying in a heartbreaking way on a neighbouring boat.

The sailors went to inquire, and were told that the junk, like theirs, had come from the Kingdom on Earth with merchandise to sell, but that it had been damaged during the storm at sea. Merchant

Lin and Tang Ao offered to have the junk repaired for these people, since there were two men in the crew who knew how to do it. When the women heard this, they stopped crying, and all was quiet at last.

Yet, when day broke, they heard a loud rabble on shore, and when Tang Ao, Merchant Lin and Old Tuo hurried to the helm to see what it was, they discovered that the junk was surrounded by about a hundred husky bandits, all of whom wore turbans, and had soot smeared on their faces. They held weapons in their hands and pointed these at them, shouting, 'Hand over the money!'

Merchant Lin immediately went down on his knees. 'We are a small junk with little merchandise on board,' he cried. 'Please let us go! We have no money to give you!'

'If you won't listen to talk, maybe you'll listen to force!' said the leader of the bandits, and leaped up on the junk with his knife.

Suddenly a shower of pellets fell with force, as if from the sky. The bandit chief fell flat on his back.

A beautiful young girl was standing on the neighbouring junk, wearing a blue silk scarf on her head and an onion-green archer's shirt, with purple trousers. Single-handed, she felled most of the bandits with her pellets (shot from her bow and arrow) and the others ran for their lives, dragging the wounded with them.

When the bandits had disappeared, Tang Ao thanked the girl and asked her who she was. The girl said that her name was Beautiful Hibiscus. Tang Ao in turn told her who they were.

'But could you be Uncle Tang from Lingnan?' Beautiful Hibiscus cried. 'Do you remember me? My father was Shu Ching-kung. When my Uncle Shu Ching-yeh was wanted for his part in the Rebellion, we changed our name to Chang and fled abroad. We have been living on the junk and trading for a living. But my parents died three years ago and I was left with no one except my nursemaid. Not knowing what to do, nor how things were at home, we went on with the trading and lived on our junk. But last night, our junk was damaged. Who would have thought that it was you who sent the sailors over to help!'

She had only finished speaking when Young Shu leaped over to her junk and took his cousin in his arms, and the two wept with joy at their reunion.

But it was not long before a band of men and horses were coming toward them in a cloud of dust.

'They must be the bandits who have come back with more men for revenge,' cried Old Tuo. 'What shall we do?'

'I left my weapons in the Country of Scholars,' said Young Shu. 'Are there any on board?'

'There is a long spear which used to belong to father,' said Beautiful Hibiscus. 'The sailors cannot lift it. Will you have a look at it?'

Young Shu hurried into the cabin and came out with the spear. The men and horses were already very close. They were wearing scholars' green costumes and turbans, and Young Shu knew that they had been sent by the Royal Son-in-law. He leaped ashore with the spear and was met by a general on horseback, who was holding a banner-of-order.

'By order of the Royal Son-in-law, I, General Szekung Kei, have come to escort you back to the Country of Scholars to undertake an important mission,' he said. 'If you don't come back with me we have orders to cut off your head and take that back instead.'

'I must decline the honour,' said Young Shu. 'Please convey my regrets to the Royal Son-in-law.'

Szekung Kwei cried, 'Arrest him!' and brandished his banner-of-order. His men immediately advanced on Young Shu, but the latter thrust his spear forward and pierced Szekung Kwei in the leg, and wounded several others. The rest, seeing their general fallen, beat a hasty retreat.

Young Shu was returning to the junk when another group of men, bandits this time, appeared and swarmed around him, carrying weapons. Their leader was wearing a pair of pheasant's feathers on his head and carrying an arch. 'Where is the girl who dared to harm my men?' he cried, and raising his arch, let pellets fly.

There was a swoosh. Young Shu parried with his spear and dashed the pellets to the ground. He charged and the bandit answered by producing a sword. Young Shu found himself fighting a hard battle. He was just holding his own when the bandit suddenly fell to the ground and dropped his sword. It was Beautiful Hibiscus who had splayed the air with pellets and knocked the bandit-chief to the ground, and was turning back his men.

Only then did Young Shu return to the junk and take his cousin over to Merchant Lin's junk to meet Marsh Orchid, Mistress Lu and Pleasant.

When Beautiful Hibiscus's junk was repaired, Young Shu decided to go on it and return with his cousin to the Kingdom on Earth. Tang Ao suggested that for the sake of convenience, he and Marsh Orchid should be married before they went back, but Young Shu did not want to have a hasty ceremony, and said that he would rather wait until he was back at home, and had proved himself worthy of Marsh Orchid by helping to bring the Emperor back to the throne, before he married her.

So after two days, Tang Ao and Merchant Lin said goodbye to

them but not before Mistress Lu had sewn them sets of clothes and quilts and mattresses, and they had been given money to use on the way.

When Merchant Lin's junk reached the Country of Flaming People, it found itself surrounded by the natives, who spewed jets of flames from their mouths at them. The junk caught fire, the sailors' hair was singed, and Lin lost his beard and was burned. But just in time many naked women came up out of the sea and sprayed the junk with jets of water from their mouths and put out the fires.

When the Flaming People had been beaten off, the travellers discovered that the women were in fact the mermaids whom they had saved in the waters of the Country of Black-bottomed People, and who had come to help them in their time of distress.

Old Tuo was deeply touched. 'Animals, crustaceans, fish and birds alike must all have souls,' he said, 'and can tell the difference between good and bad, and right and wrong, like human beings. Therefore, every time we kill an animal in order to eat it, we must not only be offending the will of heaven, but the animal kingdom as well.'

Lin complained of the burns on his face, and Old Tuo said that he had a simple remedy.

'Fill a bottle half full of sesame seed oil, and add to it fresh sunflowers until the bottle is full. It is good for treating burns or scalding from hot water. Apply repeatedly, and the skin will be healed. When sunflowers are not available, mix sesame seed oil with powder of rhubarb and apply.'

'Indeed,' said Tang Ao, 'often the simplest and cheapest remedies prove to be the most effective. When I was a boy, I grew a wart the size of a yellow bean on my face. It didn't hurt, but it was unattractive. Some one told me to take a prune, stone it, pulverize the meat and reduce it by roasting into a powder. I mixed it with clear water, and spread it on the wart. After a few days, the wart disappeared.'

Merchant Lin mixed rhubarb powder with sesame seed oil, and put it on his burns. In a few days he was completely recovered.

Now they sailed into a very hot climate, and the sailors were prostrate with heat. After passing the Flaming Mountain, they came to the Country of Long-armed People. The travellers saw the people fishing on the seashore, and their arms were twenty feet long.

'It merely illustrates that people have to be discriminating about what they go after in life,' sighed Old Tuo when he saw them. 'If they stretch out their hands and try to grasp everything within reach which may yield a profit, in time their arms lengthen, and this is what happens.'

After passing the Country of Winged People, who laid eggs and had long heads because they loved to wear high hats, the Country of Pig's-snout People, and the Country of Sleepless People, who never slept for fear of never waking up, the travellers arrived, after some time, at the Country of Witches, where Lin was anxious to sell his silk and brocade. For although there were many mulberry trees here (on which silkworms fed), the people did not cultivate silkworms, and all wore cotton, which was grown in abundance.

Tang Ao remembered that he had a letter for a girl called Hsueh Sweet Asarum from Red Lotus of the Mountain of Eastern Opening, and went on shore with Lin and Old Tuo. After walking for some time, they came to a jade green forest. A man was hiding in one of the trees.

Soon, an old woman and a young girl came along. When the man in the tree saw them, he jumped down and went after them, brandishing his sword.

Tang Ao and his friends hurried after him. 'Now you shall die, little girl! The days of your evil-doing are over!' shouted the man as he went up to the two women. Raising his arm with the sword held in it, he was on the point of bringing it down forcefully, when Tang Ao sprang on his back, and with his powerful arms, which had the strength of a thousand catties in them ever since he had eaten the magic plants, brought the man over backwards and almost threw him to the ground. The sword flew from his hand.

'Hold still there!' Tang Ao ordered. 'Explain yourself! What has this girl done?'

The man looked him up and down and said, 'According to your dress, you look like a gentleman from the Kingdom on Earth. I am not doing wrong. You had better ask this evil girl to tell you what *she* has done.'

The old woman and the young girl were both crying.

'Tell me, what is your name and where do you come from?' Tang Ao said to the girl. 'And what have you done to this man?'

'My name is Yao,' replied the girl in tears. 'I am called Fragrant Angelica, and I am fourteen years old. My nursemaid and I were on our way to visit the graves of my parents when we met this man. Thank you for saving our lives. I am like yourself from the Kingdom on Earth, but I have lived here for several years, and raise silkworms for a living. Since my parents died I have been living with my aunt.'

'You have ruined tens of thousands of families with your evil worms!' the man said.

93

'What do you mean by that?' said Lin. 'You'd better begin from the beginning and tell us the whole story.'

'I am the official broker of this country,' said the man. 'I am in charge of its cotton and cotton produce. Since this girl came here, she has been raising countless detestable silk-producing worms, and weaving silk material to sell in the market. We don't like competition, but we did not really mind until she began to teach her black art to the people, so that many of them began to raise these filthy worms and to weave silk, too. The families who lived on cotton were ruined, and no longer have any income. I came especially to kill her. But if she is to be allowed to live, she must leave this country at once. If not, I have other means to deal with her!'

He picked up his sword, and went away in a temper.

Fragrant Angelica said to Tang Ao, 'My father was Yao Yu, Governor of Hopei. We escaped from the Kingdom on Earth during the Rebellion, and I have been staying with my aunt, Mistress Hsuan. Luckily, her daughter Sweet Asarum knew how to weave, and since I had brought some silkworms' eggs from the Kingdom on Earth, we went into the silk-weaving trade to keep ourselves. We did not know that we were doing any harm to anyone.'

Tang Ao introduced himself and said, 'Sweet Asarum's father and I are old friends. Tell me, how is he?'

'Unfortunately, he passed away some time ago,' said Fragrant Angelica.

She invited Tang Ao and his companions to her home. When they approached the house, they saw that it was surrounded by a crowd of people, who were shouting for the life of the 'weaving maid'. Fragrant Angelica was frightened.

Tang Ao and his companions went forward, and saw the man they had met in the woods among the crowd.

If the reader wants to know what happened, please read the next chapter.

12

'Please stop shouting,' said Tang Ao to the crowd. 'I have something to say to you. We three have come to take the Hsueh family back to the Kingdom on Earth. They are leaving very soon. Now please return to your homes.'

The big fellow believed Tang Ao, and led the others away.

It was only then that Fragrant Angelica dared to come forward, and call for her aunt to open the door.

Sweet Asarum was still trembling when she and her brother Select came to meet the guests. Fragrant Angelica told them what happened, and Mistress Hsuan begged Tang Ao to save them.

Tang Ao gave the letter from Red Lotus to Sweet Asarum, and Lin told them that he had seen a junk whose owner he knew only the day before, and was sure that they could go on board, and return to the Kingdom on Earth.

Then Tang Ao remembered the son and daughter of the Wei family of Unicorn and Phoenix Mountain, and told them about it. Mistress Hsuan was delighted at the thought of finding a son- and daughter-in-law on the way home, and looked forward to stopping at Unicorn and Phoenix Mountain on the way, with Tang Ao's letter of introduction.

After the visit, Tang Ao made Select take him to his father's tomb, and arranged for the removal of the remains to the junk which was bound for the Kingdom on Earth. The travellers then left some money, and bade them farewell.

When the Hsueh family stopped at Unicorn and Phoenix Mountain and visited the Wei family, they took to each other at once. Mistress Wan persuaded Select, who, like the male members of his family, was skilled at using the repeating rifle, to stay on in the mountain and take up the commission of killing the wild beasts, so the Hsueh family did not go on to the Kingdom on Earth. Later, when Red Lotus wrote to them from Narcissus Village, the two families left Unicorn and Phoenix Mountain to join her, and went back to the Kingdom on Earth together.

Not long after, Lin's junk arrived at the Country of Split-tongued People, who had in their possession a rhyme scheme which was a jealously guarded national secret. It was said that once a man learned the rhyme scheme and knew the language of the Split-tongued People, he could learn other languages and dialects with no difficulty whatsoever.

The travellers tried to offer the two-headed birds Lin bought in the Country of Restless People for the rhyme scheme, but discovered that the people were under orders from the King not to divulge the secret to any foreigners. Old Tuo spent a day in the wine shops talking to the young people, but as soon as he mentioned the word 'rhyme', they immediately turned away from him. At last he found out that if a man disclosed the secret to a foreigner, he would be banished to another country to live a life of celibacy.

Tang Ao was quite discouraged when Old Tuo returned to the junk and told him this. But when Lin came back with his birds in a cage, he was grinning all over his face.

'Why, what happened?' asked Tang Ao.

'I met an official today who offered to pay me many times more for these birds than I was going to ask. I was going to sell them to him, when one of his subordinates said, "My master wants to present these birds to the Prince. If you hold out, he is sure to raise his offer. I shall find out what I can for you. All I ask is that you remember me when you conclude the deal." It was getting late, so I immediately put up my price and left. The subordinate told me to go back in the morning. His master was sure to meet my price.'

The next morning, Lin got up before dawn and left with his pair of birds.

Not much later, however he came back with the birds still in their cage, and looking very unhappy.

'What happened? Did the subordinate play a trick on you?'

'No, when I arrived I was told that the official had indeed agreed to my price, and I was going to conclude the deal when the subordinate said that his master had an audience with the King this morning, and was in a hurry. If I held out a little more, when he came back he was sure to make an even better offer. I waited until the official finally came back, and then was told that he was no longer interested. The Prince had gone hunting that morning, fallen from his horse and lost consciousness. The King is already preparing his coffin. Of course the official was no longer interested in buying the birds.'

Sighing, Lin left with the birds again after lunch, saying that he would try his luck with some other people, but hardly hoped to make even half of what he was expecting.

With nothing to do after he had corrected a few of Pleasant's verses, Tang Ao decided to go for a stroll in the afternoon with Old Tuo. When they arrived at the city centre, they saw a crowd of people gathered around the posting board reading a royal proclamation which had just been put up.

It was an appeal by the King to any physician or man of high learning who could save his son, who was now on the brink of death. A reward of five hundred pieces of silver would be given to any person of the Split-tongued Country who could save his life, and of ten thousand pieces of silver to anyone from a foreign country who could do so.

When Old Tuo read the proclamation, he stepped forward and detached it from the posting board.

As soon as the Palace guards saw that he was a foreigner, one flew off to find an interpreter, while others immediately summoned horse and carriage to escort the old man in style to the official guest residence.

Tang Ao was flabbergasted by what Old Tuo had done. When the interpreter arrived, he said that his surname was Chih, and his given name Chung. In turn Tang Ao and Old Tuo introduced themselves and told him where they came from.

'Although I am not an expert in medicine, my ancestors have passed on to me many secret prescriptions which are very effective for treating those who have suffered falls and injury through violence,' said Old Tuo. 'Treatment depends on whether the injuries are internal or external, and how serious they are. These prescriptions I have can snatch life back from the jaws of death.'

Old Tuo turned to Tang Ao, and asked him to go back to the junk and fetch his medicine, as the interpreter went ahead to inform the King. Soon, the two of them were being taken to the inner apartments of the Palace.

The Prince was lying in bed, completely unconscious, bleeding from head wounds, with concussion of the skull and injury to both his legs.

Old Tuo told the interpreter to bring half a bowl of boy's urine and mix it with half a bowlful of rice wine. He forced this slowly through the clenched teeth of the Prince. Then he took a bottle from his pocket, and applied the contents to the cuts and bruises on his head. As he applied the medicine, Old Tuo fanned the patient fiercely with a paper fan.

When the palace people saw this, they all began to shout. The interpreter said, 'Would the Learned One please stay his hand! The Prince is susceptible to draughts in his condition. Aren't you adding fuel to the fire?'

'The medication I am giving him is called Iron Fan Mixture,' said Old Tuo. 'It must be fanned upon immediately after application to stop the bleeding and prevent complications. I have used the remedy for many years. I would not toy with human life. It would work even if you fanned the patient with a fan as heavy as iron, and that is why it is so-called.'

He did not stop fanning while he talked. Not long after, the bleeding stopped, the blood congealed on the surface of the wounds, and the Prince slowly returned to consciousness, mumbling something in his sleep.

'You have brought him back with your magic drug!' said the interpreter. 'But his legs are broken. The ligaments are torn. Have you any remedy for that?'

'For the treatment of torn ligaments and broken bones, whether the condition is light or serious, take a bowl of boy's urine and half a bowl of yellow wine, warm, and give to the patient three times a day, even if he is unconscious,' said Old Tuo. 'In a few days, the patient should be completely recovered. When we have a man who dies of this kind of injury it is usually due to internal haemorrhage and blood clotting. Yellow wine and urine stops pain and restores the circulation and the life-force, and therefore possesses the remarkable power of snatching life back from the jaws of death. But it must be taken soon after the injury has been sustained. When the injury is very severe, take a raw crab and pulverize it. Steep it in the best warm wine, and give it to the patient every day. A poultice should be made of the crab pulp after it has been steeped, and applied to the injury, while boy's urine and yellow wine must be taken every day. In the absence of fresh crab, a dried crab will do, but only if it is roasted and reduced to ashes by pulverizing, and taken in wine. However, I have brought the Seven-*li* Mixture which will do equally well.'

Old Tuo took a bottle from his pocket and weighed seven *lis* of it, and dissolved it in warm rice wine, and gave it to the Prince. He again dissolved some more of the medicine in wine, and applied it to the injuries on the legs.

The Prince now seemed more restful, and slowly fell asleep. When he woke up after a nap, Old Tuo again gave him a bowl of boy's urine and wine.

'The Prince is now out of danger,' he told the interpreter. 'Please tell His Majesty not to worry. Continue to give him as much yellow wine and boy's urine as he can drink, and apply the medication to his leg injuries. I shall come to see him tomorrow with some more medicine. He will be recovered in a few days.'

'His Majesty desires you to remain in the guest residence for a few days in order to be near the patient,' said the interpreter. 'Your dinner is waiting for you there.'

Old Tuo and Tang Ao spent the night as the King's guests. The next day, Old Tuo again gave the Prince a dose of Seven-*li* Mixture, and applied poultices and other medications to his injuries. The Prince had a great capacity for wine, so he drank his medicine as though it were tea. Not many days later, he felt restored again, although he was still not able to use his legs.

Old Tuo could have left now, but as he was still bent on getting the rhyme scheme, decided to stay on for a few more days. But even by the time the Prince had made a complete recovery, he had still found out nothing.

At the banquet for the departing guests, the King took a thousand ounces of silver and gave it to Old Tuo together with an additional two hundred ounces, if he were willing to divulge the secret of his prescriptions.

'Please tell His Majesty that I am not interested in money,' Old Tuo told the interpreter. 'I should be glad to give you my prescriptions if I can have in return a book of rhyme scheme, or an explanation of your rhyme theory.'

But the King said that he could not comply, although he would be willing to increase the amount of silver.

The interpreter said, 'The rhyme scheme is a state secret. The King would not disclose it in any event, even at the best of times. And now his wives are sick, and he has a lot on his mind. I dare not press him.'

'What ails the Imperial Concubines?' Old Tuo asked.

'One of them is five or six months pregnant. Yesterday she carelessly lifted a heavy object, and has not felt well since. There is a slight pink discharge, pain in the abdomen, and disturbance in the womb. The other Imperial Concubine has had an abscess in the breast for two days. It is swollen and painful, but the abscess has not yet come to a head. The King is greatly concerned for them.'

'If the discharge is not heavy, there is an even chance that a miscarriage can be avoided. As for an abscessed breast, treatment must never be delayed. It would be most difficult to treat if pus has already formed inside but has not yet come to a head on the skin. However, you say she has only had this for two days, so pus may not have formed yet, and there is an even chance of curing it. I have secret prescriptions for treating both the ladies. But would the King be willing to divulge the theory of rhyme to me in return?'

The interpreter conveyed this to the King, who had no choice but to give in.

Old Tuo was extremely pleased, and begged Tang Ao to return to the junk and fetch a prescription, which he had given to Merchant Lin's wife, who was pregnant.

When Tang Ao returned with the prescription, Old Tuo gave it to the interpreter, who read :

PRESCRIPTION FOR SAFE PREGNANCY

chien (one *chien* is one tenth of a Chinese ounce, or ·22 milligrams)

1·5   angelica polymorpha (*ligusticum acutilobum*)
·8   milkvetch (*astragalu reflexistipulus*)
·1   bell-wort, pulverized (*uvularia cirrhosa*, also called *fritillaria*)
1·5   Japanese dodder (*cuscuta japonica*)
1·5   angelica sylvestris
·5   liquorice plant, roasted (*glycyrrhiza glabra*)
·7   *magnolia hypoleuca*, sautéed in ginger root
1·5   thistle (*carduus officiale*)
·6   hedge-thorn, sautéed in wheat bran (*aegle sepiaria*)
·7   tarrogan (*artemisia vulgaris var indica*)
·8   Japanese catmint (*nepeta japonica*)
1·8   peony albiflora (*paeonia albiflora var hortensis*) sautéed in wine, to be used in all seasons except winter.
3 slices ginger root.

This prescription is especially for calming the foetus in the womb, and takes effect instantaneously. If due to over-taxation there is a show of blood but no injury has been done to the womb, this prescription will prevent miscarriage after repeated doses have been taken.

'Have you a remedy for an abscessed breast?' asked the interpreter.

'Take the juice from the bulbs of one catty (1⅓ lbs.) of onion,' said Old Tuo, 'and mix with the best wine. Heat and drink in two doses. Bathe the breast frequently with broth made from one ounce of wheat sprout (malt) cooked with shrimp cream. The salt in the shrimp cream softens what is hard, and shrimp helps the circulation of the breast. As soon as circulation has been restored the swelling will go down. Take an old comb, and gently comb the breast. These are effective methods for treating an abscessed breast, but since the patient has had it for two days, no time must be lost in treatment.'

The interpreter accordingly gave the instructions to the people in charge, and after a few days the Imperial Concubines recovered.

The King was delighted, but at the thought of disclosing the rhyme scheme to Old Tuo, felt sorry that he had promised, and sent the interpreter several times to tell Old Tuo that he would give him silver instead. But Old Tuo would not hear of it. The King at last discussed the matter with his ministers. After three days, he produced a sealed envelope with a few words written in it, and gave it to the interpreter for Old Tuo.

As soon as the latter received it, he wrote down his prescriptions for Iron Fan Mixture and Seven-*li* Mixture on paper for the King.

IRON FAN MIXTURE

chien

4   elephant hide (thinly sliced, held over a small flame with iron tongs until dry and yellow)

4   dragon's bone (fossils) use the best, whitest portions

ounces (one Chinese ounce is 2·2 milligrams)

2   old lime (must be several hundred years old)

2   alum ash (cook raw alum in pot until done)

2   black cypress resin

2   pine resin (dissolve these two together in water, remove from fire, allow water to evaporate).

Mix and pulverize all into a fine powder and keep in an earthenware jar. In case of cut-throat, broken belly or similar injury, apply mixture to the wound, and fan steadily. The bleeding will stop at once, and the wound will dry up. Patient must lie in a cool place. If there is swelling near the wound, make a broth of bitterwort and brush on swollen area with a feather.

SEVEN-*LI* MIXTURE
(one *li* is one thousandth of a Chinese ounce.)

chien

·5   musk

·5   Borneo camphor

5   spear flower (*ardisia crenata*)

5   *hibiscus rosa*

6   frankincense

6   myrrh

ounces

2   catechu

4   gum of dragon's blood (*calamus draco*)

Grind into powder all the ingredients, and keep in an earthenware jar and seal with yellow wax. Although the ingredients may be collected at any time, it is best to collect and take this mixture at noon on the fifth day of the fifth month. A pious attitude and attention to cleanliness are most important.

This mixture is especially meant for treating bones and torn ligaments, and injury sustained from falls or fights. If there is bleeding, apply to the wound and bleeding will stop at once. If bleeding is internal, take seven *li* of the mixture with warm wine and give to the patient orally. The wine must be made from yeast. This mixture also treats cut-throat and other injuries to the throat.

The interpreter thanked Old Tuo profusely for the prescriptions. When Old Tuo and Tang Ao returned to the junk in horse-carriages, the ministers came to see them off on behalf of the King. The interpreter also came with bearers carrying the silver. Old Tuo did not want to accept it, but Merchant Lin thought that it would be more gracious for him to do so.

The interpreter bowed to them all and said, 'I have taken the liberty of bringing my daughter to see you, Learned One, in the hope that you can save her life. She is called Melody Orchid, and is fourteen years old. Since she was a little girl, she has had an illness which caused her abdomen to become swollen and tight as a drum. We have tried all sorts of remedies, but to no avail, and lately, she seems to have become worse. If you would have a look at her, I shall tell her to come in.'

Old Tuo said that of course he was willing to have a look at her, and the interpreter told his daughter to come into the cabin with her nursemaid. They were all impressed by her simple beauty, the almond shape of her eyes and beautifully arched eyebrows, and yet the girl was sallow and of bad colour, and her stomach was indeed swollen and as tight as a drum. Her father explained that she had been like this since she was five or six years old.

Old Tuo, however, could not say what was wrong with her. But Tang Ao said that he knew a prescription passed down from his ancestors which was sure to cure her condition, which he diagnosed as a case of worms.

'Take five *chien* of thunder pills (*mylitta lapidesce*) and two of Rangoon creeper (*quisqualis indica*) and cook together in water. Peel the thunder pills and sautée until dry. Remove the shell from the Rangoon creeper and sautée with five *chien* of shredded meat, mix with thunder pills and give to the child in six doses. It may be added to beaten eggs and scrambled in oil, scallion or garlic. Taken twice a day, the patient will discharge the worms after a few days.'

While Tang Ao wrote this down for the interpreter, Mistress Lu invited Melody Orchid into the back cabin and introduced her to Pleasant. As Melody Orchid knew how to speak thirty-six languages, she conversed with Pleasant without any difficulty, and in no time at all, was fast friends with her.

The interpreter and his daughter left soon afterwards, but just as the junk was about to leave, appeared again. The interpreter ran on board without any ceremony and said in tears that the two herbs Tang Ao prescribed could not be found in the country, although he had inquired everywhere. Unfortunately, there was none on the junk, either.

Father and daughter broke down and wept. Melody Orchid fainted from emotion, and was revived only after the greatest effort by her nursemaid.

The interpreter, after much thought, whispered something to his servant, and knelt down before Tang Ao and said, 'If you cannot save my daughter's life, I and my daughter shall soon perish together. Since Melody Orchid's mother died from worrying about her, I have nothing to live for except her, and if she cannot live, I will not live, either. I remember now that a stranger once told me that Melody Orchid's fate lies abroad, and that if she should meet an Immortal named Tang, she should go with him in order to prolong her life. It is no mere chance that your name is Tang. If you would take her with you and save her life, I shall give her to you as your adopted daughter, and be forever grateful to you.'

When Melody Orchid heard this, she began to cry again, and said that she could not leave her father. But the interpreter convinced her that if she did not go, they would both die. So she bowed to Tang Ao as her godfather, and accepted the decision.

Soon, the interpreter's servant appeared with loads of silver, followed by others carrying eight leather trunks. 'There are a thousand pieces of silver here,' said the interpreter to Tang Ao. 'Half of it is an expression of my gratitude to you, and the other half is for Melody Orchid's medical, food and marriage expenses. I had long ago prepared her trousseau, which I would like her to take as well.'

Tang Ao refused to accept the silver, but the interpreter insisted, and Old Tuo suggested that Tang Ao should take it and hold it for the girl later as her dowry. It was only when this was settled that father and daughter took leave of each other in tears, and Melody Orchid was taken inside, and told to call Mistress Lu her Maternal Aunt and Pleasant her cousin, and shown where she and her nurse-maid were to sleep.

At last they cast off, and Tang Ao opened the sealed envelope which contained the rhyme scheme, and what he saw appears on page 104.

When Tang Ao saw the list of words, he could make neither head nor tail of it, but Melody Orchid explained it to him, and the three men had a good time talking to each other in code (see Notes).

After some time, the travellers arrived at the Country of Intelligent People. Tang Ao went ashore to buy the herbs Melody Orchid needed, but none could be had here, either. However, he found that he could send for them from a neighbouring country, and when they arrived he made a medical brew. Melody Orchid was given six doses in three days, discharged the obstruction in her abdomen, and was well again.

'We should take her back to her father, now that she is cured,' said Tang Ao.

Melody Orchid was delighted and Merchant Lin had the vessel turned around. However, as soon as they crossed over to the waters of the Country of Split-tongued People, Melody Orchid became ill again. She retched and fainted, and was in a serious, delirious condition.

	ang, uang	en, in	ung, iung	u, ü	ai, iao	ai, iai	i, ih ǐ	eh, ieh, ueh	au	ŝn, iŝm	ucen, yœn	ou, iu	o, io	a, ia	uei	uen, ün	eng, ing	uan	uo	ua	uai	uang
ch´, ch´u																						
m																						
y, yu																						
t´ i																						
ch´i, ch´ü																						
sh, shu																						
ts´i, ts´ü																						
li, lu																						
n, nu																						
h, hu																						
p´i																						
f																						
ti																						
chi, chu																						
mi																						
s, su																						
l, lu																						
k´, k´u																						
ts´, ts´u																						
w																						
n, nu																						
p´																						
hsi, hsu																						
t, t´u																						
tsi, tsu																						
t, tu																						
j, ju																						
pi																						
p																						
k, ku																						
ts, tsu																						
ch, chu																						
si, sü																						

Lin thought that she must suffer from 'homesickness', that was, as soon as she was home she was sick, but she was well when she was abroad. He tried turning the junk back to foreign waters, and the girl recovered at once.

They told the girl that it must be her destiny to spend her life away from home, and when Melody Orchid was convinced that it was the only way she could stay alive, she accepted their invitation to stay on board, although she was sorry not to be reunited with her father.

The junk headed back to the Country of Intelligent People. It was the Autumn Moon Festival, and the sailors all wanted to go ashore to have a few drinks and celebrate, so Lin had the junk tied up early in the day, and they all went ashore to enjoy themselves.

When they approached the town, they discovered that the people were actually celebrating New Year's Day, and not the Autumn Moon Festival. When Tang Ao asked the reason why, Old Tuo said that being intelligent people, they thought that the biggest festival of the year should be celebrated when the weather was fine and there was a full moon, and not when it was freezing cold.

'I remember you said once that the natives of the Country of Restless People live to a grand old age, and that the people here are shortlived,' said Tang Ao. 'But they all look like old fellows to me.'

'They may look old, but they are in fact only thirty or forty years old,' said Old Tuo. 'The reason for this is that since they are intelligent people, their minds never stop working. They are for ever trying to outwit one another. Although they are skilled in a hundred arts, and wonderfully educated in astrology, mathematics, scorcery and fortune-telling, their hair turns white before they are thirty years old, and when they are forty they look eighty. But compared to the natives of the Country of Worried People, they may be said to enjoy a long life, for those people seldom reach the age of forty.'

'No wonder they called me "little brother",' said Lin. 'They would never guess from my appearance that I am older than they are!'

Tang Ao learned that the people here were all wizards at mathematics, and that there was one man called Mi who was best at it. They went to call on him, but discovered that he had taken his daughter Orchid Fragrance back to visit relatives in the Kingdom on Earth.

Nevertheless, they all enjoyed themselves guessing riddles and watching the fireworks, and did not return to the junk until it was dawn, where they had a few further cups of wine. When the sun rose, the sailors cast off once more.

Melody Orchid had written a letter to her father, explaining what happened, and was soon quite contented, spending her time reading and receiving Tang Ao's instructions in poetry together with Pleasant.

After a few days, the travellers arrived at the Country of Women. If the reader wants to know what happened there, please turn to the next chapter.

When Tang Ao heard that they had arrived at the Country of Women, he thought that the country was populated entirely by women, and was afraid to go ashore. But Old Tuo said, 'Not at all! There are men as well as women, only they call men women, and women men. The men wear the skirts and take care of the home, while the women wear hats and trousers and manage affairs outside. If it were a country populated solely by women, I doubt that even Brother Lin here would dare to venture ashore, although he knows he always makes a good profit from sales here!'

'If the men dress like women, do they use cosmetics and bind their feet?' asked Tang Ao.

'Of course they do!' cried Lin, and took from his pocket a list of the merchandise he was going to sell, which consisted of huge quantities of rouge, face power, combs and other women's notions. 'Lucky I wasn't born in this country,' he said. 'Catch me mincing around on bound feet!'

When Tang Ao asked why he had not put down the price of the merchandise, Lin said, 'The people here, no matter rich or poor, from the "King" down to the simplest peasant, are all mad about cosmetics. I'll charge them what I can. I shall have no difficulty selling the whole consignment to rich families in two or three days.'

Beaming at the prospect of making a good profit, Lin went on shore with his list.

Tang Ao and Old Tuo decided to go and see the city. The people walking on the streets were small of stature, and rather slim, and although dressed in men's clothes, were beardless and spoke with women's voices, and walked with willowy steps.

'Look at them!' said Old Tuo. 'They are perfectly normal-looking women. Isn't it a shame for them to dress like men?'

'Wait a minute,' said Tang Ao. 'Maybe when they see us, they think, "Look at them, isn't it a shame that they dress like women"?'

'You're right. "Whatever one is accustomed to always seems natural," as the ancients say. But I wonder what the men are like?'

Old Tuo discreetly called Tang Ao's attention to a middle-aged woman, who was sitting in front of her doorstep, sewing on a shoe. Her hair was braided and coiled smoothly on top of her head, and decorated with pearls and jade. She was wearing long golden loops of earrings with precious stones in them, and wore a long mauve gown with an onion-green shirt underneath, from which peeped the toes of tiny feet shod in red silk shoes. With long, tapering fingers, the woman was doing embroidery. She had beautiful eyes and was carefully powdered and rouged, but when she lifted her head, they saw that her lip was covered by a thick moustache.

Tang Ao and Old Tuo could not help laughing out loud.

The 'woman' looked up and said, 'What are you laughing at, lassies?'

The voice sounded as deep and hoarse as a cracked gong. Tang Ao was so startled that he took to his heels and ran.

But the 'woman' shouted after them, 'You must be women, since you have whiskers on your faces. Why are you wearing men's clothes and pretending to be men? Aren't you ashamed of yourselves! I know, you dress like this because you want to mingle with the men, you cheap hussies! Take a look at yourselves in the mirror. Have you forgotten that you are women? It's lucky for you you only met up with me! If it had been somebody else who had caught you casting those sneaky glances, you would have been beaten almost to death!'

'This is the first time I have ever had such an experience,' muttered Tang Ao. 'But I suspect Brother Lin will receive better treatment at their hands.'

'Why?' said Old Tuo.

'Well, he is very fair, and since he lost his beard at the Country of Flaming People, he may be mistaken by these people for a real woman. But come to think of it, isn't it worrying?'

As they walked further on, they saw some 'women' on the streets as well as 'men'. Some were carrying babies in their arms, and others leading children by the hand. All the 'women' walked on dainty bound feet, and in crowded places, acted shy, as if they were embarrassed to be seen. Some of the younger ones were beardless, and upon careful study, Tang Ao discovered that some of the ageing or middle-aged 'women' shaved their lips and chins in order to appear younger.

The two returned to the junk before Merchant Lin. But when the latter did not come back at supper time, and it was past the second drum, Mistress Lu began to be worried. Tang Ao and Old Tuo went on shore with lanterns to look for him, but discovered that the city gates were shut for the night.

The next day, they went to look again, but found not a trace of

Lin. On the third day, some sailors went with them, but still they could not find him.

When a few days had passed, it seemed as if Merchant Lin had vanished, like a rock sinking to the bottom of the sea. Mistress Lu and Pleasant wailed with grief. Tang Ao and Old Tuo went to make inquiries every day.

They could not know that Merchant Lin had been told by one of his customers that the 'King's uncle' wanted to buy some of his goods. Following instructions, he went to the 'Royal Uncle's' Residence in the Palace, and handed his list of merchandise to the gatekeeper. Soon, the gatekeeper came back and said that it was just what the 'King' was looking for for his 'concubines' and 'maids', and asked Lin to be shown into the inner apartments.

The attendant led Merchant Lin through guarded doors and winding paths until he was at the door of the inner apartments, where a guard told him, 'Please wait here, madam. I shall go in and inquire what the royal wishes are.' She took Lin's list, and after a short time, returned and said, 'But madam hasn't put any prices on her list. How much do you charge for a picul of rouge? How much is a picul of perfumed powder? And hair lotion? And hair ribbons?'

Lin told her the prices, and the guard went in and came out again and asked, 'How much is a box of jade ornaments, madam? And your velvet flowers? How much is a box of your fragrant beads? And what about the combs?'

Merchant Lin told her and the guard again went to report, and came back and said, 'The King has been choosing imperial concubines and wants to buy some of your goods for them. He invites you to go inside, since you come from the Kingdom on Earth and we are friendly allies. However, madam must behave with courtesy and respect when she is in the presence of His Majesty.'

Merchant Lin followed the guard inside, and was soon in the presence of the 'King'. After making a deep bow, he saw that she was a woman of some thirty years old, with a beautiful face, fair skin and cherry-red lips. Around her there stood many palace 'maids'.

The 'King' spoke to Lin in a light voice, holding the list of articles in her slender hands, and looking at him with interest as he answered her questions.

'I wonder what she is staring at me like this for,' Merchant Lin thought to himself. 'Hasn't she ever seen a man from the Kingdom on Earth before?'

After a while, he heard her say that she was keeping the list of goods, and ordered palace 'maids' to prepare a feast and wine for the 'woman' from the Kingdom on Earth.

In a little time, Merchant Lin was ushered to a room upstairs, where victuals of many kinds awaited him. As he ate, however, he heard a great deal of noise downstairs. Several palace 'maids' ran upstairs soon, and calling him 'Your Highness', kowtowed to him and congratulated him. Before he knew what was happening, Merchant Lin was being stripped completely bare by the maids and led to a perfumed bath. Against the powerful arms of these maids, he could scarcely struggle. Soon he found himself being anointed, perfumed, powdered and rouged, and dressed in a skirt. His big feet were bound up in strips of cloth and socks, and his hair was combed into an elaborate braid over his head and decorated with pins. These male 'maids' thrust bracelets on his arms and rings on his fingers, and put a phoenix headdress on his head. They tied a jade green sash around his waist and put an embroidered cape around his shoulders.

Then they led him to a bed, and asked him to sit down.

Merchant Lin thought that he must be drunk, or dreaming, and began to tremble. He asked the maids what was happening, and was told that he had been chosen by the 'King' to be the Imperial Consort, and that a propitious day would be chosen for him to enter the 'King's' chambers.

Before he could utter a word, another group of maids, all tall and strong and wearing beards, came in. One was holding a threaded needle. 'We are ordered to pierce your ears,' he said, as the other four 'maids' grabbed Lin by the arms and legs. The white-bearded one seized Lin's right ear, and after rubbing the lobe a little, drove the needle through it.

'Ooh!' Merchant Lin screamed.

The maid seized the other ear, and likewise drove the needle through it. As Lin screamed with pain, powdered lead was smeared on his earlobes and a pair of 'eight-precious' earrings was hung from the holes.

Having finished what they came to do, the maids retreated, and a black-bearded fellow came in with a bolt of white silk. Kneeling down before him, the fellow said, 'I am ordered to bind Your Highness's feet.'

Two other maids seized Lin's feet as the black-bearded one sat down on a low stool, and began to rip the silk into ribbons. Seizing Lin's right foot, he set it upon his knee, and sprinkled white alum powder between the toes and the grooves of the foot. He squeezed the toes tightly together, bent them down so that the whole foot was shaped like an arch, and took a length of white silk and bound it tightly around it twice. One of the others sewed the ribbon together in small stitches. Again the silk went around the foot, and again, it was sewn up.

Merchant Lin felt as though his feet were burning, and wave after wave of pain rose to his heart. When he could stand it no longer, he let out his voice and began to cry. The 'maids' had hastily made a pair of soft-soled red shoes, and these they put on both his feet.

'Please, kind brothers, go and tell Her Majesty that I'm a married man,' Lin begged. 'How can I become her Consort? As for my feet, please liberate them. They have enjoyed the kind of freedom which scholars who are not interested in official careers enjoy! How can you bind them? Please tell your "King" to let me go. I shall be grateful, and my wife will be very grateful.'

But the maids said, 'The King said that you are to enter his chambers as soon as your feet are bound. It is no time for talk of this kind.'

When it was dark, a table was laid for him with mountains of meat and oceans of wine. But Merchant Lin only nibbled, and told the 'maids' they could have the rest.

Still sitting on the bed, and with his feet aching terribly, he decided to lie down in his clothes for a rest.

At once a middle-aged 'maid' came up to him and said, 'Please, will you wash before you retire?'

No sooner was this said than a succession of maids came in with candles, basins of water and spittoon, dressing table, boxes of ointment, face powder, towels, silk handkerchiefs, and surrounded him. Lin had to submit to the motions of washing in front of them all. But after he had washed his face, a maid wanted to put some cream on it again.

Merchant Lin stoutly refused.

'But night time is the best time to treat the skin,' the white-bearded maid said, 'This powder has a lot of musk in it. It will make your skin fragrant, although I dare say it is fair enough already. If you use it regularly your skin will not only seem like white jade, but will give off a natural fragrance of its own. And the more fragrant it is, the fairer it will become, and the more lovely to behold, and the more lovable you will be. You'll see how good it is after you have used it regularly.'

But Lin refused firmly, and the maids said, 'If you are so stubborn, we will have to report this, and let Matron deal with you tomorrow.'

Then they left him alone. But Lin's feet hurt so much that he could not sleep a wink. He tore at the ribbons with all his might, and after a great struggle succeeded in tearing them off. He stretched out his ten toes again, and luxuriating in their exquisite freedom, finally fell asleep.

The next morning, however, when the black-bearded maid discovered that he had torn off his foot-bandages, he immediately reported it to the 'King', who ordered that Lin should be punished by receiving twenty strokes of the bamboo from the 'Matron'. Accordingly, a white-bearded 'Matron' came in with a stick of bamboo about eight feet long, and when the others had stripped him and held him down, raised the stick and began to strike Lin's bottom and legs.

Before five strokes had been delivered, Lin's tender skin was bleeding, and the Matron did not have the heart to go on. 'Look at her skin! Have you ever seen such white and tender and lovable skin? Why, I think indeed her looks are comparable to Pan An and Sung Yu!' the Matron thought to himself. 'But what am I doing, comparing her bottom and not her face to them? Is that a compliment?'

The foot-binding maid came and asked Lin if he would behave from now on.

'Yes, I'll behave,' Lin replied, and they stopped beating him. They wiped the blood from his wounds, and special ointment was sent by the 'king' and ginseng soup was given him to drink.

Merchant Lin drank the soup, and fell on the bed for a rest. But the 'King' had given orders that his feet must be bound again, and that he should be taught to walk on them. So with one maid supporting him on each side, Merchant Lin was marched up and down the room all day on his bound feet. When he lay down to sleep that night, he could not close his eyes for the excruciating pain.

But from now on, he was never left alone again. Maids took turns to sit with him. Merchant Lin knew that he was no longer in command of his destiny.

Before two weeks were over, Lin's feet had begun to assume a permanently arched form, and his toes begun to rot. Daily medical ablutions were given to them, and the pain persisted.

'I should have thought that Brother-in-law and Old Tuo would have come to my rescue by now,' he thought one day as he was being led up and down his room. 'I have endured all I can! I'd be better off dead!'

He sat down on the edge of the bed, and began to tear off his embroidered shoes and silk bandages. 'Go tell your "King" to put me to death at once, or let my feet loose,' he told the Matron.

But when he returned, the Matron said, 'The King said that if you don't obey his orders, you are to be hung upside down from the beam of the house.'

'Then do it quickly! The quicker the better!' said Lin, impatient to have an end put to his agony.

Accordingly, they tied a rope around his feet and hung him upside down from the beam. Merchant Lin saw stars before his eyes. Sweat poured out of his body, and his legs became numb. He closed his eyes and waited for death to come to the rescue. But it did not come. At last he could stand it no longer, and began to scream like a pig being led to slaughter.

The order was given to cut him down.

From now on, Lin was completely in the power of the maids. Wanting to complete the task their 'King' had assigned them as soon as possible, they tied the bandages around his feet tighter than ever. Several times, Lin thought of committing suicide, but with people watching him constantly, he had not a chance.

In due course, his feet lost much of their original shape. Blood and flesh were squeezed into a pulp and then little remained of his feet but dry bones and skin, shrunk, indeed, to a dainty size. Responding to daily anointing, his hair became shiny and smooth, and his body, after repeated ablutions of perfumed water, began to look very attractive indeed. His eyebrows were plucked to resemble a new moon. With blood-red lipstick and powder adorning his face, and jade and pearl adorning his coiffure and ears, Merchant Lin assumed, at last, a not unappealing appearance.

The 'King' sent someone to watch his progress every day. One day, the Matron announced that the task of foot-binding had been completed. When the 'King' herself came upstairs to have a look, she saw a Lin whose face was like a peach blossom, whose eyes were like autumn lakes, whose eyebrows suggested the lines of distant hills, and who stood before her in a willowy stance.

She was delighted. 'What a beauty!' she thought to herself. 'If I hadn't seen her hidden possibilities beneath her ridiculous man's costume, her beauty might never have come to light!'

She took a pearl bracelet and put it on Merchant Lin's wrist, and the maids persuaded him to sink down on his knees and give thanks. The 'King' pulled him up and made him sit down beside her, and began to fondle his hands and smell them and look appreciatively at his dainty feet.

Lin went red with shame.

Extremely pleased, the 'King' decided that Lin should enter her chambers the very next day. When Merchant Lin heard this, he saw his last hopes vanish. He was not even able to walk without someone to help him, and spent the whole night thinking about his wife and shedding tears.

In the morning, the 'maids' came especially early to shave off the fine hairs from his face, and to powder him and comb him in preparation for his wedding. Supported by a pair of red embroidered high heeled shoes, his longer-than-ordinary 'golden lotuses' became not obtrusively large. He wore a bridal crown and gown, and with jewels dangling and waves of perfume issuing from his person, was if not notably beautiful, at least a rather charming 'bride'.

After breakfast, 'Imperial Concubines' came to congratulate him, and he was kept fully occupied until the afternoon, when maids came again to straighten his clothes and freshen up his appearance before escorting him to the Reception Hall.

Soon, palace attendants holding red lanterns came in and knelt before him and said, 'The propitious hour has come. Would Madam please come to the Main Reception Hall to await His Majesty? The ceremonies will be conducted there.'

Merchant Lin was stunned. His body and soul almost parted company.

The attendants seized him and escorted him downstairs. Countless officials and guests had come to witness the ceremony in the Main Reception Hall, which was brightly lighted with candles. As Lin walked toward 'His Majesty', swaying on the arms of attendants, he was like a sprig of fresh flowers waving in the wind. When he was standing directly in front of the 'King', he had no alternative but to tug at his sleeves and make a deep bow.

Congratulations were showered upon the 'King' by the attendants.

As Lin was about to be ushered into the 'King's' chambers, there came a great hubbub of noise from the outside. The 'King' was startled.

It was Tang Ao, who had come to the rescue. If the reader wants to know what happened next, please turn to the next chapter.

◀ *14* ▶

Ever since Merchant Lin disappeared, Tang Ao and Old Tuo had not stopped searching for him. They did not learn until the day before that Lin was being held in the palace and that his feet had been bound, and he was going to be made the Imperial Consort the following day.

When Mistress Lu learned this, she fainted, and Pleasant broke out in tears. When Mistress Lu came to, she said, 'Please save my husband,' and sank down on her knees to kowtow to Tang Ao and Old Tuo. Tang Ao hurriedly told Melody Orchid and Pleasant to help her up.

'I told one of the Ministers to tell the "Royal Uncle" that we were willing to present all the cargo on this ship to "His Majesty" if Brother Lin were set free,' said Old Tuo. 'But the "Royal Uncle" did not want to interfere, since a propitious date had already been set for the ceremony of entering the chambers.'

'The only thing we can do now is to write a direct appeal and take it to the Ministries,' said Tang Ao. 'If we find one Minister who is willing to take the appeal to the "King", we might yet save our brother.'

Mistress Lu begged for them to do this, so Tang Ao wrote an appeal for mercy, and they made many copies of it. Without eating any lunch, he and Old Tuo went to the Ministries with them. But everywhere they went, they were rebuffed with the excuse that it was none of their business. When they came back again and told Mistress Lu that their efforts were futile, she burst into tears once more, and did not stop weeping all night.

Tang Ao sat up all night, too. His heart was broken, but he could think of nothing else to do.

In the morning, he and Old Tuo went into the city again to see if they could find a way to delay the ceremonies, but when they came to the centre of town, discovered that the Imperial Consort was already being received into the 'King's' chambers. In celebration, the 'King' declared an amnesty, and all the officials were on their way to the Palace to congratulate the couple.

'I guess the rice is cooked. There is nothing more we can do,' said Old Tuo.

The prospect of breaking the news to Mistress Lu so distressed Tang Ao that he and Old Tuo decided to take a long walk before going back to the junk. At noon, they were sitting at a teahouse on the roadside having something to eat, when a soothsayer came by, and Tang Ao, having nothing better to do, drew a lot from his bamboo container.

The soothsayer took the sliver of bamboo from Tang Ao's hand and read the oracle on it. ' "Red pheasant" indicates a marriage, but unfortunately it encounters a "void". I am afraid that the couple will not live in accord together. I wonder what Madam wishes me to tell her?'

'I want to know whether this marriage will be consummated, and whether there is any way out for the party I am interested in.'

'I have already said that the marriage will be in name only. The party you are interested in has passed her crisis, and is about to be saved. However, ten more days must elapse before she is completely out of trouble.'

Tang Ao paid the woman and wondered what was the meaning of her words. If it were true that Lin had passed his crisis, how was it that ten more days had to elapse before he could leave the seat of his troubles?

Now they saw carriers file past, bearing gifts toward the palace. By nightfall, the officials in carriages and on horseback were returning from the Palace, and the prisoners who had been pardoned, wearing broad grins, were on their way home. Soon, they saw the bearers of the 'Royal Uncle's' gifts return with empty baskets.

Tang Ao and Old Tuo decided that there was little more they could do, and started back toward the junk. As they passed the centre of the city, Tang Ao remembered that he had read an official proclamation posted on the boards, appealing to anyone to come forward who knew how to mend broken canals, as the canals in this country were broken, and the fields were flooded, making many people homeless.

After a second's thought, he marched to the board and took the proclamation down. Turning on the people on the street, he declared loudly, 'My name is Tang, and I come from the Kingdom on Earth. There is nothing about canals which we people from the Kingdom on Earth don't know. I have come all the way here to repair your canals, but I will do so only on one condition.'

At the sound of his voice, people began to gather around him. Some knelt down and pleaded for him to help them.

'Please get up,' said Tang. 'I don't want any reward for my work.

What can you people offer me in treasures that we from the King-dom on Earth do not have? But if you grant my one request I shall commence work tomorrow.'

'What is the request?' they asked.

'I have a brother-in-law who has been forced against his will into the Palace to become Imperial Consort,' he said. 'If you will all go and ask the "King" to release this man, I'll start work immediately. But if the "King" will not release him, no amount of money or treasure you can offer me will prevent me from leaving this country straight away.'

The crowd had now gathered in great numbers. They gave a great cry in unison, and made for the Palace.

Old Tuo whispered to Tang Ao, 'Brother, do you know how to repair canals?'

'I haven't the slightest idea!' Tang Ao whispered back.

'Then aren't we getting into even deeper water?'

'I acted on impulse,' said Tang Ao, 'out of my desire to save Brother Lin, without thinking of what the consequences would be. Now at least the people are going to the Palace. Maybe they will manage to delay the consummation of the wedding. As for the canals, I shall go and have a look at them tomorrow, and see what I can do. If Brother Lin's five elements (which guide his destiny) are working for him, then luck is with us, and there should be a way to repair the canals, also. But if we are star-crossed, we shall at least take some cargo from the junk and give it to the governments of neighbouring countries and ask them to help.'

Old Tuo frowned and shook his head.

Now the guards in charge of the proclamation post appeared with carriage and horses and took Tang Ao to the guest residence, and Old Tuo followed behind. A feast and wine were made ready for the man who was going to repair the canals, and after they had eaten, Old Tuo returned to the junk to tell Mistress Lu the news, before coming back to wait for further developments.

As the 'King' and the Imperial Consort were receiving the con-gratulations of the guests, they heard a thunderous noise outside, and a palace attendant came in to report that the 'Royal Uncle' had urgent business to consult with 'His Majesty'. When the 'Royal Uncle' came in, she reported that tens of thousands of people were outside the Palace, demanding the release of the Imperial Consort, so that work may begin on the canal reparations the next day.

'For the sake of tens of thousands of people, please release this one,' said the 'Royal Uncle', and explained Tang Ao's terms.

'In our country once the marriage vow has been taken, it is for life,' said the 'King', 'How can I, as King, flout this law?'

'That's what I told the people,' said the 'Royal Uncle', 'But the people said that the Imperial Consort has not entered chambers, so it is different.'

'Then go and tell them that we have entered chambers,' said the 'King' after some thought. 'By tomorrow morning, the wedding will be consummated, and there will be nothing they can do.'

The 'Royal Uncle' tried to dissuade the 'King' from this, but did not succeed. She had no choice but to bow out, and report this to the people.

When they heard this, the people rose in fury and shouted louder than before. The 'King' was somewhat intimidated, and knew that by all that was right, the Imperial Consort should be released. But she found this very hard to do.

Then it seemed as if the noise were coming nearer and nearer. The people must have broken into the Palace. She became angry, and ordered the military attaché to gather troops at once in the palace, and quell the riot. Soon, guns and cannon fire shook the earth, and the buildings trembled.

But the people did not retreat. It was not until the 'Royal Uncle' had assured them that the 'woman' who had come to repair the canals would be detained until 'she' had done the job, and promised to speak to the 'King' again, that they could be turned back. The 'Royal Uncle' told them that they would have news the next day.

Now the 'King' went into chambers, and sat down beside Merchant Lin on the bed. Under the lamplight, she was tantalized by the sight of her blushing 'bride', who looked extremely pretty, although she did not care for the frown on the bride's face.

'Darling!' the 'King' cried. 'Don't you know that from now on we shall enjoy life together? I have made you the First Lady of the land. Please don't wear that sad expression on your face. All your happiness lies ahead of you! How lucky for you that you have shed your masculine attire and returned to your true self, so that we can enjoy life together! Let us drink!'

The attendants laid a banquet before them, and spread before Merchant Lin's eyes jewellery and silver and gold. But he could not be tempted, and he had not eaten for several days. It was as though his heart had become ashes, and strength had left his arms and legs. When the attendant put a cup of wine into his hands, he failed to grasp it, and it toppled over on to the table. Another cup was put in his hand, and again he dropped it. At last, the 'King' ordered an attendant to hold a cup to his lips, so that Lin could do nothing but take a gulp. Cup after cup was forced down his throat this way.

In normal times, Lin's capacity was very great. But as he was weak and drinking on an empty stomach, the wine he swallowed made him feel as though heaven and earth were spinning.

After many cups of wine, the 'King' ordered the table to be taken away, and with a broad smile on her flushed face and with wine-sodden eyes, said, 'It's late. Let us sleep.'

The attendants took off Merchant Lin's jacket and skirt and head ornaments, and the 'King' took off her outer robe. Stretching out a long, tapering hand, she grasped Lin by the wrist, and pulled him to the ivory bed, let down the bed curtains, and promptly fell asleep.

Meanwhile, Tang Ao waited at the guest residence for news, and was flabbergasted when he was told the 'King's' answer. Later in the evening, the 'Royal Uncle' had quilts sent over with attendants for him and Old Tuo saying that she would come in the morning to make the arrangements for the repair work to begin.

The next day, Tang Ao waited all day for the 'Royal Uncle', but the latter failed to appear. In fact, she had gone to speak to the 'King' again in the morning, and been told that the 'King' was unwell, and refused to see anyone. On the other hand, her own residence was surrounded by people waiting for news about the Imperial Consort's release, and the 'Royal Uncle' was afraid to go back and face them. She therefore remained in the Palace, but afraid that Tang Ao might escape, gave orders for the city gates to be shut, and had wine and meat, fish and fowl of all kinds delivered to the guest residence and to the junk.

It was not until the following day that the 'King', in a very bad mood, consented to see the 'Royal Uncle' and asked, 'Is that woman who knows how to repair canals still here?'

'Yes, and she cannot be detained much longer,' said the 'Royal Uncle'.

'For the sake of the people, I have decided to release the Imperial Consort when the repairs have been completed. If the work is successful, I shall let her go, but if it is not, then the woman must claim the Imperial Consort with silver.'

'Your Majesty is truly wise in his decision,' said the 'Royal Uncle'.

Soon, she came to see Tang Ao. 'I am sorry I could not come to see you yesterday, but I was detained by business,' she said. 'As for the matter of your relative, I have found out that while at the

Palace selling goods, she was suddenly taken ill. She will be returned to you as soon as she has recovered completely. Don't pay attention to the rumour that she has been made Imperial Consort. But about the canals, I wonder what your plans are?'

'I have not seen the canals yet,' replied Tang Ao. 'But I believe that in matters concerning the control of water, everything depends on the word "flow". When the Emperor Yu controlled the flood of nine rivers, the word "flow" was at the back of his mind, which is to say, he knew that adequate outlet must be found for incoming waters. I believe the cause of your trouble must be the problem of drainage.'

The 'Royal Uncle' went away, saying that she would come back the next day to take them to see the waters.

'I don't understand it,' said Old Tuo. 'Why is the "King" willing to let Brother Lin go all of a sudden? And à propos the canal reparations, exactly how are you going to go about it?'

'I am not worried,' said Tang Ao. 'If the trouble is what I think it is, I will ask them to broaden the outlets and deepen the canals to stop the flooding.'

'If it is as simple as all that,' said Old Tuo, 'can it be that these people have not thought of the solution themselves?'

'When you went back to the junk last night, I learned from the servants that iron is scarce here, and the people have only bamboo to use as tools. They have no implements for the job. Luckily, we have pig iron on board. I shall draw designs of what is required, and have the tools forged.

Tang Ao proceeded with the repairs when the necessary tools were made. Waterlocks were built and the canals were widened and deepened section by section. About ten days later, the work was finished, and the people were extremely grateful to him. A statue of Tang Ao was made, and erected at the canal to commemorate him.

In fact, the 'King' had been willing to let Merchant Lin go because he was a terrible disappointment to her. Lin acted as stiffly and as lifelessly as a statue, and there was no way he could be roused. Looking at him under the lamplight by the hour, the 'King's' feeling for him slowly turned from love to hate, until it seemed to her as if something evil exuded from the wooden creature seated before her. Finally, after two nights of frustration, she decided to admit defeat and banish Lin from her chambers. But there was the matter of the canal repairs. After consulting at length with the 'Royal Uncle', she decided to send Lin back upstairs to his old quarters, and abandoned any further efforts to keep his feet bound and his face powdered and rouged.

Merchant Lin heaved a sigh of relief and gratefully accepted his banishment to the upstairs rooms. It would be some time before his feet resumed their old shape, but he was thankful for the turn of events. He inquired of the attendants every day the reason for the clamouring at the Palace on the day of the ceremony, but no one would tell him anything.

One day, the 'Prince' came to see him and told him what had happened, and assured him that as soon as the man from the Kingdom on Earth had repaired the canals, he would be sent back to the junk. 'If there is anything you can do to secure my early release, I shall be very grateful,' said Lin to the 'Prince'.

'Please don't worry,' said the 'Prince'. 'I shall try to find out all the news I can,' and knelt down before Merchant Lin, who immediately pulled her up from the ground and thanked her.

From then on, the 'Prince' came to attend to him every day, since the attendants, knowing that Lin was no longer Imperial Consort, no longer bothered about him.

After about ten days, the 'Prince' told Lin, 'The canals have been repaired. My father went to look at them today, and was extremely pleased. The nobleman from the Kingdom on Earth has been escorted back to the junk in the company of ministers, with drums and music and a gift of ten thousand ounces of silver. I hear that you will be allowed to go back to your junk tomorrow.'

Lin was delighted, and said he did not know how to thank the 'Prince' for her help.

Seeing no one around, the 'Prince' suddenly dropped to her knees and said, 'There is something you can do for me. I am in great difficulties!'

'Why, what is it? Tell me quickly!' said Lin, pulling the 'Prince' up.

'I was made Crown Prince six years ago when I was eight years old,' she said. 'But since my mother died, the Concubine in the Western Palace has been the King's favourite. She has a son of her own whom she wants to see on the throne some day, so she hates me and has spread ugly rumours about me, and made the King hate me also. The King is leaving for abroad soon, and the palace attendants and ministers are all in league with the Concubine of the Western Palace. I have reason to believe that they are plotting to murder me. And how shall I, alone, outwit them all? If you would take pity on me, and take me with you tomorrow when you return to your junk, I should be very grateful.'

'But the customs of my country are different from yours. If you go to the Kingdom on Earth you must wear a girl's clothes and lead a proper girl's life. You have been brought up like a boy. Can you change?'

'I am willing to do anything if I can only escape from here,' said the 'Prince'. 'I don't mind any hardship.'

'But we shall be seen if we leave together,' said Merchant Lin. 'Have you thought of a way to escape?'

'It will not be easy,' said the 'Prince', shaking her head. 'But I shall try to hide in the sedan chair which is to carry you out of the palace tomorrow.'

Lin said that if she could do it, of course he would be glad to take her back to the junk. But the next day, when Lin was given back his old clothes, and was about to step into the sedan chair, he saw the 'Prince' standing with the others and weeping. Hurriedly, she managed to whisper, 'I couldn't manage it. I live in the Peony Pavilion. Please help me! If you don't come for me within ten days I am afraid I'll never see you again!'

Merchant Lin at last came back to the junk, and was reunited with his family. With mixed emotions of joy and anguish, he told them about his experiences in the Palace, and also about the 'Prince' who was waiting to be rescued. Convinced that she must be in real trouble if she was willing to give up the prospect of sitting on the throne, Tang Ao, Merchant Lin and Old Tuo decided to wait until dark, when Tang Ao would carry Lin on his back and vault over the Palace walls and find the 'Prince'.

'But do we know where the Peony Pavilion is?' said Lin.

'We will just have to find out after we are inside,' said Tang Ao.

Old Tuo warned them that there were guards everywhere in the Palace, and they should plan a way of escape before going in. But Tang Ao assured him that he would be extremely careful.

Accordingly, after supper that evening, Tang Ao and Lin changed into short jackets, and heedless of the pleading of Mistress Lu, left for the Palace.

At the foot of the Palace wall, Tang Ao made sure that no one was about, and with Lin on his back, sprinted to the top of it. From there, he leaped over one wall after another until at last, they were inside the Palace compound. There was a cluster of peony bushes in front of one building, and Lin thought that this must be the Peony Pavilion. Lightly, he jumped down from Tang Ao's back, and ventured into the bushes.

A pair of very large dogs sprang out from nowhere, and barked furiously, and sank their teeth into Lin's and Tang Ao's clothes.

Guards with lanterns appeared immediately and Tang Ao managed to work free and leap into the air and over the high wall.

Merchant Lin was surrounded. The guards held their lanterns up to his face and cried, 'Thief!'

Suddenly, one of them said, 'Don't talk nonsense. Don't you recognize her? She is the Imperial Consort! I wonder why she is dressed like this and comes here at this time of the night?'

A message was carried to the 'King' at once. 'He' was at a late banquet, and ordered Lin to be brought in quickly.

As soon as the 'King' set his eyes on Merchant Lin again, her heart melted, and she forgot all past anger and frustration.

'Darling! Have you come back?' she said tenderly.

If the reader wants to know how Lin replied, please read the next chapter.

◀ *15* ▶

When the 'King' cried, 'Darling! Have you come back?' Merchant Lin could only shiver, and make no reply.

The 'King' smiled. 'I know! You miss the comforts of the Palace and you would like me to take you back into my chambers, is that right? Well, as soon as your feet are bound again, there is no reason why you cannot come back, provided you behave this time, and don't act as stupidly as you did before. You will see how much good there is in store for you!'

She ordered the maids who had attended him before to escort him once more to his old quarters upstairs, where Merchant Lin was to be bathed, perfumed, and changed into women's clothes as before, and another propitious day was chosen for him to enter the 'King's' chambers.

'Brother Tang must be on the wall watching to see where I am,' Lin thought to himself. 'He'll come to my rescue. But I must do something to stop this foot-binding business from starting all over again.'

Turning to his maids, he cried, 'Nwo I have come back willingly to be installed as Imperial Consort, and I want you to remember it! If you are reasonable, I will not hold the way you treated me before against you when I am Imperial Consort. If you don't behave yourselves, I'll see that you pay for it!'

The maids immediately kowtowed and begged him to forget their past differences.

'If you want me to forget, there are three things you must consent to,' he said. 'Now get up on your feet, all of you. The first thing is, from now on you are to leave me completely alone as regards foot-binding, applying powder and rouge. Agreed?'

'Agreed,' they said.

'The second thing is, when the 'Prince' comes to see me, you must leave us by ourselves. Agreed?'

'Agreed.'

'And the last thing is, I must sleep alone in this room. Agreed?'

They were silent.

'Are you afraid I'll run away?' Lin said. 'You can bolt the windows and lock the doors from the outside every night if you want to. If I wanted to run away, would I have come back?'

The maids then agreed to this condition also, and they left, and locked him in from the outside, and took the keys away.

Soon, Lin heard them snoring outside. When it was almost the third drum, there was a tapping noise at the window. He hurried to it and whispered, 'Is that you, Brother-in-law?'

'Let me in quickly!'

'The window's locked,' said Lin. 'But I'll have a talk with the 'Prince' tomorrow. When you see a red lamp by the window, come and get me!'

Tang Ao nodded and vanished.

The next day, the 'Prince' came to see Lin, and heard what had happened.

'Tomorrow is my birthday,' said the 'Prince'. 'Say that you are giving a party for me at my pavilion, and send all your maids over to make the preparations.'

Lin agreed, and when the 'prince' left, he told his maids to go over to the Peony Pavilion and make preparations for the party.

As soon as they arrived, the 'Prince' asked them to come in, and treated them all to wine. When they had all come, the 'Prince' rushed over to Merchant Lin's room. Lin opened the window, and held up a red lamp.

From the roof Tang Ao appeared at once. The 'Prince' knew who it was, and made a deep bow.

'Let's go!' said Tang Ao, and with Lin on his back and the 'Prince' in his arms, gave a great leap, and landed on the top of the nearest wall. He jumped across several more walls, and at last was outside the Palace.

There was a crescent moon, and the three made their way safely to the junk, which took off as soon as they were on board.

The 'Prince' took off her clothes, and after changing into girl's clothes, knelt down before Merchant Lin and Mistress Lu and kowtowed to them as her adopted father and mother. She was introduced to Pleasant and Melody Orchid.

The girl said that her name was Yin Flowerlike.

When Tang Ao heard the name, suddenly he remembered the dream spirit in the old temple at home. 'Why, the dream spirit said that I was to look out for twelve kinds of flowers while I was travelling overseas, but I did not find any. Yet, every girl I have met on this journey has had the name of a flower; Flowering Maple, Red Lotus, Red Rose, Purple Lily, Purple Cherry, Scarlet Dogwood, Melody Orchid, Beautiful Hibiscus, Marsh Orchid, Sweet Asarum, Fragrant Angelica and now a girl simply called

Flowerlike! This certainly calls for some thought! Can I be approaching the realm of the Immortals?'

The next day, in the course of their conversation, Lin said that after his bitter experiences with wine at the Palace, he could no longer enjoy drinking. Nor could he be tempted any more by money, since gold and jewels had been laid at his feet every day, and yet he had felt no weakness for them. And after suffering so much physically, he thought that he had endured all the punishment of the flesh that a human being could endure.

'Why, if you can resist the temptations of wealth and wine, and suffer the mortification of the flesh, I should not be surprised if you were qualified to be a saint right away!' said Old Tuo.

'Yes, but there has never been a saint with bound feet before,' Tang Ao joked.

But by the time they arrived at the Country of the Shaft of Wheels, Lin had recovered his old cravings and was his old self again, and went on land to sell his wares. Tang Ao and Old Tuo walked to the capital, and saw many phoenixes flying in the air. The people of this country had the heads of ordinary people, but the bodies of snakes, although in their manners and clothing and speech, they were no different from the people of the Kingdom on Earth. The streets were very broad, but so crowded that the travellers could scarcely move. There were countless stalls which sold phoenixes' eggs, which looked like ordinary hens' eggs.

Suddenly, the people on the street parted to make way for some important personage to pass through, as a great noise announced his arrival. To the travellers' great surprise, they saw a person holding an immense umbrella with the words 'Country of Gentlemen' written on it. Under it, riding a tiger, was no other than the handsome and austere-looking King of that country, who wore a golden crown and a scarlet robe, with a precious sword at his waist. He was followed by a large retinue of attendants. Then came another umbrella with the words 'Country of Women' written on it, and under it, riding a buffalo, was none other than the attractive 'King' of that country, who was wearing a crown of pheasants' feathers and a robe of rainbow colours, and who was also followed by many attendants.

The travellers discovered that the Kings had come to pay homage to the King of the Country of the Shaft of Wheels, who was celebrating his thousandth birthday. He was well-known for his wisdom and charity, and the King to whom kings came when they had disputes between themselves. His fairness had saved many countries from going to war, and many lives. Now in celebration of his birthday, banquets and theatrical performances were being given on the Palace grounds, to which the people, whether soldiers or civilians, were all invited.

'Is a thousand years considered to be a long life in this country?' Tang Ao asked Old Tuo.

'The ancients say, in the Country of the Shaft of Wheels, those who die young are eight hundred years old. A thousand years is not considered to be a long life here.'

'It may not be considered long compared to the Immortals in Talotien,' said Tang Ao, 'but they must be the longest-living people on earth. I remember that when the Yellow Emperor was riding up to heaven on a dragon, some of the Ministers tried to go along by clinging on to the dragon's whiskers, and holding on to his bow, and clamoured and shouted to him. But how futile it was! If those officials were not yet ready to go to heaven, how could they hope to get there by clinging on to the Immortal? But if their hearts were as dead as ashes to the cravings of the worldly existence, and they are ready for Immortality, whither can they not enter if they want to?'

'Are you saying that your heart has become dead to the selfish cravings of the worldly existence?' asked Old Tuo.

'It became so long ago,' said Tang Ao.

'You must be joking.'

Now they saw before them a towering archway radiant in the sunlight with the words:

'Model of Conduct and Justice'

worked in gold upon it. Passing under it, they came to the Hall of Immortality through a pair of golden gates. It was an immense edifice with pavilions and towers surrounding it.

Tang Ao was anxious to see the King, so he walked straight into the Hall, and saw that it was filled to the corners with people. The King was seated in the position of the host, and wearing a golden crown and a yellow robe, with the tail of his snake-body coiled high above his crown. In the audience, he recognized the Kings of the Countries of Gentlemen, Giants, Restless People, Split-tongued People, Virtuous People, and many others, who were comparing their physical or moral characteristics with each other.

But when Merchant Lin joined them, and saw the 'King' of the Country of Women, he lost no time in beating a hasty retreat from the Palace with his friends.

After a few days, Lin had sold most of his goods, and Tang Ao received a letter from his teacher Yin Yuan which came by another junk, which told him the happy news that he had made the match between Red Lotus and Little Summit.

When the travellers were under way again and had visited several more countries, Lin had sold all the merchandise he had brought along with him. The Country of Immortality was not far away, although it lay behind many islands and was seldom visited by foreigners. But Tang Ao and Lin were both tempted by the thought of finding the tree of immortality there, and decided to go and have a look at it.

One day, as the three travellers sat chatting on the stern of the junk, Old Tuo suddenly ordered the sailors to lower the sails to half mast and tie them up securely. 'I see black clouds gathering and approaching. A hurricane is upon us,' he said.

Tang Ao could see nothing but a small speck of black cloud in the distance, in a perfectly clear sky. He could not help smiling and said, 'Is that what you call a hurricane?' pointing to the black cloud.

'It's a hurricane cloud,' Merchant Lin began to say, but before he could finish the sentence, they were enveloped by howling winds on all sides, and were being carried into the storm without their being able to do anything about it.

For three days, the junk was buffetted by hurricane winds, and pitched and rolled upon the high seas, until at last, the hurricane subsided, and they tied up at the foot of a mountain.

'I have never in all my years at sea encountered such a storm,' said Lin. 'If it had not blown over, I shouldn't have been surprised if it had carried us home in a couple of days, if the wind were blowing in the right direction.'

'Where are we?' Tang Ao asked.

'I remember that this is called the Bay of Putu,' said Old Tuo. 'There are many extremely steep mountains inland, but I have never been up them. By my calculations the wind travelled three to five thousand *li* a day. After three days, we must have been carried well over ten thousand *li*.'

'When I told you before we set out that we are never sure when we shall return, this is what I meant !' Lin said.

Tang Ao looked around. The mountain which was nearest was higher and broader than even the Mountain of Eastern Opening, and Unicorn and Phoenix Mountain. From a distance, it seemed to be giving off a radiance which made him long to have a closer look at it.

He decided to go and explore it with Old Tuo, since Lin had caught a cold.

'I have never been up the mountains, although I have passed through here many times in my youth,' said Old Tuo. 'This is the southern-most country abroad. I understand that there is a mountain hereabouts called Little Penglai, but I don't know which one it is. If we meet someone, we can ask him.'

After crossing mountains and walking for some time, they saw a stone tablet on the roadside with the words 'Little Penglai' carved on it.

'You're right,' said Tang Ao. They climbed steep precipices and through dense forests until they came to a clearing which afforded them a panoramic view. The scenery was matchless. The waters and mountains became increasingly beautiful as they walked on, until it all seemed like a fairyland.

'I never thought that I would see more magnificent scenery than at the Mountain of Eastern Opening,' said Tang Ao. 'But this is divine! And these beautiful herons and deer let themselves be patted and stroked and are not afraid of people. The pine seeds smell so good that they must be the food of gods. Would you be surprised if in a place as beautiful as this, real fairies exist? Maybe the hurricane meant to carry me here.'

They had come a long way through difficult roads. As it was soon getting dark, Old Tuo said that they should go back, and come again the next day. But Tang Ao was enjoying himself too much to turn back.

'If we don't return now, we'll never find our way back when it is dark,' Old Tuo urged.

'To tell you the truth,' said Tang Ao, 'ever since I came here, I have felt not only as if all the vanities and cravings which tied me to the world had vanished, but as if everything about the worldly life were empty and without meaning. I feel almost reluctant to pick up the threads of my ordinary life again.'

'You must be dizzy from too much travelling,' said Old Tuo. 'Now please come along without any more fuss.'

Tang Ao only continued to look around him. Suddenly, there appeared a white gibbon with red eyes and red spots all over its fur, which stood two feet tall, and was holding some rock fungus in its hands.

'Look,' said Old Tuo. 'That must be a magic plant the gibbon is holding. Why don't we try to get it from him?'

He chased the gibbon down the road back, and Tang Ao followed. Soon, the gibbon disappeared into a cave, Tang Ao crawled in after it, and discovered that it was a very shallow one. Without much difficulty, he grabbed the gibbon and took the fungus from its hands and gave it to Old Tuo, who devoured it with great relish.

Taking the gibbon from Tang Ao's arms, Old Tuo hurriedly walked down the mountain.

Lin had already retired to bed when they came back. Pleasant

129

secured the gibbon with a piece of string, and played with it with Melody Orchid and Flowerlike.

After Tang Ao had supper, he put his things together.

The next morning turned out to be fair, and the others got ready to put out to sea again. But Tang Ao left very early in the morning for the mountain, and had not come back when darkness fell.

Mistress Lu was worried, and Lin was disconcerted. Old Tuo was not feeling well after taking the fungus, so he ordered the sailors to look for Tang Ao in many directions, but they returned without him.

After a few days, Merchant Lin recovered from his cold, and went to look for his brother-in-law himself, but could not find a trace of him.

At last, Old Tuo said, 'I think our Brother Tang came with us on this voyage with the intention of seeking Tao, although he said that he came for the travel. When we went up into the mountains the other day, he was most reluctant to come back, and would not have done so had I not made catching the gibbon an excuse, and chased it down the road back. But the next day, Brother Tang left again without a word. Isn't this a sign that he is ready to take leave of us, and make a break with his worldly ties? You must remember that he had already laid a moral foundation. And is it mere chance that on this trip, although we three have always been together, he alone seemed to have the opportunity to consume all the magic plants? And what about the Split-tongued people saying that an Immortal by the name of Tang was going to pass through their country? The way I see it, we would be wasting time trying to find him.'

Lin knew in his heart that Old Tuo was right, but he could not leave until all hope was gone. Every day, he went into the mountains to search for Tang Ao, until the sailors grew impatient and said, 'We have already been here too long. If we don't take advantage of the fair winds and sail now, we shall be stuck here with little water and food, and all perish in this forsaken place. Master Tang has been gone for a long time. There is not a single soul living in the mountains, but there are plenty of wild beasts. If he has not already been eaten by the beasts, he will have died of starvation by now. If we don't leave now, the same fate will fall on us.'

Lin was in a dilemma.

From inside the cabin, Mistress Lu said, 'You are right. However, you must remember that Master Tang is our relative. What will it be like for him to find us gone when he comes back? I suggest that we wait another fortnight, and if he is not back by then, we will sail without him.'

The sailors grudgingly agreed to this compromise.

Lin stared into the mountains expectantly every day. When the fortnight had passed, he persuaded Old Tuo to go with him once more into the mountains for a last look. But it was all in vain.

When they were coming back, they saw some fresh writing on the stone tablet inscribed with the words 'Little Penglai'. The ink was still wet on it. It was a poem which read :

Though this life has not been completely in vain,
Like Flotsam I have drifted as the ripples carried me;
Today at last I have returned to the Source,
How can I leave it and travel on?

It was dated and signed, 'Tang Ao, on the occasion of his taking leave of the world and returning to Little Penglai.'

There was no more room for doubt.

When they returned to the junk, Old Tuo wrote the poem out for Mistress Lu and the young girls, who burst into tears when they read it.

Lin ordered the sailors to cast off and sail for Lingnan.

Six months later, Lin's junk arrived in Lingnan. He said goodbye to Old Tuo, and returned with Mistress Lu, Pleasant, Melody Orchid and Flowerlike to his home. When the sailors brought the things from the junk, they found all Tang Ao's things in order, except that his ink slab and writing brush were missing.

Lin explained what happened to his mother-in-law Mistress Chiang, who sighed and said, 'Your sister has been waiting anxiously for her husband's return, and constantly sent for news from us. Now you have come back you should send word to her.'

Lin stamped his foot in frustration and said, 'How am I going to break the news to her? What if she takes the news too hard, and we lose another life in addition to the one we have already lost?'

'I think it would be wiser if we told her that Brother-in-law has gone to Changan for the Imperial Examinations upon his return, and that he will come back after he has taken them,' said Mistress Lu. 'This way we gain time to think of what to do.'

Lin agreed, and decided to go and see his sister the next day, but cautioned his wife to hide Tang Ao's things well, in case his sister should come back with him.

Melody Orchid should have gone with Lin to pay her respects to her godmother, but Lin was afraid that the girl might blurt out the truth unwittingly, and decided that it would be safer if she and Flowerlike were to spend a few days in the home of Old Tuo. The girls did not know what was going on, but did not dare to ask. Old Tuo was glad to have them, since two of his nieces, Tien Phoenix-in-Flight and Chin Little Spring, were staying with him. The girls soon settled down and began to sew and study in the company of the other talented young ladies.

Lin came back to his own home after thanking Old Tuo for his trouble, and the next day, hired a small boat, and with a few sailors carrying the money Tang Ao had received in the Country of Women, went to see Mistress Lin.

If the reader wants to know what happened when he arrived there, please read the next chapter.

◀ *16* ▶

Tang Ao's wife, Mistress Lin, had not heard from him directly for two years. When she received the news that he had passed the Imperial Examinations and been awarded the rank of *Tan-hua,* she looked for him to come home every day. Then she heard that her husband was deprived of that title, and was too humiliated and unhappy to come home, although he had returned to Lingnan, and that he was going with her brother and sister-in-law to travel abroad. She was none too pleased when she heard this, and begrudged her brother taking her husband away.

Little Hill also missed her father very much. One day, she wrote a poem to him :

> Dreaming of glory, you are rudely awakened,
> Abandoning home, you travel afar;
> Though greater realms may beckon you there,
> Forget not your daughter who awaits you here.
>
> Cold moon shines on autumn chrysanthemums,
> Fairyland looks upon a wandering star;
> No matter I was not born a lad,
> I'll cross oceans to bring you back !

She showed this to her uncle Tang Min, who read it and said, 'You have made great progress in your poetry, but how would you set about looking for him in the immense overseas?'

Little Hill looked at her uncle and said, 'You seem extraordinarily happy today, Uncle. Could it be that you have some good news?'

'I have just read an extraordinary Imperial Edict which is unprecedented in history,' said Tang Min.

'What is it about?' Little Hill cried. 'Don't tell me that the Empress has decided to award official posts to all the *Hsiu-tsai,* and Uncle will be an official from now on?'

'Don't be silly,' said Tang Min. 'If she had done so, there would be no scholars left to teach the students. No, the reason for the edict is this : next year the Empress celebrates her seventieth birthday. She has been on the throne for more than a decade, and there has been prosperity and peace during her reign. To celebrate the Female Emperor's birthday, she has issued twelve decrees, besides granting official promotions and scholastic honours to the meritorious. These twelve decrees all concern women. That is why I say it is unprecedented.'

'Please tell me what these decrees are,' said Little Hill.

Tang Min said that they all had to do with women's welfare. Those who performed distinguished service in the home to their parents or parents'-in-law would be publicly honoured. Widows who remained chaste all their lives would be publicly recognized. Homes to care for aged and infirm women, orphanages to take care of girls, and allowances for the support of widows would be set up.

To girls who were twenty years old but not yet married because they lacked dowries, the Empress would give dowries. Women's clinics would be set up throughout the country by renowned physicians who would travel its length and breadth. The Empress would provide funerals for women who left no money behind, and if a woman had no family to remember her in prayers, she would be publicly remembered in official memorial rites held in the spring and autumn of each year, provided she had been a virtuous and filial woman.

'But best of all,' said Tang Min, 'the Empress has decided to hold Imperial Examinations for Women in order to discover talented girls to come and help her in the affairs of the country. She thinks that there is no reason why women should not bring glory to their families as well as men. Title and rank will be awarded according to merit. Here is your chance, Little Hill! You asked me last year whether there were official examinations for women. Now your wish has come true. If you study hard, I am sure you can pass.'

Little Hill was very happy, but she said, 'I wonder when the examinations are to be held? If they are not to be for some time, I may have a chance. But how can I hope to pass if they are to be held very soon? I have such a lot of studying to do. And besides, I may be too young to participate.'

'Everything depends on yourself,' said Tang Min. 'But as far as age is concerned, the younger the better. I urge you to work very hard from now on. There is no reason why you should not take part in the Examinations if they are held next year.'

From then on, Little Hill studied very hard. The following year, details of the Examinations for Women were issued by the Empress. Little Hill read the Empress's declaration eagerly:

By Divine wish the Empress declares:

That Heaven is not discriminating in endowing human beings with the pure essences and fine savours of the Universe. Although men may be as brilliant as jade, women are no less so. In my search for people to help me with affairs of the nation, a ministry is given to fine men of learning and ability. But so far, the source of talented women has not been explored. Although talented men have been recommended to me, and there are none too many of these, no talented woman has been singled out.

Now since the pure essences and fine savours of the Universe have been concentrated upon a woman (myself) for so long, it follows that the glory and talent of women should be promulgated and propagated.

After consultations with my officials, I have decided to hold Imperial Examinations for Women on the Third Year of *Sheng Li*. May the Ministries and Officials take heed of the following rules.

Among the rules for the candidates were these : that the name, date, place of birth and family background of candidates should be submitted to county officials in the Second Year of *Sheng Li*, and that County Examinations should be held in August of that year. Successful candidates would participate in District Examinations, which would be held in October. Candidates must not be accompanied by their teachers or advisers, but may be accompanied by one or two women relatives.

Successful candidates of County Examinations will be known as 'Damsels of Literature'. Successful candidates of District Examinations will be known as 'Virtuous Ladies of Literature'. These will participate in Ministerial Examinations. Successful candidates of Ministerial Examinations will be known as 'Talented Ladies of Literature', and participate in Palace Examinations at the capital. Those who pass the Palace Examinations with the highest honours will be known as 'Lady Scholars'. Those who pass with second-class honours will be known as 'Lady Doctors', and those who pass with third-class honours will be known as 'Lady Masters', and all will be invited to attend the Banquet of Literary Celebration. Those who wish to serve in the Palace in their literary capacities may do so on a trial basis for a year. Those who fail in the Palace Examinations will receive a length of satin and may, if their age permits, take the Examinations when they are held again.

The parents, parents-in-law or husbands of Lady Scholars will be promoted one grade in rank if they already hold official positions of the fifth rank or above. Those who hold official positions below the fifth rank will be promoted to be officials of the fourth rank. Those who do not hold official positions will be awarded titles of the fifth rank, and all will be given appropriate official robes. The parents, parents-in-law and husbands of Lady Doctors will be awarded the title and robes of officials of the sixth rank. The parents, parents-in-law and husbands of Lady Masters will be awarded accordingly to the title of officials of the seventh rank, and appropriate official robes will be presented.

All County, District and Ministerial Examinations will be held on the subjects Poetry and Prose. Candidates will enter Examination Hall between four and six a.m. and leave between five and seven p.m. Candles are forbidden. All Examination papers will be copied before they are submitted for grading, in order to avoid partiality.

Those who fail to attend County and District Examinations due to illness may take them when they have recovered, while those who fail to take the Ministerial Examinations due to illness or failure to arrive at the capital on time may take them at a later date if the official responsible thinks that the candidate merits it.

Palace Examinations may not be taken at a later date than that designated.

Passage will be given to those participating in Ministerial Examinations who have far to travel. The successful candidate of District Examinations and her family will be exempt from government service.

Sixteen years is the age limit of candidates. Girls who are divorced, disfigured or who come from dishonourable families are disqualified.

In order to give time for the necessary preparations it is decided that the Ministerial Examinations will be held in March of the Third Year of *Sheng Li* and Palace Examinations in April of the same year.

Yea! Those whose prose is like brocade and whose calligraphy is as beautiful as a maiden with flowers in her hair will attend the Banquet of Flowers! From now on talent will fill the Court. Is it possible that a female Hsiangju will be left out?

May all officials take heed and act accordingly to accomplish this worthy task.

Little Hill was delighted. 'I was afraid that I would not have time to prepare for the Examinations,' she said. 'But if they are not to be held for two years, I'll have plenty of time to prepare, and I shall be exactly sixteen years old.'

'I was glad for you when I read it, too,' said Tang Min. 'And besides, you are outstanding in poetry and prose. I don't think you will have any difficulty.'

Now Little Hill applied herself diligently to her studies, but both she and her mother were worried about Tang Ao, from whom they had received no news for so long. Mistress Lin sent messengers constantly to Merchant Lin's home to ask if there was any news.

One day, just as Mistress Lin was thinking about her husband, her brother walked into the house with Tang Min.

At the sight of her brother, Mistress Lin assumed that her husband had come back, too. Overcome with joy, she invited Merchant Lin to sit down, and Little Hill and Little Summit rushed out to greet their maternal uncle.

'We have been grievously worried for two years,' said Mistress Lin. 'That you should take your brother-in-law overseas on such a long journey as this!'

'Where is my father?' Little Hill burst out.

'When we arrived yesterday, your father was overcome suddenly with humiliation for having been deprived of the rank of *Tan-hua* and could not come home to face you and his friends,' lied Merchant Lin. 'He insisted on going to the capital again to prepare himself for the next Examinations, and said that he would not come home until the rank of *Tan-hua* was restored to him. Your aunt and I tried to stop him, but he would not listen. He asked me to bring the silver he received overseas to you. He has already left for the capital.'

Mistress Lin and Little Hill were flabbergasted.

'I always knew that my brother cared very much for honour and acclaim,' said Tang Min. 'But I never thought that he cared this much, and that he would not even come home although he was practically at the doorstep. What if he does not receive the rank of *Tan-hua* again? Does he mean never to come home?'

'I tried to tell him this also,' said Lin. 'I said that people at home would like to have him back whether he had a title or not, but he would not listen.'

'Well, you shouldn't have taken him with you in the first place, brother,' admonished Mistress Lin. 'He has travelled so much he has quite forgotten about home!'

'I didn't want to take him,' Lin said, 'but he insisted on coming with me. How could I stop him?'

'It's all your doing,' cried Little Hill. 'You took him overseas, and now you have let him go to the capital without even coming home. I don't think there is anything you can do now except take me to the capital and find him! Even if I cannot persuade him to come home, I shall feel better for having seen him again!'

Lin was dazed. 'You are so young, how can you travel to the capital?' he cried. 'Your father has always come back before from his travels, and he will, this time, too. It is several thousand *li* from Lingnan to the capital, across high mountains and over deep waters. Ask your paternal uncle if it is the kind of journey for a young girl to contemplate. If he says so, then let him take you.'

'The way I see it,' said Tang Min, 'Little Hill must prepare for her Examinations next year. If she passes them, she will go to the capital and see her father anyway when she is taking the Ministerial Examinations. As for my brother, I know that he is never happy when he is cooped up at home. He loves to travel, and he is in good health, and he has been away from home for more than a year or two at a time before, since our parents died. So I think it is unnecessary to worry about him. He is actually happier away than at home. Little Hill, your mother understands this.'

Little Hill could do nothing but weep and say, 'Uncle is right.'

Lin spent an uncomfortable evening at his sister's home. Mistress Lin and Little Hill could not stop blaming him for taking Tang Ao abroad. So after supper, having turned over the ten thousand ounces of silver to his sister, and the precious pearl which Flowering Maple had given to Tang Ao, he bade a hasty farewell and returned to his own home.

Lin sold the birds' nests he received at the Country of Gentlemen for a handsome profit, and bought a few plots of land. After some time, Mistress Lu gave birth to a son, and the news was carried to Mistress Lin's house by a messenger.

When Mistress Lin heard it, she was delighted for her brother that he now had an heir. After three days, she went with her son and daughter to offer her congratulations.

Unfortunately, Mistress Lu was not well. She had caught a chill after childbirth, and suffered great loss of blood. Fortunately, the county official was in the act of carrying out the Empress's orders to set up clinics for women, and a renowned physician gave her two doses of medicine, so she was on her way to recovery. Still, she was extremely weak, and Mistress Lin decided to stay on at her brother's home in order to help look after her.

One day, Little Hill was in Mistress Chiang's room when the white gibbon which had been brought back from Little Penglai dragged Tang Ao's pillow from underneath the bed.

'What a mischievous gibbon!' said Little Hill. 'But why have you put a perfectly good pillow under your bed?' she asked Mistress Chiang.

Then she recognized the pillow. She lifted the bedcurtains and discovered a bundle under the bed.

'Why that's my old bedding, tattered and torn,' Mistress Chiang cried. 'Don't touch it!'

Startled by Mistress Chiang's voice, Little Hill became suspicious, and dragged the bundle out from under the bed. When she had a good look at it, she recognized it to be her father's things. She was going to ask Mistress Chiang for an explanation when her mother walked in and saw her husband's things lying on the floor, and the frightened expression on Mistress Chiang's face. Sensing that this could not mean anything good, she broke out into loud wails. Little Summit rushed in, and burst into tears also.

Little Hill controlled herself. She walked over to Mistress Lu's room, and asked Lin to come in. Pointing to the bundle, she asked what it meant.

Lin knew that he could no longer keep Tang Ao's intentions a secret.

'My brother-in-law is in good health and has not met any calamity,' he said. 'He is in the mountains cultivating his spirit and preparing himself for Tao. There is no need to cry like this. If you would control yourselves, I'll explain it all to you in detail.'

Mistress Lin then suppressed her outcries, and Lin did the best he could to explain how the hurricane had carried them to Little Penglai, and how Tang Ao disappeared, and how they looked and waited for him for a whole month, and did not leave until they were in danger of starving to death.

The more they heard, the harder Mistress Lin and Little Hill cried. 'You should have told us this as soon as you came back,' said Little Hill. 'If I had not discovered father's bundle today, we should still believe that he was in the capital! Are you going to let my father stay abroad forever? If you don't give my father back to me, my life is in your hands!'

Lin could make no reply. Mistress Chiang at last persuaded mother and daughter to go to Mistress Lu's bedroom, where the latter pried herself up from her pillow and tried to comfort them. But Little Hill could not be comforted, and kept demanding her father's return.

Exasperated, Lin said, 'How am I going to give your father back to you when he is not here? The only thing I can do is wait until your aunt has recovered, and then go and look for him again overseas.'

'You must listen to reason,' said Mistress Lu. 'When we go abroad again to sell our goods, we will of course do all we can to look for your father.'

Lin showed them the poem Tang Ao had written on the stone tablet on Little Penglai. 'From the last two lines, it should be very clear to you that he has abandoned the entanglements of the world, and seeks the world of Immortals. I don't think I could find him again.'

'At least now we know where he is,' said Little Hill thoughtfully. 'We shall just have to be patient and wait until Maternal Aunt is well again. Then I'll come with you to find Father.'

'No, I'll go with them,' said Mistress Lin. 'How can a young girl like you make such a voyage? And you should stay at home and prepare for the Examinations. If you win honours at the capital, you will not only benefit yourself but your parents also.'

'How can I think of the Examinations now!' cried Little Hill. 'And besides, Mother should stay at home to look after my brother. And I fear that if I don't go, Father will not come back.'

'Why do you say that?'

'Well, supposing you meet Father, and he says that he refuses to come back because he has detached himself from worldly life. What can you do about it? But I could tell him that I have come a hundred thousand *li*s to find him because Mother is ill. Who knows but that he might be touched by my filial heart and come back with me? And besides, Mother cannot go anywhere she pleases and show her face to people without discrimination, but I (being a child) can. How would you go about looking for him in the first place?'

Mistress Lu maintained a thoughtful silence.

'And who says you may show your face in public, young lady?' said Lin. 'Don't any of you go. I'll go. It will be simplest.'

'And if you don't bring him back, I'll not stop hounding you until you do. But if I go and see for myself, I will be satisfied one way or another. I think that for the sake of peace, you may as well let me go now and have done with it.'

Lin saw that she was stubborn, and knew that there was nothing else he could do. 'Well, then, at least let us wait until your Maternal Aunt has passed the full month after her childbirth,' Lin said.

It was decided that Little Hill and Lin and Mistress Lu would leave on the first of August, with the junk loaded once more with merchandise to sell abroad.

Mistress Lin and her children returned to their home, where she told Tang Min what had happened, and began to get her daughter's things ready for the voyage.

Time slipped by, and soon it was the last day of July. Little Hill, with her nursemaid, took leave of her mother and paternal aunt and brother in tears. Tang Min took her as far as Lin's home, and handed over a thousand ounces of silver as Little Hill's passage.

Reluctant though Old Tuo was to go overseas again, after receiving a thousand ounces of silver at the Country of Split-tongued People, which would enable him to retire and enjoy a life of comfort at home, he allowed himself to be persuaded to make another trip. It was decided that Melody Orchid should go and live with her godmother Mistress Lin, and take the place of Little Hill in her absence, while Flowerlike, being Merchant Lin's adopted daughter, for no better place to stay, should come on the voyage with them, and keep Little Hill company. They would find a good match for her upon their return.

On the last evening, Old Tuo came over with his nieces and the girls fell to discussing the coming trip and the Examinations.

'Will you be back by June next year?' asked Phoenix-in-Flight, for that was the date of registration.

'I fear not,' said Lin. 'Last year we left in January and did not come back until June of this year. How can we hope to be back by June of next year, leaving now? I was hoping, too, that Pleasant might try to pass the Imperial Examinations, and maybe win her father an official rank! Alas, it looks as if I will not be wearing any silk hats in this life! But it is really a shame that Little Hill will be missing the chance of a lifetime to win some honour for her mother and father.'

'If I were so bent on seeking honour that I forgot my father, should I not be called unfilial even if I brought home silk hats for my parents to wear?' said Little Hill. 'And what would be the good of a beast decked out in raiments of honour, which is what I would be?'

The next morning, Merchant Lin said goodbye to his mother-in-law, who had taken Melody Orchid to Mistress Lin's house and come back, and left with Mistress Lu, Pleasant, Little Hill and Flowerlike on a small boat which took them to the junk which was anchored at sea.

If the reader wants to know what happened next, please turn to the next chapter.

◀ *17* ▶

Three months later, Merchant Lin's junk came to Portage Mountain. Lin, afraid that Little Hill should be homesick and bored, took her up to see the sights whenever he could, but the girl was sad and not interested, and often in tears.

'I don't understand it,' said Lin to Old Tuo. 'Her father loved travelling and enjoyed strange and exotic scenery, but Little Hill only gets sadder and sadder.'

'Miss Tang has no eye for beautiful scenery now, because her heart is set on finding her father,' said Old Tuo.

One day, Lin found his niece sitting in the cabin. 'You have brought books along. Why don't you get them out and study them, just to pass the time? If we are lucky and the wind is with us, who knows but that we may be back in time for you to take the Examinations after all? You must stop counting the days, or it will seem as if we will never arrive at Little Penglai.'

'I don't feel like studying any more,' Little Hill said. 'But I am not impatient. I wouldn't mind going on for two or three years if I can find my father at the end of the voyage. But I doubt if we will be able to get back to Lingnan in time for the Examinations even if the wind is with us.'

Lin tried to amuse his niece by telling her stories about the different people in different countries, and bought her novelties from different places. Little Hill had read a great many ancient books, and had never known whether to believe some of the things she read in them. Now she began to ask questions, some of which Lin could not answer. So he waived the taboo of men and women mixing socially, because of Old Tuo's great age, and because he was also a distant relative, and brought him inside the cabin to help answer some of Little Hill's questions. Their discussions helped to pass the time, and the young ladies found that they learned many new things.

However, Little Hill was not used to sea-travelling, and became ill, and was confined to bed for a month. When she was up on her feet again, although still feeling rather wan, it was already the beginning of spring.

At the Mountain of Eastern Opening, Lin thought of Red Lotus, and decided to call on her.

Little Hill said, 'Let me come with you! If she can come along with us, she'll be very helpful indeed if we meet tigers on Little Penglai Mountain.'

'You are still weak. How can you climb mountain roads?"

'If I don't give my legs some exercise, and get them used to climbing mountains, how shall I look for my father when we arrive at Little Penglai?' said Little Hill. 'And besides, the change will do me good.'

So Lin consented, and set off with the three young ladies and a few sailors carrying arms. The girls held one anothers' hands and walked slowly, often stopping to rest.

After many such rests and much time, they finally arrived at the Lotus Temple. There was not a soul in sight. After a while, two farmers came by, and Lin asked them what happened to Lo Lung.

'We used to work for the old gentleman,' said the farmers. 'After he died, Miss Lo gave this land to us, and moved to live in Narcissus Village. This January, she had her grandfather's coffin taken to Narcissus Village, saying that she was preparing to return to the Kingdom on Earth. We don't know when she will come this way, though. We of the mountain are indeed grateful to her for killing all the tigers here.'

Little Hill was disappointed not to find Red Lotus. When they were not far from the junk, they saw Old Tuo talking to an old Taoist nun on the bank. The nun was in rags, and holding a sprig of clear tinder. Her face was a frightening green colour.

'Why bother talking to such a crazy beggar?' said Lin as he approached. 'Ask the sailor to give her some money and send her on her way.'

'She seems crazy, but she is no beggar,' said Old Tuo. 'She was asking if she could come along with us, and wanted to pay us with her plant. When I asked her where she wanted to go, she said, "To the shore of the Turning of the Head." I have never heard of such a place. She is crazy.'

Suddenly, the nun began to sing.

'I am the Fairy of a Hundred Plants from Penglai
Whom you have not met for so long,
I have crossed the seas to help you,
Won't you take my magic plant, and remember me again?'

When Little Hill heard this song, she was shaken. Hurriedly, she said to the old nun, 'If you want to reach "the other shore", I'll take you. Are you really going to give me that magic plant?'

'If you would be so kind, Bodhisattva, of course this magic plant is yours. You have been ill. Without this you will not fully recover.'

'In that case, please come on board.'

Lin and Old Tuo could do nothing but let her come on board, and cast off.

'Miss Tang should be careful,' said Old Tuo. 'That plant of hers may not be a magic plant of the Immortals, but of evil spirits. You should consider carefully before taking it. Last time I took a "magic plant" I was sick for days. Even now I feel more easily tired because of it.'

'That is because you had no business taking it,' retorted the nun. 'For instance, something that agrees with a human being may disagree with a cat. It all depends on whether a person is suited to it. This plant is the magic plant of the Immortals, and those who are fit to take it will join the ranks of Immortals when they take it. But if a cat swallows it, who can tell what will happen?'

'Touché!' thought Old Tuo to himself, seething with wrath.

Little Hill invited the nun into the cabin, and introduced her to Pleasant and Flowerlike. The nun gave the clear tinder to Little Hill and said, 'Please, will the Bodhisattva take of this, and cleanse herself of the cravings of the earthly existence. Then perhaps she will remember the past, and we can have a good talk.'

Little Hill thanked her, and took the clear tinder and ate it. Suddenly, she felt extremely clear-headed, and when she looked at the nun, the latter was no longer ugly or green of face, but seemed extremely kind and divine looking.

Suspiciously, she whispered into Pleasant's ear, 'That nun doesn't look so horrible now, but most kind and charitable. Do you notice?'

'How can you say that?' Pleasant whispered back. 'She still looks as hideous as ever.'

'In the *Book of Songs* it says, "How does one distinguish between a male and female bird?" He who is not a bird himself cannot make the distinction.'

'But those of a species can tell the difference at a glance,' said Little Hill.

'Since this is so, Immortals should recognize each other at a glance (although those who are not cannot tell). In the *Book of Changes* it says, "Only those who are kind can recognize kindness. Only those who are wise can recognize wisdom." From this the Bodhisattva should understand my meaning.'

Little Hill thought to herself, 'How does this nun know what I said to Pleasant in a whisper? Isn't it strange?' Aloud she said, 'May I ask your honourable name?'

'I am a friend of a hundred flowers,' said the nun.

When Little Hill heard the words 'hundred flowers', it was as though there were something she should recall, but she did not know what it was. 'I wonder if it has anything to do with my hidden destiny?' she thought to herself. 'This nun says she is the friend of a hundred flowers, I wonder who she is herself? The proverb says, "An Immortal never reveals his identity." Let me see if I can find her out.' So she asked politely, 'Please tell me where you come from?'

'I come from the Path of Transmigration from the Cave of Vexation at the Mountain of Lack of Forbearance.'

Little Hill thought, 'Because of lack of forbearance, there is vexation, and one is on the path of transmigration. I wonder if she means herself the friend, of "a hundred flowers"? Her words smack of Taoist mysticism. How interesting !'

'And where are you bound?' she asked.

'I am going to the Shore of the Turning of the Head across the Bitter Sea.'

Little Hill thought, 'According to the Taoists, "The Bitter Sea (of births and deaths) is infinite, but turning the head, one sees the shore".'

'On the Shore of the Turning of the Head, is there a famous mountain and a fairy cave?' she asked quickly.

'There is a fairy island there called the Island of Return to the Element, upon which there is a fairy cave called the Cave of Return to the Source.'

Before she finished talking, Little Hill asked, 'Whom are you looking for?'

'I am looking for the incarnate of the Fairy of a Hundred Flowers.'

When Little Hill heard this, she became dazed. It was as though she were half drunk and half awake, and felt an indescribable turmoil in her heart. She was lost in a stupor for a few moments. Suddenly, she fell on her knees and said, 'Your humble pupil seeks the compassion of the Immortal. If you will show me the way to cross the bitter sea safely and free me from the coils of mortal strife, I shall become your disciple.'

All this time, Old Tuo, stung by the caustic remarks of the nun, had been eavesdropping with Merchant Lin in the forward cabin. When he heard what Little Hill said, he said, 'I think your niece must have come under the evil spell of this nun. If we don't get rid of her in a hurry, I fear for Miss Tang's life !'

Before he finished talking, Lin broke into the inner cabin, and pointing his finger at the nun, cried, 'If you don't get out of here quickly, you weird creature, you will get a taste of my fist! How dare you come on my junk and practice sorcery . . .'

Little Hill quickly held her uncle back and cried, 'Uncle! She is an Immortal! Don't touch her!'

The nun said to herself, 'I came here today to try to help her out of a difficulty, because the Scarlet Child said that friends should help each other. Well, it seems there is nothing I can do now. Never mind, she will meet others.' She said to Little Hill, 'I will have to take leave of you now, but we shall meet again, probably on the Shore of the Turning of the Head.'

So saying, she left the junk.

Little Hill told her uncle that he should not have offended the nun.

'If it hadn't been for you, I would have given her a sound beating,' said Lin.

The junk was under way again, and after a little while, Little Hill felt completely well again for having taken the magic plant. When they arrived at Narcissus Village, she asked her uncle to go up and inquire the whereabouts of Red Lotus. Lin found out that Red Lotus had, with Flowering Maple, already returned to the Kingdom on Earth.

When he returned to the junk, Lin saw hundreds of weird creatures leap from the sea and surround the junk. They had green faces with long, sharp teeth. Some of them had leaped on the junk. All the sailors happened to be on shore.

'Hurry up, get on the junk and open fire!' Lin cried to the sailors. But before they could reach it from their sampans, the weird creatures of the water emerged from the cabin with Little Hill between them, and plunged into the sea with her.

When Lin at last boarded the junk himself, he found Mistress Lu, Pleasant, Flowerlike, and Little Hill's nursemaid all wailing with grief.

'Did you see what happened?' Mistress Lu asked through her tears. 'We were just sitting around talking, when all of a sudden, those strange creatures appeared and dragged Little Hill away.'

'I saw it,' said Lin, stamping his foot. 'What are we going to do?'

Old Tuo came from the stern of the ship and said, 'First of all, we must send some sailors into the sea to see what kind of creatures those are, before we decide what to do.'

He and Lin went on deck, and ordered the sailor who dived into the sea after Flowering Maple to dive in. But the sailor was afraid of the creatures and said he would not go unless another went with him. So two sailors dived in together, and after a while, came up and said, 'We could not find a trace of them. The water isn't very deep here, and we don't know where the devils could have hidden themselves. Everything was quiet down below.' They went to get out of their wet clothes.

Lin cried, 'Oh, my niece! What a terrible death you have met! How am I going to face your mother? I might as well go with you!' At these words he jumped overboard.

Old Tuo was not in time to catch him, and shouted for help. The two sailors had just begun to strip off their wet clothes when they heard him cry out, and jumped into the sea in their underclothes. After a long while, they hauled Lin back up on the junk, but his stomach was already distended like a drum, and he was no longer breathing. Mistress Lu, Pleasant and Flowerlike melted in a puddle of tears. Old Tuo ordered the sailors to take a big (semicircular) cauldron and set Lin upon it gently, and after a while, the water began to come out of his mouth, and the swelling in his stomach went down. He had barely recovered consciousness when Pleasant and Flowerlike helped him into the cabin, and changed his clothes, while Lin mumbled, 'Niece! Niece! What a tragic death you have met!'

Old Tuo said, 'You have swallowed a great deal of sea water, and your stomach must be upset. You must not grieve. I have just remembered, perhaps Miss Tang will be saved after all.'

'I swallowed only a few mouthfuls of sea water, and lost consciousness as a result. She has been down there this long time. How can she be saved?'

'That crazy nun we met mumbled something about helping her in a difficulty, and also that Miss Tang would meet others to help her,' said Old Tuo. 'Maybe she was an Immortal after all.'

'You are right,' said Lin. 'I must pray for help immediately.'

He took a cane, and wobbled on deck, and had the sailors carry an altar to the shore, where he knelt down, lit a few sticks of incense, and began to pray for help.

When it was growing dark, Old Tuo said, 'You should go back for a rest. You are still weak, and it is late. You can continue to pray tomorrow.'

'No, there will be a full moon. I have resolved not to leave this altar until help comes, and I don't care if I do not get up from this spot in this life again.' He began to wail aloud, and Old Tuo stood beside him helplessly and sighed.

When the third drum was struck on the junk, and the moon was high in the sky, Lin saw two Taoist priests coming towards him, holding switches in their hands.

In the moonlight, they looked like monsters. One had a yellow face with long tapering teeth, and the other a black face with long, pointed teeth, and both had their hair tightly bound together with gold bands. Four boys followed them.

Lin immediately kowtowed and cried repeatedly, 'Please save my niece!'

'Please rise,' said the priests. 'We have come to do what we can. There is no need to plead.' Turning to two of the boys, they said, 'Dragon-killer Boy and Turtle-killer Boy, go to the Bitter Sea and arrest the Errant Dragon and the Bad Oyster and have them brought here for questioning.'

The two boys immediately dived into the sea.

Lin stood up and said, 'My niece is in the sea now. Please have compassion for her.'

'Of course,' said the two priests. They turned and spoke to the other two lads, who also leapt into the sea.

Not long after, they came back and reported, 'We have returned the incarnate of the Fairy of a Hundred Flowers to the junk.'

The priests waved their switches and they went to stand obediently behind them.

Then the Turtle-killer Boy emerged from the sea holding a large oyster, which he placed at the feet of the black-faced priest.

The Dragon-killer Boy also came up, and said to the yellow-faced priest, 'The Errant Dragon refuses to come. I was going to kill him but dared not do so without your order. I have come to request further instructions.'

'Let me deal with that disobedient character myself!' said the yellow-faced priest. He sprinted, and soon was standing on the surface of the water in the middle of the sea. He brandished his switch, and the sea parted and opened a lane into which he disappeared.

After a while, he came back with a blue dragon.

'You no-good beast!' he addressed it. 'Haven't you learnt your lesson? You should be atoning for your sins by behaving properly after being banished into the Bitter Sea for disobeying the rules of Heaven. Instead, you are up to no good again. Explain this to me!'

The dragon prostrated itself on the ground and said, 'I have never misbehaved since I was banished to the sea. But yesterday suddenly there came from the shore wafts of rare perfume, which penetrated even to the bottom of the sea. The Big Oyster told me that it was the daughter of the Immortal Tang who was passing through, and that if I married her, who was the Fairy of a Hundred Flowers incarnate, I would become an Immortal too. I would never have thought of this myself, but at the Big Oyster's suggestion I decided to abduct the girl. She swallowed a lot of sea water and lost consciousness when I got her to the bottom of the sea, but I was going to the island to seek help, when I met the Fairy of a Hundred Plants at Penglai, and begged her to give me a plant to return her to life. I have just come back with it and was arrested. See here, I have the magic plant for proof! Please have mercy upon me!'

The black-faced priest said to the Big Oyster, 'Explain yourself! You have been cultivating your soul for so many years. Why have you now hatched this evil plot?'

'Two years ago, when the Immortal Tang went through here, he saved the life of the filial daughter of the Lien family. To repay him, the girl killed my son and extracted from him a bright pearl. When I heard that the Immortal Tang's daughter was passing through the Bitter Sea, I decided to avenge my son. Honestly, is this wrong?'

'Your son was a greedy and selfish bully who killed and ate indiscriminately. That is why I had him killed through the Lien family's daughter's knife. How could you try to avenge him by plotting the abduction of the Immortal Tang's daughter? Muddle-headed no-good evil-doer, you will not be allowed to live and do any more harm. Crustacean-killer Boy! Open him up immediately and slaughter him!'

The yellow-faced priest intervened. 'Please wait a minute. Although these two, one a plotter of evil and the other a licentious good-for-nothing, should be punished by death at once, yet it is against the will of Heaven to kill. Besides mercy should be shown the Errant Dragon for finding the magic plant which will not only bring Hundred Flowers back to life, but return her to the ranks of Immortals once more. I suggest that these two be punished by being banished to live in the latrines of the Country of Intestineless People, to pay for their crimes by feeding on the wastes amid the faecal streams and vapours.'

'You are right,' said the black-faced priest.

The yellow-faced priest took the return-to-life-plant and gave it to Lin, saying, 'If you give this to your niece, she will return to life. Now we take leave of you.'

Lin took the plant and knelt down to thank them. 'Please tell me your names, so that I shall know to whom to be grateful.'

The yellow-faced priest pointed to the black-faced priest and said, 'He is the Spirit of a Hundred Crustaceans. Your humble Fairy is the Spirit of a Hundred Scaly Animals. There is no need to thank us. We happened to come this way, and were glad to be of help.'

The sailors who had been watching from afar were aghast at the goings-on. When the priests and their boys left, Old Tuo and Lin returned to the junk, where they forced the magic plant into Little Hill, who expelled several mouthfuls of sea water, and immediately regained consciousness and felt extremely well. They were all delighted and congratulated her on her return to life.

'I don't mind any kind of suffering, so long as I can find my father and bring him back,' said Little Hill.

Lin told her the news from Narcissus Village, and they sailed in the direction of Little Penglai once more.

After much time had passed, the junk finally arrived at the spot where they encountered the hurricane which carried them to Little Penglai the year before. However, now there was no hurricane, and when they were at the border between the Country of Little People and the Country of Husbands, Old Tuo and Lin went on shore to ask the way.

The people were alarmed when they heard that they wanted to go to Little Penglai.

'On the way to it about a thousand *li* from here there is an island called Tien-mu, on which there is a mountain called Hai-mu,' they said. 'Every ship which has passed it has come to a bad end. It is populated with all sorts of demons which do harm to people.'

The sailors were extremely reluctant to go on when they heard this, and Lin and Old Tuo were equally alarmed. However, Little Hill insisted upon it. Both Lin and Old Tuo knew that it would be useless to dissuade her since they had come so far already, so they decided to risk it and sail ahead.

One day, they arrived at an island with a large range of mountains around which they had to navigate. As they went around it, they saw all kinds of trees laden with heavy, fragrant fruit – peaches, pears, tangerines, dates and other fruit of all seasons.

The helmsmen and oarsmen steered the junk towards the bank when they smelt the irresistible aroma of the fruit, and dropped anchor. The sailors scrambled on shore and began to pick the succulent fruit from the trees and eat them, exclaiming that they were delicious.

Old Tuo and Lin went on shore as well, and after they ate their fill, took many peaches, pears, tangerines and dates back for Mistress Lu and the young ladies.

'Why has Uncle dropped anchor here?' asked Little Hill. 'Don't you remember we were told there are demons on this island?'

'Who cares about demons! When I smelled that tempting fruit, it was as if I cared for nothing on earth but to stop and taste it,' said

Lin. But going on deck, he shouted to the sailors, 'Let's go! We don't want to meet any demons!'

But they replied, 'After eating this fruit, we feel tipsy, almost drunk, and our legs are weak. How wonderful! Who has the energy to go back to work?' And they soon fell asleep under the trees.

Old Tuo and Lin, standing at the bow of the ship, also began to feel as though their bones were melting, and heaven and earth were spinning around. They wanted to do nothing but lie down.

Suddenly from the mountains came a swarm of women who boarded the junk and led Mistress Lu, Little Hill, Pleasant, Flower-like and the nursemaid to the shore. Two others took Old Tuo and Lin by the hand, and led them on to land also. Several score of others led the sailors into the mountains.

Now although they realized what was happening, none of the travellers could speak, and they were powerless to resist. Only Little Hill still had her willpower, but as she saw that the others all were spellbound, and she could do nothing alone, she pretended that she was drunk also, and allowed herself to be led away without any struggle.

After a short while, they came to a stone cave. Inside, there were two courtyards, and behind these a parlour, in which a vixen sat facing them, wearing a phoenix headdress and embroidered robe, and upon whose face was a bewitching fingerprint. Beside her sat a wizard of not more than twenty years, who had snowy white teeth and scarlet lips, and was powdered and rouged like a girl. A little beneath them sat two other wizards, one with a face the colour of black dates, and the other orange-coloured, with red hair flaming over their heads.

The vixen cackled. 'I knew that there would be no difficulty in leading them to us after they had eaten the fruit which is fermented. What a marvellous lot for us to savour and enjoy slowly!' Addressing the wizards, she said, 'Darlings, I wonder if you have any novel suggestions as to the best way to cook them?'

The powdered and rouged wizard said, 'These humans must still taste of wine, since they have just eaten a lot of yeast. I don't think we should cook them the usual way. But why don't we try something new, and make human wine out of them? Does my dearie think that is a good idea?'

'Why, that's a splendid idea!' said the vixen.

The date-faced wizard said, 'It's a good idea, but to bring out their true flavour, I don't think we should mix the males with the females. We shall brew two separate lots in order to have a light wine, and one with a fuller body.'

'Why don't we let them drink as much as possible so that they get really soaked,' said the orange-faced wizard. 'Wouldn't that help in their fermentation?'

'Good idea, my beloved,' said the vixen, and ordered attendants to lead the humans inside, where they should be given as much wine to drink as they could hold, to hasten the process of brewing.

Little Hill went down on her knees and prayed secretly. 'Please come and help, divine spirits! I, Tang Little Hill, am in the hands of demons! If help comes, I shall prostrate myself at the feet of Buddha and forfeit this worldly existence in gratitude.'

A Taoist nun appeared. 'Don't be afraid,' she said. 'I have come to help you.'

If the reader wants to know what happened, please read the next chapter.

Quickly, the Taoist nun mingled with the others. As the demons brought them their wine, the nun said, 'Watch me! Watch me! See how much I can hold!'

The demons thought that they had made a mistake in counting, and there were really six instead of five human females. The Taoist nun began to swallow cup after cup of wine, so fast that the demons were kept running to fetch her more. When she had drunk all the wine in the cave, she was still asking for more.

The attendants reported to the vixen, who would not believe it, and came with her three wizards to see for themselves.

When the nun saw them, she opened her mouth and spewed wine at them, which came from her belly like a stream of white light. The cave was filled with the aroma of the fruit from which the wine was made. While she sprayed the demons with wine, the nun stretched out her arm and opened her fist. There was a clap of thunder. A coloured cloud appeared over her palm and rose into the air. Peaches, pears, tangerines and dates rained from it and pelted down on the heads of the four demons.

'You good-for-nothing beasts!' the nun shouted. 'Return to your original forms at once! What are you waiting for?'

As fruit rained upon them, the four demons suddenly seemed to disintegrate, and became no more than four little pips which the nun grasped in her hand. The attendant-demons also returned to their original forms and changed into mountain spirits and water sprites, and fled in all directions.

All those in Lin's party woke up as from a dream.

'Please, would the Immortal tell me her name?' said Little Hill to the nun. 'And who are these four demons?'

'I am the Fairy of a Hundred Fruits,' said the Taoist nun. 'I have come to help you.'

She opened her fist and said, 'Look.'

They crowded around to see, and discovered the pips of a pear, a peach, a date and a tangerine.

'Why, the earth abounds with pips like these,' cried Old Tuo.

'Do you mean that these things can become demons, or are these pips of a special nature?'

'No, they are perfectly ordinary pips,' said the nun. 'But they existed in the Chou Dynasty, and are about a thousand years old. The pear was eaten by the famous beauty Shi Shih, and Mi Tse-hsia shared the peach with Duke Ling of Wei. The tangerine was given to the King of Tsu by Yen Tse, and the date was eaten by Tseng Chih. Thus, one came into contact with the lip-rouge of a beautiful woman, and another absorbed the influence of a sage; still another came to know sodomy from the lips of a handsome boy, and the last received courage from the mouth of a good minister. In time, their tempers received the essence of the sun and the florescence of the moon, and were brought to life.'

'So the vixen was like Shi Shih (the beauty) and the wizard made up in lip-rouge and powder was like Mi Tse-hsia (the handsome boy),' said Old Tuo. 'I can understand how these two, who put their good looks to evil use, became models for demons to emulate. But Yen Tse and Tseng Chih were both good men. Don't tell me they looked like the date-faced and orange-faced wizards?'

'No indeed,' said the nun. 'Shi Shih and Mi Tse-hsia both put their good looks to bad use, and it was easy for evil spirits to imitate them. But the reputations of Tseng Chih and Yen Tse are incorruptible, although their bodies have perished. Therefore although the date pip and the tangerine pip absorbed their influence, they cannot imitate them. It is what we call "There is no substitute for the genuine article." No matter how hard they try, they still look like what they are, a black date and a yellow tangerine.'

Little Hill asked the nun, 'Please, would you tell me how far it is from here to Little Penglai?'

'It is as far as the edge of heaven, and as near as right in front of you,' came the reply. 'Know the answer in your heart. Do not ask me.'

So saying, the nun took the four pips and disappeared. Old Tuo and Lin made sure that everyone was accounted for, and they returned to the junk.

They could not stop talking about the miraculous appearance of the nun when the junk was at sea again. Old Tuo said, 'It must be due to Miss Tang's extraordinary filial piety that time and again, help has come from unexpected quarters when she needed it. If we are to believe the Big Oyster, Brother Tang has already joined the ranks of the Immortals.'

'It seems quite likely,' said Lin. 'As they say, "Officials look after themselves." It would not surprise me if Immortals also looked after their own kind. What troubles me is the meaning of "a hundred flowers". Can my niece really be the incarnate of the spirits of a Hundred Flowers?'

'How can that be?' said Little Hill. 'If that is what "a hundred flowers" means, the spirits of a hundred flowers should be scattered in the persons of a hundred girls. And if it could be possible for one girl to be the incarnate of a hundred flowers' spirits, I would not want to be it, thank you.'

'Why not?' asked Lin.

'Why, because flowers are vegetable life. You have heard that for a fox to become an Immortal, it must first lay a moral foundation and cultivate his soul to the level of human beings. Only when it has done so can it cultivate its soul toward Immortality. If it is so hard for an animal, think how hard it must be for vegetable life, which has even less moral foundation.'

'If that is your reasoning,' replied Lin, 'I do hope that for your sake what you say is true, so that we may have some peace and quiet! I think we have had enough intimations of Immortality for awhile!'

Soon, they heard the sailors saying, 'Isn't it odd? We are making so many turns.' They came upon another island with a steep mountain around which they must navigate.

'Last year when we were here there did not seem to be so many islands with such high mountains,' said Old Tuo as they began to weave in and out of them.

'I don't know how we will ever get there at this rate,' said Lin.

When they drew up alongside an island, Old Tuo and Lin went on shore to ask the way. After walking some distance, they came to a stone tablet with the words 'Little Penglai' carved on it.

It wasn't until then that they realized they had arrived at their destination. 'As the nun said, it is as far as the edge of heaven, and may be as near as right in front of our eyes,' said Old Tuo.

Little Hill was delighted when she heard the news. As it was already evening, she said her prayers, and the next day, rose at dawn to go into the mountains. After breakfast, Lin, with a few sailors who carried weapons, led her, Pleasant, and Flowerlike into the mountains, up winding roads which were thick with vines. The girls clung to them for support as they made their way up slowly, and rested often when they came to a stretch of level ground.

At last, they came to the stone tablet. The ink with which Tang Ao had written the poem on it was still wet.

Tears rolled from Little Hill's eyes when she saw the majestic scenery. Peak after peak rose in brilliance and splendour around her, and she felt as if she had left the world behind, and escaped into the regions of heaven, and could not blame her father for wanting to stay here.

But she knew that it would not be easy to find her father. They could do nothing but take a general look around first, and return to the junk in the twilight.

After supper, Little Hill said, 'From what I saw today, there are mountains upon mountains on this island. It won't be a simple task to find Father. If we don't have a plan, we might never find him even if we looked for a year. What I want to do is go into the mountains alone and spend a few days exploring them, and then decide the best way of approach.'

Lin said, 'How can you go in there alone? I'll come with you.'

'No,' said Little Hill, 'you must stay behind with the ship. I may be gone a month, at least two weeks. I will come back at the end of that time in any case, to tell you what I plan to do. But if you come with me, Uncle, and something happens to you, what will all the people on the junk do?'

'In that case, I'll come with you,' said Flowerlike. 'In the Palace I learned to ride, shoot and use a bow and arrow. And I think it would be better if two of us travelled together.'

When Pleasant heard this, she wanted to go, too, but Little Hill said, 'No, Sister Pleasant and Nursemaid must stay behind. They are not used to walking long distances, while Sister Flowerlike was brought up like a boy, and used to all kinds of exercise. Indeed, I would like to have her company.'

'But what will you do for food and shelter?' said Mistress Lu.

Little Hill gave this some thought, and said at last, 'There are all sorts of crags and rocks in the mountains. We can hide under them for shelter at night, or take refuge in the thick pine forests. As for food, didn't the ancients live on grass and tree bark? Besides, there are pineseeds and fruit of all kinds in the mountains, which will serve us amply.'

'But you cannot live on that alone,' said Mistress Lu.

Then she remembered that there was some bean meal on board, which Tang Ao had once taught her how to prepare. After taking a meal of it, a person did not have to eat again for seven days, and after taking it a second time, he did not have to eat again for forty-nine days. There was also a meal made of the seeds of hemp, which, mixed with water, will prevent a person from becoming thirsty for many days. According to Tang Ao, the recipe was given to the official Liu Ching-hsien in the time of Emperor Huei of Chin dynasty during the Second Year of Yung-ning in a time of famine, by a recluse of Tai-pai mountain.

The recipe was this: Wash five piculs of large black beans. Steam three times and remove the skin. Pound the beans into a paste, and form into a ball the size of a fist. Place in an earthenware crock and steam from between seven and nine p.m. to between eleven and one a.m. Remove from crock between four a.m. and six a.m. At twelve noon, dry in the sun until all the moisture has evaporated. Crush into powder.

Taken as one full meal, a person will not feel hungry for seven days. After the second meal, he need not eat again for forty-nine days. After the third meal, for three hundred days, and after the fourth meal, he need not eat again for the rest of his life.

For the meal which prevents thirst: Take three piculs of hemp seeds (*cannabis savita*) and soak overnight and steam it three times. Remove the skin (from the seeds) and pound into paste. Steam and dry as for the black beans. This mixture, taken in water, cleanses the internal organs and prevents thirst.

To return to a normal diet, take 6.6 ounces of sunflower seeds, brew it, and drink the tea, cold. The faeces discharged will be golden in colour.

The next day, Little Hill and Flowerlike rose early, and after washing and combing, got dressed. Little Hill put on a bright red archer's costume of felt made of monkey's fur, and an archer's cap. Flowerlike was dressed in a similar costume of almond yellow. Both carried swords tucked into the silk sashes which were tightly wound around their waists. Their cotton garments, bean and hemp meal, ladles of coconut shell and other things were folded into the bundles of their bedding, which they would carry on their backs.

After a meal of the bean mixture, the two young ladies said farewell to Mistress Lu and Pleasant.

'Heaven will take compassion on this filial heart of yours and protect you,' said Mistress Lu in tears. 'Please take good care of each other and be careful, and find safe shelter in the evenings. I hope you will find your father and come back soon!'

Lin took the girls to the first plain, and watched until they disappeared into the distance before returning sadly to the junk.

Little Hill was afraid they would not be able to find their way back through the treacherous winding paths, and left her name carved on the trunks of trees or rocks at every corner they turned. After many *lis* and crossing many mountain peaks, they came at last to a stretch of level ground. In the evening, they found a hollow tree trunk and spent the night in it. It was comfortable to sit on the pine needles, and soon, both young ladies fell asleep, tired after a long day's walk.

In the morning, they woke up early and continued to walk into the mountains. At noon, they took out their coconut shells and mixed some hemp meal with water from a mountain stream. That evening, they found a stone cave and spent the night there.

After several days of walking through mountains of unmatched beauty, with rare flowers and trees and exotic bamboos and plants everywhere, the mountain ranges still stretched before them one after another as far as the eye could see.

Little Hill said, 'We promised Uncle that whether we found my father or not, we would go back and give them some news after a fortnight. I fear that if you don't go back now, we shall not be able to keep our word. It looks as if these mountains cannot be penetrated in a matter of a few days.'

"I don't think it would matter if we are a few days late,' said Flowerlike. 'We should go a little further.'

'I said what I did not only because I want you to take news back, but because I should like to go on alone,' said Little Hill.

Flowerlike was startled. 'Why?'

'The further we go into these mountains, the longer it will take for us to get back. I have vowed not to go back until I find my father. But I cannot ask you to do this, and keep Uncle waiting forever. You go back and if you should leave without me, I would be happy to spend the rest of my life with my father, cultivating my soul and preparing ourselves for Immortality.'

'I wouldn't have come with you if I were afraid to go into the mountains,' said Flowerlike. 'Do you think that I came with you because of any selfish desire, or that I wanted to be well-thought-of by others? Do you think I came just for the sake of taking a walk? I came because I respected your sense of filial piety. If my godfather cannot wait for us, it does not matter if he goes back to the Kingdom on Earth without me. For I should be glad to remain here and cultivate my soul with you. I am alive today only because I was snatched out of a tiger's lair just in time. What hold can the temptations of life have for me? I can see through it all.'

Tears welled in Little Hill's eyes. 'How can I thank you?' she said. 'I cannot repay you, but I will remember it for the rest of my life.'

It was eight days since they had come into the mountains, and they both felt a little hungry. Little Hill picked some pineseeds and kernels and found them extremely fragrant and delicious, and they decided to subsist on these from now on. So, talking about olden times and about prose and poetry to help the time pass, they walked on.

Six or seven more days later, they met an old woodcutter with white hair. It was the first person they had seen since they left the junk, and Flowerlike wondered if they could be coming to a village.

'Please, old gentleman, would you tell us what is the name of this mountain, and whether there are people living up ahead?' said Little Hill.

'These mountains are called Little Penglai,' said the old man, 'but this peak is called the Peak of Flowers in the Mirror. Beneath it, there is an abandoned tomb. Pass it, and you will come to the Village of the Moon in the Water. Only a few simple mountain folk live there.'

'I am looking for a Mister Tang from the Kingdom on Earth who came to these parts last year,' said Little Hill. 'Might he be living in the village ahead?'

'Do you mean Tang Yiting of Lingnan?' asked the woodcutter.

Little Hill trembled with excitement. 'I mean the very same person! Do you know him?'

'Of course! We live together! Day before yesterday he asked me to take a letter from him down to the seaside to be posted to Hoyuan in the Kingdom on Earth.'

He took the letter and put it on the handle of his axe and passed it to Little Hill. She recognized her father's handwriting right away. But the writing on the envelope said, 'To my daughter, Daughter of Tang'.

Little Hill was puzzled. 'Read the letter, then go to the Lament for Beauty Pavilion and enjoy the view. You will then understand the meaning of the letter,' said the woodcutter and floated away.

Little Hill and Flowerlike read it together.

'My father says that he will not see me until I have passed the Imperial Examinations and become a Talented Lady,' said Little Hill. 'Why? When I am here already and it would be so easy for us to meet? And why does he call me Daughter of Tang?'

Flowerlike said, 'It must have a hidden meaning, and I think it is this. Now the Empress has changed the name of the dynasty in the Kingdom on Earth from Tang to Chou, and your father wants you to remember when honours are given to you in the Examinations in the name of Chou dynasty that you are really a subject of Tang dynasty. If the letter says you should return quickly to the Kingdom on Earth to be in time for the Examinations, we should not tarry here any longer.'

But Little Hill said that since they had come so far, they should have a look and see if they could not find her father anyway.

After crossing another peak, the young ladies came to the old tomb which the woodcutter mentioned. On the precipice of a mountain behind it, there were these words carved into the rock : 'Tomb of Flowers in the Mirror'.

They did not know what this meant, and were sorry that they could not ask the woodcutter about it. After a little rest, they climbed the precipice and soon came to a pavilion of white jade with the words 'Village of the Moon in the water' carved on it. There was no one about. A long stream blocked the way to the mountains ahead, and there was no bridge. But an immense pine tree had fallen across the stream. Clutching its branches, the two girls crossed over to the opposite side.

It was dense with pine trees. After walking for about half a *li*, they finally emerged from the forest and came upon a view of breathtaking beauty. Far away, on top of a mountain, there seemed to be caves of jade with golden palaces and altars in front of them. They were enthralled by their magnificence, and looked at them spellbound. Suddenly, a brilliant cloud circled the sky. Its purple mists parted, and revealed a red pavilion in the midst of the mountain and waters.

If the reader wants to know what happened next, please turn to the next chapter.

◄ *19* ►

The red pavilion was bathed in a golden aura which lit up its surroundings brilliantly. Towering bamboos and vines surrounded it like a tapestry of jade. Many kinds of rare flowers and plants grew near it.

A large plaque suspended from the front of the pavilion was inscribed with the words 'Lament for Beauty Pavilion'. A couplet was inscribed on either side :

Peach blossoms fade, water flows away,
Bright moon, clear breeze are everywhere.

The writing was in *chuan* characters.

There came a blinding flash of red light and a rumble from within the pavilion. The Star of Literature, breathtakingly beautiful, and holding a writing brush in one hand and a dipper in the other, flew out on a rainbow-coloured cloud, surrounded by the brilliant red light, and floated into the air in the direction of the Palace of the Big Dipper.

'We have always worshipped the Star of Literature,' said Flowerlike. 'But I did not know that it had a female form.'

'When we go home, I will have a female image made at the Temple of the Star of Literature, and have it installed beside the male image,' said Little Hill.

When they walked into the pavilion, they saw a jade altar in the middle with stone pillars on either side, with this inscription carved on it :

Say not there are few beautiful girls on earth,
Hard luck accompanies those whose names are carved on this tablet.

There was a tablet of white jade upon the altar, which was eight feet high and several yards wide, with the names of a hundred girls inscribed on it :

Talented Lady No. 1   Trumpet Flower Spirit, Shih Quest-for-Seclusion
Talented Lady No. 2   Poppy Spirit, Ai Fragrant Grass
Talented Lady No. 3   Loru Spirit, Chi Profound Fish

Talented Lady No. 4   Blue-purse Spirit, Yen Brocade Heart
Talented Lady No. 5   Yellow Day Lily Spirit, Hsieh Literary Brocade
Talented Lady No. 6   Lichen Spirit, Chih Orchid Language
Talented Lady No. 7   Rose Spirit, Chen Virtuous Beauty
Talented Lady No. 8   Yellow Pimpernel Spirit, Pai Charming Beauty
Talented Lady No. 9   Suisheng Spirit, Kuo Good Omen
Talented Lady No. 10   Mimosa Spirit, Chou Wide Celebration
Talented Lady No. 11   Spirit of a Hundred Flowers, Daughter of Tang
Talented Lady No. 12   Peony Spirit, Yin Flowerlike
Talented Lady No. 13   Magnolia Cuspicua Spirit, Yin Clever Prose
Talented Lady No. 14   Carnation Spirit, Pien Precious Cloud
Talented Lady No. 15   Orchid Spirit, Yu Fair Heroine
Talented Lady No. 16   Chrysanthemum Spirit, Lin Fragrant Book
Talented Lady No. 17   Hortensia Spirit, Sung Wise Maxim
Talented Lady No. 18   Lotus Spirit, Chang Virtuous Orchid
Talented Lady No. 19   Plum Flower Spirit, Yang Fragrant Ink
Talented Lady No. 20   Begonia Spirit, Li Brocade Spring
Talented Lady No. 21   Cassia Spirit, Tien Peaceful Blossom
Talented Lady No. 22   Almond Blossom Spirit, Lu Purple Lily
Talented Lady No. 23   Peony Albiflora Spirit, Yeh Fragrant Spring
Talented Lady No. 24   Jasmine Spirit, Shao Red Feather
Talented Lady No. 25   Indian Lotus Spirit, Tsu Painted Flower
Talented Lady No. 26   Meadowsweet Spirit, Meng Purple Mushroom
Talented Lady No. 27   Bignonia Spirit, Chin Little Spring
Talented Lady No. 28   Magnolia Fuscata Spirit, Tung Blue Ornament
Talented Lady No. 29   Rhododendron Spirit, Chu Fragrant Moon
Talented Lady No. 30   Yulan Spirit, Szetu Marsh Orchid
Talented Lady No. 31   Wintersweet Spirit, Yu Beautiful Hibiscus
Talented Lady No. 32   Narcissus Spirit, Lien Flowering Maple
Talented Lady No. 33   Fig Spirit, Lo Red Lotus
Talented Lady No. 34   Aster Spirit, Lin Pleasant
Talented Lady No. 35   Camphor Spirit, Liao Glorious Spring
Talented Lady No. 36   Sago Palm Spirit, Li Red Rose
Talented Lady No. 37   Green Peach Spirit, Yen Purple Jade
Talented Lady No. 38   Hydrangea Spirit, Chiang Spring Glory
Talented Lady No. 39   Laurel Magnolia Spirit, Yin Scarlet Dogwood
Talented Lady No. 40   Begonia Evansia Spirit, Wei Purple Cherry
Talented Lady No. 41   Alhagi Manna Spirit, Tsai Jade Moonlight
Talented Lady No. 42   Lily-of-the-Valley Spirit, Meng Orchid Mushroom
Talented Lady No. 43   Cotton Blossom Spirit, Hsueh Sweet Asarum
Talented Lady No. 44   Tecoma Grandiflora Spirit, Yen Purple Silk
Talented Lady No. 45   Yingnien Spirit, Chih Melody Orchid
Talented Lady No. 46   Banksian Spirit, Yao Sweet Angelica
Talented Lady No. 47   Touch-me-not Spirit, Yu Purple Caltrop
Talented Lady No. 48   Chinese Mallow Spirit, Tien Phoenix-in-Flight
Talented Lady No. 49   Rambling Rose Spirit, Chang Red Pearl
Talented Lady No. 50   Anemone Spirit, Yeh Fragrant Jade
Talented Lady No. 51   Honeysuckle Spirit, Pien Rainbow Cloud
Talented Lady No. 52   Passion Flower Spirit, Lu Yellow Lily
Talented Lady No. 53   Hydrangea Hortensia Spirit, Tso Melting Spring
Talented Lady No. 54   Tsewu Spirit, Meng Honeybush Mushroom
Talented Lady No. 55   Vervain Spirit, Pien Green Cloud
Talented Lady No. 56   Artichoke Spirit, Tung Precious Ornament
Talented Lady No. 57   Daphne Spirit, Shih Luxurious Spring

Talented Lady No. 58   Kayanut Spirit, Tou Country Smoke
Talented Lady No. 59   Monthly Rose Spirit, Chiang Pretty Glory
Talented Lady No. 60   Swallow-wort Spirit, Tsai Fragrant Orchid
Talented Lady No. 61   Opium Poppy Spirit, Meng Bright Mushroom
Talented Lady No. 62   Pink Spirit, Pien Brocade Cloud
Talented Lady No. 63   Blue Chrysanthemum Spirit, Chou Complaisant
                        Spring
Talented Lady No. 64   Lilac Spirit, Chien Noble Jade
Talented Lady No. 65   Japanese Kerria Spirit, Tung Flowery Ornament
Talented Lady No. 66   Magnolia Denudatat Spirit, Liu Graceful Spring
Talented Lady No. 67   Globe Everlasting Spirit, Pien Purple Cloud
Talented Lady No. 68   Pink Mullien Spirit, Meng Jade Mushroom
Talented Lady No. 69   Balsam Spirit, Chiang Moon Glory
Talented Lady No. 70   Lyre Flower Spirit, Lu Precious Lily
Talented Lady No. 71   Sky-blue Passion Flower Spirit, Tao Fair Spring
Talented Lady No. 72   Gamboge Spirit, Chang Black Pearl
Talented Lady No. 73   Campion Spirit, Chiang Star Glory
Talented Lady No. 74   Seven Sisters Rose Spirit, Tai Red Jade
Talented Lady No. 75   Red Poppy Spirit, Tung Peark Ornament
Talented Lady No. 76   Wild Scarlet Lily Spirit, Pien Fragrant Cloud
Talented Lady No. 77   Plantian Lily Spirit, Meng Fairy Mushroom
Talented Lady No. 78   Burning Bush Spirit, Chang Many Pearls
Talented Lady No. 79   Gardinia Spirit, Chiang Autumn Glory
Talented Lady No. 80   Yellow-wort Spirit, Tsu Jade Clasp
Talented Lady No. 81   Chinese Rose Spirit, Pien White Cloud
Talented Lady No. 82   Marigold Spirit, Chiang Lovely Tower
Talented Lady No. 83   Honeybush Spirit, Mi Orchid Fragrance
Talented Lady No. 84   Tumeric Spirit, Tsai Silver Moonlight
Talented Lady No. 85   Shrubby Althea Spirit, Pan Beautiful Spring
Talented Lady No. 86   Hollyhock Spirit, Meng Fragrant Mushroom
Talented Lady No. 87   Cockscomb Spirit, Chung Embroidered Field
Talented Lady No. 88   Iris Spirit, Tan Fragrant Marsh Orchid
Talented Lady No. 89   Okra Spirit, Meng Lustrous Mushroom
Talented Lady No. 90   Sambac Spirit, Chiang White Glory
Talented Lady No. 91   Pear Blossom Spirit, Lu Fair Lily
Talented Lady No. 92   Wisteria Spirit, Tung Jade Ornament
Talented Lady No. 93   Arundo Spirit, Chang River Pearl
Talented Lady No. 94   Smartweed Spirit, Ching High Spring
Talented Lady No. 95   Sunflower Spirit, Tsui Little Canary
Talented Lady No. 96   Myrtle Spirit, Su Orchid
Talented Lady No. 97   Peach Blossom Spirit, Chang Baby Phoenix
Talented Lady No. 98   Apple Blossom Spirit, Wen Fragrant Plant
Talented Lady No. 99   Water Caltrop Spirit, Hua Fragrance Returns
Talented Lady No. 100   Lilium Spirit, Pi Completely Virtuous.

Little Hill was puzzled. She was listed as Daughter of Tang, and
the names of Flowerlike, Pleasant, Melody Orchid and others were
all there. After most names there was a cryptic poem. But she
could not understand what connection they had with the spirits of
flowers.

'Could these be oracles?' she asked Flowerlike.

'But all the writing is in *chuan* characters,' said Flowerlike. 'I don't understand a word of it. What are you talking about?'

Little Hill said, 'Are you making fun of me? If so, please tell me.'

'What do you mean?'

'The characters engraved here are perfectly ordinary characters. Why do you say they are *chuan* characters?'

Flowerlike rubbed her eyes and took another look at the words on the tablet. 'But these are all antiquated characters, just like the couplet inscribed on either side of the tablet. I am not making fun of you. On the contrary, you must be making fun of me. There isn't a word I can read!'

'I expect it depends on who is looking at it, then,' said Little Hill. 'Those who are meant to can read it at once, but those who are not cannot read it.'

'Since that is so, would you mind telling me what is said on it?'

'I dare not,' said Little Hill. 'In any case, the meaning of the oracles will be revealed to those who concern it in due time. I am afraid that I would be disclosing heavenly information which I have no right to reveal, if I were to tell you, since you say you cannot read it.'

'Maybe you are right,' replied Flowerlike. 'Just looking at the red light radiating from the tablet has made me dizzy. Why don't you stay here while I go for a stroll and wait for you outside?'

'There doesn't seem to be any red light to me,' said Little Hill. 'But there is a clear luminance. But if you see a red light, it must presage good fortune for you.'

'What good fortune can my life hold?' said Flowerlike sadly. 'If there were to be any, I would not have been forced to leave my home and come abroad. I should be satisfied if I could just pass the Imperial Examinations.'

Tears rolled from her eyes. She took off her pack and put it on a stone bench and went outside.

Little Hill returned to the tablet. After the list of a hundred names, there was a passage which read:

Vast, vast the wilderness,
Incredible, incredible the destinies involved;
If Tang meets Tang,
Carry the news back to the Kingdom on Earth.

After giving this some thought, Little Hill decided, 'The first Tang must refer to the Tang Dynasty. The second Tang must mean me, since my surname is Tang. Does it mean that if someone by the surname of Tang sees what is written on the tablet in Tang

dynasty, he must take the messages written here back to the Kingdom on Earth? But there are a hundred names, how shall I remember them all?'

She took off her pack and sat down on a stone bench for a rest.
'It clearly means that I am to take this information back,' she
thought. 'But I have not brought my writing brush. What shall I
do?'

She tried to commit it all to memory, but it was very difficult.
Just then, Flowerlike returned. She asked Little Hill what she was
doing, and why she did not come out to have a look at the splendid
view. Little Hill told her her trouble.

Flowerlike went out again, and soon came back with some
banana leaves and some splinters of bamboo. 'Try writing on these,'
she said.

Little Hill put the leaves on the stone table, and began to scratch
words on them with the bamboo splinters. It worked very well, and
she said, 'Let's leave this and come back later. Just now, we saw
beautiful caves and palaces high on top of the mountain. It looked
like heaven. Why don't we go and have a look for my father there?
I have a feeling he is there.'

Little Hill and Flowerlike took up their packs again, and went
towards the jade cave. But as they came near it, suddenly, there
came a roar like thunder, and a waterfall many yards wide spilled
across the road, dividing this side of the mountain from the other
like a curtain. There was no way to go near the jade cave.

'I think we must take the hint of the woodcutter,' said Flowerlike. 'He was no ordinary mortal. He said that he and your father
live together. I fear that we would be looking for him in vain if we
don't heed his counsel and fulfil his wishes before coming back and
looking for him. You would save your mother a lot of worry, too, by
returning as soon as possible. Why don't we go back and copy the
inscription on the tablet, and then go back to the junk?'

Little Hill knew that she was right, but she was loath to leave
without meeting her father after coming so far, and feeling that he
was so near. Suddenly she noticed a stone wall on the roadside which
had not been there before, with this verse written on it:

The love of father and daughter is human nature,
    How can you forget me?
But you'll look for me in vain though you go to
    The edge of the sky.
For us to meet, you must first recall the past,
Home awaits you on top of Penglai.

It was dated and signed, 'Tang Yiting, in view of immediate circumstances'.

'Why, this has just been written!' cried Flowerlike.

Little Hill was stunned. It seemed as if there were something in her past which she should remember, but she could not think what it was. She stared at the stone wall in a stupor.

'I think the meaning is very clear. Your father is telling you that it would be futile to look for him now, but you'll meet when you have gone back and taken the Examinations. Don't you see? He calls Penglai his home. That means he has joined the Immortals. And look, this stone wall has appeared from nowhere. Isn't that proof enough? We had better do as he says and return to Lingnan. Who knows but that after some time your father will help you to become an Immortal, too?'

She led Little Hill back to the Lament for Beauty Pavilion, and picked a few pine seeds to eat on the way.

There were many words to copy down, and Little Hill could not do it in one day. The next morning, when she woke up after spending the night in the Pavilion and looked at the tablet again, she was startled to find that more words had been added to it. Under her own name, there was the message, 'Because of one false move, she must endure the trials and tribulations of the seven emotions.' Beneath Flowerlike's name, there was the message, 'Though she missed being Queen of the Flowers, she will eventually reign over a foreign country.' There were messages under the names of Melody Orchid, Pleasant and the others, too.

Little Hill was puzzled. 'What false move did I make?' she wondered, and felt extremely confused. As Flowerlike waited outside, she went on copying the names and messages. Out of curiosity, Flowerlike came in and discovered that Little Hill was writing in *chuan* characters, and asked her when she learned it.

'But I am not writing in *chuan* calligraphy, but in ordinary characters!' protested Little Hill.

'Is there something the matter with my eyes?' said Flowerlike. 'But while you have been working so hard copying, I have been outside enjoying the marvellous scenery.'

'And I have been learning something about the destinies of you and Pleasant and all our girl friends,' said Little Hill. 'Isn't that even better?'

'What! Do you mean that you know what will happen to us in the future?'

Perspiration broke out all over Little Hill. 'Please don't ask me, sister, if you don't know. I cannot tell you whether I know or don't know. If you don't mind, go out and amuse yourself again while I finish copying this.'

'You may think that it is well for you to know,' said Flowerlike, 'but it is well also that I do not know. In any case, when the end comes, whether we know or not, don't we all perish alike into fine dust? Or do you think there is some magic which will save us from death?'

Little Hill was confused and could not answer. After a long pause, she took up her task again, and kept at it until it was dark.

The next day the copying was finished. So the two girls took up their packs once more. Little Hill knelt down before the altar, and kowtowed. Tears flowed from her eyes.

Then they started on their way back. Little Hill could not stop weeping, and kept turning her head back to look. But after they had crossed the pine forest and the stream, and passed the Village of the Moon in the Water and climbed the Cliff of Flowers in the Mirror, she thought of nothing but returning to the junk.

After two days' walking, they came to a large waterfall with the words 'Jade Waterfall' inscribed on the face of a precipice. The waterfall made the surrounding roads slippery and difficult to follow. Little Hill remembered that she had left her name carved on rocks and tree trunks along the way, and looked for them. But when she found them, the characters had been changed from 'Tang Little Hill' to 'Daughter of Tang'.

'It must be the work of your father,' said Flowerlike.

Relieved, they followed the trail back to the junk. But one day, they came to a steep cliff which had not been there before, and there was no way for them to get across except by climbing it, clinging on to the trees and vines which covered it thickly. Half way up, Flowerlike was exhausted, her feet ached, and she sat down and wept.

Suddenly, the leaves began to fly, and a strong wind with a carnivorous smell in it blew their way. A leopard appeared and came charging at them with flashing eyes, and opened his mouth and let out a terrific roar. Little Hill and Flowerlike both took their swords out and stood trembling to await the leopard.

But it charged past them like a gust of wind. Turning, the girls saw the leopard devour a goat which had been grazing behind them, and spit out its horns in a trice. Then it turned around and charged at the girls again, and letting out a tremendous roar, lifted a front paw and wagged its tail, and started to lunge at them.

Before the girls could cry out, there was a thunderburst of drums. From the top of the cliff a strange white horse with a single hump on its back galloped toward them as if on wings, making the noise which had sounded like the roll of drums. It had a tiger's claws and a black tail.

As soon as the leopard saw it, it fled for its life.

The horse stopped in front of the girls, and lay down peacefully and began to eat the green grass. Little Hill stroked it and said, 'I have heard of a leopard-and-tiger-eating horse called the *Pu* which looks like this one. A good horse has supersensory perceptions. I wonder if it will let us put a rein around its neck, and ride it over the top of the cliff? Let us try.'

She took off her silk sash, and said to the horse, 'I am Daughter of Tang, and this is my companion Sister Flowerlike. I came here to look for my father, and we are having difficulty in getting across this cliff. If you would carry us across, I shall erect a tablet to you when we return to the Kingdom on Earth, and burn incense at your shrine every day to repay my gratitude to you.'

If the reader wants to know whether the horse consented to let the girls ride it, please turn to the next chapter.

◄ *20* ►

As Little Hill spoke, she tied the sash around the horse's neck. Grasping hold of the hump on its back, the girls both climbed on its back, and the horse carried them safely to the top of the cliff. There, they saw the leopard down below, chasing some wild animal.

The *Pu* horse let out a drum-roll noise, and started to make for it. Quickly, Flowerlike pulled at the sash, and stopped it. They dismounted and untied the sash, and the horse disappeared in the direction of the leopard.

After a little rest, the two young ladies walked several more *li*s and stopped early at a cave to pass the night. The next morning, Flowerlike said that she was feeling weak, and had another bean meal. But Little Hill said that since she began eating the pine seeds in the mountains, she did not feel tired or hungry.

Two days later, Little Hill said, 'We were a fortnight arriving at the Cliff of Flowers in the Mirror, and it is seven days since we left the Lament for Beauty Pavilion. We must be about half way back. Uncle and Aunt must be frantic about us!'

Suddenly, someone called from the forest, 'At last! At last, you have come back!'

Startled, they both put their hands at the handles of their swords, and stood still, only to find Merchant Lin coming panting toward them.

'What a relief! I thought it must be you two when I saw two people walking in the distance, wearing hats and carrying packs on their backs!'

'Is everything all right?' asked Little Hill. 'Why have you come all this way to look for us?'

'How many days is it since you left the junk?' asked Flowerlike.

'You must be lost,' said Merchant Lin. 'The Little Penglai tablet is only a little distance behind me. I was worried after you failed to come back when three weeks had passed, and came here every day to look out for you.'

When they heard him say this, Little Hill and Flowerlike felt as though they had awakened from a dream, and as if a strange power of magic had enchanted them for the past weeks.

Together, they went downhill to the junk, where Little Hill's nursemaid helped them to take off their clothes and change into others. Little Hill told them all of the meeting with the woodcutter, and showed her uncle Tang Ao's letter.

'Good,' said Lin after he read it. 'You will see your father in a year.'

'That is what he says,' said Little Hill regretfully. 'But how will I come back here again, since no ships ever call?'

Lin was afraid that Little Hill might change her mind and decide to go back into the mountains, so he said hurriedly, 'Your father would not deceive you. After you have passed the Examinations, I shall bring you here again, since I make frequent trips abroad. Now we must lose no time in getting back. Your mother must be very anxious about you.'

It was just what Little Hill wanted him to say, and she was very pleased.

'There must be a reason for your father wanting you to change your name to Daughter of Tang,' said Lin, and told everyone that from now on, they were to call Little Hill by her new name.

Daughter of Tang put her father's letter away, and the junk was under way again. The three young ladies devoted all their time to studying prose and poetry. When she had a chance, Daughter of Tang copied the inscription from the tablet from the banana leaves on to paper, and threw the leaves, carefully wrapped up, into the sea.

She showed her copy to Pleasant, who could not read a word of it, either. This pleased Daughter of Tang, who thought, 'I shall not know whether the oracles revealed to me on the jade tablet come true until after all these hundred girls have lived their lives. I wonder if one day a scholar will match their lives with the oracles, and write an historical romance about them for the sake of posterity?'

As she was about to put her copy book into her trunk, the white gibbon which had become Pleasant's pet snatched it from Daughter of Tang's hands, and held it between its fingers, apparently reading it.

Daughter of Tang laughed. 'Don't tell me that you can read it? I have seen that you abstain from eating meat and you meditate, too. Maybe after a few hundred years you will acquire Tao, and then you will help me find a writer who will record all the events for us?'

She took the copy book back from the gibbon's hands, and put it away in her trunk. The gibbon made her think of the *Pu* horse, and she set up a spirit tablet in its honour on the junk, and burned incense before it every morning and evening.

From now on, there was smooth sailing, and time passed quickly. But when they arrived at the Country of Two-faced People, a storm came up, and they had to take refuge by its shores until it was over.

'Of all the countries overseas, including the Country of Women,' said Lin, 'it is the Country of Two-faced People I detest the most. I hate their wearing turbans to hide their ugly faces. I would sooner they came right out with them, and told me they were interested in nothing but my money.'

Daughter of Tang asked him what he meant, and he told her about the bandits they had met, and how Beautiful Hibiscus and her cousin saved them.

'Then we must take precautions. Tonight, the sailors must shoulder rifles and keep watch,' said Flowerlike.

Lin agreed, and gave the order to the sailors. As soon as it was dark, bells were struck, and Lin and Old Tuo themselves came out of the cabin from time to time to see that everything was all right.

When the sun came up, the storm had passed over, and they were preparing to get under way again when a swarm of small boats appeared, and surrounded the junk, followed by the sound of gunfire. Bandits from the boats boarded the junk. Their leader walked into the forward cabin and seated himself in its most prominent position, while the others guarded him, carrying knives. Everyone was wearing a turban, and looked very threatening.

In the inner cabin, Daughter of Tang and her cousins were shivering. Before long, other bandits came in with Old Tuo and Lin and some of the sailors, and brought them before the bandit chief.

Lin recognized him as the bandit chief whom Beautiful Hibiscus had wounded the year before.

'Let us see the women on this junk,' the bandit chief said.

The others went inside, and dragged Mistress Lu, the nursemaids, Daughter of Tang, Flowerlike and Pleasant into the forward cabin.

'The one who shot me isn't among them,' said the bandit chief. 'How much cargo is there on this ship?'

'There is not much,' said Lin. 'A hundred or so piculs of rice, about twenty piculs of glutinous noodles, the same of fresh vegetables, and several trunksful of clothes.'

'It isn't much, but since you have brought it from so far, I will gracefully accept it,' said the bandit chief, laughing. 'But these three young ladies are very pretty. How did they know that my wife was wanting in slave girls? I would be unkind if I didn't take them along to the mountain fortress and hand them over to her.' To the bandits he said, 'Take them, and mind you don't lose them on the way, or you'll lose your heads!'

Old Tuo and Lin fell on their knees to plead with them, but the bandits forced Daughter of Tang, Flowerlike and Pleasant out of the cabin and into a small boat. They unloaded all the food and trunks of clothing from the junk, too, and made off.

Mistress Lu shook convulsively with tears. Lin beat his breast and stamped his foot, and then hurriedly got a sampan with Old Tuo to go after them. But the bandits hoisted the sails of their boats and sailed away as if on wings.

The three girls tried to jump overboard, but were surrounded on all sides. After a while, they were taken to the mountains and arrived at the fortress. The bandit chief led them inside.

An enchanting woman of about thirty, heavily powdered and rouged, and wearing silk gauze, came out and said, 'What kept you so long, my lord?'

'I was afraid the black girl I found for you yesterday did not please you, so I have found these three for you, and that is why I was so long,' said the bandit chief. To the girls, he said, 'Hurry up and kowtow to Madam.'

The young girls had no alternative but to go forward and mumble, 'Ten thousand good-fortunes,' to the woman.

'What, have you no manners? Don't you know how to knock your heads on the ground? You are no better than the black girl!' said the bandit chief. 'Do you like them, Madam? Do you find them attractive?'

The woman studied the three girls, and suddenly blushed red in the face. 'Let us have a banquet in celebration of their joining us,' she said, and to the old women who attended her, she said, 'Set the table here.'

Soon, the bandit chief and the woman sat down opposite each other, and the bandit chief said, 'Madam should have the old women teach these three and the black girl how to serve. Otherwise, how will they ever learn?'

The woman nodded, and had the black girl called in. She was fifteen or sixteen years old, quite pretty, and she was crying. The old women made the girls stand two at each side of the table. The bandit chief could not take his eyes off the young girls, and began to drink rather quickly. 'Why don't you ask these four slave girls to pour for us? Let us have a good time!' he said to the woman, who made a noise through her nose and said, 'You four, take turns and pour for the Chief!'

The girls answered yes, but made no move.

'Why don't we get the bandit drunk, and then ask the woman bandit to let us go?' Flowerlike thought to herself. She stepped forward, and poured full cups for both of them, and gave the others a glance. The young girls understood her meaning, and began to pour for the bandit and his wife in turn.

The bandit chief was extremely pleased. As wine poured into his intestines, he felt better and better. The four girls did not stop, and soon he was feeling extremely happy, and began to stare and grin at them foolishly.

'I see my lord has taken a fancy to them,' sneered the woman.

The bandit chief grinned even more broadly, but dared not say anything, and began to giggle.

'If you like them, why don't you take them for concubines? I have old women to serve me,' said the woman.

When Daughter of Tang heard this, she thought, 'Here's where I must take leave of the world!'

The bandit stared at the woman and said, 'Do you mean it?'

'Why not? And when they beget children, won't that be reward for your trouble, since I haven't given you any?'

The girls looked at one another frantically. Daughter of Tang pulled at Flowerlike and Pleasant's sleeves and whispered, 'What shall we do?'

'Can we find some knives in the kitchen and kill ourselves?' said Flowerlike.

Just as they were whispering, they heard the woman say, 'If you agree, I'll pick a propitious day.'

The bandit chief made a deep bow to the woman and drooled, 'The idea of taking concubines has been on my mind constantly, but I was afraid that you would object, and never dared mention it. Since you have brought it up yourself, this is just what I have been longing for . . .'

Before he finished speaking, there was a crash of plates and cups. The woman overturned the table and food and furniture began to fly in the air.

'Beast! I thought you had my comfort in mind when you found these girls! So this is what you had in mind all along! Well, since it is so, why should I continue to live and be a thorn in your eye?' So saying, she got up, took a pair of scissors and pointed them at her throat. Clenching her silver teeth, furrowing her brows, and with tears pouring from her eyes, she was going to cut her throat when the bandit seized the scissors from her hand and fell down on his knees in front of her.

'I am sorry. I did not know what I was saying because I was drunk. Please forgive me, Madam. From now on I will cease to entertain these ignoble thoughts!'

The woman howled that since he no longer loved her, she must end her life, and taking a ribbon, started to loop it around her neck. The bandit took that away from her, too. She tried to smash her skull against the wall, and the bandit stopped her.

He began to kowtow to her. 'I swore to you I would not entertain such evil ideas from now on, but Madam would not believe me. Then cane me. If I should ever err again, I shall be glad to be caned twice as many times.' Turning to the old women, he told them to fetch four caning boys.

'Due to my careless talk while intoxicated, I have offended my wife and caused her to become angry and want to commit suicide. May I trouble you to cane me twenty times? It will be to your credit if you beat me to such a condition that Madam takes pity on me and forgives me. But don't talk about it afterwards. I may be hen-pecked, but I have my pride.'

He prostrated himself on the ground. The caning boys raised their sticks and began to beat him lightly. The bandit chief pretended to cry out in pain and ask the woman's pardon.

When the twenty strokes were delivered, the woman pointed to him and cried, 'Well, since you are willing to suffer for your mistake, I will not try to take my life again. But to give vent to my anger, twenty more strokes must be delivered.'

The bandit chief knocked his head on the ground repeatedly and said, 'Yes, m'am! If you will just stop being angry, and forget about the whole thing, I will gladly let you beat me as many times as you like!'

The woman said to the caning boys, 'Since he is willing, you apply yourselves to the job properly now! If you don't, look out for your lives!'

At this, the caning boys went to work. Two of them held the bandit chief down, while the other two took up big planks, and applied them to the bandit's body. His skin split open and his flesh tore. The bandit screamed. When the twenty strokes had been given, the boys stopped.

'Twenty more!' the woman cried. 'This heartless bandit is not going to get off so easily!'

The bandit chief sobbed, 'Please, Madam! I cannot endure any more!'

'Then why has the idea of taking concubines been on your mind constantly? Would you like it if I took a gigolo, and cast you aside? In times of poverty, you men sometimes know what is right and what is wrong. But when you get rich, you forget not only your old friends and relatives, but even the wife who struggled with you in your hard days! And with your nose up in the air, you think only of yourselves! For that alone you ought to be cut up into ten thousand pieces, and you are still thinking of taking concubines! I am beating you for no other reason than that you are selfish, and never think of other people. I am going to beat you until you have not a shred of pride left, and show some humility! After today, I will not interfere with you any more. If you don't want to take concubines, all right. If you do, all right, too. But find me a gigolo first. This gigolo, or what the ancients call "Face and Head", will be handsome in the face, and have a full head of hair on his head. And I will not be setting any precedent either, but only following the customs of ancient times.'

The bandit chief said, 'What is the difference? If you want a male-concubine, go ahead. Why be afraid of setting a precedent? But please, do not destroy my pride. It is what we bandits of the forest live by.'

'Pride is a bad thing,' said the woman. 'Why not let me destroy it?'

'We bandits live by our pride! If we have no pride left, how can we be bandits? It is something that cannot change until we die!'

'I will see if that is true!' the woman said, and told the caning boys, 'Continue!'

Eighty more strokes were delivered. The bandit, lying on the ground, fainted several times, and finally cried out, with tears rolling down his face, 'Madam, you had better start making the funeral arrangements! I have nothing to leave behind except to caution posterity, "Don't lose your pride!" ' So saying, he fainted again.

The woman saw that he could not take any more, and ordered that he be carried to bed. 'So, he would not relinquish his pride even though he was near death!' she thought. 'If I had known this, I would not have had to go to so much trouble!' She told the attendants, 'Take the three girls away. Their boat must be still at the foot of the mountain. Let the black girl go with them, as she is of no use here, and give them back all their clothing, so that we will have no more trouble. Hurry! If there is any mistake, you will be seeing me next with severed heads!'

'Yes, m'am!' the attendants said, and hurriedly took the four girls down the mountains.

Old Tuo and Lin were overjoyed to see them back. When the trunks of clothing were being brought, however, one of the attendants secretly held one back, and cried, 'Hurry up! Get going before the chief comes after you! If you tarry here, there is no accounting for what may happen to you!'

Lin and Old Tuo quickly took the girls and the trunks on board the sampan and made for the junk.

When Merchant Lin learned what happened, he could only thank Buddha for showing his mercy.

Old Tuo looked at the black girl and said, 'Who are you? How did you come to this place?'

'My surname is Li,' said the girl. 'My name is Red Rose, and I come from the Country of Black-toothed People. My father was a second-lieutenant in the army. When he died, I came overseas with my uncle to trade, but the bandits killed my uncle, and abducted me into the mountains. I am an orphan now, with no one to turn to!'

Old Tuo remembered her. She was the scholarly girl whom he and Tang Ao had met in the Country of Black-toothed People, and told the others about it. When they were on the junk, Red Rose paid her respects to the people on the boat, and when Mistress Lu was told what had happened, she could do nothing but sigh.

Daughter of Tang said, 'It must have been fate that we meet like this. I have a lot to learn from you. Will you condescend to become our sworn sister?'

Red Rose said, 'I am an orphan with no one to turn to. How dare I presume to become your sworn sister?'

'Oh, don't be so modest!' Merchant Lin said. 'My niece's father was a *Tan-hua*. Miss Li's father was a second-lieutenant. You are both girls of good family.' So Red Rose consented, and the four girls became sworn sisters. Red Rose was the eldest, and Flowerlike was second. Daughter of Tang was the third sister, and Pleasant was the youngest.

The sailors were overheard saying, 'We are dizzy from hunger. All our grain was taken by the bandits. We haven't the energy to cast off!'

'It is lucky we still have the bean meal Brother Lin brought,' said Old Tuo.

'I would never have thought that we had to fall back on that, when we had a hold full of white rice yesterday,' said Merchant Lin. 'It is lucky that the bandit chief's wife returned the trunks to us, otherwise we would have starved to death!'

It was not until then that Lin discovered that the trunk which contained the bean meal was missing.

176

'The attendants must have thought that there was money inside, and taken it,' Lin said. He went on shore again, but of course the attendants were not in sight. Lin decided that it would not be safe to go inland to buy rice, and the Country of Scholars was still far away, and the sailors would rather endure hunger than return to the Country of Two-faced People. They decided that they had no recourse but to sail ahead, and hope to meet a friendly junk soon, and buy some grain from it.

However, they met no junk for two days. Instead, there was a typhoon. The sailors' faces became dark with hunger, and there were moans and sighs to be heard from bow to stern. Lin could do nothing but order that anchor be dropped on a strange shore, to wait out the typhoon.

Sitting in the cabin, the sworn sisters looked out of the window and saw a thin and sickly-looking Taoist nun come up to the junk with a basket in her hand to beg for food.

The sailors cried, 'We haven't eaten for two days! We have nothing to give you!'

When the Taoist nun heard this, she sang:

'I am the Fairy of a Hundred Grains from Penglai,
How long we have been companions together!
I've crossed the sea because of my compassion for you,
To give you the clear-intestine grain, for old times' sake.'

When Daughter of Tang heard this, she remembered the nun she had met at the Mountain of Eastern Opening, who had sung a similar song, but she did not know what 'clear-intestine grain' was. She took her three sisters up to the bow of the ship and said, 'Please, will you come on board for a cup of tea and a talk?'

'I have to go sight-seeing, I have no time to talk!' the nun said. 'If you will give me a vegetarian dinner, I'll be on my way.'

'Please, may I ask,' said Daughter of Tang, 'are nuns interested in sight-seeing, too?'

'Bodhisattva, you should know that once you have seen all, it is over!'

'Is that so?' said Daughter of Tang. 'Please tell me, where have you come from?'

'I come from the Cave of the Turning of the Head on Reunion Mountain,' said the nun.

Daughter of Tang was struck by her words. 'Where are you going?' she said.

'I am going to the Cave of Ultimate Happiness on Flight Island.'

'Can it be that after one has "seen all", he "turns back" and finds happiness?' Daughter of Tang thought. She asked, 'Please tell me, where is the Cave of Ultimate Happiness on Flight Island, geographically speaking?'

'It is in the Area of the Heart,' said the nun.

Daughter of Tang nodded and said, 'I see! I wish I could give you something, but we have been without food for days ourselves.'

The nun said, 'I beg only where I am destined to beg. There might be a place where the grain is piled high like a mountain, and I will not go there to beg. But if I meet someone I was meant to meet who is without grain, then I have some grain in my basket which I can give to help out.'

Flowerlike smiled and said, 'It does not look as if that basket could hold very much grain.'

'My basket may look small,' said the nun, 'but it is large or small, depending on the need.'

'How large can it be?' said Red Rose.

'It can be as large as to hold all the grain in the world.'

'And how small can it get?' asked Pleasant.

'At its smallest it will provide enough food for those on board for three months.'

'Can it be that we on board this junk were destined to meet you?' said Daughter of Tang.

'There are more than thirty on board,' said the nun. 'I could not have been meant to meet every one of you.'

'How about we four sisters?' said Daughter of Tang.

'We were not only destined to meet, but our destinies are entangled,' said the nun. 'Because they are entangled, they are knotted. Because they are knotted, there must have been old threads. Because there are old threads, there must be a common resolution. Once there is a common resolution, there will be detachment.' So saying, she threw the basket on the deck. 'Too bad there is not much grain left in this basket. Everyone can be only half of half full.'

Pleasant removed the grain from the basket, and asked a sailor to hand it back to the nun. The nun took it and said, 'Blessings, Bodhisattva! We shall meet again. I must go now.'

After she left, Pleasant said, 'Look, sisters, the nun left eight grains of rice, each grain a foot in length!'

They did not understand what kind of grain it was until Old Tuo came and said, 'This is the clear-intestine grain. One grain will do for a person for a year. There are thirty-two of us on board. We will break each grain into four sections, so that everyone has a piece. Thus, none of us should know hunger for at least three months.'

'So that is why the nun said the grain would make us only half of half, or a quarter full!' said Flowerlike.

Old Tuo and Lin took the rice to the galley, and had each grain cut into four sections, and cooked. Everyone had a meal, and felt well again, and was grateful to the nun for it.

If the reader wants to know what happened next, please read the next chapter.

21

The next day, the junk was on its way again. Daughter of Tang had a chance to mention the Imperial Examinations for Women to Red Rose, but Red Rose said with a sigh, 'I am afraid that I am not interested, because what is the use of being talented, if a person does not come from the right kind of family? That is how successful candidates are determined in my country.'

Nevertheless, as she had no one to turn to, she agreed to go to the Kingdom on Earth with her sworn sisters. Speaking of the Country of Black-toothed People, Red Rose remembered her friend Purple Lily, who was now also without a family, and wondered whether she could be persuaded to go to the Kingdom on Earth too, for surely, she had more than enough talent to pass the Examinations with honours.

Remembering her, Lin and Old Tuo both said that Purple Lily was probably not the sort of girl who could be persuaded.

'Why not?' said Flowerlike. 'Is she not a person who is made of flesh and blood, or does she have six arms and three heads?'

'She may be made of flesh and blood,' said Lin, 'but her tongue is made of steel. I remember the sweat Old Tuo got into, just talking to her! If you really want to see her, you had better brush up on your classics! We shall stop over in the Country of Black-toothed People to buy rice, and then you will have a chance to discuss literature with her.'

When they arrived at that country, Lin and Old Tuo led the sailors ashore to buy rice. Daughter of Tang wanted Red Rose to come with her to see Purple Lily, but Red Rose said, 'Uncle Lin knows where she lives. There is no need for me to go. If I went, and she thought that she had to come for my sake, it would be embarrassing. Why don't you go alone, and say that you want to talk to her? Whether she agrees or not, I shall go over later and convey your beautiful wish for her to go to your Kingdom. That way, she will not despise me.'

Flowerlike agreed to go with Daughter of Tang, and they went into the city with Merchant Lin. Soon, they came to a narrow alley and saw the words 'Female Institute of Learning' written in big characters upon a doorway.

A girl dressed in purple opened the door when they knocked. Lin recognized her as the girl he had met the year before last with Tang Ao. When the girl knew who they were, she invited the young ladies to step inside, while Lin waited in a small room nearby. In the study, Purple Lily asked Flowerlike and Daughter of Tang to sit down, and after they had exchanged names, Daughter of Tang said, 'I have long heard of your reputation, and wanted to pay my respects to you when I passed this way last year, but I was afraid to incur your laughter because of my poor learning.'

'How dare I presume to be so honoured!' exclaimed Purple Lily. 'I remembered that a Sage named Tang came with the Old Gentleman Tuo last time. Is the Sage of one family with you?'

'He is my father,' said Daughter of Tang.

Purple Lily stood up at once and made another bow to Daughter of Tang. 'I did not realize!' she said. 'I had the honour to receive his instruction a year ago. Since his departure, there has been no one from whom to seek advice in literary matters.' Daughter of Tang said, 'What is it you wish to know?' whereupon Purple Lily, Daughter of Tang and Flowerlike became involved in a discussion of the names and dates and historical interpretations of Confucius' *Chun Chiu*, and Purple Lily demonstrated that she knew all the royal designations of the years of all the emperors' reigns.

When Red Rose appeared, she told Purple Lily of the misfortunes she had met overseas, and after she stopped crying, she said, 'Sister, do you know why these young ladies have come to call on you?'

'I dare not say that I do,' said Purple Lily.

Red Rose thereupon told her about the Imperial Examinations for Women, and the young ladies' wishes.

After giving this some thought, Purple Lily said, 'I appreciate your kindness, but I have a widowed mother who is sixty years old. How could I go and leave her here, although I have always wanted to take part in an Examination of this kind?'

'Why can't you bring Auntie along too?' asked Daughter of Tang.

Purple Lily sighed and said, 'I've thought of that. Unfortunately, we have only a few meagre acres of land to live on. Even if we sold them there would not be enough money to pay for the passage and maintain us in the Kingdom on Earth. And what would we live on afterwards?'

'If only Auntie is willing to come, the rest is easy,' said Daughter of Tang. 'You don't have to spend anything on the passage if you come with us, and as for food and clothing in the Kingdom on Earth, my family can give you what you need, although we are not very well off, and have but a few good acres of land and a few rooms in Lingnan. You need not spend anything. Don't sell the land, but ask some relative to take care of it while you are gone.'

'How dare I impose on you when we have only just met?' said Purple Lily. 'Please allow me to ask my mother's opinion about it, then I shall come to pay my respects to you on the junk before you leave.'

'Nonsense!' said Red Rose. 'You may have just met Sister Daughter of Tang, but you have not just met me. I think that you should accept her kind offer. Look at me, if it were not for her, would I be here today? Why don't you ask your mother now, and see what she says?'

So saying, she took Purple Lily's hand, and went inside to tell Mistress Tsu about it.

Mistress Tsu herself was a woman who had grown up with books and poetry. In her youth, she had also taken part in the Examinations for Women in this country, but had not passed, although she was learned. When she gave birth to Purple Lily, she and her husband devoted all their efforts to teaching her, hoping that one day the girl would win a place of honour for them. Her husband had died in regret because they had not gained any honours as the judges were partial to influential families, not poor ones.

Now hearing that an opportunity had come again, Mistress Tsu's own ambition was reawakened. She came with her daughter and Red Rose to the outer room and met Daughter of Tang and Flowerlike and said, 'Any achievement that my daughter may win in the future will be all due to your love for her. I am sixty years old, but my spirit is still young. It has been my ambition in life to pass the Examinations. Only I am afraid that the age limit prevents me from taking advantage of this once-in-a-lifetime opportunity! Is there anything you can do to fulfil my wish?'

'How can I not try to help if I can?' Daughter of Tang said. 'What a fine spirit you have! You could of course lie about your age when you register, were it not for the white hairs on your head and wrinkles on your face. How can we hide those?'

Mistress Tsu said, 'Now why could I not dye my hair? As for my wrinkles, I shall put two boxes of "protocol soap" on my face, and then cover it with powder. I don't need to walk with a stick yet . . . But if I can't take part in the examinations, I do not want to make a long journey like this.'

Daughter of Tang thought hard for a while and said, 'I suppose Auntie could get past the supervisors in the County and District Examinations. But supervision is very strict at the Ministerial and Palace Examinations. I dare not say that you will not be detected.'

'Oh, I should be satisfied if I just pass the District Examinations and obtained the rank of "Virtuous Lady",' said Mistress Tsu. 'I wouldn't want to try for anything higher.'

Daughter of Tang could only answer, 'I shall try my best to help you when the time comes.'

So it was agreed that Mistress Tsu and Purple Lily would come to Lingnan with them. Purple Lily ordered two servants to pack, and put the land, house and their sundry belongings in the care of relatives. When this was done, it was already dusk. Merchant Lin told the porters to carry the baggage and led the party back to the junk.

On board, Mistress Tsu and Purple Lily were introduced to Mistress Lu, and Purple Lily also became a sworn sister of the girls. As Red Rose was still the eldest, she became the second, before the other three girls. From now on Purple Lily, Red Rose and Mistress Tsu shared one cabin, while Daughter of Tang, Flowerlike and Pleasant another.

The wind was with them all the way, and soon it was summer.

One day, Merchant Lin was chatting with the sisters, and Flowerlike asked, 'How many days more will it be before we arrive in Lingnan?'

'How many more days?' Lin said with a laugh. 'How easily said, indeed!'

'Does Uncle mean that it will be a few more months before we arrive?' said Red Rose.

'We won't arrive even then,' said Lin.

Pleasant snorted, 'Then do you mean it takes half a year or a year?'

'Maybe a year,' said Lin, 'but certainly more than half a year. It is only two months since we left Little Penglai. Now it would be a hundred days at least with fair winds if we could go in a straight line through Portage Mountain. As we have to make so many detours, it will take a least half a year. If the winds are against us, then it will take longer. This is my experience from many trips abroad. Have you forgotten how we had to wind our way out of Portage Mountain last year?'

'I did not notice it last year as the only thing on my mind was finding my father,' said Daughter of Tang. 'But if it is as you say, we shall not arrive before next spring, and we shall miss the Examinations.'

Lin said, 'As long as you arrive in time for the Palace Examinations in April, it will be all right. The other examinations can be made up.'

'The County Examinations take place in August, and the District Examinations in October,' said Purple Lily, 'and the Ministerial Examinations in March next year. How will we have time to make up these three examinations if we arrive so late?'

'I did not know that there were these requirements,' said Lin. 'We will just have to make our way the best we can. If only they could delay the examination date !'

Daughter of Tang was unhappy, and let out long sighs every day.

Mistress Lu was afraid that she would get sick from worrying, and was sorry that her husband had told them the truth. One day, both she and Lin tried to assure Daughter of Tang. 'Although it is far away, if we meet a great wind which is blowing our way, we could cover several days' distance in a day. Please don't worry. The heaven will look after one such as you who have such a filial heart. Buddha would not let you miss the Examinations because you had come to find your father.'

'I am not worried about myself,' said Daughter of Tang. 'If I took the Examinations so seriously, would I have come on the trip at all? But I have persuaded Red Rose and Purple Lily to come across thousands of miles of ocean. How did I know that it would be in vain?'

Although Lin knew that it was hopeless, he said, 'When one is travelling on the seas, there is really no telling what will happen. If we meet a great wind, we may travel three or five thousand *li* a day . . .'

One day, there was a fair gust of wind, and the sailors said, 'This is strange. The wind is blowing upwards and does not touch the water at all.'

Lin came on deck and asked, 'Why is it like this?'

'Look, the ship is being pushed ahead by the wind as though it were on a cloud, faster than steeds can gallop. And there are no ripples on the water. It is a shame that Portage Mountain blocks our way, so that no matter how fast we travel, we shall not arrive before spring.'

After some time, they were indeed at the foot of the mountain. Lin walked to the tower and heard Old Tuo laughing.

'Now, Brother Lin, I want to ask you a question. What is the mountain which is facing us?' he said.

Lin said, 'Why do you ask? Isn't it Portage Mountain?'

'I shall tell you a strange phenomenon I have observed,' said Old Tuo. 'When I travelled on the seas as a young man, I met an old man and asked him, "Why is Portage Mountain so called, since there is no portage, but the mountain blocks the entrance to the Kingdom on Earth?" and the old man said, "It is so called because in the time of Ta Yu (a legendary Emperor) he opened a tunnel through it (to ease the floods). However, in time the tunnel was blocked again, and no ship could pass through it." Just now I was thinking that since the young ladies are so anxious to go to attend the Examinations, if the tunnel could be opened up again, we could sail straight through it and arrive in time. As I was so thinking, I heard a noise like a thunderclap, and saw a pass in the mountain open up through which we can travel !'

Lin leaped up and down with happiness before Old Tuo finished speaking, and truly saw waves rolling in the middle of the mountain. Before he could make out the tunnel clearly, the ship had been sucked into the opening and was sailing through it.

Overjoyed, he rushed into the cabin to tell the others the news. The next day, they had passed out of the tunnel to the other side of the mountain.

'Now the mountain spirits have opened the way for you,' Lin said to Daughter of Tang, 'and the wind spirit has helped, too! When you become a lady of rank, you must thank them properly !'

The sisters laughed, but Daughter of Tang said, 'Wait until we arrive, and even then, I wonder if I shall pass the Examinations. In any case, I shall have to trouble Uncle to take me on another journey afterwards if father has not come back by himself !'

'Of course I shall,' said Lin, 'since I gave you my promise.'

The junk arrived in Lingnan at the end of July. Lin took leave of Old Tuo, and took the sisters home with him.

Daughter of Tang's mother, Mistress Lin, had taken Little Summit and Melody Orchid to her maiden home on a visit when she did not hear from her daughter for a year. She and Mistress Chiang were thinking and talking about them when the party appeared. After shedding many tears of joy and sorrow, Daughter of Tang handed her father's letter to her mother, and told her what had happened.

Mistress Lin was saddened to hear that her husband had not come back, but comforted to have his letter in his own handwriting, and by the thought conveyed in it that they would meet again soon.

After Daughter of Tang introduced Mistress Tsu, Red Rose and Purple Lily, Mistress Lin said, 'We are indeed honoured to have you. It must have been so destined. Now that you are sworn sisters, you must look after each other.'

Everyone promised. Daughter of Tang thanked Melody Orchid for taking care of her mother for her, and Mistress Lin said, 'It is lucky that she was with me to prepare my medicines and serve me after you left, for I was often ill. Now I am in good health. But we must discuss the coming County Examinations with your uncle, and see that you are all registered.'

'Mother's words are wise,' said Daughter of Tang.

'I do not know anything about registration procedures,' said Lin. 'You will have to take Flowerlike and Pleasant with you.'

'I know how to do these things,' said Daughter of Tang. 'But will Sister Flowerlike have to use a pseudonym, and change the place of her birth?'

'What for?' said Lin. 'She was to have been the "King" of the Country of Women. I want her to put down her real name and the country she comes from, so that later, when she wins a rank, she will be partially avenged for the humiliation I suffered at the hands of those traitors who chased her out of her own country, and took the throne away from her.'

'Very well,' said Daughter of Tang. 'Red Rose and Purple Lily and Melody Orchid will also put down the real places of their origin, so that Flowerlike will not be the only person from a foreign country to take the Examinations.'

'The Empress should be glad that candidates have come from abroad to take part in the Examinations,' said Lin. He also gave the names and dates of Tien Phoenix-in-Flight and Chin Little Spring to Daughter of Tang, and asked her to register for them.

So Mistress Lin took her daughter and son, Red Rose, Mistress Tsu and Purple Lily, and returned to her own home by a small boat. Little Summit was enchanted with the white gibbon and asked Pleasant if he could have it. Pleasant agreed, so he took it home.

Mistress Shih (Tang Min's wife) was glad to see that the travellers had come back, and told Daughter of Tang, 'Your Uncle is quite occupied these days, and leaves early in the morning to return at night. He is teaching the daughter of the Governor of this district, Yin Clever Prose, as well as the officials of nearby in preparation for the Examinations. So he is busy all day, and does not come home until late.'

'If the daughters of officials are participating in the Examinations, why are they not returning to their own counties to take the examinations?' asked Daughter of Tang.

'It is inconvenient for them to go back,' said Mistress Shih.

'If they pass the Departmental Examinations they will have to go to the capital, and they don't want to travel too much,' said Mistress Lin. 'Also, because in September your uncle will be fifty years old, they want to celebrate his birthday here.'

'We shall have a great celebration then,' said Daughter of Tang.

When Tang Min returned, he was glad to see Daughter of Tang

again, and reading his brother's letter, was comforted. He said, 'Now my niece will have many companions to go with her to take the Examinations.'

Now, Mistress Liang, Lien Flowering Maple and her brother Brilliant and Lo Red Lotus (who had come from Narcissus Village in the Country of Gentlemen) arrived, and Mistress Liang told Mistress Lin how Tang Ao had saved the life of her daughter and also, that of her son and that Yin Yuan (Tang Ao's teacher) had proposed a match between Red Lotus and Little Summit.

Mistress Lin was delighted when she heard this, and extremely happy to have a daughter-in-law who was accomplished in both literature and the arts of war. Mistress Liang therefore turned Red Lotus over to Mistress Lin. As it happened, the latter had bought a house next door. Now she had a door made in the wall which separated it from her home, and Mistress Liang and Flowering Maple, Mistress Tsu and Purple Lily would live in it. Red Rose shared a room with Mistress Tsu and Purple Lily, and Daughter of Tang, Red Lotus and Melody Orchid shared a room upstairs. Little Summit and Brilliant slept in the study. When this was all settled, a great banquet was laid.

When everyone was seated, Daughter of Tang said, 'I heard in the Village of Narcissus that you had left in the spring. How is it that you have only just arrived, Mistress Liang?'

'The winds were against us,' said Mistress Liang, 'and we had to make a big detour around a mountain before we arrived in Lingnan.'

'That is the Portage Mountain,' said Flowering Maple. 'There is really no portal in it. We must have spent half a year going around it, with the wind against us. Luckily, after we had circumvented the mountain, it was smooth sailing, otherwise we would have been at sea for two months more.'

Mistress Lin said, 'Since your son is engaged to the daughter of the Yin family, why did your future daughter-in-law not come with you, Mistress Liang?'

'The Yin family are from Chien-nan,' explained Mistress Liang, 'and have taken Scarlet Dogwood back there with them.'

Tang Min wrote down everyone's name and age. Red Lotus had changed her surname from Lo (horse radical) to Lo (water radical), in order to avoid detection, since her father was the rebel Lo Pinwang. There were Daughter of Tang, Melody Orchid, Pleasant, Flowerlike, Red Rose, Purple Lily, Flowering Maple, Phoenix-in-Flight and Little Spring, ten girls in all, beside Mistress Tsu, who took a false name, who must be registered for the County Examinations.

When the banquet was over, and they had bid Mistress Liang and Mistress Tsu goodnight, Daughter of Tang, Melody Orchid and Red Lotus went upstairs to their room. They opened the window, and sat down in the cool of the evening to chat.

Daughter of Tang took out the notes she had made in the Lament for Beauty Pavilion to show her companions, but none of them could read a word. When they learned what the notes were, the two girls both stuck out their tongues in amazement. The white gibbon came over, and taking the notes from Daughter of Tang's hands, looked at them.

'Can the white gibbon read?' said Melody Orchid, laughing.

'I wouldn't know,' said Daughter of Tang. 'When I was copying the notes on board the ship overseas, the white gibbon stood beside me and watched. At that time I said to it in fun, if there was a man who could record the history of the lives of the people whose names are carved on the jade tablet for posterity to enjoy, would it please go and find him, and do us all a great service? I wonder if the gibbon intends to do so?'

'No wonder he is reading so intently!' said Red Lotus, joking, and said to the gibbon, 'Are you going to undertake the job?'

The white gibbon gave a snort and nodded, and taking the notes with him, leaped out of the window, and from below, made a funny face at them.

Suddenly, there was a noise from outside, and a girl who was dressed entirely in red, with a red fisherwoman's turban on her head, red embroidered shoes on her dainty feet, and a red sash around her waist with a dagger tucked into it, leaped into the room from the window. Her face was deep red too, and extremely beautiful. She seemed to be fourteen or fifteen. The three girls were startled at the sight of her.

'Please, may I ask who you are and what you are doing here this time of night?' asked Daughter of Tang.

If the reader wants to know who the red girl was, please turn to the next chapter.

22

The red maiden said, 'My surname is Yen. Are you Sister Little Hill?'

'My surname is Tang,' said Daughter of Tang. 'I used to be called Little Hill, but my father wishes me to be called Daughter of Tang now. How did you know my humble name?'

The girl prostrated herself immediately. Daughter of Tang returned the courtesy, and after the girl had learned the names of Melody Orchid and Red Lotus, she sat down and said, 'My name is Purple Silk, and I also live at Hundred Fragrances Crossroads, in fact only a few houses from here. My grandfather was Governor of Kuan-nei. After he died, my father became very poor, and we farmed to keep ourselves alive. Last year, my parents died also. There is only grandmother at home, who is eighty years old, for three years ago, my brother Cliff went to the capital to take the Military Examinations, and has not come back. When I heard that the Empress was holding Examinations for women, I was very happy, but I cannot go to the capital alone. May I come with you?'

Daughter of Tang said, 'I have long heard of your grandfather's reputation. Of course I shall be happy to have your company. But how did you get here?'

Purple Silk said, 'As a child, my father taught me the art of swordsmanship, and now I can travel very fast. I can cover miles in a few seconds.'

'Did you see anything on your way over here?' said Daughter of Tang.

'I saw a monkey going off with a heavenly record book,' said Purple Silk.

'How do you know it is a heavenly record book?'

'The book gave off a red light, and the heavenly monkey was heading toward the clouds. That is why I did not dare to stop him.'

'The book belongs to me,' said Daughter of Tang. 'Do you think you can get it back for me?'

'If it was stolen from you, of course I can get it back for you,' said Purple Silk. 'But this white gibbon had a spiritual light on top of his head, and a rainbow-coloured cloud at his feet. It must be the product of a thousand years' cultivation of Tao, and in the twinkling of an eye, can travel ten thousand *li*. So I don't think I can catch it. Besides, if it is a gibbon which has acquired Tao, then he must have a reason to take the book away. But I wonder where the book and the gibbon both came from?'

Daughter of Tang told her the story, and Purple Silk said, 'The gibbon must have had a reason to take the book away. Did he ever reveal any hint to you?'

'No, he never gave me any indication,' said Daughter of Tang. 'But once I told him something in fun.' She repeated what she said to the gibbon to Purple Silk, who said, 'I am sure that the gibbon has gone to carry out your mission, and has gone to look for some scholar who will do as you desire.'

'I should like to know who it is,' said Daughter of Tang. 'Will you please find out for me if you can?'

'If I knew, would I not be a spirit, also?' said Purple Silk.

Red Lotus said, 'You travel like the wind. Can you teach us this skill?'

'I can teach you to travel fast within an area of a few hundred *li*.'

'Daughter of Tang wants to send a letter to her cousin Pleasant who lives about thirty *li* from here. Would you deliver it for her?'

'Do you mean the one whose mother is Daughter of Tang's aunt? I'll take it,' said Purple Silk. She took the letter, and said, 'Beg your pardon!' and turning around, vanished through the window.

Melody Orchid sighed and said, 'Strange things happen here indeed! There is every type in the Kingdom on Earth! With her coming to the capital with us, we shall not have to worry much along the way!'

'Was there a person like her described on the tablet?' Red Lotus asked.

'I remember that there was a phrase, "Brought up on swordsmanship, at home in the original elements". I don't know if it described her. It is too bad that the record is lost. I should have committed the whole thing to memory! If the gibbon really finds the rightful owner of it, then I shall not have gone to so much trouble in vain.'

Red Lotus said, 'I did not know that it was a heavenly gibbon. But Miss Yen could tell at a split-second's glance that it was one, which shows that her eyesight must be uncommon. I am sure the phrase described her.'

They had not spoken a few more words, when Purple Silk came back through the window. 'Your letter has been delivered. It is late now, so I shall come again tomorrow,' she said, and flew out of the window again, leaving the three sisters speechless with surprise.

The next morning, the sisters arose early to await Pleasant and the young ladies who lived in her house. But there was no trace of them. Melody Orchid said, ' I know, the girl in red never delivered the letter (asking them to come), and was only fooling us.'

However, at about noon, Pleasant, Flowerlike, Phoenix-in-Flight and Little Spring came hand in hand, and after paying their respects to Mistresses Lin and Shih, joined Daughter of Tang, Melody Orchid, Red Rose, Purple Lily, Red Lotus, and Flowering Maple.

Red Lotus asked them if they had received a letter last night, and Flowerlike laughed.

'Pleasant and I were going to sleep last night, right after the second drum had been struck, and Pleasant had just taken off a shoe, when the door burst open. Pleasant was so frightened that she crawled under the bed with only one shoe on. Luckily, I kept my nerve, and asked the person who she was, and was given the letter from you. Pleasant dared not come out until she had gone.'

Everyone burst out laughing, and Pleasant said, 'Can you blame me for being frightened? Who expected a letter to be delivered in the middle of the night! I was in fact quite brave, otherwise would I not have been frightened literally to death?'

'You may not have been frightened to death, but from the fact that you did not even put the other shoe on, you must have been frightened enough!'

Flowering Maple said, 'Whom did you send with a letter that made Pleasant so frightened?'

Daughter of Tang told them about Purple Silk, and Red Lotus said, 'When I first saw her through the window, giving off a red light, I was frightened, too. Upon a closer look, we saw that she was completely red, even her face. But in the light of the lamp, she was quite attractive.'

'Why then is she not called Red Something, but Purple Silk?' said Little Spring. 'And Red Rose has a black face, and yet is called Red Rose.'

Phoenix-in-Flight said, 'Who said that names have to be like how we look? What would Purple Lily have to look like then, and what about Flowerlike, would she be expected to have a blossom on her face?'

'I have observed that since Red Rose and Purple Lily came to the Kingdom on Earth, they are losing their colour,' said Flowerlike. 'But speaking of blossoms, there is something I would like to ask you.'

'What is it?' said Daughter of Tang.

'I have heard that there is a disease here which is called the "heavenly blossom" disease, or "small pox". Foreigners all get it when they come here. Now both Red Rose and Purple Lily are losing their colour since they have come. I am afraid that eventually, all five of us who are from overseas will get the smallpox, and I am worried.'

'Yes, that is something to worry about,' said Red Rose and Purple Lily. 'But what is there to do? If we get it I suppose we will just have to die.'

'If one is certain to die of it, then that is one way out,' said Flowering Maple. 'What I am afraid of is that the pox blossoms will leave many hideous marks on the face. How awkward that will be!'

'Not only awkward, but you will have a difficult time finding a husband!' said Pleasant, laughing.

'I guess you are not worried about that, since your face is as smooth as though not a hair could grow on it,' joked Flowerlike. 'However, if you hop about barefooted too often, and let your feet grow big, will it be easy for you to find a husband?'

'Oh, don't tease each other,' said Daughter of Tang. 'You should take precautions against smallpox. It is lucky that Old Tuo has many secret remedies. We will ask him. Would Little Spring write a letter to him for us?'

'There is no need to write to him,' said Phoenix-in-Flight. 'I know a preventive formula from home. I used it as a child, and have never had smallpox, which shows that it works.'

'I wonder what the preventive formula is?' said Flowerlike, 'and would you be willing to reveal it?'

'It is no secret, but nobody believes it, because people think that only medicine which is expensive is effective, and this calls for cheap ingredients only. This formula our family uses costs only a few pennies, and that is why it has never become well-known. It is this: For a child under three, use nine (dried) Persian lilac blossoms (*melia Japonica*), for a child under five, use eleven, and under ten years, use fifteen blossoms. On a propitious day, make a broth of the blossoms, and bathe the child with it. Then use a cloth dipped in the broth and apply it all over the skin and allow it to dry. Bathe a child like this ten times a year, in May, June and July, because these are warm months and there is less risk of catching cold, and he will not get smallpox. If he does, it will be an extremely light case with a few poxes only, which will fade almost as soon as they blossom. If you don't believe it, when you bathe yourself with this broth, leave a finger out, and see if that finger does not get a lot of pox while the rest of you is immune from attack. If you five sisters want to try it, I should think that you must use about thirty blossoms each.'

Everyone was glad to hear it, and Melody Orchid said, 'If children bathe ten times a year, we must do it more often for it to be effective. There are thirty-six propitious days in a year. I guess we will just have to bathe ourselves on each one of them. I was practically brought up on medicine when I was a child. Now that I should be bathing myself in it as well, we might truly say that "the wrapping of the parcel matches what's inside!"'

Little Spring said, 'But I have heard that Lady Pox is in charge of smallpox, and Brother Pox is in charge of the smallpox of boys, and Sister Pox in charge of that of girls. I think that you five girls from overseas should also pray to Lady Pox and Sister Pox, otherwise, if the formula is not effective, not only will it be hard to find husbands for you, but you will have trouble applying face powder on rough surfaces. And can you get rouge into the bottom of each hole in the face?'

'Where does this lady live?' said Red Rose.

'She is a spirit, and we must pay tribute to her in the temple,' said Daughter of Tang.

'What shall we do then (since young ladies are not supposed to go to public places)?'

'It is permissible for women to go to temples to burn incense, but there are shrines of Lady Pox in nunneries,' said Daughter of Tang. 'Last year before I went abroad, I went to ask permission from the Goddess of Mercy. Now that I am back, I should go and tell her. We shall ask my mother whether my paternal aunt might come with us tomorrow, and we shall do the two things at the same time.'

'I should like to go, too, and ask an oracle of the whereabouts of my brother,' said Red Lotus.

Daughter of Tang received her mother's permission to go to the nunnery with her sisters, and Mistress Shih agreed to go with them to the White Robe Nunnery nearby, where there was a shrine of Lady Pox.

The next day, they went there. An old unshaved nun called Ultimate Emptiness showed the party to the main hall. Everyone burned incense and kowtowed to the Goddess of Mercy. Red Lotus drew an oracle (by drawing a bamboo lot), and received the answer 'Up and Up' to her question, and she was very happy.

Ultimate Emptiness led the party to the inner hall, where the shrine of Lady Pox was, and after the girls from overseas had kowtowed to it, and burned some paper money, Daughter of Tang said, 'Is there a shrine of the Star of Literature?'

'There is one next door in the Happy Spirit Temple,' said Ultimate Emptiness. 'It, too, is run by nuns. I will come with you if you like.'

'Is the likeness of the Star of Literature a man or a woman?' said Daughter of Tang.

'I do not know, for I have never seen it,' said Ultimate Emptiness. 'If you would like to have a likeness of the Star of Literature installed, it can be done easily. But have a rest and a cup of tea first, before we go over.'

She took her guests to the Hall of Contemplation, where they sat down, and tea was served. Ultimate Emptiness asked her guests' names, and when she heard the name Lo Red Lotus, the nun looked at her again and again, and said suddenly with tears in her eyes, 'Aren't you the progeny of Master Lo Pinwang? I have a novice here who would like to know what happened to Young Master Lo. Perhaps you can tell me!'

Red Lotus was afraid to be discovered and said quickly, 'You are mistaken! My surname is Lo of the water radical.'

Ultimate Emptiness turned to Daughter of Tang and said, 'Please, Miss Tang, would you tell me what relation is Tang the *Tan-hua* to you?'

'He is my father,' said Daughter of Tang.

The nun said, 'Then I am not mistaken! You need not be afraid that I will get you in trouble, Miss Lo. When Master Tang became *Tan-hua,* he and Master Shu Ching-yeh and Master Lo Pinwang became sworn brothers in Changan. My husband was there, and saw it with his own eyes. My novice is in fact the fiancée of Young Master Lo. That is why I asked.'

Red Lotus cried, 'What is the name of your novice, and who is she?'

'Her father was the ninth son of Emperor Tai Tsu, called the Ninth Prince. He was also called the Brave Duke, after he helped to resist foreign invaders. He and Master Lo were good friends, and so he promised his daughter to Master Lo's son for a wife. The Princess is called Lee Wise Maxim, but she changed her surname to Sung because she is afraid of the Empress's detection.'

Red Lotus said, 'You are mistaken. I know a few things about the Lo family, although I am not one of them. It is true that Master Lo's son was engaged to the daughter of the Ninth Prince, but the Princess has been dead for a long time.'

Ultimate Emptiness said, 'You don't know the true story. Let me tell you. My surname used to be Chi. My husband's name was Chiao Chin. He was a tutor to Young Master Lo. When the match was made between the Young Master and the Royal House, Master

Lo recommended me to be tutor to the Princess. Before a year was over, however, the Princess died. I wanted to come back, but the Ninth Princess would not let me. At that time she was expecting again, and promised Master Lo that if she gave birth to a daughter, she would become Young Master Lo's wife. However, Master Lo took his son and went to help Master Shu in the Rebellion before the Ninth Princess was delivered. My husband died in fighting. The following year, the Ninth Princess gave birth to another daughter. I looked after her and tutored her, preparing her for the day when she would become Young Master Lo's wife. However, during the Rebellion, the Ninth Prince and Yao Yu, the Governor of Hopei, met with disaster, and the Emperor was banished to Fangchow. I and the eunuch Tsui Chuang took the little princess and the little White Prince and fled. We met soldiers on the way, and the eunuch and the little White Prince became separated from us. After a great many trials and tribulations, I succeeded in taking the princess to this nunnery. The Mother Superior, after learning our story, was willing to let us keep our hair and stay here. When she died, I came in charge of the nunnery, and I have been in charge for seven years, although I have still kept my hair. The Princess is now fifteen, and nobody knows she is here, because she never goes out of doors, but spends her time reading books and poems and Buddhist sutras.'

Red Lotus thought the nun's story sounded true, since she had heard her mother talk about the second match to be made for her brother and knew about the tutor Chiao Chin and his wife. Then her brother's fiancée must be here!

'I did not realize that you were Mistress Chi!' she said. 'That is why I concealed my identity from you. I beg your pardon. Where is my future sister-in-law? I should like to see her!'

Ultimate Emptiness said, 'I shall ask her to come in.'

She went inside, and soon appeared with Sung Wise Maxim. Everyone was struck by the princess's beauty. After they were seated again, Ultimate Emptiness told Wise Maxim what it was all about, and Red Lotus said in tears, 'I did not know that we would meet here today! How sad it is that your family had met the same kind of fate as mine!'

Wise Maxim's tears fell like rain. After awhile, she said shyly, 'I heard that your grandfather and mother had fled overseas. How are they, and how did Sister come here?'

Red Lotus sighed and said, 'Unfortunately, they are both dead. I was lucky to meet Uncle Tang and receive his help, otherwise I would never have come back.'

She was going to tell her experiences overseas, when Mistress Shih said, 'We had better not talk here. Why does the Princess not come home with us, since she is our relative?'

Wise Maxim said, 'I am afraid you will have to excuse me, for I have never left the nunnery.'

'Surely you can come with us, and return in the evening, since we live very near here?' said Daughter of Tang.

Wise Maxim allowed herself to be persuaded. The young ladies and Mistress Shih took leave of Ultimate Emptiness, and returned to the Tang home, where they told Mistresses Lin and Tsu what happened. Wise Maxim and Red Lotus exchanged much news about the hardship they had suffered in the past years. In the evening, Mistress Lin wanted Wise Maxim to stay, but she could not be persuaded. However, the sisters sent for her things, and Wise Maxim at last agreed. Daughter of Tang put her name down for registration at the County Examinations, and from now on, Wise Maxim remained with them.

The eleven young ladies spent their time together, and studied. On every propitious day, Flowerlike and those young ladies from overseas, as well as Mistresses Liang and Tsu, bathed themselves with the broth of Persian lilac. Daughter of Tang remembered the promise she made at the Lament for Beauty Pavilion, and had a female likeness of the Star of Literature installed in the White Robe Nunnery.

On the day of the County Examinations, Mistress Tsu went with the eleven young ladies. Luckily, the Empress said that every candidate could be accompanied by one or two relatives. Therefore, she got in without any difficulty. When the roll was called, a maid-servant took Mistress Tsu's place in answering it, and then Mistress Tsu took the examination herself, because the supervisors were not very strict. When the results were published, Daughter of Tang was first, and Flowerlike second. Red Rose and Purple Lily were also high on the list of successful candidates. Purple Silk was not good in calligraphy, but with the help of her sisters, she, too, passed, and everyone was very happy, although Mistress Tsu came in last.

When the time came to take the District Examinations, everyone thought that Mistress Tsu should not trouble herself to take them, but the old lady said, 'There must be someone in all of the Kingdom on Earth who recognizes my talent! Maybe I will meet him this time!' and insisted upon going. When the results were published, everyone was surprised to learn that she had come in first. Flowerlike was second, and Daughter of Tang third. Even

Purple Silk passed with the help of the others, and all of the young ladies became Virtuous Ladies of Literature.

However, Mistress Tsu pleaded illness, and did not go to pay her respects to the official examiner. She said, 'I really did not want to take the District Examinations, for I was afraid that I would come in number one again – backwards! But I had a dream, and in it I was told that if I did not go, one person would be missing from the roster of the hundred successful candidates in the Palace Examinations. How could I have known that I would come out first! But what use is it, since I don't think that I will be permitted to take the Ministerial Examinations!'

'If it were not for your age, I am sure you would take first place even in the Palace Examinations,' said Daughter of Tang.

'Twenty candidates passed the District Examinations, and twelve of them are in this family,' said Mistress Lin. 'If we were to hold a celebration for each one of them, we would be feasting for twelve days. However, tomorrow we will celebrate your success and Tang Min's birthday together.'

The next day, plays were staged in the Tang house. The officials of the area whose daughters Tang Min was tutoring all came to pay their respects, followed by their daughters, the Misses Yin Clever Prose, Tou Country Smoke, Chu Painted Flower, Su Orchid, Chung Embroidered Field, and Hua Fragrance Returns. Everyone was very gay, but Mistress Tsu sat apart from the young ladies, afraid of being recognized. After morning noodles, Daughter of Tang showed the guests her study, where books filled the shelves and the brushes and inks and ink-slabs were much admired.

Clever Prose said, 'When my father read your prose, he remembered the Empress saying, "Talent is not restricted to men!" Your prose was distinguished for its clarity and uncluttered style, while Flowerlike's was distinguished for its regal and splendid style. But the first place was given to the one who had the best calligraphy. Her handwriting was really superior to both of yours, and it did not seem like that of a young girl's but to come from a practised hand. My father decided that she must have worked very hard, so the first place went to her.'

After a great deal of merry-making, Purple Silk said, 'We are so happy, and it is such a rare chance for us to be together. Why do we not become sworn sisters? Then, when we go to the capital, we shall look after each other, too.' Everyone agreed, but as Fragrance Returns had expressed the thought that she would come in first in the Palace Examinations, because the Empress might take a liking to her name, remembering how the hundred flowers bloomed at the same time, she was not included by the sisters.

A maid servant brought in a red carpet and the sisters kowtowed to each other, and became sworn sisters. When the party was over in the evening, Country Smoke, Clever Prose, Painted Flowers and others travelled back to the districts they came from, to take the District Examinations. Purple Silk became Tang Min's pupil, and all the sisters studied very hard for the Ministerial Examinations.

If the reader would like to know what happened at the Ministerial Examinations, please read the next chapter.

In January, Daughter of Tang and her sisters prepared to go to the capital to take the Ministerial Examinations. Mistress Tsu wanted to go too, but was persuaded by Mistresses Liang and Shih to stay at home.

Tang Min was afraid that the old nursemaids would not be adequate to take care of the young ladies on the difficult journey, and after discussing it with Merchant Lin, asked Old Tuo and Ultimate Emptiness to go along, and gave them a lot of silver. Old Tuo was going to take his nieces Phoenix-in-Flight and Little Spring to the capital anyway, and Ultimate Emptiness was going to take Wise Maxim, and they were both glad to be paid for the journey.

Ultimate Emptiness put on her ordinary clothes, and came to the Tang house. On a propitious day in the middle of February, Mistress Lin gave them a farewell banquet. The next morning, Daughter of Tang took leave of her mother, uncle and aunt, and told Little Summit to take good care of them, and with Purple Silk, Pleasant, Red Lotus, Flowering Maple, Phoenix-in-Flight, Little Spring, Wise Maxim, Red Rose, Purple Lily, Melody Orchid and Flowerlike, and their attendants, left for the Western Capital. They had meant to leave earlier, but because Red Lotus had written to Fragrant Angelica and waited for her reply, they had been delayed. Pleasant said that Beautiful Hibiscus and Marsh Orchid had not been heard from either, so they left without further delay.

What happened was that after Young Shu took leave of Tang Ao, he and Beautiful Hibiscus and Marsh Orchid returned to Huainan, after he had changed his name to Yu for self-protection, to find Wen Yin, the Governor of the district.

On their way, one of the sailors became sick, and was replaced by a man from another ship. This sailor turned out to be the husband of Beautiful Hibiscus's nursemaid, and was called Shuen Shin. He had worked for the Governor for more than ten years, and was in fact on his way to Huainan himself.

Young Shu was very happy, and asked him about the Wen family, whom he had never met. Shuen Shin said, 'Governor Wen

comes from Kiangnan and is an only son. His wife, Mistress
Chang, has given him five sons. There are two daughters by a
concubine who has died. The eldest of the sons is called Honeybush, and the second is called Sedge. The third is called Shep-
herd's Purse, the fourth, Cabbage, and the youngest is Senega.
All are husky lads of around twenty. The eldest and the fourth
are especially talented, and people call them the Five Wen
Phoenixes. Governor Wen is not yet fifty, but he is not in good
health, and seems more. Many times, he was ordered to fight the
Japanese invaders, and riding on horseback has exhausted him.
Now there is peace, and the five sons rule for him. Often, Master
Wen has thought of retiring, but since the Emperor is still banished in Fangchow and is not yet restored to the throne, he does
not think that he should do so until the Emperor has come
back.'
    'How old are the two daughters?' Beautiful Hibiscus asked.
    'Fifteen and sixteen. The elder is called Fragrant Book, and
has been promised to Lin Brave, the son of an official. The
younger is called Fragrant Ink, and is promised to Governor
Yang's son, Extraordinary.'
'Are the five sons engaged to be married?' said Young Shu.
    'Yes,' said the man, 'they are engaged but not yet married,
because the young ladies are going to take the Examinations.
Honeybush is engaged to Beautiful Orchid, the daughter of
Governor Chang of Shan-nan. Sedge is engaged to Red Feather,
the daughter of Governor Shao of Chowchow. Shepherd's Purse
is engaged to Red Jade, the daughter of the Librarian Tai, and
Cabbage to Fair Heroine, the daughter of the Military Attaché
of Hsuchow, Yu. Senega is engaged to Chien Noble Jade, the
daughter of the Cavalry Officer of Liuchow. The boys' mother is
Mistress Chang, the sister of Governor Chang Ken of Hotung,
and a kind person. She does a great deal of charity work, and is
called the Living Buddha by the people of Huainan.'
    'I did not know that there were Imperial Examinations for
Women,' said Young Shu. 'That evil woman is thinking up new
tricks indeed while she sits on the Emperor's throne!'
    Young Shu asked Shuen Shin about Mistress Chang's family,
and learned that Governor Chang Ken had three brothers. Between them, they had four daughters and ten sons, who came to
live with him when the Governor's brothers died. The ten Chang
boys were brave and husky, and called the Ten Chang Tigers.
The eldest was called Prince's Feather, and engaged to High
Spring, the daughter of the Cavalry Officer Ching. The second
was called Mushroom, and engaged to Melting Spring, the
daughter of the Governor of Huei-chi, Tso. The third was called
Asarum, and engaged to the Governor of Chien-nin's daughter
Liao Glorious Spring. The fourth was Hibiscus, who was engaged
to Miss Fragrant Spring, the daughter of the Military Attaché Li

of Wulin. The fifth was Basil, and engaged to Brocade Spring, the daughter of the Librarian Li. The sixth son was called Wildhop, and engaged to the daughter of the official of the Ministry of Appointments Chou, Complaisant Spring. The seventh son was called Begonia, and engaged to the daughter of the Cavalry Officer Shih of Changchow, Luxurious Spring. The eighth was called Parsley, and engaged to the daughter of the Conscription Officer Liu, Graceful Spring. The ninth son was called Fragrant Weed, and engaged to Doctor Pan's daughter Beautiful Spring. The tenth son was called Artemisia, and engaged to the daughter of the Cavalry Officer Tao of Loyang, Fair Spring.

The four daughters of the family were Fragrant Orchid, who was engaged to Tsai Noble, the son of the Official Tsai; Fragrant Marsh Orchid, who was engaged to the son of the *Hanlin* Tan, Ultimate; Fragrant Jade, who was engaged to the son of the Scholar Yeh, Ocean; and Fragrant Moon, who was engaged to the scholar Chu's son, Tide.

Mistress Chang had given her prospective daughters-in-law names with the word 'Spring' in them so that it would be easier to remember, and all her daughters and nieces had names with the word 'Fragrant' in them. Because the young ladies were connected with the Rebellion through their families, they would use the surnames of their fiancés when they took the Imperial Examinations.

Young Shu took many days to reach Huainan because the wind was against him. When he arrived at last, and the junk was anchored at the river, he took a small boat, and went to the Governor Wen's house with Shuen Shin, who announced him. Young Shu at last delivered to the Governor the letter in blood which his father had given him.

Governor Wen was deeply moved to read the message and said, 'Thank goodness you are safe and sound after going through such hardship. I am so happy to see you.' Fingering his beard, he added, 'I am not yet fifty, but my beard is white, and I am ill and tired. You can imagine what my life has been like since your father and I took leave of each other more than ten years ago. But I will not give up this life until the Emperor comes back to the throne. I have looked for a chance to help in this cause, but the Empress's forces are getting stronger every day, and it would be like moths flying into the fire, or smashing eggs against rocks for us to move. I don't know whether I will live long enough to see my wish fulfilled. I am ill, and my five internal organs have been reduced to cinders.' He sighed for a long time, and then told the servants to escort the two young ladies to the inner rooms. Marsh Orchid and Beautiful

Hibiscus were received by Mistress Chang, and met Fragrant Book and Fragrant Ink.

Young Shu met Mistress Chang also, and was introduced to the five Wen brothers, and liked them extremely.

Honeybush said, 'I admired your father greatly for his loyalty and his spirit. He did all a man could. Whether he succeeded or not was in destiny's hands.'

Senega said, 'If I had my way, we would have made war on the Western Capital already. But my Fourth Brother believes in astrology, and wants us to wait until the right element enters the right constellation before we set out, and when heaven and earth are in harmony.'

Shepherd's Purse said, 'I wish we could charge up to Changan at the slightest excuse, and show Wu what stuff the Wen family is made of ! What do I care about astrology !'

But Cabbage said, 'My brothers should not be so impatient. Now the Purple Constellation is on the rise, so is the fortune of the Emperor, and the light of the Heart-Moon Fox is diminishing. I think that Wu's time is limited. Give her three or five years at the most, and our time will come. But if we move now, we would not only be going against the stars, but we would be doing the Emperor harm. Have you forgotten the fate of the Ninth Prince?'

Senega said, 'I remember you said last year that Wu's time was up. How can you now say that she has three or five more years?'

Cabbage said, 'At that time, her time was up, and the Heart-Moon Fox Spirit was in the descendant, but recently, she has emitted another ray of strange light, obstructing the light of the Purple Constellation. I thought that it was merely a reflection, but it turned out to be a benevolent light.'

'What happened to cause this strange manifestation?' said Young Shu.

'On the occasion of her seventieth birthday, she proclaimed an amnesty and reduced taxes, and issued twelve edicts for the welfare of women. Because of this, the suffering of many people lessened, and the atmosphere of relief turned into a benevolence which was carried to heaven and resulted in this strange light. However, she has only three to five more years to go, because of her record of cruelty. If you don't believe me, you have only to wait and see.'

'What do you mean?' said Young Shu.

'I have been observing the sky over Lung-yu for many nights, and saw signs of fighting there, but the omens are not good. I think that Uncle Shih must have listened to rumours, and believed that it was only a reflection that cast the light on the Heart-Moon Fox Spirit, and started to fight. I predict that no good will come of it.'

Soon, news was carried to them that indeed, Governor Shih Yeh of Lung-yu had been defeated in his manoeuvres against the Empress. Empress Wu has sent three hundred thousand troops under the command of her brother Wu Number Nine, and most of the troops had been slaughtered.

The brothers of Cabbage had to argue that he was right.

'If Uncle Shih has met defeat, I wonder what has happened to Young Lo, who was to have gone to find him with his letter written in blood?' said Young Shu.

The Wen brothers decided to go to Lung-yu and find out. But Wen Jin received orders to proceed to Chien-nan with troops to fight the Nipponese invaders, and Honeybush had to remain to act for the Governor. Wen Yin took his sons Cabbage and Senega and a thousand troops and left for battle at once. Sedge, Shepherd's Purse and Young Shu, therefore, told Mistress Chang that they were going to burn incense at the Five Altars, and went to Lung-yu to try to find out what had happened to Young Lo. Honeybush tried to tell them not to go, but could not stop them. He therefore sent men to follow them in secret, in case they met with danger.

After many days' travelling, the three advanced on Lung-yu, and heard that Governor Shih Yeh had been killed. But they could not be sure whether this was true. When they arrived at last at Lung-yu, they learned that Governor Shih had retreated to Takuan under the advance of Wu Number Nine's troops, and was still in retreat. The three young men could not learn any news of Young Lo either, and had to start back for Huainan in disappointment.

One day, as they were walking at the foot of Little Yingchow Mountain, the young men saw a band of men fighting a girl on top of one of the peaks, and she seemed to be fighting a losing battle.

Young Shu thought, from the distance, that the leader of the men looked like none other than Young Lo. 'If it is him, we should give him a helping hand!' cried the Wen Brothers, and brandishing their swords, charged up to them and cried, 'Hold on there, female! Here we come!' and leaped into battle.

'Is it Brother Lo up there?' Young Shu called.

It was indeed him. Young Shu hurried up and explained to Young Lo who he and the Wen brothers were, and that they were looking for him, and asked what he was fighting the girl for.

'It is a long story,' said Young Lo. 'Let me kill her first and tell you later.'

Therefore he and his men lifted their swords and advanced on the girl together.

The girl retreated, although she was skilled in the art of war.

But suddenly, there was a cry from a young man hurrying towards them. 'Please stop! Don't kill my sister-in-law! I'm coming!' he shouted.

When the young man had identified himself, he turned out to be the son of Governor Shih Yeh himself. The men stopped fighting, and Narrator took them to their hideout in the mountain fortress. There, Narrator explained that he had arrested the girl in the mountains, only to discover that she was none other than his relative, for his maternal uncle had the name of Tsai Tsung and was Governor of Lung-yu long ago. His wife Mistress Shen had two daughters, Silver Moonlight and Jade Moonlight, and the girl they were fighting was none other than Jade Moonlight, who with her sister, mother and two cousins Fragrant Plant and Completely Virtuous, were on their way to the capital. Jade Moonlight was looking out for beasts, afraid that her mother would be frightened, when they were mistaken for spies and almost killed.

The three young men identified themselves, and Young Lo told Young Shu that he had delivered his letter in blood to Governor Shih, and changed his name to Lo (water radical) after he arrived at the Governor's house. He was trained in the art of war, and now he, together with the Shih brothers and a thousand men, were hiding in the fortress in the mountains from the soldiers of Empress Wu, and there were several hundred bandits in the mountains, too, who had joined their forces.

It happened now that they heard that the family of Wu Number Nine were passing through this way, and Young Lo wanted to kill them. But Young Shu said, 'The family will be guarded by soldiers. If you attack them, you will bring the weight of Tai Mountain upon yourselves and be crushed like eggs. My idea is that it is better to wait here and bide your time, and spend your forces more effectively later. The land here is fertile. You can grow grain and raise horses here, and build up your men until the time comes to avenge the Emperor.'

To this, the others agreed.

The three young men stayed a few days more, and returned to Huainan to report to Honeybush. Young Shu told his fiancée Marsh Orchid and his sister Beautiful Hibiscus what had happened, and the latter said that Mistress Chang wanted them both to take the Examinations. Since it would be at least two years before the young men would rise and wage war against the Empress's forces, Young Shu thought that it was just as well for them to go.

Beautiful Hibiscus and Marsh Orchid were delighted, and Fragrant Book and Fragrant Ink were happy to have their company on the journey. One of the nursemaids of the family had a daughter, Little Canary, who wanted to go, too, and they agreed to go together.

In time, the daughters of the Chang family came for the daughters of the Wen family, and together with Beautiful Hibiscus, Marsh Orchid and Little Canary, the nine girls went to Kiangnan and passed the County Examinations. They returned to Huainan, and after a time, left for the Western Capital. On the way, they met Daughter of Tang and her party, and the twenty girls proceeded together to Chang-an. Pleasant, Beautiful Hibiscus and Marsh Orchid were very happy to see each other again, and Marsh Orchid thanked Daughter of Tang for her father's help in saving her life, and was glad to hear that Tang Ao was in Little Penglai contemplating Tao. Red Lotus was relieved to hear of her brother Young Lo's safety, and told the news to Wise Maxim, Young Lo's fiancée.

That evening at the inn, the young ladies saw a party of soldiers surround a wooden cage in which there was a young soldier who was tied up with rope. They overheard the soldiers say that the prisoner was called White, and that his surname was Lee, but that he had changed his name to Sung and escaped to these parts because he was the son of the Ninth Prince, but now he was apprehended at last. When Wise Maxim found out that it was her brother the White Prince, she was desperate, and wanted to free him.

Old Tuo learned that when the White Prince escaped, he had hidden in the home of a rich man who was called Sung Sze, who took him as a son, and later on betrothed to him the daughter of a friend in a neighbouring village, Yen Purple Jade. The White Prince's right eye had two pupils, and when the Empress suddenly remembered this, she issued an order to the officials throughout the country to be on the lookout for a man with two pupils in one eye. Although the White Prince was skilled in fighting, and people called him the 'Three-eyed Tiger', recently he had been ill, and that was why he allowed himself to be arrested by a man called Big Bear.

When Purple Silk ascertained that the White Prince had committed no crime, she decided that she would go and free him. That evening, Wise Maxim invited Red Lotus, Daughter of Tang and Purple Silk to dinner, and after toasting Purple Silk respectfully, said, 'It is time for you to go now.'

'There is no hurry,' said Purple Silk. 'Even if they have taken him far away, I can go on a "spirit horse", and will catch up with them no matter where they are.'

If the reader wants to know whether Purple Silk succeeded in freeing the White Prince, please read the next chapter.

◄ *24* ►

'I wonder if ordinary people may ride on the "spirit horse" too?' said Wise Maxim.

'Why not? If you only repeat some spells, you can ride on the "spirit horse", too.'

'Then may I come with you?' said Wise Maxim.

'You may, but to travel fast, one must have abstained from eating meat.'

'Don't listen to her,' said Red Lotus. 'She does not need any "spirit horse". She delivered a letter for us in Lingnan and covered a distance of fifty, sixty *li* in less than half an hour.'

'Well, it is getting late now, and you must go,' said Daughter of Tang.

Purple Silk changed into her red travelling clothes, tied a silk sash around her waist, a fisherwoman's turban on her head, and carried a sword at her breast. She began to give off a red glow. She had just tied the knot in her sash when she said, 'I'm going now,' and was gone.

'Strange!' said Wise Maxim, and rushed to the door to see. But Purple Silk was already nowhere in sight. Turning around, Wise Maxim said, 'I am sure she will succeed in freeing my brother.'

'If she did not have extraordinary powers, she would not have dared to go,' said Daughter of Tang. 'The female swordsmen of ancient times were capable of doing extraordinary things, but first they had to make sure that they were on the side of right. You noticed that Purple Silk made sure that the White Prince had not committed any crime before agreeing to help him.'

'I wonder if you saw which direction she went when you went to the door?' Red Lotus asked Wise Maxim.

'I saw a sky which was bright with a full moon and stars, but not a trace of her,' said Wise Maxim.

The three girls chatted a little while, and then saw Purple Silk fly in, with another girl behind her who was wearing a purple outfit just like hers, and who had a peach complexion.

'Did you free my brother?' Wise Maxim said. 'And who is the young lady you have brought?'

'Who do you think she is?' said Purple Silk. 'It is none other than the fiancée of your brother, Purple Jade, of Hotung, who has learned the art of swordsmanship from your brother since childhood. She was also on her way to help the White Prince when we met. We went on together, and while I engaged the soldiers in battle, she went in and freed the Prince. I shook off the soldiers and caught up with Purple Jade, who took the Prince back to her home in the Village of Yen, and he is hiding there now. However, the guards are searching the village from house to house, and it is not safe to keep him there. We have come back to ask you what to do.'

After Purple Jade had asked everyone's name, and paid her respects to them, Purple Silk said, 'I wonder if Sister Wise Maxim knows a place of concealment for him, since they are searching both the Village of Yen and the Village of Sung, and it will not be safe for him to go back to the Sung family?'

Wise Maxim shed tears and said, 'How I wish that I did! But the room I lived in in the nunnery was not more than ten feet long. I was cooped up in it for eight years, with only the stars to look at. Because the nunnery was near the village, many people passed by the place, and the door was always securely locked in the daytime, and I never saw what the sun was like. It is no place for my brother.'

'What if we take him back to Lingnan and he stays in my home until it is safe for him to go back to the village of Sung?' said Daughter of Tang.

'No!' said Red Lotus. 'Old Tuo said that the Empress had issued an order to all the officials in the country to be on the lookout for the Prince. I think that it would be best if he were to join my brother in the hideout in Little Yingchow Mountain. If you agree, I will write a letter.'

'You are right,' said Purple Silk. 'Please write the letter, and the sooner Purple Jade can go to join him there, the better.'

Purple Jade blushed and said, 'He has been ill, and Little Yingchow is far away. I don't know if I can manage it without Purple Silk's help.'

'I shall come with you,' said Purple Silk. 'Little Yingchow is several hundred *li*s from here. As it is almost dawn now, we cannot be back before morning. The rest of you had better leave here as planned, and we shall catch up with you at the next inn tomorrow evening.'

'Why don't we stay and wait for you here another day?' said Daughter of Tang.

The young ladies decided that this was the wisest course, so Red

Lotus wrote the letter, and Purple Jade and Purple Silk made their farewells and left.

In the morning, Daughter of Tang pretended that she was not feeling well, and they stayed on for another day at the inn. At the third drum in the evening, Purple Silk came back and said, 'This morning we went to Purple Jade's home and saw Mistress Yeh and told her our plan. Although she and her husband were reluctant to let him go, they thought that it would be the best thing to do. We waited until evening, and then took the White Prince to the mountain fortress and delivered the letter and came back.'

'Where is Purple Jade now?'

'She is at home in the Village of Yen, which is on our way. She is preparing to welcome us to her house, and she is coming to the capital with us.'

After travelling fifty *li*s the next day, the young ladies arrived at the Village of Yen. Servants of the family were waiting to greet them when the sisters arrived at the Yen residence.

Purple Jade introduced the young ladies to her mother. Her father was a retired official named Yen Yi, who was a general in the army when he was young. Now he was seventy, and retired. He had a son, called Courage, who was skilled in the art of war, and away taking the War Examinations at the capital. The Yen family was extremely wealthy, and in retirement, Yen Yi had many of the sons of friends who lived nearby come to his home, and hired instructors to teach them the art of war, so that one day they would be ready to rise against the Empress. When he heard that his daughter was inviting the daughter of Tang Ao and the daughter of Lo Pinwang to dinner, he was delighted, and ordered a feast. His nieces, Chiang Lovely Tower and Chang Baby Phoenix, were also going to the capital to take the Examinations.

There were twenty-four girls altogether, who sat around five tables. Purple Jade was a good hostess, and made everyone feel extremely at home.

Pleasant said, 'We have only just met, but it seems that we have known you for a long time. Could it be that we met in our previous lives?'

'Everyone must return to the King of the Wheel after each death before he is reincarnated,' said Little Spring. 'We all must have met there some time.'

Everyone laughed. Lamps were lit, and the young ladies were talking gaily when a girl wearing a pink costume flew into the hall, and startled most of them.

'Who is it that kidnapped Sung White?' cried the girl. 'Come forward!'

Purple Silk took her sword and stepped forward and said, 'It was I, Yen Purple Silk.'

Purple Jade also took her sword and said, 'It was I, Yen Purple Jade. Who are you, and why do you ask?'

The girl in pink looked them up and down and said, 'I thought it was someone with three heads and six arms who could do it! It was only the two of you! Well, swordsmen live by honour, and what is wrong must be put right. Sung White is guilty of committing a crime and was under arrest. How dare you interfere with royal soldiers and free him? Hand him over right away if you know what is good for you! Big Bear is my cousin, and when my father was alive, he was an important official in the court of Emperor Tang. Grandfather was Commander-in-Chief of the armed forces. In gratitude for Imperial favour to our family, we have come to capture rebels. My name is Yi Purple Caltrop!'

'You talk as though reason were on your side, but how do you know that we don't have a good reason for freeing Sung White, and do you know what he is like as a man?' said Purple Jade.

'His name is not Sung!' said Purple Caltrop. 'He is the rebel Ninth Prince's son. I have known that for a long time.'

'Since you know, so much the better,' said Purple Jade, smiling. 'Please enlighten me, when you said your family was grateful for Imperial favour, do you mean the Imperial favour of the Royal House of Tang?'

'Of course!'

'Then you must realize that the Ninth Prince was not only the direct descendant of the Royal House of Tang, but also one of its most loyal subjects. He worked ceaselessly to restore the Emperor to the throne after it was stolen from him, and lost his life because of it. But heaven has justice, and left him an heir. I did not think that since your family was grateful to the Royal House of Tang, you would devote your efforts to killing the sons of Tang to win glory. If you do this, the foul reputation of your family will linger after you for ten thousand years, and you will also have forgotten the swordsman's sense of honour. If you can explain your behaviour, please do so in front of these young ladies. If the White Prince is guilty of some crime, please tell us.'

Upon hearing this, Purple Caltrop became speechless, and stood like a wooden figure in the middle of the hall.

Red Lotus, seeing this, took Daughter of Tang by the hand and went up to Purple Caltrop's side and said, 'If you have anything to say, why don't you sit down and let us talk slowly?'

Purple Caltrop put her sword back in its scabbard, and sat down. After everyone was introduced to her, and Daughter of Tang explained that they were on their way to the capital to take the Imperial Examinations, Red Lotus said to Purple Jade, 'I think Sister Purple Caltrop is an extraordinary person. Since her family has been in the favour of the Royal House, she will not turn against us. She does not seem like someone who shifts loyalties easily ...'

Before she could finish talking, Purple Caltrop said, 'If I were a subject of the Chou (Empress Wu's) Dynasty, I would not hesitate to carry out her orders even though I knew that Sung White is a descendant of the Royal House of Tang. However, I came today only on my cousin's behalf. I would like to take leave of you now. We shall meet again at the capital.'

Purple Jade would not let her go before she had had some wine. A place was set for Purple Caltrop at table, and in the course of dinner, it transpired that Purple Caltrop was going to the capital, too, and it was agreed that they should go together.

As she was leaving to pack, Purple Silk said, 'What will you tell your cousin when you go back?'

'I shall say that I could not find you,' Purple Caltrop said, and leaped into the air and flew away.

Those in the banqueting hall like Fragrant Book, Fragrant Orchid, and Marsh Orchid who had never seen people fly were stunned and cried out, 'We did not know such extraordinary people existed!'

'Now with Purple Caltrop and Purple Silk with us, and Purple Jade who can talk her way out of any difficulty, as she has just demonstrated, we will have no fears on the way,' said Beautiful Hibiscus.

The young ladies joked and made merry, and then said good night to Mistress Yeh and retired.

The next morning after breakfast, Mistress Yeh asked the slave-girls to accompany the young ladies to the garden for a walk.

It was almond-blossom time, and the willows were beginning to turn green. The garden was filled with a beautiful spring air, and after awhile, Purple Jade said, 'This garden is really not very interesting. The only unique thing about it is that you can enjoy a good cup of tea here, if you like tea.'

'Why, do you have a special source of spring water?' said Melody Orchid.

'We have a sweet spring, and also several good tea trees,' said Purple Jade. 'I don't usually make tea with fresh leaves, but the colouring is very good.'

'Take us to have tea made with fresh leaves then!' said Fragrant Ink. 'It will be a novelty!'

Purple Jade led the way, and the young ladies came to a little pavilion which was surrounded with tea trees. Some were tall and some were small, but they were all jade green, and extremely fragrant. The young ladies sat down in the pavilion, and saw that it was called 'Fragrant Green Pavilion'.

Slave-girls and women servants became busy outside the pavilion. Some fetched water, others fanned the fire, and still others picked the leaves and washed the cups. Soon, tea was made, and a cup was served to each young lady.

The young ladies tasted it, and found that the fragrance was quite unique, and unlike ordinary tea. The colour of the brew was greener than spring onions. Everyone liked it very much, and Pleasant laughed and said, 'If you had this good tea, why didn't you serve it last night?'

Purple Jade said, 'My father is the tea-lover of the family. He could not get any good leaves, so he had tea trees brought here from many places. But tea trees do not take to transplanting, and not one tree grew again in our garden. These dozen-odd trees you see here were cultivated from seeds he brought from Fukien, Chekiang and Kiangnan, and therefore not uniform in size. My father has written a book called *On Tea* in ten volumes. When it is printed, I shall give each of you a copy.'

Red Rose said, 'In the *Six Classics* the word tea cannot be found. Tea is seldom found abroad. Perhaps you can tell us about its origin?'

Purple Jade said, 'The word *cha* (tea) comes from the ancient word *tu* which means bitter grass. In the *Book of Poetry* this word occurs several times, but it did not mean tea, although it was pronounced *cha,* at the time, as Yen Shih-ku, of Han Dynasty ascertained. Later, people thought that the two words were one, since the character *tu* has only one more stroke than the word *cha,* and that the two words were interchangeable. Now we make the differentiation in pronunciation. As for tea itself, apart from quenching thirst, nothing good can be said about it. In the *Book of Medical Plants,* it says tea will take off fat and make a person thin. Tea taken too often makes all kinds of illness converge in the body. In my father's book, he also counsels people not to drink too much tea. He often tells me, it is better to drink less tea than more tea, and to drink no tea than little tea. There are few good teas, and many bad ones. If tea is good, it is habit-forming, and too much tea-drinking will impair the principal element in the body and cause the blood and vital essences to be reduced, and cause stomach trouble, stones in the stomach, as well as paralysis, both the painful kind and the kind which is not painful. It will cause the small intestines to swell and be obstructed. People who have diarrhoea, or vomit, or stomach ache, or are thin and sallow-complexioned due to internal injury can often find that tea is the cause of it. But few people know this, and seldom blame tea for their illness. The ancients lived for a long time, but nowadays people do not enjoy such longevity. That is because tea and wine are taken in too great quantities and do harm to the internal organs. Those who like tea and wine always burst out laughing when they hear this argument, and say that it is not true. People say that tea is a great purger of the impurities of the body, but are not aware of its hidden bad effect, which works slowly in the body. My father therefore says that tea is the opposite of the olive, which is sour when it is in the mouth, but leaves a sweet after-taste, while tea tastes good in the mouth, but does no good once it is in the body.'

Fragrant Jade said, 'Since it is so, why does your father plant so many tea trees here?'

'My father has formed the habit of drinking tea and drinks it all day long. He discovered that it was not good for him only when it was too late. Now he is ill, but his health gets even worse if he stops drinking tea. He knows that it is too late for him to abstain from tea, but has written a book to warn posterity about the evils of it. When he finished the manuscript last year, he suddenly had a stomach ache, and threw up an object which looked like a cow's stomach, but which had eyes and a mouth. He poured tea into it and filled it with five bowlsful, which was the number of bowls my father used to drink at a time. Ever since he got rid of this object, his health has improved.'

'I am sure it was an act of heaven,' said Flowerlike. 'Your father is a man of honour, and heaven has rewarded him. Now he will live for a hundred years.'

'I only hope that it is true,' said Purple Jade. 'The only kinds of tea which are not harmful are chrysanthemum tea and mulberry tea. Also, tea made of cypress leaves and locust leaves are good. According to the *Book of Medical Plants* cypress leaves are not harmful, although they taste bitter. That is because the cypress is a durable tree of hard wood, and therefore a tree of long life. Drinking tea made of its leaves will rid a body of germs and help the female element. Hair will not turn white and a person will have better resistance against heat and cold if he drinks it. The Taoists drink it, and people take it on New Year's Day to get rid of hangovers. Deer eat the cypress leaf and get their musk from it. That shows how good it is. As for the locust leaf, it is also non-poisonous although it tastes bitter. Tea made from it taken regularly will not only prevent hair from turning white, but invigorate a person, brighten his eyes and help his brain to function, and prolong his life. The poet Sou Chien-wu drank locust tea, and still had black hair on his head when he was eighty, and could read fine print in the dark.'

That evening, as tables were being prepared for supper, gardeners carried in a lot of luggage. Purple Jade thought that it belonged to Purple Caltrop, but upon inquiry, learned that it belonged to young ladies who were on their way to the Examinations, who had no place to stay because the drivers and carriers in her guests' party had taken up all the rooms in the inns in the village, and the young women, having learned that the Yen residence extended its hospitality to travellers, had come to spend the night.

The young ladies let down the blinds in the hall, and watched as the travellers went by. Red Lotus saw two girls with their nursemaids, and thought that one of the girls looked like Sweet Asarum.

She was so thinking, when Flowering Maple said, 'Look, does the one in green not look like Scarlet Dogwood?'

'Do you know them?' said Purple Jade.

'We know two of the girls,' said Red Lotus. Purple Jade therefore asked the young ladies to come in, and Sweet Asarum and Red Lotus were very happy to see each other again. Scarlet Dogwood was overjoyed to see Red Lotus and Flowering Maple, and Fragrant Angelica was glad to meet Pleasant again. Purple Cherry of Phoenix and Unicorn Mountain had also come. She was introduced to Daughter of Tang, and the latter expressed her admiraation for Purple Cherry for dressing up as a boy in order to kill the beasts in the mountains.

When the young ladies sat down to dinner, someone flew into the room. Sweet Asarum was so frightened that she trembled, and dropped her chopsticks, and Fragrant Angelica hid under the table. But it was only Purple Caltrop, who had come back. After she had put down her parcel, she greeted everyone, and Purple Jade pulled Fragrant Angelica from under the table, saying, 'Why are you so frightened?'

'I was frightened by bandits in the Country of Witches, and from that time on, have been very timid,' said Fragrant Angelica. 'I am sorry I forgot my manners, but please don't laugh at me.'

When everyone was seated again, a slave girl took Purple Caltrop's parcel away, and Daughter of Tang said, 'You really travel light.'

'If I hired a carriage to load baggage I would not get here for two or three days,' said Purple Caltrop. 'I wonder when we are leaving?'

'If nothing detains us, we plan to leave tomorrow morning,' said Daughter of Tang.

Purple Jade tried to persuade them to stay longer, but the young ladies thought they should be going, especially since Old Tuo was becoming impatient. Therefore they packed after dinner, and Baby Phoenix and Lovely Tower returned to their homes, saying that they would come in the morning to go together. Purple Jade told the slave girls to give Purple Caltrop some bedding, since her parcel did not appear to hold any.

The next morning, the twenty-nine young ladies took breakfast, said goodbye to Mistress Yen, and headed for the north.

The young ladies travelled by day, and stopped at night. At last, they arrived in Chang-an. Old Tuo went ahead to look for a place for them to stay.

Empress Wu, expecting many talented girls to come to the capital for the Imperial Examinations, had set aside the estate of the Ninth Prince for them, and had many more rooms added to the spacious grounds, and changed its name to the Feminine Literary Inn. Old Tuo therefore submitted the young ladies' credentials, and after giving some money to those in charge, secured a large courtyard on the premises for the young ladies, and took them into the city.

A building of six stories, with a courtyard and a centre door which could shut it off from the rest of the estate, was put at their disposal. Daughter of Tang was grateful to Old Tuo for securing the place for them, and there were more than enough rooms and halls.

'I spent some time and money before I secured it,' said Old Tuo. 'The other houses are of three to five rooms, at most ten. I think two or three hundred candidates have already arrived. This was reserved for the daughters of the First and Second Ministers of Rituals and Examinations, the Pien and Meng families. But as they are not going to take the examinations, we have been given these quarters.'

'How many daughters have the two families, that they need so many rooms?' said Red Lotus.

'The Pien family has seven daughters, and the Meng family eight. Besides, there are relatives and cousins, thirty to forty girls altogether.'

'Why are they not taking the examinations?' said Pleasant.

'I hear that for some reason they have not been allowed to,' said Old Tuo.

When the young ladies' baggage arrived, they were carried into the different rooms. Five girls shared each room, and soon, their bedding and bed-curtains were in place, and Old Tuo went to see to the kitchen.

The next day, he came with a record book of the young ladies who were living in the residence, and Fragrant Book and Fragrant

Orchid found the names of some of their brothers' fiancées in it. So, together with Fragrant Marsh Orchid, Fragrant Jade, Fragrant Moon, Fragrant Ink and Little Canary, they went to look for them. The boulevards in the estate were broad, and there were not many people, for guards prevented anyone who was not supposed to from coming in, and there were no peddlars and loiterers. Soon, they found the future daughters-in-law of the Wen family, Virtuous Orchid, Red Feather, Red Jade, Fair Heroine, Noble Jade, and Fair Heroine's cousin Tien Peaceful Blossom. When the young ladies came back, the future daughters-in-law of the Wen family came to return the call, bringing with them the ten future daughters-in-law of the Chang family, High Spring, Melting Spring, Glorious Spring, Complaisant Spring, Fragrant Spring, Luxurious Spring, Graceful Spring, Beautiful Spring and Fair Spring, who sat down in the hall, and exchanged names with the other young ladies.

Daughter of Tang was delighted to have the young ladies' company, and asked them to move in, since so many rooms were vacant in their courtyard. The young ladies agreed, and ordered their maids to bring their belongings over. Ultimate Emptiness showed them where to put the beds and arrange the furniture, and in the evening, there were ten tables for dinner. There were forty-five young ladies altogether: Daughter of Tang, Pleasant, Red Lotus, Flowering Maple, Red Rose, Purple Lily, Melody Orchid, Flowerlike, Phoenix-in-Flight, Little Spring, Purple Silk, Wise Maxim, Beautiful Hibiscus, Marsh Orchid, Scarlet Dogwood, Fragrant Book, Fragrant Ink, Little Canary, Fragrant Orchid, Fragrant Marsh Orchid, Fragrant Jade, Fragrant Moon, Purple Jade, Baby Phoenix, Lovely Tower, Purple Caltrop, Sweet Asarum, Fragrant Angelica, Purple Cherry, Virtuous Orchid, Red Feather, Red Jade, Fair Heroine, Noble Jade, Peaceful Blossom, and the ten 'Spring' girls, who sat down according to age, and had a very merry time.

Daughter of Tang said, 'I have heard my uncle say that the Empress decided to hold the Examinations for women because she admired two girls, Shih Quest-for-Seclusion and Ai Fragrant Grass, who unravelled Su Orchid's famous "Tapestry Poem" (which could be read in many combinations). I have long heard of their reputations, and would certainly like to meet them.'

'I did not see their names in the record book yesterday,' said Fragrant Book.

'But we shall certainly meet them during the Ministerial Examinations,' said High Spring.

After supper, the young ladies strolled in the courtyard, and were attracted by the fragrance of some Banksian rose which grew at the foot of a wall. There, they heard someone weeping outside, and wondered who it was. Little Spring said, 'It must be a girl who is homesick.'

'Let us ask Old Tuo to find out whether she is in any difficulties,' said Daughter of Tang.

'Oh, I know who it is and what is troubling her,' said Fair Heroine. 'When Peaceful Blossom and I came here, we met her on the way, and became friends with her. She has left her books and credentials at home in Chien-nan, and that is why she is crying.'

'That is too bad,' said Red Lotus. 'However, if she forgot them, she has no one to blame but herself.'

'Fair Heroine has given her own books and credentials to her,' said Peaceful Blossom. 'I don't know why she is still crying.'

Fragrant Book and Fragrant Ink were astonished.

'How can you do it, after coming so far? Do you mean that you are not going to take the Examinations yourself?' said Fragrant Book.

Fair Heroine said, 'I have not been feeling too well, and again, I know that my scholarship is poor, and I would rather not take the Examinations and reveal my shortcomings. On the other hand, this girl is learned, and it would be a shame for her to come all this way and not take the Examinations. That is why I told my nursemaid's husband to give my papers to her.'

Just then, the nursemaid's husband came back and said, 'Miss Tsu told me to thank you very much, but she does not want you to give up your own chances for her sake. She has asked me to return the papers to you.'

He handed the papers to the slave girls, and left.

'You have done what you thought you should,' said Daughter of Tang, 'and she has also acted as her heart dictated. The way I see it, if she is destined to take part in the Examinations, she will do so even if she has not brought her papers. But as the ancients say, talent and destiny go together, and a woman's destiny depends a great deal on her virtuous conduct. Without virtuous conduct, talent is not enough. Virtuous conduct is like the advance guard of an army. Success or failure depends on it.'

Peaceful Blossom said, 'Oh, this young lady's conduct is virtuous. On the way, she has been constantly uneasy because whenever we stopped at an inn, the innkeeper, on learning that we were on the way to the capital, would kill chickens and ducks and present them to us for supper. She was troubled by all this unnecessary killing, and told the innkeepers to stop, but they would not do so. She realized then what they really wanted was to make a profit, so she began to ask what the price of fowl was before the innkeepers could kill them, and gave the innkeepers what they were worth, saying that it was not necessary to kill. In this way, she has saved many lives. If you say that virtuous conduct is the advance guard of destiny, then why is she not taking the Examinations?'

'If she is such a charitable person, I am sure heaven will protect her, and she will not only take part in the Examinations, but perhaps a great destiny even awaits her,' said Daughter of Tang. 'What is her name?'

Fair Heroine said, 'Her name is Tsu Jade Clasp. She comes from Chien-nan, and is sixteen years old.'

'Then I guarantee that she will have a chance to take the Examinations,' said Flowerlike.

The others did not understand. If the reader wants to know why Flowerlike said this, please read the next chapter.

25

The other young ladies did not understand why Flowerlike said what she did. 'Oh, I think it must be because you are going to become "King" of the Country of Women, so you are going to give your papers to her,' said Melody Orchid. 'Am I right?'

'If I become "King", will you become my minister?' said Flowerlike, laughing.

Melody Orchid smiled. 'If you become "King", of course I shall become your minister."

Flowerlike took Daughter of Tang aside and said, 'Do you remember when Mistress Tsu wanted to take part in the County Examinations, and we thought of a false name for her? Well, since she had a jade clasp in her hand at that time, I thought of the name "Jade Clasp". I did not want to put down her place of origin as Lingnan, since there were already too many of us from there, so I put down Chien-nan. Now there is a girl who is really from Chien-nan and who is really called Tsu Jade Clasp! I have brought Mistress Tsu's papers. Isn't it a coincidence?'

'How wonderful!' said Daughter of Tang. 'But we must not tell the others, in order not to embarrass Purple Lily (Mistress Tsu's daughter). We shall only say that we found these papers at home, and brought them along.'

Flowerlike took the papers, and told Fair Heroine, who exclaimed that there could not be a greater coincidence. Purple Lily of course understood what it was all about, and said, 'These are genuine papers, signed and sealed. Please don't delay in giving them to the girl.'

The nursemaid's husband took the papers and went. In a short while, Jade Clasp herself came in and after greeting the others, thanked Fair Heroine repeatedly, and asked her where she found the papers. Flowerlike said, 'Please don't worry about them. We would not give you these papers unless we knew that they were perfectly in order.'

Jade Clasp thanked her profoundly, and left.

On the third day of March, Daughter of Tang and her sisters and friends, together with many learned young ladies of the land, went to the Ministry of Rituals and Examinations to take the Ministerial Examinations.

The Minister of Rituals and Examinations was Pien Pin, and the Vice-Minister was Meng Mo. Together with other examining officials, he read the papers, and chose a propitious day to proclaim the results. Before they did so, however, an official memorandum was received from the districts of Kiangnan, Huainan, Hopei and Hotung, in which it was said that ten girls had failed to take the District Examinations because of illness, or one reason or another. They were at the capital, and wanted to be allowed to take an examination in four subjects as well as the District and Ministerial Examinations, they were willing to be punished if they failed to finish their Examinations in one day, or if their compositions contained absurdities. The girls' names were Shih Quest-for-Seclusion, Ai Fragrant Grass, Chi Profound Fish, Yen Brocade Heart, Hsieh Literary Brocade, Shih Orchid Language, Chen Virtuous Beauty, Pai Charming Beauty, Kuo Good Omen and Chou Wide Celebration.

The examining officials Pien Pin and Meng Mo did not dare to decide, and asked Her Majesty what to do. The Empress thought that since the young ladies were willing to be tested both in the District and Ministerial Examinations in a day, they should be given the chance. She ordered that the Ministry of Rituals and Examinations should choose the subjects, and that the girls should be present at the Ministry to take the examinations at dawn the following day.

When it was so done, the Ministers hurriedly corrected their papers, and found them to be excellent, and submitted them to the Empress with the question as to whether the girls should be permitted to take the Palace examinations since they were late, and were not properly registered.

The Empress read the papers herself, and found them to be superb, and ordered that the results of the Ministerial Examinations should not be proclaimed until all the candidates were tested in the second examination. The examining officials were ordered to select another propitious day for the second Ministerial Examinations to be taken again, and the thirteenth day of March was chosen.

The Minister Pien Pin was from Kuangling in the Huaunan Corridor. Since childhood, he had filled himself with learning, and won the rank of *Chin-shih* in the Imperial Examinations. He came from a family whose wealth would make those who loved luxury lose heart, but on the other hand, give inspiration to those who were poor. He was also called Pien Million Acres, because that much land had been left to him by his grandfather.

His great grandfather was Pien Hua, a man who loved luxury above all else. Although his ancestors left him a fortune of many hundred thousands, between him and his wife, they squandered it so that when he was fifty years old, it was all gone. It was too late for regrets. From eating rich food and wearing silk, they were reduced to eating porridge and wearing coarse cotton. In a couple of years, they both died of unhappiness, leaving a son to whom they gave the name of Thrift when they were dying.

Thrift and his wife Mistress Chin sold the house to pay for his parents' funeral, and went to live in a straw hut in the country. Thrift was a hard-working scholar, and spent all his time in study, and depended on the needlework of his wife for support. But sometimes, he went to collect kindling to add something to their meagre income. In this way, they had barely enough to live on.

One cold winter, Thrift had only a single thin garment to wear and was very cold, so he went to bed early. When he woke up at about the fifth watch, he saw that his wife was still sewing under the lamplight. 'Why don't you go to sleep? Why work so hard on such a cold night?' he said. Mistress Chin said, 'You have only a thin cotton garment to wear. I want to make a few extra coppers so that you will not have to climb the mountains to collect kindling in this weather.'

'But you have never been strong yourself,' said Thrift. 'What if you get ill from working too hard! And again, if I don't collect some kindling to help meet the expenses, I would feel very bad indeed.'

When it was morning, Thrift opened the door, and found that the earth was covered with snow. There was only enough rice and kindling left for one meal, and Thrift could not go out to collect any since snow covered everything. So they had one meal, and waited for it to stop snowing so that Mistress Chin could sell her needlework.

The next day, it still snowed, but Thrift braved the weather, and took the needlework into the city to sell. All doors were closed to him, and he failed to sell anything. When he came home, he thought for a while and said, 'We have a chicken and a duck, who usually find food to eat on the ground, and lay us eggs. Why don't we sell them to buy some rice?'

Mistress Chin shook her head and said, 'No! I mean to make a fortune by them! If we sell these fowl now we shall not be able to buy another pair for many times the money we get for them. Their eggs will soon hatch. When the chicks and ducklings grow big, we will have hopes of making more money.'

The couple starved for another day, and when it stopped snowing, continued to live in their frugal fashion.

In the spring, the hen and duck laid twenty eggs each. The hen sat on her eggs, and the couple hatched the duck eggs with the help of a fire. Soon, the chickens and ducklings were big enough to sell. They kept a few which laid eggs, and sold the rest. With the money, they bought two pigs, who eventually gave birth to litters. In a few years, they had a farm of pigs and sheep, and water buffaloes. They built another straw hut, and bought another piece of land. Thrift planted vegetables on the land, and sold the vegetables at a good profit. The couple were so hard-working that they still wore cotton clothes, and ate simply, and did not hire any help to do the work for them. In thirty years, they became very rich, and their granaries were full. Their son, Pien Chi, was also hard-working and thrifty, so that when Pien Pin was born, the family had a million acres.

One year, after Pien Pin became a scholar, there was famine and fighting in the land, and the treasury was in dire straits. Pien Pin sold half a million acres of land and gave the money to the government. He was summoned to Court, and found to be not only a scholar, but an expert in music, chess, painting, medicine and astrology. He was very generous, and never refused help to those who were in need.

Now, the only regret in Pien Pin's life was that he had no son.

He had had two sons, who both died at the age of three. Although he had taken several concubines since he turned forty, now in his fifties, he still had only daughters, seven of them.

When Pien Pin's second son Badge died from convulsions, the family let out loud wails. A Taoist beggar changed to pass by, and asked what the matter was. When he saw the child, he said, 'There is hope for him, but not in this city. If you will give him to me, I shall return him to you when he is grown up, and his years of hard luck are over.'

Pien Pin did not believe him, since his son was dead, but his wife Mistress Cheng insisted, saying that it could do no harm, and Pien Pin complied. However, ten years had now passed, and there was no news of the child, so Pien Pin took him for dead.

But Pien Pin treasured his daughters as though they were flowers, and whenever he had time, taught them to write and make verse. In the County Examinations the year before, he did not want to be accused of partiality, so he sent his daughters back to their hometown to take the examinations. The young ladies, whose names were Precious Cloud, Rainbow Cloud, Brocade Cloud, Purple Cloud, Fragrant Cloud, White Cloud and

Green Cloud, all passed with distinction, and also came within the first ten in the District Examinations. But because their father was Chief Examining Official, they were prevented from taking the Ministerial Examinations, and were extremely disappointed. To cheer them up, Pien Pin invited some of his nieces to come and stay. These were the daughters of Meng Mo, the Vice-Minister of Rituals and Examinations, who had married Pien Pin's sister, and Meng Mo's deceased brother. There were eight girls altogether, called Orchid Mushroom, Bright Mushroom, Fragrant Mushroom, Honeybush Mushroom, Lustrous Mushroom, Fairy Mushroom, Purple Mushroom and Jade Mushroom. They came with widow Mistress Pien to live in Pien Pin's residence, together with the daughters of the other examining officials. Chiang Chin had four daughters and a son called Worthy. The daughters were called Spring Glory, Autumn Glory, Star Glory and Moon Glory, and two nieces by a widowed sister-in-law named White Glory and Pretty Glory.

The Examining Official Tung Tuan had five daughters called Precious Ornament, Pearl Ornament, Jade Ornament, Flowery Ornament and Blue Ornament. The Examining Official Chang Chung had three sets of twins of four girls and two boys. The girls were called Red Pearl, Multiple Pearls, Black Pearl and River Pearl. The Examining Official Lu Liang had three daughters, Yellow Lily, Propitious Lily and Fair Lily.

On the thirteenth of March, the Ministerial Examinations were held once more. Pien Pin and Meng Mo and the other officials graded the papers and took the passing papers to Court to show Empress Wu. The Empress read them and said, 'We really have many extraordinary girls in the country, and I am glad that some girls have come from overseas to take the Examinations, too.' But when she looked at the names, she sighed and said, 'What happened to some of the girls who passed the District and County Examinations with top honours? I remember that many had the name of Pien and Meng.'

Pien Pin explained that they were daughters of Examining Officials, and so prevented from taking the Ministerial Examinations. The Empress remembered that these were outstanding girls, and issued a decree allowing thirty-three daughters or nieces of Examining Officials to be allowed to compose a prose-poem as their Ministerial Examinations, and to be graded according to their merit. Those who were deemed worthy would be allowed to take part in the Palace Examinations.

The Pien sisters and Meng sisters were overjoyed to hear the news, and on the twenty-third day of March, went to the Ministry of Rituals and Examinations to write their prose-poems. In view of the fact that the Feminine Literary Inn was nearer the Palace, and would be more convenient for them when they took the Palace Examinations, the young ladies came to live there when they heard that there was room for them.

Daughter of Tang and the young ladies at the courtyard were delighted, especially since all forty-five of them had passed with honours, with Flowerlike coming in first, and Daughter of Tang second. The six pupils of Tang Min had also passed.

They arranged for a great celebration banquet to be held. In the midst of it, old Tuo came in and said, 'There is someone outside who wants to see Miss Flowerlike. The servants asked his name, but he would not say. I looked at him, and it is none other than the "Royal Uncle" from the Country of Women. I don't know why he has travelled thousands of miles to come here to see you.'

When Flowerlike heard this, she was flabbergasted. 'The people from my country don't as a rule come here. He must have a reason for coming, and I wonder how he knew where I was?' she said.

'Since you came in first in the Ministerial Examinations, he must have had no difficulty in finding you,' said Old Tuo.

'Since he is here, and Flowerlike is his relative, is there anything we can do but invite him in?' said Daughter of Tang.

Flowerlike asked Old Tuo to have the visitor shown to the library, and went in to meet 'him'.

It was, indeed, the 'Royal Uncle'.

'I am glad to see you!' she said. 'How is my father? Why have you come suddenly to the Kingdom on Earth?'

The 'Royal Uncle' shed tears and said, 'It is a long story. After you left, the King and I went to the Country of the Shaft of Wheels to attend the birthday celebrations of their King. The traitors of the Western Palace took the opportunity to have the Concubine's son installed as King. When we came back, they would not let us into the Palace, and we had to escape to the Country of the Shaft of Wheels. The new King was a ruthless ruler, and mistreated the people, and lived on wine and women. Before a year was over, the people rose against him, and killed both him and the Concubine of the Western Palace, and welcomed the King your father back to the throne. The ministers thought of you, and want you to come back. The King has no heir, and cannot refuse the wishes of the ministers and the people. Therefore, we borrowed a flying carriage from the Country of Plenty, which can travel two or three thousand miles in a day if the wind is with it, and seats two people. I was sent here to ask you, my nephew, to return to our country. I arrived several days ago, and did not know where to look for you.

Then I saw the results of the Examinations and had no difficulty finding you. When my nephew reads it, he will understand.'

Flowerlike read the letter and sighed and said, 'I did not know that all this had happened in the last two years, although I might have guessed it. But I have no desire to return to my country. Unworthy as I am, I have become a Lady Scholar by decree of the Empress, and will surely be given an official post. Is there anything more I can desire? There are others in my country who can become King. It does not have to be me.'

The 'Royal Uncle' said, 'How can you say that? If it were not for your father wanting to see you again, after having endured so much, would I have spent so much time and money to borrow the flying carriage to come here? If you do not go back you will not only disappoint your father, but also the people of your country. I am afraid that you will regret it if you do not come now, and it may not be so easy to come back later.'

Flowerlike said unhappily, 'I am sure that I will not regret it. I would not have left my country in the first place if I were going to regret it. In any case, I am not going back, and I should be grateful if you would not mention it again.'

Flowerlike's heart could not be shaken. After lunch, she wrote a letter hurriedly in reply to her 'father's', and resisted all the 'Royal Uncle's' efforts to make her change her mind. The latter could do nothing but take the letter and leave.

When Flowerlike came back from seeing her 'Uncle' off, Daughter of Tang said, 'We overheard your conversation. I was going to come in and tell you to take his advice, but dared not. Had I known that your "Uncle" was a woman dressed up as a man, I would have come in!'

'It would not have made any difference. My mind is made up, and nothing can change it,' Flowerlike replied.

Little Spring said, 'If the "King" wants you to go back so badly that he went to the expense to borrow a flying carriage, how do you know that he has not sent gold and silver to Uncle Lin, and told him to make you go?'

'Even if my godfather told me to, I would not go,' said Flowerlike.

'But Uncle Lin would be embarrassed for you to stay in Lingnan after that,' said Little Spring. 'I think that the best way out for you is to get married. Then, if anything happens, you have your husband to protect you.'

They were still talking when Jade Clasp came to call, and invited Flowerlike, Daughter of Tang and Peaceful Blossom to dinner to thank them for their help. The next day, the young ladies invited her back.

There were several days' parties, and soon it was the first of April. Daughter of Tang got up at the fifth drum, and went to the Forbidden City with the other young ladies. Many Talented Ladies had already arrived at the Palace, and gathered at the Imperial Hall.

When Empress Wu came in, the young ladies exclaimed their salutations, and stood in two rows on either side of the hall. The Empress walked past them, and saw that indeed the Court was filled with beauty and talent, and was extremely pleased. She said a few words to Quest-for-Seclusion, and had a few words for Fragrant Grass, and summoned Daughter of Tang, Good Omen and Wide Celebration and said, 'Did you three take your names only recently?'

'My father was told by a dream-spirit that the name Daughter of Tang would appear in the list of successful candidates at the Ministerial Examinations, and so gave me this name to remind me to study hard,' said Daughter of Tang.

Good Omen said, 'My name was given to me last year.'

'The names Good Omen and Wide Celebration are both timely, so I thought they must have been recently given. But I was wrong about Daughter of Tang,' said the Empress.

She summoned the Meng and Pien sisters next, and had a few words of praise for them. Then she announced the subject for the Examination. The Talented Ladies went to their seats and started to do the Examination, as the Empress herself supervised them.

When the papers were collected, the Empress ordered the Imperial Concubine Shangkuan Waner to look at them, and ordered the six Ministers to grade the top ten papers. The third day of April was chosen to make known the results, at the fifth drum.

When the young ladies heard that the results would be announced the following day, they were both nervous and excited. Little Spring and Pleasant who shared a room with Peaceful Blossom and Fair Heroine could not sleep. They had several cups of wine each, and after failing several attempts to go to sleep, sat up and talked, and sighed and worried. At the fourth watch, Fair Heroine was awakened by the noise they made, and said, 'Please go to sleep! Why are you jumping up and down and crying and laughing at the same time?'

'Why do you think?' said Peaceful Blossom. 'They are anxious about the results to be announced tomorrow!'

Fair Heroine said, 'Listen! The cock has crowed several times. It must be dawn. There is no need to go back to sleep now.'

'We have already asked Old Tuo to go to buy the list of results as soon as they are issued,' said Pleasant. 'He left in the second watch and should be back soon.'

She had not finished speaking when there was the sound of a boom from the distance, which sounded like a cannon being fired, and shook the windows. Soon, maidservants and slave girls came in and said that it was people from the Palace, who had come to announce good tidings, by firing the cannons outside the residence.

Pleasant opened the door of her room, and Little Spring sent for Old Tuo, but the second gate to the courtyard was locked, and they could not go out. There came another boom, and Little Spring asked the slave girls to hurry and find the key. Other booms came in succession now.

'They fire the cannon once for every girl who has passed,' said Fair Heroine.

'I wonder where the other young ladies are?' said Peaceful Blossom.

'They must all be counting the booms of the cannon in their room like us,' said Little Spring. 'They will not come out until they hear forty-five of them!'

When thirty-three cannon shots had been fired, Little Spring looked into the sky and cried, 'Star of Literature! Please be kind and let the cannon sound twelve times more! If it stops now, I shall die . . .'

Three more shots were heard, followed by another one. But the cannon became silent after firing thirty-seven times. Pleasant was speechless, and thought that she was going to die.

Day had broken, and all the girls were in their rooms listening and waiting, but nothing more could be heard. Fair Heroine and Peaceful Blossom hurriedly got dressed, and after washing and combing their hair, prepared to go to the hall, where the young ladies had agreed to meet. Pleasant and Little Spring sat with tears rolling down their faces like broken strands of pearls, but Fair Heroine and Peaceful Blossom managed to get them into the main hall.

The other young ladies were all there, sitting staring at each other with faces the colour of paper, and no one said a word. When breakfast was served, no one ate anything.

Little Spring started to tremble so hard that her chair began to shake, and Pleasant said, shivering, 'I . . . I cannot stand it . . . I shall die . . . right now . . .'

Daughter of Tang sighed and said, 'It does not seem as if any more shots will be fired, and eight of us have failed. We must have the second gate unlocked, and see if Old Tuo has come back with the list.'

Pleasant said, crying, ' . . . At first I was impatient . . . now I would rather not know . . . I think I would rather die . . .'

'There is nothing we can do about it,' said Flowerlike. 'Remember when Daughter of Tang saw the jade tablet she saw all forty-five of our names there. Now only thirty-seven of us have passed. However, we must find out sooner or later who they are. It would be best to wait until Old Tuo has come back with the list.'

'You are quite right,' said Daughter of Tang, and told the slave girls to go and see, but Old Tuo had not returned.

'Don't worry,' said Daughter of Tang. 'There must be a great crowd waiting to buy the list, and it is not strange that he has not come back yet.'

'I think something is wrong,' said Fair Heroine. 'If the results have been issued, he should have come back already.'

Suddenly, Old Tuo could be heard talking outside. Daughter of Tang hurriedly told the slave girls to let him in. In a short while, the old man came in, his face dripping with sweat.

'Congra . . .' he started, but could not finish what he was going to say because he was panting so hard.

Little Spring, trembling, and Phoenix-in-Flight helped their uncle to sit down, and tea was brought to him.

In tears, Little Spring said, 'Have I passed?'

Old Tuo could not speak, but he nodded.

Pleasant also said in tears, 'Old Tuo . . . have I?'

Again, Old Tuo nodded.

'Have you brought the list of results?' said Daughter of Tang.

Old Tuo pointed to his breast, and Phoenix-in-Flight took the list from his pocket and gave it to Daughter of Tang.

If the reader would like to know which young ladies were successful in the Palace Examinations, please read the next chapter.

26

On the list which Phoenix-in-Flight took from Old Tuo's pocket, it was written, 'Fifty Lady Scholars, forty Lady Doctors and ten Lady Masters have been selected . . .'

Flowerlike read the list out loud so that all the girls would know the results at the same time. It was this :

No. 1	Shih Quest-for-Seclusion
No. 2	Ai Fragrant Grass
No. 3	Chi Profound Fish
No. 4	Yen Brocade Heart
No. 5	Hsieh Literary Brocade
No. 6	Shih Orchid Language
No. 7	Chen Virtuous Beauty
No. 8	Pai Charming Beauty
No. 9	Kuo Good Omen
No. 10	Chou Wide Celebration
No. 11	Daughter of Tang
No. 12	Yin Flowerlike
No. 13	Yin Clever Prose
No. 14	Pien Precious Cloud
No. 15	Yu Fair Heroine
No. 16	Lin Fragrant Book
No. 17	Sung Wise Maxim
No. 18	Chang Virtuous Orchid
No. 19	Yang Fragrant Ink
No. 20	Li Brocade Spring
No. 21	Tien Peaceful Blossom
No. 22	Lu Purple Lily
No. 23	Yeh Fragrant Spring
No. 24	Shao Red Feather
No. 25	Chu Painted Flower
No. 26	Meng Purple Mushroom
No. 27	Chin Little Spring
No. 28	Tung Blue Ornament
No. 29	Chu Fragrant Moon
No. 30	Szetu Marsh Orchid
No. 31	Yu Beautiful Hibiscus
No. 32	Lien Flowering Maple
No. 33	Lo Red Lotus
No. 34	Lin Pleasant
No. 35	Liao Glorious Spring
No. 36	Li Red Rose

No. 37   Yen Purple Jade
No. 38   Chiang Spring Glory
No. 39   Yin Scarlet Dogwood
No. 40   Wei Purple Cherry
No. 41   Tsai Jade Moonlight
No. 42   Meng Orchid Mushroom
No. 43   Hsueh Sweet Asarum
No. 44   Yen Purple Silk
No. 45   Chih Melody Orchid
No. 46   Yao Fragrant Angelica
No. 47   Yi Purple Caltrop
No. 48   Tien Phoenix-in-Flight
No. 49   Chang Red Pearl
No. 50   Yeh Fragrant Jade
No. 51   Pien Rainbow Cloud
No. 52   Lu Yellow Lily
No. 53   Tso Melting Spring
No. 54   Meng Honeybush Mushroom
No. 55   Pien Green Cloud
No. 56   Tung Precious Ornament
No. 57   Shih Luxurious Spring
No. 58   Tou Country Smoke
No. 59   Chiang Pretty Glory
No. 60   Tsai Fragrant Orchid
No. 61   Meng Bright Mushroom
No. 62   Pien Brocade Cloud
No. 63   Chou Complaisant Spring
No. 64   Chien Noble Jade
No. 65   Tung Flowery Ornament
No. 66   Liu Graceful Spring
No. 67   Pien Purple Cloud
No. 68   Meng Jade Mushroom
No. 69   Chiang Moon Glory
No. 70   Lu Propitious Lily
No. 71   Tao Fair Spring
No. 72   Chang Black Pearl
No. 73   Chiang Star Glory
No. 74   Tai Red Jade
No. 75   Tung Pearl Ornament
No. 76   Pien Fragrant Cloud
No. 77   Meng Fairy Mushroom
No. 78   Chang Multiple Pearls
No. 79   Chiang Autumn Glory
No. 80   Tsu Jade Clasp
No. 81   Pien White Cloud
No. 82   Chang Lovely Tower
No. 83   Mi Orchid Fragrance
No. 84   Tsai Silver Moonlight
No. 85   Pan Beautiful Spring
No. 86   Meng Fragrant Mushroom
No. 87   Chung Embroidered Field
No. 88   Tan Fragrant Marsh Orchid
No. 89   Meng Lustrous Mushroom
No. 90   Chiang White Glory

No. 91   Lu Fair Lily
No. 92   Tung Jade Ornament
No. 93   Chang River Pearl
No. 94   Ching High Spring
No. 95   Tsui Little Canary
No. 96   Su Orchid
No. 97   Change Baby Phoenix
No. 98   Wen Fragrant Plant
No. 99   Hua Fragrance Returns
No. 100 Pi Completely Virtuous

When Flowerlike finished reading the list, the young ladies' anxiety turned into happiness.

Old Tuo was asked, 'Why then were eight cannon shots missing this morning? Where did you get this list?'

He replied, 'I was there waiting beside the proclamation board at the third drum, and after giving some bribes, found out that Miss Daughter of Tang was placed first, and Miss Flowerlike second. However, the Empress changed her mind at the last moment, and thought that Miss Quest-for-Seclusion and Miss Fragrant Plant should be rewarded for their poetry, and so shifted the first ten and the second ten around. The list had to be re-copied, and it took a lot of time, and it is not yet on sale. But I knew that you were anxious, so I copied each name as it appeared on the proclamation board, and then ran back as fast as I could, because the successful candidates must lose no time in going to the Palace to thank the Empress. You had better have some food and go right away.'

He had not finished speaking when eight cannon shots were heard.

'Those are for the young ladies who came in the first ten,' said Old Tuo. 'They were afraid that the Empress would change her mind again, so the last places were announced first, and the first places were not announced until the end. Now I have not slept all night, and must have some rest. Tomorrow I shall offer my congratulations to you properly.'

The young ladies hurriedly made themselves ready, and after breakfast, left for the Palace, where the Empress conferred the degrees of Lady Scholar, Lady Doctor and Lady Master upon them, and presented each girl with a pair of gold flowers, and ordered a great feast to be prepared in celebration.

For three days, the Empress celebrated the selection of the successful candidates, after which Princess Taiping gave a feast which lasted for two days. The successful young ladies had ample opportunity to know each other well, and when the five days were over, they were sorry to have to part.

On the sixth day, the young ladies finally thanked the Empress and the Princess, and prepared to call on the Master of Examinations, Pien Pin, at his residence.

Pien Precious Cloud hurried home ahead of the young ladies to warn her father that they were coming, and Pien Pin hurriedly ordered a banquet and wine to be made ready.

As the girls arrived at the residence, each left her card and gifts for the Master of Examinations. Pien Pin stood at the second gate to receive the callers, who, except for his own daughters and the Meng daughters, went in according to their rank, and upon passing through the second gate, went into the reception hall and were shown into the Frozen Jade Pavilion by the slave girls.

Pien Pin said to the young ladies, 'I suggest that we dispense with the ceremonious greetings, otherwise we should be doing nothing else but greeting one another all day.'

But Quest-for-Seclusion said, 'We must go through the full ceremonies, since this is the first time that we are calling on the Master and the Master is of the older generation.'

Fragrant Grass said, 'If the Master is afraid that it will take too long, we shall do it ten persons at a time, and it will soon be done.'

Quest-for-Seclusion forthwith ordered the slave girls to put the kowtowing cushions in place. Pien Pin had no choice but to receive their ceremonial greetings.

When these were over, his own daughters came up and also kowtowed to him. The slave girls were going to take the cushions away when Quest-for-Seclusion said, 'We would like to meet and greet the Mistress.'

Pien Pin therefore sent for his wife. Soon, his daughters escorted their mother Mistress Cheng into the pavilion, and the young ladies paid their respects to her. After the young ladies also paid their respects to the Pien sisters, Pien Pin said to his eldest daughter Precious Cloud, 'I have already ordered dinner. Will you and your sisters and my nieces entertain the guests for me? It is but a simple meal.'

So saying, he left and told his man Pien Piao, 'Please tell the young ladies that I will not accept their gifts. If they feel that they must give me something, then let them give me their own paintings and samples of their calligraphy.'

Mistress Cheng chatted with the young ladies and said, 'I have no presents for any of you. But I wish you all a long and happy life!'

The young ladies said, 'Your blessings are received with thanks. Since you are blessed with longevity and good fortune yourself, what you say is naturally propitious !'

'Please make yourselves at home,' said Mistress Cheng, 'as it is indeed the home of your teacher and elder. Dinner will soon be served, and you must not feel like guests.'

She then left with her slave girls.

Just as Precious Cloud was going to seat her guests, Quest-for-Seclusion's slave girl said, 'Men have come from the Palace summoning you to go to receive your presentations of writing brushes and ink-slabs. The Empress also wants to talk to Miss Flowerlike.'

The young ladies therefore left hurriedly to go to the Palace. The Empress received them, and after presenting them with writing brushes and ink-slabs, summoned Flowerlike, who knelt before the throne and said, 'Yin Flowerlike answering Your Majesty's summons.'

'I have received a communication from the sovereign of your country, and learned that you have come here because of trouble at home. I am glad that you have received the title of Lady Scholar. Please read the communication first, then I shall give you your title, so that you may return to your own country by flying carriage with the emissary.'

Flowerlike took the communication from an official's hand and read :

'The King of the Country of Women bows to the Empress of the Kingdom on Earth. I have long heard of your illustrious reputation, and regret that distance keeps me from paying my respects to you personally. Your recent achievements in gathering the talent of the land to Court are well-known, and I am extremely grateful to you for selecting my son Flowerlike for a high rank in the Examinations.

'I am forty years old, and have had only two sons. Flowerlike lost his mother as a child, and because of intrigue within the Court, was forced to flee from this country. My other son was not good. Due to difficulties which he got himself into, he has met with a bad end. I am now in very poor health, and in my loneliness and sorrow, wish that Flowerlike should return and take up the duties of the throne. I regret that I did not do my duty as a father toward him, and hope that I shall be forgiven. If the Empress will allow Flowerlike to come back, I shall be eternally grateful.'

Tears rolled down Flowerlike's face after she read the communication. She said, 'When I left my country two years ago, I was afraid for my life. Since coming here, I have had the good fortune to receive Your Majesty's favour. How can I think of leaving, not knowing what my fate will be when I return to my own country? I should like to remain in the Kingdom on Earth and serve Your Majesty for the rest of my life. Please take pity on me!'

The Empress was touched by her plea, but she had received many treasures from the sovereign of the Country of Women, and as she valued treasure more than talent she said, 'When you left your country, there were plots against you. Now the "Concubine of the Western Palace" and "her heir" are both dead, and you may go back without fear. It is your "father's" wish that you fulfil your destiny, and "he" has already expressed "his" regret for "his" past negligence of you. Now you should go back and assume your duties. Let no more be said about it. I hereby confer upon you the title of Princess of Glorious Literature, and present you with a ceremonial robe and jade belt. You must return to your own country for the sake of your "father" and your people as soon as possible.'

Flowerlike kowtowed and said, 'I am deeply grateful to Your Majesty for conferring so many honours on me. But I am in a difficult position. When I was a child, I devoted myself to studying, and did not bother about the affairs at Court. Now although the people of the Western Palace have been vanquished, there is still a great deal of intrigue. How shall I, a mere girl, go back and try to rule, without ministers to help me and loyal officials behind me? If Your Majesty would lend me three or four able ministers, I shall go, and with their help, make my position secure. When I no longer need them, I shall return the ministers to Your Majesty, and be forever grateful!'

The Empress said, 'I can understand your predicament. But able ministers are hard to find in Court, and I have none too many of them. I cannot spare you two or three. If I should send you less capable officials, would I not be asking for the ridicule of the people of your country?'

'I have three people in mind whom I would like to take to help me,' said Flowerlike. 'With Your Majesty's permission, I should like to name them.'

The Empress said, 'Who are they?'

'They are among the newly-made Lady Scholars,' said Flowerlike. 'One is Chih Melody Orchid of the Country of Split-tongued People. The other two are from the Country of Black-toothed People : Li Red Rose and Lu Purple Lily, whom Lin Chih-yang the merchant adopted as daughters and brought to this Kingdom to take part in the Examinations. They are all three girls of exceptional talent and character. If the Empress gives permission, I should like them to come with me.'

The Empress said, 'Since they are from abroad, it is appropriate for them to go with you. Later they can return to their own countries.'

She therefore told her ministers to summon the three young ladies, who advanced to the throne and knelt.

The Empress conferred on Melody Orchid and Purple Lily and Red Rose the titles of Scholars of the Eastern Palace, and presented them with ceremonial robes and jade belts, and ordered them to go with Flowerlike to the Country of Women to help her rule and then return to their own countries, and decreed that Flowerlike and the three young ladies should leave the Kingdom on Earth within ten days.

When the young ladies were dismissed, Precious Cloud invited them to return to her home for dinner, but as the young ladies still had to call on the Examination Official Meng and others, they thanked her and declined her invitation.

When the young ladies returned to the Feminine Literary Inn, Pleasant shed tears and said, 'I am heart-broken because Flowerlike has to go back. Now the Empress has ordered Melody Orchid, Red Rose and Purple Lily to go too! Why not cut out my five internal organs and have done with it! Why should I live anymore?'

Everyone began to cry, and Flowerlike, Melody Orchid and Red Rose cried especially hard. Only Purple Lily remained composed and smiling.

When Pleasant saw her, she said, 'Why are you smiling? Do you mean that after we have been together for so long, you feel nothing at leaving us? Are you satisfied merely because the Empress has conferred a title upon you?'

Purple Lily stopped smiling and said, 'Do you think that I care for the title? I am happy first because I shall have the company of three sisters, and also because now I have something worthwhile to do, instead of spending my days in vain. If I can help Flowerlike, either in establishing the customs of her country, or purging it of evil, and help to make the country peaceful and prosperous, I should be very proud. I thought that you would understand this. As for the happiness of our being together, if we were to prolong it, what would it do to Flowerlike? It is not that I do not know the sorrow of parting, but there is no feast which does not end in life. We still have ten days in which to be happy together. If we spend it weeping and being sad, won't they be hard to endure? My suggestion is for us to forget the word "parting" for the next ten days, and make the most of the time which is left to us. Or, as the ancients say, "Make merry while we may". What do you say if we have a series of parties and take turns to be hostesses?'

The girls agreed, and dried their tears. Daughter of Tang said, 'We have been so busy that we have not yet had time to celebrate. Now we shall follow Purple Lily's suggestion, and I shall be hostess first.'

'I shall be hostess tomorrow,' said Pleasant.

When this was decided, Purple Lily wrote a letter to her mother Mistress Tsu, and asked Old Tuo to send it for her.

Soon, the 'Royal Uncle' appeared and was shown into the study. Flowerlike received 'him' and said, 'How is the "King"?'

'When I returned to our country after travelling for six days because the wind was against me,' said the 'Royal Uncle', 'I found that your father's health had worsened. His heart was broken when he received your letter, and after some thought he decided to write to the Empress, and present a great deal of money and treasure to her. He ordered me to take them here, in order that my nephew should be allowed to return to our country. I had to borrow two more flying carriages from the Country of Plenty to carry everything. Now the three carriages will carry my nephew and his three friends back.'

When the 'Royal Uncle' left, Flowerlike asked Old Tuo to find out where 'he' lived, and returned the call.

Daughter of Tang and the others decided to present the four young ladies who were leaving with a gift of painting, on which each girl would inscribe a poem. Fragrant Ink was asked to do the painting, and she consented, saying, 'Although I do not paint well, it will be a little shower of ink to have with them when they are upon their windy journey.'

When Flowerlike returned from paying her courtesy call to her 'uncle', the gatekeeper came in with invitations saying, 'Master Pien has sent these invitations for the young ladies to have lunch tomorrow. Morning noodles will also be served.'

The next morning, Pien Pin ordered twenty-five tables to be laid for the banquet at the Frozen Jade Pavilion. The pavilion faced an open air stage, and was banked by red cassias on either side, and surrounded by a forest of rockery, pines and cypress. Pien Pin liked to hold his banquets here because it was such a beautiful place when the cassia flowers were in bloom, and the pavilion was surrounded by greenery, and the perfume of the pines filled the air. The twenty-five tables were set up in five rows, with four people to be seated at each table.

Precious Cloud acted as hostess as her father was away on official duty, and Meng Orchid Mushroom said that her father would entertain the young ladies the following day at this same place.

When Precious Cloud asked the young ladies to be seated for breakfast, Quest-for-Seclusion, showing due modesty, refused to be seated in the place of honour, and said that they should be seated according to age, in which case Completely Virtuous and Fragrance Returns would be seated first.

'How can I be seated first, when it is destined that I should be seated last?' said Completely Virtuous.

'Yes, it is so destined,' said Fragrance Returns. 'Let me explain a strange phenomenon to you. When we were taking the Ministerial Examinations, I sat quite near Daughter of Tang and Completely Virtuous, and I sighed, saying, "I am afraid I shall never succeed in the Imperial Examinations," and Daughter of Tang said, "You will, but you will be next to the last, and Completely Virtuous will be first – counting from the end." She also said that she would be number eleven, and that a girl called Quest-for-Seclusion would be first, and that a girl called Fragrant Grass would be second. I wrote it down, and now it has all become true. Isn't it extraordinary?'

'Really!' said the others. 'Could Daughter of Tang be a living fairy who knows the results before they are announced?'

'Yes, and we would like to know what she meant when she said that her name was suggested by a fairy in a dream,' said Precious Cloud.

'It is really a long story,' said Daughter of Tang. 'If my sisters will all be seated, I shall try to tell you.'

'No, tell us first,' said Purple Mushroom. 'We are not afraid of our feet growing big from standing too long.'

'Well, it is a very bizarre affair, but I saw it with my own eyes when I went abroad to look for my father,' said Daughter of Tang. 'But I must tell you everything from the beginning for you to understand.

'My father saw through the vanities of the worldly life, and travelled abroad with my maternal uncle on his merchant vessel. One day, a hurricane blew the junk to the foot of Little Penglai Mountain, and my father went on shore to explore its scenic beauty, but he never returned. When I learned this, I went overseas with my uncle, and in the company of Flowerlike, went to the mountains to look for him. After travelling for a fortnight, we came to a pavilion which gave off a red light, on which was written three big characters: "Lament for Beauty Pavilion". There was a jade tablet inside the Pavilion, with an inscription on it which said, "Say not there are few beautiful girls on earth. Hard luck accompanies those whose names are carved on this tablet." On the tablet were the names of a hundred girls, which are the names of the hundred of us here today, with an oracle after each name. At the end there was a seal carved in *chuan* characters with the message :

Vast, vast the wilderness,
Incredible, incredible the destinies involved;
If Tang meets Tang,
Carry the news back to the Kingdom on Earth.

I copied down what was written on the tablet, and on my way back met a woodcutter who gave me a letter from my father, asking me to come home to take part in the Examinations and saying that we would meet again after I had done so.'

'Will you let us see what is copied from the tablet?' said Purple Mushroom.

'I took the copy back to Lingnan, but a white fairy gibbon snatched it away, so I haven't got it any more,' said Daughter of Tang.

'Where did this gibbon come from?' Precious Cloud asked.

'My father caught it in Little Penglai and Pleasant brought it back to Lingnan. Every time I looked at what I had copied down, it would stand beside me and watch. One day I said to it in fun, "You don't eat meat, and you have a contemplative air. What do you know about this record? I would like to find a scholar-writer who will write about the lives of the people whose names are here. Will you help me?" To my surprise, he nodded, and taking the record from my hands, disappeared.'

'Isn't it a shame?' said Purple Mushroom. 'But do you remember what you wrote?'

Daughter of Tang said that she remembered some of the oracles, but she could not remember all. She would try and write down what she remembered.

Slave girls brought writing brush and paper and ink-slab, and Daughter of Tang begged the young ladies' pardon and sat down, and wrote down most of what was written on the tablet. Everyone was astonished by it.

Orchid Mushroom asked Quest-for-Seclusion, 'From the words "hard luck accompanies those whose names are carved on this tablet", does it mean that most of us will meet with bad ends?'

'It is difficult to say,' said Quest-for-Seclusion. 'If it is so, would it not have said so more plainly?'

'And yet, the pavilion is called "Lament for Beauty". That does not seem to be very auspicious,' said Precious Cloud.

'I think that hard luck for some of us may not be avoidable,' said Orchid Language. 'It would be hard to expect all of us to enjoy both long life and wealth, in view of the name of the Pavilion and the couplet. However, the ancients say, "Do your best for now, and don't worry about the future." It is also said, "Good and bad luck are like shadows which follow a person's form." If a person acts with reason in big affairs and small towards everyone, it is all that can be asked of him, and the rest is up to destiny.'

At last, Purple Mushroom said, 'We had all better sit down and have some breakfast, for everyone's feet must be aching. Since Quest-for-Seclusion and Fragrant Grass's names are inscribed at the head of the fairy tablet, let us be seated accordingly.'

After some further demonstration of modesty, the young ladies finally seated themselves, with the Meng and Pien daughters acting as hostesses at the tables. Flowerlike suggested that they dispense with further formalities, and wine and several courses of food were served.

After their noodles, the young ladies went out into the garden, where some continued their literary discussions, and others played on musical instruments. Others walked past the vegetable gardens and farms where the Pien family raised cows, pigs, sheep and horses, and at last they all met again at the Peony Pavilion, where refreshments were served. Precious Cloud had ink and painting brushes brought, and several of the young ladies began to paint on fans, while others played chess, and still others played on the lute.

Some young ladies sat on the swings, others played shuttle-cock, and dice, and recited poetry, and played guessing games, and fished, or simply talked.

After a morning of amusements, the young ladies sat down to a wine banquet and began a guessing game based on their knowledge of ancient classical texts, with the loser having to tell a joke and drink a cup of wine as forfeit.

When Purple Mushroom had to tell a joke, she said, 'Once there was a very poor man who met the Immortal Lu Tung-pin and asked for his help. Lu took pity on the man and using his magic finger, pointed to a stone and turned it into gold, and presented the man with it. From then on, whenever the man met the Immortal, he asked for his help, and Immortal Lu always pointed to a stone with his finger, and turned it into gold for him. One day, the man, who had become very wealthy, met Lu again, and the latter turned an unusually large piece of stone into gold and gave it to him. The man said, "I am extremely grateful to you for helping me so often, and I have given you no end of inconvenience. I dare not ask you for help again. I would be satisfied if you give me one last thing." Immortal Lu said, "What do you want? Tell me and I shall give it to you." The man went up to the Immortal and chopped off his finger. "I only want this pointing finger which turns stone into gold," he said.'

Painted Flower said, 'That was funny, but it did not make us laugh out loud.'

'Well, I shall tell you another,' said Purple Mushroom. 'Once a rich man was travelling with his servant and felt hungry. They went into a restaurant to eat. When the bill was tendered, the rich man discovered that while he had eaten only two bowls of plain white rice, the servant had ordered himself a dish to go with it. The rich man paid, and the two left the restaurant and continued on their journey. The rich man became angrier and angrier, thinking about what had happened, and after a few steps, turned around and told his servant who was following behind, "I am your Master, not your horse (which goes into battle first to meet the enemy's arrows), why are you walking behind me?" The servant hurried to the front of his master, and they walked for a little while this way. Then the rich man said, "I am not your servant, why are you walking in front of me?" The servant backed up a few steps, and the two walked shoulder to shoulder for a while. Then the rich man said, "You and I are not equals. Why are you walking shoulder to shoulder with me?" The servant said, "What shall I do, then, if I am not to walk behind you, or ahead of you, or shoulder to shoulder with you?" The rich man said angrily, "Well, to tell you the truth, you'd better pay me back for that dish you ordered!" '

Soon, slave girls came to report that the Empress had delivered paper, and ordered the talented young ladies to compose a poem in praise of Governor Wen Yin's success in resisting the Nipponese invaders. The Empress had ordered Shangkuan Waner to compose forty verses of eighty lines each, five words to the line in praise of the occasion, and wanted the young ladies to write a verse each and have them delivered at the Palace in the morning.

The young ladies thought that they had all better go back and start work, so Precious Cloud ordered that the meal should be served quickly so that the guests could leave.

When the young ladies had delivered their poems in the morning, they came to the Pien residence again, and compared notes. After morning noodles, they strolled again in the garden under the willows and around the fish pond.

Purple Mushroom took a few of the young ladies to a long track where her father practised archery. It was a covered way, at the end of which the targets were set up.

'I suppose the canopy is to protect the track when it rains?' said Orchid.

240

'Yes,' said Fragrant Cloud. 'My father likes to practise archery when he has nothing to do. The covering is to prevent the feathers on the arrows from getting wet.'

The young ladies discovered that they all knew how to shoot with bows and arrows, and each had a few shots at the target to loosen their muscles.

Purple Mushroom said, 'People always say archery loosens the muscles, but my arms always ache afterwards, and my heart beats quickly. Is it because I use too much force in my left arm?'

Orchid said, 'When I was learning archery, I found this verse in *Hsi Chiang Yueh* which my father said were the rules which a person must follow in archery :

"The body must be straight, the breath must be deep,
Arms, shoulders and the centre of the head level.
Feet must be firmly planted."

'This means the body and face must face the target squarely. When drawing the bow, one must bend at the waist to allow the chest to relax, and exhale slowly. Otherwise, one is quickly out of breath. By arms, shoulders and the centre of the head being level, it is meant the end of the arrow must be against the mouth, and the bow must be held against the body, with the string against the right ear. If a person does not stand straight, and one shoulder is higher than the other, this position cannot be achieved. When drawing, one must pull the arrow back instead of pushing the bow forward, using equal strength in both hands, as though one were opening a pair of doors. If strength is used only in one arm, one cannot help looking like a teapot. When ready to shoot, one should pause, and then let go the entire hand which holds the arrow, and not just one finger.'

'When I was learning archery,' said Purple Mushroom, 'I remembered people saying that as long as the arrow is aimed at the target, it does not matter what the posture is. I remembered people saying, "The right arm should be as strong as if it were supporting a mountain, and the left arm as careful as though it were holding a baby." '

'That is where one often gets into trouble,' said Orchid. 'If one arm is supposed to be supporting a mountain and the other holding a baby, there is imbalance of weight. One shoulder is bound to be higher than the other, and the arrow will go off the mark. However, if you say, "One arm is blocking a mountain", then all is right. The arm will be straight, and the wrist and shoulders are level.'

Green Cloud said, 'Why is posture so important?'

'It is very important,' said Orchid. 'People practise archery for the exercise. It loosens the muscles and helps the circulation, and improves the appetite and the health. However, if no attention is paid to posture, instead of getting any benefit from archery, a person will get a backache and a stiff arm, and have chest pains and palpitations of the heart. If he tries to support a mountain as well, it is no wonder that he will suffer.'

When the slave girls served refreshments in the Peony Garden, Daughter of Tang said, 'I have heard my father say that there is an extraordinary mathematician in the Country of Scholars. When he visited the country, the mathematician and his daughter had come back to the Kingdom on Earth. This must be Orchid Fragrance. I have not had the opportunity to benefit from your wisdom.'

Orchid Fragrance said, 'I learned a few methods of calculation from my father, but I am not good at it. But if you would like to hear about it, I should be glad to tell you.'

Blue Ornament pointed to the round table which was in front of them and said, 'What is the circumference of this table?'

Orchid Fragrance asked for a ruler, and discovered that the diameter of the table was thirty-two inches. She drew a chart of calculation like this:

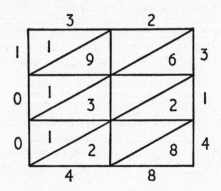

'The ancients in doing a multiplication problem drew a diagram like this, and put the figure to be multiplied on the top of the square, and the multiplying figure on the right-hand side of the square,' she said. 'The numbers are multiplied with each other, and the products written inside the square, the units in the bottom triangle of each rectangle, and the tens in the top triangle of each rectangle. The figures in each diagonal column are then added, and the sum written on the bottom and left-hand sides of the square. Reading down from the top of the left-hand side, one obtains the answer. The answer to this problem is 10048, or, the circumference of the table is 10.048 feet.' (One Chinese foot is ten inches.)

Spring Glory said, 'The circumference is usually three times the length of the diameter, isn't it?'

'It is roughly that. It is actually 3.14159265 times the size of the diameter, but it is accurate enough to multiply the diameter by 3.14.'

'If the area of this round table is made into a square table, how long would the sides be?' said Glorious Spring.

Orchid Fragrance said, 'Its sides would be twenty-two and a half inches long.'

Precious Cloud pointed to a set of gold cups on the table and said, 'There are nine cups of graduating sizes on this table. If 126 ounces of gold were used to make these cups, how much does the largest one weigh, and how much does the smallest one weigh?'

Orchid Fragrance said, 'I use the Method of Difference to calculate this. If 9 plus 1 make 10, and 9 times 10 are 90, half of 90 is 45. 126 divided by 45 is 2.8. This is the weight of the smallest cup.'

She told her slave girl to take the twice times multiplication table and the 8 times multiplication table out of her bag, and placed the twice times table over the 8 times table like this :

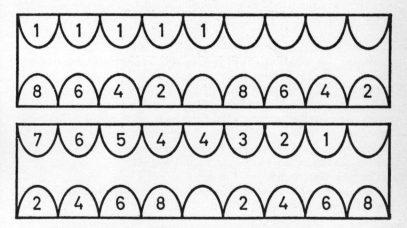

After calculating for a while, Orchid Fragrance wrote,

The largest cup weighs 25·2 ounces   The sixth cup weighs 11·2 ounces
The second cup weighs 22·4 ounces   The seventh cup weighs 8·4 ounces
The third cup weighs 19·6 ounces   The eighth cup weighs 5·6 ounces
The fourth cup weighs 16·8 ounces   The ninth cup weighs 2·8 ounces
The fifth cup weighs 14 ounces

'Isn't it an ordinary times table you used?' said Precious Cloud. 'How can you know how much each cup weighs just by a glance?'

Orchid Fragrance said, 'Just now I divided 126 by 45 and got 2.8. I therefore took the twice times table and the 8 times table, and placed the two directly over each other. If you read the figures of the first column on the left, you get the weight of the first, or largest cup, which is 252 (by adding the two middle figures. As 8 plus 7 make 15, the 1 is added to the 1 in the top semi-circle), and if you read the numbers in the first column on the right, you get the weight of the ninth, or smallest cup, which is 2.8.'

As Orchid Fragrance finished talking, it began to rain, and there was a clap of thunder. She said, 'I can tell how far away the thunder is.'

'How can you tell?' asked Moon Glory.

'Thunder travels at 1280 feet 7 inches a second,' said Orchid Fragrance. 'The thunderclap was ten *li* (11280 feet) away.'

'You are really too clever if you even know where thunder is,' said Completely Virtuous.

When it cleared up, Mistress Cheng had some tea served which had just been delivered by Precious Cloud's nursemaid's husband. Precious Cloud asked the man to come in and tell them the news from the south, where he had just come from. The man said, 'There was a big wind last year which blew the well in my courtyard clear out of the wall.'

'I have never heard of wind doing that,' said Green Cloud.

The man said, 'The wall which surrounds our house is made of bamboo. The wind blew it in toward the house, so it blew the well outside it. Why do you think I say this? Because although Miss Precious Cloud has been presented with riches and honour, I still have only a bamboo fence around my house . . . However, a person must not be bitter, and have bad thoughts or Father Thunder will strike him. In my village just now a man was struck dead by thunder. He was a man who had done no good in life.'

'How far away is your village?' said White Cloud.

'It is ten *li* from here,' said the man.

Everyone was astonished by the accuracy of Orchid Fragrance's calculation.

After refreshments, the young ladies played at guessing games based on quotations from the classics, and riddles. In the evening, they sat down to a banquet and played guessing games based on rhyming, with the girls having to drink up as forfeit. Some of the young ladies became drunk, and after they took turns in reciting Buddhist sutras, there came a gust of fresh wind from the pine forest, and the girls shivered.

Daughter of Tang said, 'I wonder where this sudden breeze comes from, which carries such a clear fragrance?'

'It smells like red cassia,' said Peaceful Blossom. 'I did not know that they are in bloom at this time of the year.'

'No, our perennial cassia have been given to the Palace in tribute,' said Precious Cloud. 'But this is an unusual fragrance. Can it be that the Cassia Spirit has come to earth to help me entertain my honoured guests?'

Slave girls came in and told Precious Cloud, 'There are two young ladies outside who say that they are Talented Ladies of the Fourth Rank (which is non-existent), and would like to come in and see whether the young ladies present are really superior to them. But if the young ladies do not want to show themselves up, they need not trouble to meet these two, and they will leave. The man Pien Shing did not dare send them away.'

Precious Cloud was silent.

Daughter of Tang said, 'Tell them to leave. Say that we passed our Examinations fairly and that it is late, so we shall not ask them to come in.'

'That would save us a lot of trouble,' said Flowerlike.

But Red Rose, Painted Flower, Spring Glory and Blue Ornament all said, 'NO! If we send them away it will seem as if we had something to hide. Why don't we let them come in and show them what we are worth?'

After some discussion it was decided to do this and the visitors were admitted. They entered hand-in-hand.

The older girl wore a blue robe, and the younger a white robe, and both were of extraordinary beauty and carried themselves in the manner of distinguished persons. The young ladies stood to greet them when they saw them, and were told that the one in blue had the surname Feng (Wind) and the one in white the surname Yueh (Moon). Precious Cloud asked them to sit down.

When the young ladies had told them their names, the girl in white said to Daughter of Tang, 'In the Imperial Examinations a composition was written on the subject "Angels Scattering Flowers" which was excellent. Unfortunately, it is kept in the Palace, so that we cannot enjoy it. Will you compose another prose-poem using the five words in the title as the rhyme?'

Daughter of Tang was astonished and said, 'How can I do this?'

The young lady in blue said, 'If you do not grant this wish, you will be hurting my friend's feelings and also spoiling the reputation of you Talented Ladies.'

Red Rose said, 'Daughter of Tang took the Imperial Examinations on orders from her father. Now she is in no mood to compose another prose-poem. If you will let me I shall do it for her, although I am not as gifted as she is.'

'No,' said the girl in white. 'We don't want to trouble you. It is Talented Lady Tang we want to trouble, since she was supposed to have come first during the Examinations, and we want to see what she can do. However, if she will not comply with our wishes, will she at least write one or two sentences for us?'

Daughter of Tang did not want to do it, but as everyone saw that there was nothing else she could do, she had writing materials brought, and sat down and began to think hard.

The lady in white said, 'If a girl is really gifted, she should not have to make a draft copy and should not have to make any corrections.'

Daughter of Tang gave this some thought, and after a while, took writing brush in hand. Her characters flew on paper as if they were dragons. The others were stunned by her performance, and when she finished it, she handed the paper to the visitors.

The young lady in white read it, and was extremely angry, for in it Daughter of Tang disparaged the Lady of the Moon.

In fact, the visitors were no other than the Lady of the Moon herself, who had quarrelled with the Fairy of a Hundred Flowers and thus plotted to have her sent to earth, in the hope that she would receive her punishment there, and Aunt Wind. When the Lady of the Moon heard that the Empress had conferred honours upon her, she was extremely upset, and together with Aunt Wind, decided to come as the girl in white and the girl in blue to cause trouble.

If the reader wants to know what kind of trouble they caused, please read the next chapter.

◀ 27 ▶

When the girl in white read Daughter of Tang's prose-poem, she cried, 'Your subject was on flowers, not the wind and the moon! It proves that the results of the Imperial Examination are absurd. It was lucky that the Empress made you the eleventh instead of the first in rank. That you were a successful candidate at all was due to the Empress's indulgence. Instead of being ashamed, you are showing off with this composition!'

Aunt Wind said, 'You say that flowers are not afraid of the wind. Are they made of copper stems and iron petals? They cannot stand a cool breeze, if you ask me.'

Before she finished talking, wind started up from four sides, and the young ladies were frightened and cold, and began to shiver.

In the midst of their predicament, there came from heaven a red beam of light which shone directly on the Frozen Jade Pavilion. When the light came near, out of it stepped an extremely beautiful maiden. The wind subsided when the red light appeared, and the young ladies were frightened. Purple Silk, Purple Jade, Purple Caltrop, Purple Cherry, Beautiful Hibiscus and Jade Moonlight took their swords from their scabbards and stood in readiness. The beautiful girl, who held a dipper and a writing brush in her hands, said to Aunt Wind and the Lady of the Moon, 'You are in charge of the wind and the moon. Why are you interfering in literary affairs? Is this behaviour becoming to the stars of heaven? I am in charge of the literary affairs of the talented girls. May I ask if you realise your mistake? If you do, leave here at once and we will save ourselves a lot of trouble. If not, you will bitterly regret it.'

The Lady of the Moon said, 'I am settling a private quarrel. What does it have to do with you?'

The beautiful girl was furious, and was going to answer back in no uncertain terms, when the slave girls announced, 'There is a Taoist nun outside who wishes to come in.'

Before the slave girls had finished talking, the nun was already inside, and made her greetings to the beautiful girl. Then she said to the Lady of the Moon and Aunt Wind, 'Please go back. These flower-spirits have almost served their terms on earth, and we shall

247

soon see each other again in heaven. You had your misunderstanding, but a great deal of time has passed since then. Why pursue it? From now on I hope that we shall be able to live peacefully together, and that you will forget past differences. If you cannot do that, can you not wait for the flower-spirits to return to their original forms before taking up the quarrel? I am afraid that the rest of the stars will not think well of you for rushing down here and carrying on like this.'

Aunt Wind nodded and said, 'Your treatise is quite correct, and I shall not argue with you. I only came because she wanted me to. I shall obey you and make my exit.'

The Lady of the Moon said, 'I quarrelled with her and had her sent to earth as a punishment. Instead since she arrived she has had a good time, and has travelled everywhere. I was not happy, so I came here to see her especially. However, since the Immortal has spoken, I shall forget the past, and never bring it up again. Heaven be witness if I go back on my word, I shall gladly be sent to earth myself!'

So saying, she and the girl in blue went away. The girl who had stepped out of the red light also disappeared.

The Taoist nun was also going to leave, but the talented girls now knew that she was an Immortal, and would not let her go. So the nun consented to sit down at table.

Precious Cloud said, 'May I ask the Immortal's name?'

The nun stretched out her two hands and said, 'This is my name.'

'You have such long fingers,' said Precious Cloud. 'Are you are the Fairy of Long Fingers?'

'I come from Long Finger Mountain,' said the nun.

'The girl with the writing brush I have seen before when I was abroad with Daughter of Tang,' said Flowerlike. 'When we came back we had a likeness of her installed in a nunnery. She must have been the Star of Literature. May I ask who those persons in white and blue were?'

'Consider their names and you will know,' said the nun.

Daughter of Tang respectfully toasted the nun with a cup of vegetarian wine, and offered her some fruit, Purple Mushroom whispered to the young ladies, 'This is a nun of unusual origin. She must be clairvoyant. Why don't we ask her about the future?'

The young ladies thought it was a good idea, and asked the nun to tell them a thing or two about their future.

'Although I know a little about fortune-telling,' said the nun, 'there are a hundred of you. How can I hope to do it all?'

'Can you tell us about things generally?' said Daughter of Tang.

The nun said, 'When I was overseas, I saw a long poem, which seemed to have some connection with you talented girls. If you will not be bored, I should like to recite it to you.'

'That would be wonderful,' said Daughter of Tang, 'and we can ask you questions if we do not understand.'

'The poem is indeed long, and cryptic,' said the nun. 'You must pay close attention.'

'If it is so, why don't we write it down?' said Daughter of Tang.

The Taoist nun nodded and said, 'I shall recite it and try to explain as much of the meaning as I can.' Turning to Painted Flower, she said, 'Is your name not Painted Flower? Since I understand that this poem was composed to paint a picture of the flowers, why don't you write it down?'

Everyone was astonished by the nun's words.

The nun proceeded to recite the poem, and Painted Flower wrote it down. Cryptic as the poem was, the nun and the young ladies stopped often to decipher the lines' meaning. As line after line was explained, it became clear that the future boded no good for many of the young ladies. Much tragedy would befall many of them. Many of them would die of broken bones and mortal wounds, and others would commit suicide.

The girls were aghast, and many of them trembled and shed tears as their names were revealed in the poem.

'Oh, the worst is yet to come,' said the nun. 'There are others of you who will be pierced by arrows, and your bodies spattered all over the ground.'

Little Spring, Pleasant and Blue Ornament cried and said, 'How tragic this is! We cannot bear to think that it will happen to any of us!'

'Many of you will be widows,' said the nun.

Jade Mushroom said, 'From what you have said, it seems that the couplet inscribed on the jade tablet about hard luck accompanying us is quite right!'

'Is it because we have done some great wrong that so many of us will not meet with a happy end?' said Little Spring.

'If you had done some great wrong, would your names be passed down to posterity, carved on the jade tablet?' said the nun.

'Then what is the reason for our having such sad destinies?' said Little Spring.

'It depends on how you look at it,' said the nun. 'If you think that suffering physical injury is a tragedy, then it is sad. But if in the pursuit of a worthwhile cause, a person does not consider his life, then he has also reduced the importance of death.'

'There are many good people on earth who meet with sad ends, and many bad people who enjoy a long life. Why is this?'

'It is because good men often sacrifice themselves for a purpose, while bad men think only of themselves, and will yield to circumstances,' said the nun. 'In life, as long as a person's purpose is clearly defined, and the values of life and death are in their proper places, his good name will be passed on to posterity (although he lives but a short life). Even if a man lives to be a hundred, he cannot avoid death. When the time comes, is it not better to die with a smile, rather than be greedy for life? When I say, "die with a smile" I mean, there are several of you who must choose to do so. But the affairs of life are hard to define, and a person can only understand them when things actually happen to him.'

When the nun finally left, Jade Mushroom said, 'Her words have upset me. However, when she said that some of our names would be passed on to posterity, it made me think. Perhaps I would rather die with honour, and have my name live for generations afterwards!'

'No, I would rather live as long as I can, and I don't care what kind of reputation I leave after I die!' said Fragrance Returns. 'If you asked me to seek death in order to leave a fair name to posterity, I would not do it.'

Completely Virtuous and Fragrant Grass agreed with her. 'Wouldn't it be crazy to give up happiness on earth for an empty name in death!' they said.

The girls remembered that they had not finished their games with wine when they were interrupted by the visitors, and went on with it. When at last the party was over, Jade Mushroom said, 'I would like to know what is the best remedy for a hangover, since we have drunk so much wine today?'

Beautiful Spring said,

'Take 8 *chien* of *ligusticum acutilobum* (sometimes called *eumenol*, or *angelica polymorpha* of the *Umbelliferae* family)
  3 *chien* of Hemlock parsley (*conioselinum univattatum*)
  3 *chien* of Lion's tail (Siberian motherwort, or *Labiatae sibiricus*)
  1 *chien* of liquorice
  5 *fen* ash of ginger
  10   peach stones (ground into powder)
  1   bowl of water
  1   bowl of rice wine,
and simmer until liquid is reduced to one bowl, and take the brew warm.'

When it was almost dawn, the young ladies at last thanked their hostesses and departed.

The next day, the young ladies of the Chiang, Tung, Chang and Lu families also borrowed the Frozen Jade Pavilion to give a party, and the day after that Daughter of Tang, Flowerlike and Quest-for-

Seclusion returned the dinners at the same place, which was followed by farewell parties for the departing girls. When the painting was finished, and several thousand verses had been inscribed in it by the young ladies, it was a work of four volumes, and called 'Memento on Leaving Chang-an'. The existence of such a work became known to all in the Kingdom, and the Empress and the Princess also contributed prose-poems to it.

Finally, the day of departure came for Flowerlike, Melody Orchid, Red Rose and Purple Lily. After saying goodbye to the examining officials, the four young ladies returned to the Feminine Literary Inn to find that emissaries from the Ministry of Rituals and Examinations had come from the Empress to summon them for an audience.

The four young ladies prepared incense altars to receive the summonses, and then made themselves ready and went to the Palace to thank the Empress. The 'Royal Uncle' had also received the Empress's Summons, and returned from the Palace with the young ladies.

Because the 'Royal Uncle' was actually a woman in man's clothing, she met the hundred young ladies and sat down to a wine banquet with them.

When the banquet was over, the three flying carriages were already waiting in the courtyard, facing the west. Each carriage was about as high as half a man, and four feet long and two feet wide, woven from willow branches, and therefore very light, and covered on the outside with shark's skin. There were compasses in all four directions of the cabin, and a little wooden rudder at the back rather like that of a ship. The wheels of the carriage were made of brass, and of various sizes, the large ones as big as basins, and the little ones like winecups. There were several hundred wheels, very thin but very strong.

It was decided that the 'Royal Uncle' and Flowerlike would ride in the first carriage, Red Rose and Purple Lily in the second, and Melody Orchid and the servants in the third. The 'Royal Uncle' handed the keys to the servants and to the three young ladies and said, 'One key is for starting the carriage. The second is to make it go up, and the third key is to make it come down. They are clearly marked. If you want the carriage to turn right, steer the handle to the left, and if you want the carriage to turn left, turn the handle to the right. Follow close behind me, and you will not make a mistake. There is a small sail made of shark's skin in front of the carriage, and if we meet a fair wind, we will hoist it, and it will help us to travel.'

Then the 'Royal Uncle' got into the first carriage.

Tears fell like rain from the eyes of Flowerlike, and the three young ladies who were leaving. The other young ladies joined in the crying, too.

Purple Lily told Daughter of Tang, 'I sent a letter to my mother, telling her where I am going but I don't know when she will receive it. Please tell her not to worry when you return to Lingnan. When I arrive in the Country of Women, I shall ask Flowerlike to appoint someone to come with me when the time comes to send for her. Please look after her for me, and accept my eternal gratitude!'

So saying, she knelt down and wailed and kowtowed without stop, and collapsed on the ground. Daughter of Tang thought of her parent, who was in the faraway mountains, and wept tears of sorrow, and knelt down and wailed also. The 'Royal Uncle' tried to hurry them into the carriages. Finally, Pleasant and Little Spring, themselves in tears, helped the two up from the ground, and Purple Lily, dazed with sorrow, fainted again several times. But the emissaries from the Palace who had come to witness their departure were waiting, and Old Tuo did not want them to exceed their time limit in the Kingdom on Earth. He told the slave girls to help Purple Lily and Red Rose into the flying carriage, and Flowerlike and Melody Orchid also got in sadly.

Soon, the carriages were in motion. The copper wheels, both horizontal and vertical, moved very fast, some in an up-and-down motion, and the carriages began to spin like a pinwheel, and lifted from the ground. They went straight up in the air for about a hundred feet, then headed west. After they were out of sight, the young ladies returned sadly indoors.

After a few days, the young ladies all prepared to leave the capital. Daughter of Tang, Pleasant, Little Spring, Phoenix-in-Flight, Red Lotus, Flowering Maple, Wise Maxim and Purple Silk returned to Lingnan together. Beautiful Hibiscus, Marsh Orchid, Fragrant Book, Fragrant Ink and Little Canary went back to Huainan. Scarlet Dogwood, Purple Cherry, Sweet Asarum and Fragrant Angelica all returned to their homes, too, and the talented young ladies were scattered in four directions.

After leaving Chang-an in the flying carriages, Flowerlike and her party met unfavourable winds, and did not arrive in the Country of Women until ten days later. When she arrived, her 'father' the 'King' had already died, out of longing for her and the sorrow of losing 'his' second 'son'. The officials at Court immediately made Flowerlike 'King', and Melody Orchid, Red Rose and Purple Lily became her Ministers. When this was established, Purple Lily returned with the Ministers of the Country of Women to the Kingdom on Earth to thank the Empress, and took the opportunity to go to Lingnan and take her mother Mistress Tsu back with her to the Country of Women.

Mistress Lin was delighted when Daughter of Tang and the other young ladies returned, and ordered a great celebration banquet to welcome them back. Daughter of Tang found that during her absence, Little Summit and Brilliant had both abandoned their studies and taken up the art of war. Tang Min asked Old Tuo to sit down with the boys' tutors, and after the dinner, Pleasant, Little Spring and Phoenix-in-Flight took leave of Mistress Lin and returned with Old Tuo to his home.

Upon returning to Hundred Fragrances Crossroads, Purple Silk discovered that her grandmother had died, and hurriedly, she and her brother Cliff (who had come back from the War Examinations) left to escort her body back to their birthplace for burial. Wise Maxim and Mistress Chi stayed on in Daughter of Tang's home, and the Lien family, Mistress Liang, Flowering Maple and Brilliant, lived in the new house. Red Lotus, Wise Maxim and Daughter of Tang shared a room upstairs.

The day after she returned, Daughter of Tang told her mother that she wanted to find her father in Little Penglai, but Mistress Lin said, 'I know that you are anxious to go, but Red Lotus is of age now, and she and Little Summit should be married in the autumn. Can you wait until they are married before you go?'

Daughter of Tang had to comply. A month after Red Lotus was married to Little Summit, Yin Yuan sent for Brilliant and Flowering Maple to be married to Scarlet Dogwood and her brother Jade, and they left with Mistress Liang.

Then Pleasant was engaged to Ting Courtier, Phoenix-in-Flight's brother, and Merchant Lin had to wait until Courtier's father returned in retirement from his post as Commander-in-Chief in Shannan before he could leave.

Many people also sent matchmakers to ask for the hand of Daughter of Tang, but Mistress Lin and she both felt that they should wait for Tang Ao to return before making any decision, and turned the matchmakers away.

In April of the following year, Pleasant was at last married. Now Young Lo sent for Wise Maxim to be married in the fortress at Little Yingchow Mountain. Mistress Lin prepared a dowry for Wise Maxim, and Mistress Chi went with her.

At last in July, Daughter of Tang and Merchant Lin were free to set out for overseas to find Tang Ao.

The evening before her departure, Daughter of Tang was packing in her room upstairs when there was a sudden noise and a red light, and Purple Silk appeared in the room.

Daughter of Tang quickly asked her to sit down and said, 'I knew that you had gone home to your birthplace with your grandmothers' remains. I did not know that you had already come back.'

Purple Silk said, 'When I learned that you were going overseas, I hurried back first to bid you farewell, and also because I have something to discuss with you. Now that Pleasant is married, it will be lonely for you on the journey. I wonder if I could come with you, since there is no one to tie me down here any more?'

Daughter of Tang was delighted by the suggestion, but she had a few considerations which she could not very well tell Purple Silk. She hesitated and said, 'I should like you to come very much, but if I fail to find my father, or if he refuses to come back, I would have to stay overseas, and don't know when I shall be coming back.'

'I see it this way,' said Purple Silk. 'From a mortal point of view, of course you should find your father and bring him back to be reunited with your family. But after you are reunited, what of it? In a few decades, will all not be returned to nothing? For who can escape death? If I come with you, I would not mind not coming back if your father does not wish to. Perhaps I, too, shall be able to escape the mortal coil in the bitter sea of transmigration.'

Daughter of Tang thought to herself, 'She really understands.' To Purple Silk she said, 'If you feel this way, we are of one heart. Please come tomorrow so that we may go together.'

Purple Silk agreed, and disappeared.

The next morning, she returned with her baggage. Mistress Lin was glad to have a companion for Daughter of Tang on her journey.

Daughter of Tang bade farewell to the spirits of her ancestors, and said goodbye to her mother, uncle and aunt. She told Little Summit, 'You are already a grown man, and I don't have to repeat to you what your duties are. In a word, be a filial son and a loyal subject. If you remember this, and do nothing which you need be ashamed of, you will be all right.'

She knelt down in front of Red Lotus, who hurried down on her knees as well, saying, 'How dare I?'

Daughter of Tang said, 'You are a filial daughter who avenged your mother, and took care of your grandfather in his old age. Now I am going far away, and I leave the care of my mother to you. Please allow me to thank you.'

They both got up in tears. After Mistress Lin cautioned her daughter to take care of herself again and again, Daughter of Tang, Purple Silk and their nursemaids left for Merchant Lin's home.

Pleasant and Phoenix-in-Flight had come to see them off. Old Tuo was not going overseas this time because he was feeling tired, and Little Spring had not come because she was unwell.

Merchant Lin had bought some merchandise to take overseas, and leaving his mother-in-law Mistress Chiang in charge of his house, took leave of those at home, and together with Mistress Lu, their young son, Daughter of Tang and Purple Silk, went on board the sea-going junk, and set sail for Little Penglai.

Lin sold some goods on the way, but did not dare to tarry at any place for long. In April of the following year, they arrived in Little Penglai. Daughter of Tang and Purple Silk alighted from the ship, and went into the mountains to look for Tang Ao. Merchant Lin waited for two months, and when they failed to return by then, became very anxious, and went to look for them every day in the mountains, but could not find them.

A month later, one day in the mountains, he saw a little Taoist nun picking flowers. The girl handed two letters to him and said, 'These are letters which the Taoist Immortals Tang and Yen want to send home.'

As Lin read the letters, the girl disappeared, and in front of him stood a green-faced fox-toothed ogre who let out a terrible screech. Lin cried, 'Oh!' and ran down the mountain, with the ogre in hot pursuit. When he reached the junk he ordered the sailors to fire, but the ogre took no notice of the firing, and kept on roaring and tried to leap on board. The sailors cast off immediately.

Lin was frightened and exhausted after searching for the girls in the mountains for so long, and was feverish and ill all the way back. When the junk arrived in Lingnan in March of the following year, he was still convalescing. He gave the two letters from Daughter of Tang and Purple Silk to his wife to give to Mistress Lin.

Mistress Lin knew after she had read her daughter's letter that the latter had given up the vanities of the world, and would not return. She gave Purple Silk's letter to her brother Cliff (who had married Little Spring), and Cliff learned the same thing about Purple Silk. In the letter, Purple Silk told him to go to Little Yingchow and find Young Lo in the mountain fortress, and join him in the mission of restoring the Emperor to the throne.

Cliff asked Pleasant's husband Courtier to go with him, and sent word to Little Summit to go also.

On the way to Little Yingchow, the three young men met Brilliant, Yin Jade, Wei Warrior and Hsueh Select, and went on together with them.

When they arrived at the foot of Little Yingchow Mountain, Cliff handed his sister's letter to a soldier. Shih Narrator, Young Lo, and the White Prince came to meet them, and after exchanging names, Cliff told them about what had happened to Daughter of Tang and Purple Silk.

Narrator was extremely impressed by the seven newcomers, for they were as fierce-looking as tigers, and took them into the mountain fortress, with a soldier leading the way.

If the reader would like to know what happened when they reached the fortress, please turn to the next chapter.

When the seven newcomers arrived at the hideout in the mountains, two husky fellows came out to meet them. One had a big, golden face, and the other a craggy, red one. Both were wearing tiger skins on their backs, and bearskins around their waists, and were extremely impressive to look at.

Young Lo said, 'This is the son of the Minister of Rituals and Examinations, Pien Pin's son Badge. And this is the brother of Purple Jade, Courage.'

The newcomers learned that Narrator had married Silver Moonlight, and Courage was married to Jade Moonlight. The White Prince had married Purple Jade, but Badge was not yet married. Young Lo and Wise Maxim were married, and the families were living in the back of the camp. The newcomers were told that they should also send for their wives.

Narrator ordered a banquet, and the twelve young stalwarts sat down at table according to their age. After several cups of wine, Cliff said, 'Why hasn't Brother Pien followed his father's footsteps in taking up an official career at the capital? How many years have you been here?'

Badge said, sighing, 'It is a long story. When I was three years old, I suffered from convulsions, and my family took me for dead. A Taoist beggar happened to come by, and took me away and cured me.'

'Who was this Taoist who could do this extraordinary thing?' said Brilliant. 'Is he an immortal?'

'No, he was not really a Taoist,' said Badge, 'but a scholar who had failed in the Imperial Examinations, and was stranded in the capital. My father was impressed by his learning, and made him a keeper of books and documents at home. When his father died, my father also helped him with the burial. The man was very grateful. When I became sick, he knew a remedy to cure me, but because my parents had already lost another boy at the age of three through convulsions, he dared not tell them what the remedy was, for fear it would not work, for they had turned it down once before. So he found a Taoist, and by this ruse, took me out of the house.

When I was cured, the man left my father's home, and took me to Lung-yu, where I stayed for many years.'

Select said, 'Who was he, and when he cured you, why did he not take you back home?'

'His name is Shih Victory, and he was a physician, but because he could not cure his mother's illness, he swore not to practise again. When he cured me in order to repay my father for his kindness to him, there was a very good reason why he did not return me to my father.'

'What reason was that?' said Courtier.

'His reason was that he believed a child gets convulsions because of overheating, or excessive cold, or because of exposure to the wind, or from food which does not agree with him, but a rich man's son suffers from convulsions often because he is overprotected, and so has no resistance to the assaults of heat and cold. He did not want me to go home for fear that I should fall sick again. Instead, he took me to his own home, and trained me in riding and in the art of war. He treated me like his own son, and as luck had it, things began to go well for him. He cultivated land and harvested crops where the land had been arid and barren before, and his family enjoyed a change of fortune. When he heard that Brothers Shih and Lo were here, he brought me here three years ago.'

Warrior said, 'What remedy did he give you and is it an infallible cure?'

'Epileptic convulsions are not easy to cure,' said Badge, 'and have taken the lives of many children. Most doctors do not ask what causes them, and prescribe the same medicine, with the result that the child often becomes an idiot or a useless person. But there is a remedy which cures convulsions, and that is to take a live scorpion and wrap it up in four peppermint leaves, and roast it over a fire until it is burnt crisp. Grind it into powder, and mix it with hot water and drink it. The scorpion regulates the circulation of the twelfth pulse. If a live scorpion cannot be had, a preserved one can be used if the salt (used as preservative) is washed away, but it is not as good as a live one. I had several dozen live scorpions, and took medical tea to disperse the fever in my system, and was cured.'

The newcomers soon joined the others in the fortress in horseback riding and practising swordsmanship as their daily routine. Select practised on his repeating rifle, and perfected this art of war. After some time had passed, the seven young men returned to Lingnan secretly, and brought their wives to the fortress.

When a year had passed, Young Lo wanted to go to Huainan to see the sons of the Wen family and find out if there were any plans for starting the rebellion.

But Narrator said, 'I remember the sons of the Wen family told us that we should not risk going to Huainan for fear of discovery. When the time comes to rise in arms, they will send Brother Shu with news.'

As he was speaking, Young Shu himself arrived.

'After Uncle Wen pacified the Nipponese invaders, he stayed on in Chien-nan until the Talented Ladies returned from the capital, and ordered his five sons to be married,' said Young Shu. 'Soon afterward, he became ill and died. Luckily, the Empress remembered that Honeybush performed the duties of Governor well in his father's absence, and made him Governor. The period of mourning was over last year. Now the light of the Heart-Moon Fox is diminishing, and it is time to strike. I have come secretly to tell you that on the third day of March next year, we shall rise in arms and defeat the Wu brothers who guard the Passes to the capital.'

'What are these four Passes called?' said Brilliant.

'To the north is the Water Pass, and to the west the Knife Pass,' said Young Shu. 'To the east is the Treasure Pass, and to the south the No-fire Pass.'

'Which of these is easiest to break into, and which is the hardest?' said Select.

'The Water and the No-fire Passes are the easier ones, and the Knife Pass is the hardest,' said Young Shu. 'I have been sent here by the Wen brothers also to discuss the tactics for breaking the Passes with you. Then I must go to Hotung to meet the ten brothers of the Chang family.'

'Why are you not planning to discuss matters with Uncle Chang?' said Young Lo.

'Governor Chang died three years ago. Now Prince's Feather, the eldest son, has assumed the Governor's post,' said Young Shu.

'Which Pass should we attack first, according to the Wen brothers?' said the White Prince.

'Some people think that we should attack the hardest first, but Honeybush thinks that we should go for the two easier ones first. Once we have two of the four Passes, the enemy will suffer a blow to their morale, and the remaining two should be less hard to attack.'

The young men thought that this was right, and they should attack the Water and No-fire Passes first.

After a while, Young Shu left, saying, 'I cannot delay. I must go to Hotung to inform them of the news, and then return to the Wen family.'

'Where shall we meet when the time comes?' said Badge.

Young Shu said, 'If we attack the southern and northern Passes first, we shall meet at the Water Pass. When the time is near, further news will be sent to you. The Wen brothers say that we must take our families with us in the attack, for if we suffer defeat, we would not want them to be tortured at the hands of the Wu brothers, and it is better to go down in battle together.'

Young Shu then left, and told the ten brothers of the Chang family the news, and returned to report to the Wen brothers in Huainan. He had married Marsh Orchid, and Fragrant Book and Fragrant Ink were also married. But Beautiful Hibiscus was not yet married because she had been hiding in the Wen residence. Young Shu therefore made a match between his sister and Badge, and Beautiful Hibiscus went to Little Yingchow to be married.

After the New Year, Wen Honeybush, Chang Prince's Feather and Shih Narrator sent messages to each other again, and agreed on the time of meeting at the Water Pass.

At the time agreed upon, the armies from Huainan and Hotung marched toward the capital with the Imperial flag of the House of Tang aloft, and Shih Narrator led his men out of the fortress in Little Yingchow.

On the third day of March, two hundred thousand men and horses were on the roads. Five *li* from the Water Pass, three cannon shots were fired as the signal, and the men stopped and encamped.

In the big camp there were the Wen brothers, Honeybush, Sedge, Shepherd's Purse, Cabbage and Senega; the Chang brothers, Prince's Feather, Mushroom, Asarum, Basil, Wildhop, Hibiscus, Bignonia, Parsley, Fragrant Weed and Artemisia. There were also Narrator, Courage, the White Prince, Cliff, Courtier, Warrior, Select, Jade, Brilliant, Little Summit, Young Shu and Young Lo. There were the husbands of the Wen family's daughters Fragrant Book and Fragrant Ink, Lin Hero and Yang Elegant, and the husbands of the Chang family's daughters : Fragrant Orchid's husband Tsai Noble, Fragrant Marsh Orchid's husband Tan Ultimate, Fragrant Jade's husband Yeh Ocean, and Fragrant Moon's husband Tsu Tide, thirty-four young men in all.

In the women's camp were Mistress Chang, the mother of the Wen boys, Mistress Hsui and Mistress Liu, the mothers of the Chang boys, Courage's mother Mistress Yeh, Little Summit's mother Mistress Lin, Brilliant's mother Mistress Liang, Warrior's mother Mistress Wan, Select's mother Mistress Hsuen, eight ladies of the older generation. The young wives were Virtuous Orchid, Red Feather, Red Jade, Fair Heroine, Peaceful Blossom, Noble Jade, High Spring, Melting Spring, Glorious Spring, Fragrant Spring, Brocade Spring, Complaisant Spring, Luxurious Spring, Graceful Spring, Beautiful Spring and Fair Spring, and Fragrant Book, Fragrant Ink, Fragrant Orchid, Fragrant Marsh Orchid, Fragrant Moon, Silver Moonlight, Wise Maxim, Beautiful Hibiscus, Jade Moonlight, Purple Jade, Little Spring, Pleasant, Sweet Asarum, Purple Cherry, Flowering Maple, Scarlet Dogwood, Red Lotus, and Marsh Orchid.

At first, it was thought that the rebels should bring Emperor Chung Tsung to camp, but the Empress had ordered him back to the Eastern Palace (from Fangchow, so it was not possible). As White Prince was a cousin of the Emperor, he was made Commander-in-Chief of the rebel army.

To accomplish their purpose, Honeybush, Prince's Feather and Narrator decided that they should attack both from outside the capital, and within the Palace itself. At the Palace, there were six officials whom they could trust, Chang Chien-chih, Heng Yen-fan, Li Tuo-hsiang, Yuan Shi-yi, Hsueh Sze-hsing and Tsui Yuan-wei. Messages were sent to them, telling them to go to the Eastern Palace and be prepared for an emergency. Of the Emperor's ministers, Chang Yi-chih, Chang Chang-tsung and Chang Chang-chi were the most hated by the people, for they had no scruples and killed without discrimination, and there was not an evil which they did not commit.

The news that the army for the Emperor was on the march was reported to Wu Number Four, who ordered his General Mao Meng to gather his armies at the Water Pass. If the reader wants to know what happened next, please read the following chapter.

◀ *29* ▶

The Empress's brother Wu Number Four ordered General Mao Meng to gather his armies at the Water Pass when he heard that the Emperor's men were on the march. The next day, Honeybush, Prince's Feather and Narrator led their men on horseback and advanced toward the Pass.

Wu Number Four sent a column of men out of the Pass to meet them. Senega galloped forward to challenge the enemy in battle, and Mao Meng came forward to meet him. After several rounds of fighting, Senega used the 'find the snake in the grass' strategy, and thrust his silver lance into Mao Meng's body. With an outcry, Mao Meng fell from his horse, his stomach pierced by the lance. Honeybush, Prince's Feather and Narrator hurried up behind Senega, and engaged the rest of the Empress's men in battle.

When Wu Number Four saw this, he himself came out of the Water Pass and bellowed, 'Wen Honeybush and Chang Prince's Feather! I have cast a spell over this Pass! If you can break the spell, I shall surrender the Pass to you! If you are afraid and dare not advance, I shall lay down my sword, and as an act of charity, let you through!'

Senega cried, 'Stop boasting, you old dog! Watch us break your dog spell!' He whipped his horse and started to gallop into the spell-bound area, but Honeybush cried, 'Fifth brother, wait! It is already late! Let us take care of the old dog tomorrow!'

He ordered the bugle to be sounded for retreat, and the men returned to camp.

'Number Four suffered great loss of men today, and his morale has suffered. I was going to conquer the spell when the going was good. Why did you stop me?' said Senega.

'I don't know what kind of magic spell he has cast before the Pass,' said Honeybush. 'We must not go in lightly. There is no hurry.'

'If we don't break the spell, how can we get to the Pass?' said Senega. 'I am going through tomorrow.'

The next day, Wu Number Four was at the head of his army again, and shouting, 'Who dares to come through the spell!'

Honeybush said, 'Wu Number Four! We had a spell too, the coiled-snake spell! Will you come and break it?'

'If I come into your spell, how do I know that hidden swords will not come down at me?' answered Wu Number Four.

'Then why do you keep telling us to go into yours?' said Honeybush.

'Because I promise you, once you are in it, not a hair on your bodies will be harmed,' cried Number Four. 'If I go back on my word, may I die under arrows and swords!'

Senega said, 'Since the old dog has so sworn, let me go ahead and see,' and urged his horse forward.

Wu Number Four had already disappeared. When Senega entered the spell-bound area, he could see only willows and clouds, and green mountains and streams. The earth was covered with verdant grass, and fine steeds neighed proudly all around. He alighted from his horse, and almost forgetting that he had come to battle, took the reins in his hand, and walked on.

There was a bamboo forest beside the road, and seven men who wore the costumes of the Chin Dynasty were having a little wine feast there. The aroma of the wine was very fragrant, and Senega inhaled it deeply. After a moment, a young man in white said, 'How is it that I feel a vulgar presence? Can it be that some vulgar person is nearby?'

Senega knew that they were referring to him, and wanted to answer back, but as these seven men did not seem to have a care in the world, he said as he walked on, 'These men must be frustrated scholars, they are so supercilious. If I start to argue with them, there will be no end of words! Let them say what they like!'

Soon, he was assailed by another wine-smelling gust of air. Covering his nose, he said, 'Where does this stinking smell come from?' and saw a pack of drunken cats advancing towards him, walking unsteadily and shaking their heads and sticking out their front paws. 'Come, come, come! Let us play three rounds of finger-guessing games before we let you go!' the cats said to him.

Senega smiled and said, 'Drunken cats! Dead drunk, from only a few cups of wine! It doesn't take much for them to show their worst qualities!'

He raised his lance, and flourishing it to the right and left, made the drunken cats scatter in four directions.

After walking some distance, Senega came upon a wine shop on the roadside with the banners flying high. The bouquet of fragrant wine was overflowing the shop. When he smelled it, his throat began to itch, and he walked toward the shop. There were many people there, some drinking alone, and others in a crowd, and everyone looked at least thirty-per-cent intoxicated. Senega sat down at a table amid the pungent aroma.

The shopkeeper came up to him smiling and said, 'What would you like to drink?'

Senega said, 'I want the best wine in the world. Do you have it?'

'Yes, indeed,' said the shopkeeper, and took the blackboard from his counter, and showed it to his guest, bowing from the waist and saying, 'We have wine from every different place, and better wine than you will find anywhere. After you have tasted our wine, you will want to come back often.'

'Do you sell on credit?' said Senega.

'Of course!' said the man. 'As long as you favour us with your patronage, we are in no hurry to settle accounts!'

Senega therefore took the blackboard and read:

> Distilled wine of Shansi
> Pei wine of Kiang-nan
> Cooked wine of Tsaochow
> Heng wine of Hunan
> Rice wine of Jaochow
> Chia wine of Huichow
> Forced wine of Shenshi
> Hsin wine of Huchow
> Tsa wine of Pahsien
> Miao wine of Kweichow
> Yao wine of Kuanghsi
> Dry wine of Kansu
> Shaoshing wine of Chekiang
> Hundred Flowers wine of Chen-chiang
> Quince wine of Yangchow
> Orchid Stream wine of Wuhsi
> Belssings wine of Suchow
> Three White wine of Hangchow
> Tunglu wine of Chihli
> Famous wine of Weihuei
> Bitter Dew wine of Hochow
> Drip Drop wine of Taming
> Golden Waves wine of Chining
> Parcel wine of Yunan
> Lu River wine of Szechuan
> Grain of Paradise wine of Hunan
> Hen River wine of Chichow
> Fragrant Snow wine of Haining
> Longevity wine of Huainan
> Curcuma wine of Chapu
> Peppery Yellow wine of Haichow
> Lamb's wine of Luancheng
> Persimmon wine of Honan
> Seasoned wine of Taochow
> Fragrant Huan wine of Fukien
> Burnt Rice wine of Mouchow

Lu An wine of Shanshi
Five Poisons wine of Chengtu
Old Cask wine of Shanyang
Double Pepper wine of Chingho
Maiden's wine of Shaoshing
White Double Brew of the Liuchiu Islands
Drip wine of Kueichu
Snow wine of Nantungchow
December Snow wine of Kashing
Grass Nectar wine of Yencheng
Grain wine of Shantung
Top of the Cask Spring wine of Kuangtung
Milin Double Brew of the Liuchiu Islands
Spring on Tungting Lake wine of Changsha
Longevity wine of Taiping Fu

As he read the names of the wines and smelled the fragrance of
the wineshop, Senega's mouth began to water. He said, 'I want to
try every kind. Please first bring a pot of each of the first ten kinds.'

The shopkeeper soon placed ten pots of wine and some appetizers
on the table, and ten winecups.

Senega thought, 'Can this wine be poisoned?' and sniffed it,
but the bouquet was irresistible. Taking up the first cup, he placed
it to his lips, and suddenly shook his head. 'No, no! I must not! I
must not!' he said, but even as he said so, he was swallowing half
of the contents of the cup. When he had swallowed half the contents of each cup, he said, 'It is beautiful wine! But I like old
wine best, and these are new wines. I shall slip out of here and see if
I can find something stronger to quench my thirst.'

So he took his lance and left. He did not have long to walk before
he found another shop. In front of it there was a scholar who held a
winepot in one hand and his clothes in another, and was asking an
old man on the street to give him some money for his clothes so
that he could buy a pot of wine. The clothes he held were of silk
and lavishly embroidered.

The old man said to Senega, 'This robe is made of the feathers of
kingfishers. The scholar you saw was Szema (Hsiangju), a great
scholar, but he loves to drink, and he has no money, so he has sold
his clothes for a pot of wine.'

Senega walked into the shop, and the shopkeeper said, 'Do you
like old wine or new wine? We have no new wine.'

'If I did not like old wine, would I come in here?' said Senega,
'How many kinds of wine do you have?'

'We have many kinds,' said the shopkeeper. 'But do you like wine
brewed by famous vintners of the past, or do you like the wines of
different famous districts?'

Senega said, 'I like the latter.'

The shopkeeper showed him his board, and Senega saw about a hundred kinds of famous wine listed. He said, 'I would like to have a bowl of each. If it is good, I shall patronize your shop again. Can you extend credit?'

'I am sorry I cannot,' said the man. 'You saw that man selling his kingfisher's coat for cash in order to buy wine.'

Senega took his sword from his body and said, 'Will you take this sword as a pledge? I should like to have a bowl of each kind of wine you have on the board. Bring thirty bowls first to quench my thirst, and serve the rest in the same manner, but more slowly, and keep it coming. If the wine is to my liking, I shall reward you handsomely after I have finished.'

The shopkeeper took the sword and went away. Soon he came back with thirty bowls of wine, whose aroma wafted into Senega's nostrils in a heady stream. It was as though from his throat there had grown a little hand, which came out of his mouth and grabbed the wine bowls one after another. He could not stop himself, and thought, 'Wu Number Four, even if you have put poison in this wine, I don't care!'

In the twinkling of an eye, he had finished the thirty bowls. Smacking his lips, he said, 'I did not know that such great wines existed. I don't blame that Mr Szema for exchanging his robe of kingfishers' feathers for it! I know wine is not good for a person, but my mouth will not obey me. I suppose I shall have to surrender my life for it. I must not drink too much, I must remember, I must remember. It is important, important!'

As he was talking to himself, the shopkeeper said, 'How many more bowls do you want?'

Senega thought to himself, 'What the hell! I shall abstain to-morrow!' and said, 'I have already told you! Why do you ask?'

The shopkeeper therefore put thirty more bowls on the table, and Senega finished them at a stretch. Soon, he had had a bowl of every kind of wine on the board, and heaven and earth were spinning around him.

Standing up, he took his silver lance and walked out of the shop. A few steps later, he fell on the ground unconscious.

Honeybush and the others waited for a long time outside, and when they did not see Senega coming, they became anxious. Select said, 'Yesterday he and I agreed that if he did not come back, I would go and look for him.'

'I'll come with you,' Sedge said.

Honeybush told them to be careful. The two mounted their

266

horses and charged into the spell. Soon, they were breathing the strong aroma of wine. Select did not drink, and the very smell alone was enough to fell him from his horse, and he fainted away. Sedge drank a few cups, and fell drunk on the ground.

When Honeybush did not see them return after a long time, he called the retreat and went back to camp.

The next morning, Wu Number Four ordered his men to carry Senega back to Honeybush's camp, and asked Honeybush to see if Senega had suffered any injury through fighting, or had been poisoned. 'If you know what is good for you, you had better retreat, or else every one of your men will die like Senega,' said Wu Number Four's soldiers.

The Wen brothers and the others gathered around Senega, and saw that his face still seemed alive. Wine was flowing from his mouth, and he exuded a strong enough alcoholic smell to repel any man. Honeybush felt his chest, and it was still warm. So he sent for a physician. But the latter could do nothing for him. After much effort, all Senega said was, 'It is too late to be sorry,' and died.

The Wen brothers wept and stamped their feet, and swore that they must kill Wu Number Four for this, and removed the body to a nearby temple. When Senega's wife Noble Jade heard the news, she almost cried herself to death.

The following morning, Wu Number Four was again in front of the spell, challenging the men into the 'battlefield'. Honeybush and Prince's Feather were going to lead their men in, but the White Prince, Courage, Little Summit and Young Lo said, 'We would like permission to go in and find Sedge and Select, and see what the spell is actually like.'

Honeybush said, 'You must be extremely careful.'

The four mounted their horses and charged into the spell-binding area, and were at once overcome by the alcoholic vapours. Those who could not drink fell down and fainted, and those who could drink, already tipsy from the smell of alcohol in the air, went on to drink and became drunk.

In this way, all who entered the area where Wu Number Four had cast the spell of wine never returned.

The rest of the men waited and saw no one come back. The next day, Honeybush said, 'We are only at the first Pass, and we have already lost so many men! What shall we do?'

They were discussing the best move to make, when it was announced that Talented Ladies Tsai Jade Moonlight and Yen Purple Jade had arrived at the big camp.

The ladies were invited in, and said in tears, 'Our husbands are in the spell-binding territory of Wu Number Four. We would like your permission to go in and find out what has happened.'

Honeybush gave them permission and told them to be careful. The ladies left the big camp, and mounted steeds, and together, charged into the area.

Honeybush again waited for a long time, and suddenly saw someone drop from the air before him. It was Purple Jade, who was panting hard, and flushed in the face. Narrator brought her a cup of tea, and after Purple Jade drank a few mouthfuls and recovered somewhat, she stood up and said, 'When we entered the area, we saw clear streams and green hills, and endless stretches of beautiful scenery. We had taken only a few steps when the aroma of wine came to our nostrils, and Sister Jade Moonlight was overcome immediately. I went on to explore, and came back to tell you that although seven of our men are drunk, they have met with no other harm. I wanted to carry Jade Moonlight away on my back, but the entire area where the spell has been cast is enclosed by the nets of the sky and the earth, and it took all my strength to escape alone. As Little Summit is in there, and he is the brother of Daughter of Tang, I would like to go to Little Penglai and find her, and see if she can help. I know she has become an Immortal, and I don't know if I can find her, but please allow me to try.'

Before Honeybush could speak, Purple Jade sprang up in the air and was gone.

She arrived at Little Penglai and went before the stone tablet where Tang Ao had left his writing. Nearby, she saw a Taoist nun gathering herbs. Purple Jade went up to her and closed her palms in greeting.

The nun returned her greeting and said, 'From where has the Bodhisattva come, and on what errand?'

'I am looking for the Immortal Tang and the Immortal Yen,' said Purple Jade, and told her where she came from.

The nun said, 'I have been here for many years, but I have never seen these two. What do you want to find them for?'

When Purple Jade told her the reason, the nun said, 'The spells binding these four Passes may be called together the "Self-destruction Spell". Although several of your men are trapped in it, they will not be harmed, for the moment a single man is harmed, the spell is broken.'

'Why do you say this, when the fifth son of the Wen family has already met his death?' said Purple Jade.

The nun said, 'Those who come to harm in the spell do so because they lack self-discipline. How can anyone else be blamed for it? That is why it is called the "Self-destruction Spell",' said the nun.

'Can you tell me if there is a way to break this spell?' said Purple Jade.

The nun smiled and said, 'A nun knows how to cultivate her soul and discipline her actions. She knows nothing about breaking spells. But why does the Bodhisattva not defeat the enemy with his own strategy?'

Purple Jade wanted her to explain, but the nun had disappeared. She realized then that it was a fairy who had come to show her the way, and she prostrated herself on the ground and gave thanks.

Upon returning to camp, she told the others what happened, but the men could not understand, either.

Honeybush said, 'The spell is cast over the town, and yet people come and go freely. How is it that only we are overpowered by wine when we go in? There must be a way of becoming immune to the temptation of wine, and that must have been what the fairy meant. We shall capture one of Wu Number Four's soldiers and see what he carries on his person.'

He ordered Badge and Narrator to do so, and Purple Jade returned to the rear camp.

Soon, Badge and Narrator captured a husky soldier, and brought him into the big camp. They found a piece of yellow paper on his person with the words 'shrine of Divine Yu' written on it. After interrogation, they found out that every soldier in Wu Number Four's army carried such a piece of yellow paper as a talisman on his chest, and then was not susceptible to the temptation of wine.

Honeybush was delighted, and ordered that the prisoner be shut up in a cage. He had several thousand such talismans made, and then he picked three thousand troops and gave a talisman to each man, and said, 'We shall advance in three columns. One thousand men will be led by Pien Badge and Yen Cliff, and advance on the centre of the spell-binding area. The second thousand of infantry led by Brothers Lin Hero and Chang Basil will advance on the left, and the third thousand men will be led by Brothers Nsai Noble and Fourth Brother Cabbage, and advance on the right side of it. Once past the spell-bound area, those who reach the Pass will fire a signal gun. Then I and Brother Shih Narrator will follow with five thousand men and horses. After we enter the Pass, we must not harm the people. Brother Prince's Feather and his brothers will guard the camp here.'

When it was around the first watch of the night, the young stalwarts led the soldiers and marched on the spell-binding area.

However, once they were in it, all six leaders and three thousand brave soldiers fell under the spell of wine, and although they did not drink, fell dead drunk on the ground.

Honeybush waited for the signal gun to be fired, and when he heard nothing after a long time, he was alarmed. He returned to camp and found the prisoner and questioned him again, and discovered that when Wu Number Four cast a spell before the Pass, his men were forbidden to drink. On the day the men entered the area, if one man violated the order, then the talismans would cease to work for all the men. Moreover, the men who wrote the talismans and everyone who carried it must burn incense and kowtow to heaven and earth, and say the word 'Abstain' the day before they entered the area. Only then would they be safe.

Honeybush ordered the prisoner to be taken back to his cage, and he and the rest of the young men bathed (to make themselves pure) and burned incense and bowed to heaven. They wrote out their talismans with great reverence, and Honeybush ordered that there should be no drinking in camp.

The following day, an altar was made ready, and after they kowtowed and burned incense and prayed again, the talismans were distributed to the men. Everyone kowtowed upon receiving it and said the word 'Abstain'.

Then Honeybush ordered Brilliant and Asarum to lead a column of men, and Elegant another, and advanced on the sides of the spell-bound area, for their own men were trapped in the centre of it, and he did not want to injure them. Honeybush and Narrator brought up the rear. Suddenly they heard the sound of guns being fired, and hurried in with their men.

When they arrived at the Pass, they saw that their own flag was already hoisted on top of the city wall.

For Wu Number Four was celebrating the capture of three thousand men and did not expect another attack. When the new men arrived, he was not prepared. He was killed by arrows, and his family was captured.

When the men entered the city, the magic spell which still lingered before the Water Pass turned into a mighty gust of wind, and blew itself away, and the men who had been trapped in it woke up, and returned to their companies. Jade Moonlight also recovered. But Sedge had been trampled upon by soldiers as he lay drunk on the ground, and died. The Wen brothers cried profusely and gave him a funeral.

The Chang brothers Wildhop, Begonia, Parsley and Artemisea

were ordered to guard the Water Pass with four thousand troops. The rest of the army rested for a day, and advanced on the No-fire Pass.

If the reader wants to know what happened at the No-fire Pass, please read the next chapter.

◄ *30* ►

When the men were five *li* away from the No-fire Pass, they made camp. Scouts reported that the binding-spell before the Pass was already cast, and that from the outside one could see neither men nor horses within the area, but only fog and mist.

The next morning, Hero mounted his horse and went to challenge the enemy in battle. He engaged Wu Number Seven in a few rounds of battle, and then Wu Number Seven turned around and went away.

'I think he must be trying to lead me into the spell-bound area,' thought Hero. 'I shall see what it is like!'

He went on, and by that time Wu Number Seven was already out of sight. Clouds billowed and fog moved all over the spell-bound area, and the distant peaks were barely visible, nor could the woods be made out clearly.

Hero dismounted, and walked into the area slowly. The fog and clouds gradually thinned out, and soon he could see the sun dimly in the sky. It was an inhabited countryside, and there were flowers everywhere, and he could hear birds chirping.

Soon, he saw an archway with the words 'Incomplete Mountain Region' facing him. Passing underneath it, he came upon a road and saw in the distance a very imposing mountain of great height. A husky fellow was standing beneath it who for some reason was very angry, and raging and shouting as loud as thunder, and knocking his head against the mountain. There was a crackling noise which made Hero's ears split. When he recovered himself, he discovered that the husky fellow had knocked off one side of the mountain, and clouds of dust were flying in the air, so that for a moment, the sky was dark, and Hero was frightened. He ran, crying, 'Oh, what a fright! I have never seen a man with such a hard head! But even if his head were made of steel, how can he knock off the side of a mountain? It must be his fury that did it!'

Another husky fellow was standing in the distance, who was also extremely angry. Suddenly, there came a fierce tiger which charged toward the fellow with all its might. Hero thought, 'This man is doomed! He is not carrying any weapon!'

However, before the tiger could spring on him, the man let out a great bellow and stared at the tiger so furiously that the corners of his eyes burst, and drops of hot blood spurted out of them and on the tiger. The tiger trembled and stumbled and letting out a roar, took flight. Hero thought, 'Just now a man knocked off the side of a mountain, and now another has repelled a tiger with the blood from the corners of his eyes. Could it be that his eyes are capable of shooting pellets? But tigers are not afraid of pellets. It must be the man's hot blood that did it. From this it can be seen that a man's wrath can accomplish extraordinary things.'

Then he saw a woman who was trying to melt a stone over a fire. Hero went up to her and asked, 'May I ask what you are melting this stone for?'

The woman said, 'Just now in knocking down the side of the Incomplete Mountain, the man shook part of the sky loose, and I am melting this stone in order to mend the sky.'

'So the sky can be mended!' Hero thought.

He walked ahead, and on one side of the road he saw a black-faced general who was leading a man in fighting and killing people. Suddenly, the general let out a shout which shattered Hero's eardrums. 'My strength can pull down mountains, and my indignation can conquer the world!'

Hero wandered on, and after some time, became hungry, and found many shops on the roadside. He went into one which was selling steamed buns and bread. There was a man sitting inside who was wearing a Chou dynasty costume, and having a quarrel with someone, and was so angry that his hair stood on end, so that his hat sat on the tips of his hair.

'If his hair is so stiff, I'd better keep clear of him so that he doesn't brush me with it!' Hero thought, and went to the next shop which also sold steamed buns. There sat another man who was so angry that his beard stiffened, and upturned the table. Hero thought, 'I'd better not tangle with him! His beard is liable to pierce a few holes in my body!'

So he went into yet another bun shop. The air was very steamy inside, and many prisoners sat at the tables, wearing handcuffs, and they were as thin as scarecrows, sighing and groaning. Hero went up to them and said, 'What serious crime did you commit, that you are sighing so? Or is it because you are being unjustly punished?'

The prisoners cried, 'We deserve our punishment! There is no injustice!' and pointed to the steaming pots and said, 'We commit crimes because of those! It is too late to regret! We wish that you would remind everyone to pay more heed to the word "forbearance". If one has forbearance, even bad luck can be turned into good, and a person will not meet the same kind of fate as we have.'

Hero was going to answer when he smelled a gust of fragrance which was like that of dates. He went into the shop which sold steamed cakes made with dates, and sat down. But everyone who was eating in the cake shop looked sickly and miserable and emaciated. Hero took pity on them and said, 'What are you suffering from? Or was it bad luck which brought you this illness?'

'It has nothing to do with luck! We asked for it!' said the customers, and pointing to the steaming pots, said, 'They are the cause of it all! Because of them, we have become, after a long time of accumulated illness, unable to swallow, and no medicine can cure us. But it is too late. We hope that you will tell all men to think constantly about "patience". Then when something unfortunate happens, calamity will turn into blessings, and they will not suffer like us.'

Hero looked at the steaming pots and said, 'How can a steamer cause men such harm? Wait until I eat some date cakes, and then I shall find out!'

He therefore called, 'Bring some cakes quickly!'

The waiter heard him, but brought cake to another table.

Hero cried, 'You convict! I suppose it is because I came in late, so you are going to serve me last! Am I a beggar that you treat me in this manner? If you don't bring the cakes you'll get a taste of my fist!'

The waiter then took some cold left-over cake from another table and gave it to him. Hero was furious. He took the plate and walked over to the waiter and threw it together with the cake at the waiter's face.

'You're killing me!' the waiter said, and fell back, his face covered with blood. When this happened, the steaming pots in the shop began to let off more steam, and the place began to get cloudy. Hero cried, 'We shall see who is going to let off steam!' and started to punch the steaming pots. His fury ignited the spell-binding vapours and from all four sides hot air invaded his mouth and nostrils, and he was overcome.

The next day, Ultimate and Ocean went into the spell-binding area, and also failed to return.

Honeybush was extremely worried, and captured a soldier of Wu Number Seven's army and questioned him. He found a piece of yellow paper on his bosom with the words 'Shrine of Lou Shih Teh of Imperial Tang' written on it.

Honeybush therefore bathed himself and burned incense, and had talismans made like it, and gave them out to the men. Like before, they said the word 'abstain' and placed the talisman on their breasts. In the evening, Warrior, Jade and Badge with a thousand men went into the spell-bound area, with the understanding that when they fired the first signal gun, Young Lo and Young Shu would follow with the rest of the men.

However, after waiting a long time, they heard nothing. Honeybush questioned the soldier again, and found out that besides the precautions they had taken, they must write the word 'forbearance' on a piece of paper, and burn it, and swallow the ashes while kneeling before the men could go into the spell. Once in, they must not lose their tempers, for once they lost their tempers, they must fear for their lives. Honeybush did accordingly, and when all was ready, he led his men into the No-fire Pass, and broke the spell.

When they entered the city from this Pass, Wu Number Seven had already escaped. But Hero, Ultimate and Ocean's anger had killed them. Honeybush had them put into coffins, and then led the main army through the Pass.

The White Prince would not let his men disturb the population. Honeybush ordered two of the Chang brothers guarding the Water Pass to come and guard the No-fire Pass, and after resting for a night, he prepared to lead his men forward to the third Pass.

Before they could set out, reports came to him that Sedge's wife Red Feather, Hero's wife and Fragrant Book, Ultimate's wife Fragrant Marsh Orchid, and Ocean's wife Fragrant Jade had all hanged themselves to preserve their chastity.

The Change and Wen brothers were much grieved by the news, and had them put into coffins with their names written on, and left soldiers behind to guard them.

Then he led his men on to the Knife Pass, and made camp. The following day, Elegant went to challenge the enemy in battle, and after fighting two rounds with Wu Number Five, was led into the spell.

When Elegant went into the spell-bound area, he was caressed by a scented wind. There were luxuriant woods in which birds were twittering, and fishes swam in the ponds. Everywhere, he saw painted pillars and carved beams in the houses, and curtains of beads and silk. It was so beautiful that Elegant thought he had entered another world.

He dismounted, and walked slowly. Soon, he heard the sound of a lady's chain tinkling, and saw two girls approaching him who were beautiful beyond description, so that the sight of them made the birds fly away and fish dive to the bottom of the pond to avoid comparison with them. As he walked on, he saw another beauty who folded her hands over her heart, and frowned attractively in a way that made his heart soft with love and pity for her. Elegant took a turning on the road, and met a succession of beautiful girls, some holding willow catkins, others pepper blossoms, and others holding circular fans, switches, and fresh flowers. Every girl was of the utmost grace and refinement, and gentle and modest beyond compare. Elegant wanted to speak to them, but the girls did not seem approachable. So all he could do was look, and after a while, had to walk away with his desire unfulfilled.

He had not gone much further, however, before he noticed that he had come to a section where there were houses of joy. Many beautiful girls could be seen inside. He was about to go into one when he was attracted by the fragrance of a particular flower, and discovered that a border of peonies grew by the side of the road, and a beautiful girl was standing in it holding a stringed instrument to her bosom, and a branch of peonies in her other hand. She came to him smiling and said, 'Your presence here is predestined. If you like me, let us be united for the rest of our lives.'

Elegant was already desirous and said, 'I am most grateful that you should bestow your love on me. Where are your fragrant apartments?'

'My home is very near,' said the girl. 'Please come through these streets of flowers and the willow lanes, pass the mulberry grove beyond, and you will find it. I shall go ahead to make tea, and hope that you come soon.'

Elegant was delighted. But as he approached the house he thought, 'Can she be trying to deceive me?' He hesitated, and then smiled and said to himself, 'Fool! Fool! How can a beautiful girl harm a person! Besides, she is of such extreme beauty, that if I do meet harm, what does it matter?'

So he hurried on happily, and fulfilled his desire.

The next day, Parsley, Shepherd's Purse and Cabbage also went into this spell, and did not return.

A day later, Wu Number Five returned their bodies to Honeybush's camp with a soldier who told Honeybush and Prince's Feather from Wu Number Five, 'Better retreat if you know what is good for you! Let this be a lesson to you!'

Honeybush and Prince's Feather were deeply saddened by the death of their brothers. When the news was carried to the women's camp, Fragrant Ink and Red Jade hurried to the big camp, and hugging the bodies of their husbands Elegant and Shepherd's Purse, wailed out loud. Then they ran their swords through their own necks.

But when Peaceful Blossom and Fair Heroine heard the news,

they each took one of Honeybush's swords, and secretly rode into the spell, crying for Wu Number Five to come out and meet them.

Soldiers reported the news to Number Five, who came out on horseback to meet them. When he saw how fair the two ladies were, he was overjoyed and thought, 'Now I have two lovely girls to keep me company in my widowerhood!'

He dashed ahead to meet them, but before he could speak to them, Peaceful Blossom and Fair Heroine raised their double-edged swords in their right hands, and holding the silk reins in their left, charged at him. Wu Number Five saw that they did not hold their swords correctly, and they were awkward riders, too, so that in spite of their fury they were the epitomy of feminine helplessness, and he gave way at once to laughter and pity. He wanted to take them both alive, but as that did not seem possible, he thought, 'Let me see, which one is less beautiful, and I will put an end to her.'

He lifted his axe and struck out at Peaceful Blossom's face. Her horse swerved and the axe missed its mark. He struck out again and Peaceful Blossom fell dead from her horse. Fair Heroine took her double-edged sword in both hands, and using all the strength she had, gave a thrust, and pierced Number Five's ribs with it. Number Five gave a cry and fell from his horse.

Fair Heroine dismounted quickly and thrust her sword into him twice more and killed him. The soldiers held back when they saw how fierce Fair Heroine was, but shot arrows at her from the distance. She mounted her horse quickly, and although wounded, urged it on, and shot back and wounded several more soldiers before she died under their arrows.

When Honeybush received the news, he came in with his troops, but the girls were already dead. However, they rescued their bodies, and brought them back to camp.

Upon his return, Honeybush discovered that his brother Cabbage had regained consciousness, and was not badly hurt.

The next day, the White Prince and Badge went into the spell-bound area, and also failed to return. So Honeybush ordered his men to capture some of Wu Number Five's soldiers to find out what made them immune to the charms of women.

Strangely enough, no prisoner could be taken. The young men in camp were worried, and did not know what to do. However, Purple Jade returned (from another expedition to Little Penglai) and said, 'I went to Little Penglai to pray for help when my husband failed to return, kowtowing every step of the way. There, I met a fairy who gave me a magic charm and a magic drug. The charm will invoke the spirit of Liu Hsia Huei (of the State of Lu, who was well-known for his indifference to "bare arms and breasts" and "the naked body"). We will burn it when the time comes, and it will protect you.'

'What is the drug for?' said Honeybush.

'It is made from the hearts of ferocious beasts. Those who take it will have courage. The men who are going to invade the Pass should take it, and write the three words "Liu Hsia Huei" on their bosoms. They will then be safe from temptation, and not come to harm. The magic spell will then be dispelled.'

On the second watch, Honeybush ordered his men to burn the magic charm and invaded the Pass and broke the spell. When he entered the city, he found that the officers who had been sent by Chang I-chih to defend the Pass had long since fled.

The White Prince and Badge had never set great store by the pleasures of woman, and were found to be unharmed. He remained to keep the peace in this part of the city, and Honeybush led the men on after resting for a night, and ordering Worship and Tide to guard this Pass with two thousand men.

If the reader wants to know what happened when Honeybush and his men arrived at the Treasure Pass, please read the next chapter.

When Honeybush and his men arrived at the Treasure Pass, Wu Number Six was ready for them. He stood at the edge of his spell-bound area and shouted, 'Come and try to break the spell!'

Prince's Feather advanced on horseback, and engaged Number Six in battle for two rounds, and then galloped into the area.

As soon as he was in it, the smell of money invaded his olfactory senses. He sighed and thought to himself, 'Scholars are always warning people of the evils of money, but that is because they cannot appreciate it's lovely smell. What a pity!'

The roads were paved with jade, and the bridges which Prince's Feather crossed were made of silver. There were scarlet portals and golden gates, and the air of affluence overflowed from every quarter. He dismounted, and led his horse toward a high archway with the words 'Money is My Brother' written in gold letters on it.

Going through the arch, he saw many people on the other side, with very happy expressions on their faces, all holding coins of different sizes in their hands. Walking further on, he saw a huge coin (suspended in the air), which was giving off a dazzling golden light. Millions of people were struggling to get up to it. Some of them were scholars, others were farmers. There were labourers, merchants, and the representatives of the three religions and nine schools of thought. There were officials stretching out their palms, and lesser officials and clerks in the act of extortion. There were some who were trying to falsify evidence and blackmailing each other in their attempt to claim the coin, and gamblers who were trying to accept bets. There were men with angry faces making terrifying threats and smooth talkers who were making false prom-ises. People were setting traps and forging papers and swindling each other. Every kind of evil was going on.

Countless ladders were suspended from the huge coin, and bodies and white skeletons were strewn across them, and piled up like a mountain beneath.

Prince's Feather saw it all, and understood, and sighed. From the hole in the coin could be seen a vista of coins shining in every direction, and jade and gold. He tied his horse at the side of the road, and climbed up a ladder himself. When he came to the hole in the centre of the coin, he crept through it, and saw jade pavilions and fairy caves beyond, and golden altars and fairy ponds. The ground on the other side was paved with green jade, and jade walls lined the street. He had never seen anything like it on this earth.

He came down on the other side of the coin, and went to look around. The more he saw, the better he liked it. 'If I could have a few rooms in this glorious place and live here for a little while, I will not have lived in vain,' he thought.

As he was so thinking, he saw a very large mansion, and went in to have a look. There were jade towers and many chambers in the front and back, with painted beams and red balustrades. The rooms were furnished with every kind of luxury. Prince's Feather was extremely taken with it all, and thought, 'To live here, one would need to have clothes to go with it, and good food.'

Then he saw that in the chambers there were piles of silk and embroidered curtains and bedding, and jade, silver, and pearl treasures, and all the delicacies of the mountains and sea. Nothing that he could think of was lacking.

'If I had known this, I would have brought my servants!' he thought.

An old man-servant appeared at that instant with a list in his hand, followed by a large retinue of other servants and errand boys. An old woman-servant also appeared, leading a retinue of maids and slave girls, and everyone bowed to him.

'What is the name of the old man-servant, and how many are there of you?' said Prince's Feather.

'I am called Old Wang,' said the old man-servant, 'and there are sixteen under me who are ready to serve you. Here is a list of their duties. Please look it over.'

Prince's Feather read the list, and discovered that Twenty Columns and Forty Columns were the Accountant and Assistant Accountant. The former checked the receipts against the payments, and the latter did the actual calculation, for the Accountant could not count. Checking Cash was in charge of the expenses of the kitchen.

'Cooks like to falsify their accounts,' said Prince's Feather. 'If you are in charge, you must see that they do not do it. But you must not falsify the accounts yourself, or else you will be dismissed.'

Checking Cash said, 'I would not dare to . . . except for such little items as tea, wine and bath.'

'As long as you retain a sense of reality,' said Prince's Feather, 'who can keep track of every penny? And furthermore, you are not aspiring to become a model of honesty, are you?'

'You are truly enlightened, Master,' said Checking Cash.

The next names Prince's Feather saw on the list were Five Per Cent and Four Coppers, who took care of the silver.

'Why are you called Five Per Cent and Four Coppers?' Prince's Feather asked.

'I am very honest,' said Five Per Cent. 'Of all the money that passes through my hands, I only take five per cent of every ounce, and never more. That is why Old Wang put me in charge of the silver.'

Four Coppers said, 'I am also very honest, and of every thousand coppers which pass through my hands, I only take four. I would never short-change anyone.'

Prince's Feather nodded and said, 'Five per cent of each ounce of silver, and four coppers out of every thousand coppers cannot be said to be unreasonable.'

The man who was in charge of the wine was called Half-Ounce.

'Why is he called Half-Ounce?' Prince's Feather asked Old Wang.

'In looking after Master's wine, he is not unscrupulous, and takes only half an ounce for himself every day, and that is why he is in charge of the wine.'

Prince's Feather said, 'Half an ounce is not much, but he must not take more.'

Half-Ounce said, 'I have a very small capacity. Even if I indulged a little, it would not be more than a few cups a day.'

'I think I can bear that,' said Prince's Feather. 'But if your capacity increases, and you throw away the ounce measure for the catty measure, and then after each cask is opened you drink half the cask, I shall not tolerate it.'

The servants all bowed, and Prince's Feather turned to the old woman and said, 'What is your name, and what are the names of the others?'

'I am called Penny Farthing,' said the old woman. 'It is not an attractive name. Would Master care to give me a more sexy one?'

Prince's Feather looked at the old woman and saw that she was trying to flirt with him, although she had not a black hair left on her head. 'Why not call yourself Greenback?' he said. 'Green has an air of youth about it. Maybe after you change your name the colour of your hair will also change.'

Penny Farthing said, 'Thank the Master very much!'

'What are the duties of these maids?' said Prince's Feather.

Penny Farthing said, 'One is in charge of the Mistress's powder, and another looks after her rouge. This one takes care of the Mistress's foot-binding cloth, and this one removes the corns from the Mistress's feet. These two look after her ornaments and jewels, and this one paints the Mistress's picture.'

Prince's Feather said, 'A person is needed to look after the foot-binding cloth, but you have assigned someone just to remove the Mistress's corns. This is very thoughtful of you, and I shall tell the Mistress to reward you. What do the eight slave girls do?'

Penny Farthing said, 'The one in white looks after the Mistress's silver, and the one in green looks after her copper coins. The one in red looks after her gambling account, and the one in yellow looks after her food bills. Their names all have the same meaning as Four Coppers and Five Per Cent, because they only pocket a very little money and never take more.'

She pointed to the four younger girls and said, 'Little Currency looks after Mistress's silk, and Little Money takes care of the tea and hot water. Little Spade looks after her towels, and Little Knife looks after the scissors which cut the Mistress's corns.'

Prince's Feather cried, 'A special person to look after the Mistress's towels and another who is in charge of the scissors for cutting her corns! This is a truly well-managed household! As they would say in official jargon, you are "clear-headed and efficient, and attentive to details in the execution of affairs".'

The servants, with their duties before them, bowed and withdrew.

The slave girls made tea, and made the bed ready for Prince's Feather. With teacup in hand, he wondered which girl he should ask to spend the night with him. As he was trying to decide, four extremely beautiful girls appeared to keep him company. Prince's Feather dined with them, and retired with them.

In the morning when he awoke, the four beauties were still by his side. Day after day, he enjoyed their company, ate the finest food, and wore the finest garments, and enjoyed all the blessings which life on this earth could yield. Soon, all four beauties were pregnant. They burned incense and bowed and prayed to the gods of heaven, earth and water, and Prince's Feather gave each of them a 'male coin' to wear, to ensure the birth of a son. The four beauties in time did indeed present him with five boys.

Prince's Feather felt that he had too many sons and wanted a daughter. So he gave several of the beauties some 'female coins', and in time, two girls were born to him. When the five boys and two girls were a little older, Prince's Feather had a tutor teach them. After a few years, the boys and girls were of marriageable age, and he arranged matches for them. In the twinkling of an eye, his grandchildren were grown up, too, and he also arranged their marriages. Before he knew it, he was eighty, and surrounded by great-grandchildren.

One day, he looked in the mirror, and saw that he was an old man whose hair was as white as snow. Suddenly, he remembered having climbed through the hole in the coin. What happened sixty years ago seemed like only yesterday. He was strong and full of spirit then, and now he was old and decrepit. Life was like a dream! Had he know that this was all that a man could hope for in life, he would have been able to detach himself from many of the cravings he thought he had to satisfy! Now it was too late. He wondered if he could find the way back to the ladder up which he had climbed so many years ago.

Prince's Feather found the coin, but when he put his head through it to look out, the hole became narrower and narrower, until he was trapped, and could neither move forwards nor backwards.

When those in Honeybush's camp did not see Prince's Feather come back the following day, the White Prince and Courage said that they wanted to go in and look for him. But Honeybush said, 'You are in command of the men in camp. How can you leave? Besides, you have suffered much at the Water Pass. No one knows what to expect now. How can I let you go?'

The White Prince said, 'How can I stay in camp when you are all here today because of my family? If I do not do something about it, my conscience will not be at ease. Life and death are a matter of destiny. Please do not try to stop me.' So saying, he rushed into the spellbound area with Courage, and did not return.

Purple Jade and Jade Moonlight were aghast the next day when their husbands did not come back, and decided that they should go to find them. If they should fail, they were ready to go to death with their husbands. They relayed the news to the big camp, and rushed in.

When Wu Number Six saw them, he at once performed his magic, and set up dense layers of sky-and-earth nets to prevent them from escaping.

Honeybush waited for the ladies, thinking that Purple Jade at least would return. He told the men, 'If she does not come back, it means that the sorcery inside is fierce indeed. I think that we should not act until we hear from her.'

Cliff was extremely depressed, and contrary to Honeybush's

orders, led a thousand men toward the Pass to challenge the enemy in battle.

It happened that Chang I-chih and Chang Chang-tsung were filled with fear after the loss of the three Passes, and Li Hsiao-yi had failed to come with the main army to support them.

Cliff wounded two of the Empress's officers, and using his silver lance, pierced the body of another high-ranking officer. Li Hsiao-yi was very angry, and rode into battle himself. Upon seeing him, Young Lo and Young Shu remembered how their father had been murdered by him. They urged their horses on and with their lances held high, engaged Li in battle. Li was wounded in the thigh by a thrust of the lance by Young Shu, and retreated in confusion.

The young men brought their men and horses into battle all at once, and killed the Empress's soldiers to the right and left. Again and again, they called for the Empress' men to come out from the spell-bound area to battle, until no one answered them, and they returned to camp.

They took a few prisoners, and searched them and found nothing on their bodies. Upon interrogation, they discovered that before Wu Number Six sent them into the spell-bound area he gave them a bowl of water to drink over which magic had been invoked.

The next day, the men went into battle again. Wu Number Six stood alone in front of the magic spell, and challenged the young men to come forward and break it, but he refused to engage them in battle. When the young men rushed near him, he retreated into the spell, and when the young men retreated, he came out again to call insults at them.

Honeybush's anger was great. He was just going to urge his horse into the spell, when Young Lo, Young Shu, Little Summit and five others said, 'For several days Prince's Feather and the White Prince have been trapped in there. Now everything depends on you. If you also go in there and become trapped, we will be without a leader. The eight of us want to lead eight hundred picked men into the spell to find out what is really going on, and come back to give you our report.'

Honeybush knew they were right, and could only give his consent, and return to camp.

The eight young men soon led eight hundred picked men and charged into the spell. But there appeared at once eight hundred and eight illusions within the area, so that each man followed his own illusion and went his own way, and lost sight of the others. Those who could not be moved by the sight of money did not come to any harm, but those whose eyes turned green with envy and whose hearts throbbed with greed met many accidents and lost their lives.

When Honeybush did not see the men return, he was frantic. The next day, he went to challenge Number Six to battle, but Number Six remained behind the protection of his spell, and taunted him with insults, and would not come out.

Honeybush thought that he was outnumbered, and did not dare to lead the rest of his men into the spell, though the men were brave.

When Marsh Orchid, Wise Maxim, Red Lotus, Fragrant Spring, Brocade Spring, Silver Moonlight, Little Spring and Flowering Maple failed to see their husbands return, they wept unceasingly, and did not know what to do. Those who had sons did not lose courage altogether, and those who were pregnant had some hope, but those who had no offspring wanted only to follow their husbands to the grave. The ladies thought of the couplets which were carved on the jade tablet on Little Penglai Mountain, and of how Fragrant Book and Fair Heroine met their deaths, and their flesh crept and their insides turned to water.

Red Lotus burned incense and prayed for Daughter of Tang to come and save her brother. Everyone followed her example and prayed, and the eight ladies prayed for three days, and abstained from food and water, and shed many a tear.

Their piety moved the hearts of the Jade Maiden and the Green Lady, who with the Scarlet Child and the Golden Infant got on their wind-fire wheels, and came to help.

When Honeybush found out, he invited the fairies to the big camp. After asking their names, he said, 'We are much honoured by the presence of the four Fairies. Now Wu Number Six has been using his evil sorcery to defeat our forces, and we have lost many men, and our Emperor is imprisoned in the Eastern Palace. Will you help us?'

The Scarlet Child said, 'We had an agreement with the Fairy of a Hundred Flowers and her ninety-nine flower-spirits that we would come to their aid when they needed us. Now we must break our vow of not killing, but that cannot be helped, since the situation is so. It is not too late for you. Tonight at the third watch, go with your men and horses into the spell, and break it. We will help you as much as we can.'

Honeybush thanked her and said, 'Can the Fairies tell me what is the evil magic which is practised in this spell?'

The Golden Infant said, 'It is the Money Spell. Since money makes the worldly life go round, and is universally loved, those who enter this spell must be very sure of their principles. If a man is easily persuaded, or hesitates, he will lose his self-control, and be lost.'

'How many columns of men should I form tonight?' asked Honeybush.

The Scarlet Child said, 'Three. When it is dark, prepare an incense altar, and we shall invoke the spirits of Wang Yen and Tsui Chun (who were known for their indifference to money) who will help us to become impervious to the smell of money. Soon the Fairy of a Hundred Fruits will arrive. When the time comes, the Golden Infant and the Fairy of a Hundred Fruits will go into the spellbound area first, and distribute walnuts to the trapped men. Then, lead a column of men with me into the centre of the spell. The Green Lady will lead a column to the left, and the Jade Maiden a column to the right, into the spell. The Wu brothers have no other tricks up their sleeve except the "Self-destruction Spell", and when this Pass has been won, you will have accomplished your mission.'

Honeybush said, 'May I ask why walnuts are to be given to the men?'

The Green Lady said, 'Those who are going into the spell must take walnuts or waterchestnuts first, to counteract the smell of money.'

'Can these two foods really counteract the smell of money?' said Honeybush.

The Jade Maiden said, 'Yes. If a child swallows a copper coin, make him eat walnuts, which will dissolve the copper into liquid. If there are no walnuts, waterchestnuts will do. If you don't believe it, chew a walnut with a copper coin, and see if the copper does not dissolve.'

Honeybush ordered his men to gather waterchestnuts and walnuts but the men could find none nearby.

When the Fairy of a Hundred Fruits arrived, Honeybush hastily welcomed her into his camp.

The Green Lady said, 'Why are you so late?'

The Fairy of a Hundred Fruits pointed to her basket and said, 'I was afraid that these would not be enough for the men, so I was delayed in looking for a few more.'

She gave her basket to Honeybush and said, 'There are walnuts here for the men. Give a few to each. Return the basket to me when you have finished, for I have other uses for it.'

Honeybush looked in the basket and saw that it was only half full.

The Jade Maiden said, 'How many men are going into battle tonight?'

'Three thousand men in three columns,' said Honeybush.

The Jade Maiden smiled and said, 'These will be enough for many times that number.'

Therefore Honeybush told Warrior and Select to pick three thousand brave men, and give ten walnuts to each. Select took the basket and walked out of the camp and said to Warrior, 'The Fairy said there are enough walnuts here for many times three thousand men. Why don't we give them twenty walnuts each and see if there will be enough. The more they eat, the safer they should be.'

So they distributed twenty walnuts to each of the three thousand men. After this was done, they looked in the basket and found that it was practically still half full.

'Since these walnuts are freely come by why don't we distribute them to the men who are not going into battle as well?' said Warrior.

'What if we finish all the walnuts?' said Select.

'If there are not enough to go round, we will leave a few in the basket and return it,' said Warrior.

After a great flurry and to-do, two hundred thousand men were given twenty walnuts each. Warrior and Select looked in the basket again, and no walnuts seemed to be missing from it except the top layer.

When they returned the basket to the Fairy of a Hundred Fruits, she looked at it and said to Honeybush, 'You saved yourself giving the men in camp a meal today.'

'What do you mean?' said Honeybush.

Warrior and Select had to laugh and confess what they had done, and everyone thought that it was most strange that the basket should contain so many walnuts.

When a vegetarian meal was prepared, the Fairies as well as the young men and ladies partook of it.

At the third watch, an altar was set up in camp, and Honeybush prayed devoutly before it. The Scarlet Child burned two charms, and with the Fairy of a Hundred Fruits and the Golden Infant, rushed into the spell.

The Green Lady, with Warrior and Mushroom at the head of a thousand men, went in on the left, and Select and Asarum led a thousand men behind the Jade Maiden and entered on the right. The Scarlet Child led Honeybush at the head of the third column of men, and advanced into the middle of the spell. In an instant, the evil spirits which had converged in it were dispersed, and paper people and paper horses fell to the ground.

Warrior and Select charged to the Pass and announced their arrival by firing cannons. Honeybush entered the city with his men, and found that Wu Number Six had fled, and his household was scattered to the four winds. Prince's Feather, Courage, Jade Moonlight and Purple Jade were beyond help, since they had been under the spell for too long, but the rest of those who went into the spell before them had come to no harm. The White Prince was trapped in the spell for many days, too, but as he had always kept his head where money was concerned, he survived the ordeal. The survivors gave the dead a funeral, and then went into the city, where the people welcomed them by burning incense.

As Honeybush was looking over Number Six's house, it was reported that the five Fairies had not entered the Pass with them, but had disappeared, and the White Prince and Cabbage were also missing. Honeybush ordered his men to look for them, but they could not be found. It was to be assumed that the two had departed from the earth with the five Fairies.

The men rested for a day, and the following day Honeybush wrote a secret letter to Chang Chien-chih and told him to be ready at the Eastern Palace and wait for him and his troops. Honeybush counted his men, and found that he had not lost too many. But he had lost Prince's Feather, Parsley, Sedge, Senega, Hero, Elegant, Courage, Ultimate and Ocean. In the women's camp, Fair Heroine, Peaceful Blossom, Jade Moonlight, Purple Jade, were dead through the evil sorcery of the Wu brothers, and Red Feather, Red Jade, Fragrant Book, Fragrant Ink, Fragrant Marsh Orchid, and Fragrant Jade had committed suicide to preserve their chastity. Honeybush had lost three brothers, and was deeply saddened, and his fourth brother was missing.

It was difficult for Honeybush to go on, but he was afraid that his mother would not be able to bear his loss too, so he decided to continue living. Every time midnight struck or dawn came, he shed tears and his face was seldom dry.

Empress Wu was eighty-one and constantly ill. For months, she was confined to her bed with only her young gigolos, Chang Chang-tsung and Chang I-chih, at her side. The Chang brothers were much hated, and began to manoeuvre for power, in case the Empress should pass away.

The rumour spread that the brothers were plotting to put themselves on the throne. A case was brought against Chang-tsung for treason, but through the Empress's intervention, the young man escaped the law. The official's patience was exhausted, and in turn Empress Wu became even more ill.

The *coup d'état* occurred a month after the Empress's intervention for Chang-tsung.

Chang I-chih, upon hearing that Honeybush's men were entering the capital, falsified orders on behalf of the Empress, and ordered four generals to lead a hundred thousand men into battle. When the armies met, Honeybush's men scattered the Empress's army, and encircled the city walls of Chang-an.

When the Emperor's sympathisers in the Eastern Palace (where he was detained) heard this, they rose, and together with Young Lo, Young Shi and Honeybush (who had entered the city) escorted Emperor Chang-tsung (from his compound, through the North Gate) to the Throne Hall.

The men set off in different directions once they entered the gate. They poured into the grounds, and a strong detachment went straight to the Empress's quarters. When the men saw the Chang brothers, they bared their knives and rushed toward them, and quickly surrounded them. Seizing the painted boys, they cut off their heads cleanly.

The Empress was aroused from her sleep by the noise and asked what was happening.

The official Li Tuo-tso said, 'I-chih and Chang-tsung were guilty of treason. By order of the Crown Prince we have killed them. I am sorry we could not inform you beforehand. Troops are in the palace. We hope that we have not been remiss.'

'Since the Crown Prince has killed them, he should now go back to the Eastern Palace,' the Empress said.

Heng Yeng-fan said, 'The Prince is already mature, and should succeed to the throne. This is the wish of the people.'

It did not take much time for the Empress to agree. She was left under guard, with the heads of the two gigolos for company.

The Emperor's supporters then arrested and killed Chang-chi and other bad ministers.

The next day, Empress Wu's officials relinquished the throne. Not long after, she was removed under guard to the royal park residence on the west side of the city.

Emperor Chung Tsung (nevertheless) bestowed upon her the title Tse-tien, Great Holy Empress (Dowager), and proclaimed an amnesty in the kingdom, and summoned those who helped to restore the throne to him to Court. He made thirty-four men including the official Chang Lien-shih and others who helped to effect the coup within the Palace, and Honeybush and his brothers-in-arms the title of Dukes, and made their wives Ladies of the First Rank. The title would be extant for three generations, and gifts of houses at the capital were presented to them. Memorials were erected to the loyalty of those men who had lost their lives for the sake of the Emperor, and memorials in commemoration of their chastity and filial piety were erected for the women who had lost their lives. Dukedoms were awarded to the sons of these men, to be passed on to their sons. The Emperor further sent officials to the four Passes to recall those who had been guarding them.

When the young men had thanked the Emperor, they returned to their homes, where the local officials welcomed them. Pien Pin was happy beyond expectation to see his son Badge again, and celebrations were held in each family where the sons and daughters had returned.

As for the white gibbon, he was a fairy gibbon who had lived in the cave of the Fairy of a Hundred Flowers for many years. When the Fairy of a Hundred Flowers was ordered to earth, he had come, too, with the intention of waiting for Daughter of Tang and returning to the cave with her. However, when Daughter of Tang told him to give the record of what was written on the jade tablet in the Lament for Beauty Pavilion, and find a scholar or historian to write about it, he went in search of him. He searched hard, but could not find the man. In the twinkling of an eye, three hundred years passed, and Tang dynasty gave way to the Chin dynasty. There was a man during the Five Generations Period called Liu Chu (who wrote the *Old History of Tang Dynasty*) who could undertake the work. The white gibbon gave the record to him, and told him what it was for. Liu said, 'Gibbon, you really aren't very bright. Look around you. There is fighting and famine, and confusion in the country, and power changes hands from one day to the next. I had all I could cope with to write the history of Tang dynasty. Who has the time or the desire to toy with this kind of work?'

The white gibbon had to take the record book back. During Sung dynasty, he found two men called Ouyang Hsiu and Sung Chiao (who wrote the *New History of Tang Dynasty*), and showed the record to them. But they said, 'We have spent seventeen years on the *New History of Tang Dynasty* and we are exhausted. Our wrists ache. We have no energy to take up this romance!'

The gibbon looked everywhere, and it was not until there was peace in the land in the present (Chin) dynasty that he found a descendant of Laotse, who had a reputation of sorts. Because the gibbon was weary of his search, he handed the record to this man, and returned to the fairy mountain.

When this man saw the scribbling in the book, he knew that it would not be easy to tell the story which had to be told. Luckily, there was peace in his time, the officials were not exacting, and left the people alone. In the harmony of the seasons, and under the peaceful rule of the land, he read some stories of adventure, and enjoyed some pleasures of life. When the spirit moved him, he took up his brush and wrote. In the long summer nights and on cold wintry ones, under the lamplight or in the moonlight, he wrote for his own amusement. One year followed another, and in the end he wrote a hundred chapters of *Flowers in the Mirror,* and had told only half the story. But those of his friends who were worried and suffering from melancholy burst out laughing upon reading it, and recovered their good spirits. They urged him, 'Since you are so lazy and write so slowly, who knows when you will ever finish the story! Why don't you send the first hundred chapters to the printers and have them blocked, so that other people can enjoy them, while you go on writing the rest?'

Well! What does it matter! The novelist has worked for more than thirty years, and what has he produced but a small, small literary work in the three thousand universes? Perhaps he has made a few flowers bloom on paper, and those who read the novel will smile, and pluck a few blossoms, and that would be destiny, too.

Notes

Shih Yi Chi and *Po Wu Chih* are both books of mythology of the Late Chin Dynasty.

Western Queen Mother. The Western Queen Mother was first mentioned in *Liehtse*. The Taoists wove endless legends around her. Her family name was given as Hou, Yang or Ho, and her maiden name as Hui. She had nine sons and twenty-five daughters, and as the sovereign of the Western Air, was the symbol of the passive, or female element. In the book of mythology *Shan Hai Ching*, she is portrayed as living in the Jade Mountain, and had a human face, the tail of a leopard, teeth of a tiger, and was an expert at whistling. Elsewhere, she is usually described as living in Kunlun Mountain, which some historians have identified as the Hindu Kush. Some people thought that there is a connection between the Western Queen Mother and the Queen of Sheba. Her palace in the Kunlun mountains has 'walls which are made of pure gold, three hundred and thirty miles in circumference, with crenelations of precious stones.' According to the *History of Chou Dynasty*, Emperor Mu in 985 B.C. was entertained by the Queen of the West at the Lake of Gems, and Emperor Wu Ti of Han paid her a visit round about 100 B.C.

The Jade Emperor heads the hierarchy of deities in Popular Taoism.

The Star Gods. It was generally believed that the celestial sphere over the earth was divided into twenty-eight constellations in accordance with the Lunar Calendar. Over each constellation presides a star god. The most important of the star gods are the Gods of Happiness, Longevity, and Affluence.

The Star of Literature. There are actually supposed to be two Stars of Literature, who lived at the Ursa Major, or the Pole. One of them was Wen Chang, who was supposed to have been a renowned scholar of Tang Dynasty, and a native of Szechuan Province. He is usually portrayed wearing a blue gown with a sceptre in his hand, mounted on a white horse with two attendants, who are called 'Deaf to Heaven' and 'Dumb to Earth', who are guardians of his secret in the disposal of intellectual talent.

The Star of Literature mentioned in this novel is Kuei Shing, who was a deformed, repulsive-looking character, and a dwarf to boot.

However, he possessed a brilliant intellect, and won first place in the Imperial Examinations. But when he presented himself at the Palace to receive his award, his appearance so shocked the Emperor that he withheld the prize. The wretched scholar, in disappointment, tried to drown himself, but a sea-monster held him up, and carried him to heaven. The Star of Literature Kuei Shing is usually portrayed mounted on a lion, which is depicted playing with a worsted ball (in order to conserve the milk which exudes from its claws).

Maku was a beautiful girl of eighteen or nineteen whose hands were like a bird's claws. She became an 'Immortal' after she retreated to the mountains to cultivate her soul.

The Ocean of Transmigration is one of the features Popular Taoism acquired from Mahayana Buddhism. According to the latter, when a person dies, his soul survives and continues to exist, taking new forms one after another until it can free itself from the cravings which bind it to the needs of the body and other transitory concerns. This continued transmigration is known as the 'ocean of births and deaths' and also the 'bitter sea'. When the soul becomes free, it becomes 'immortal'. Characteristically, the line of division between deities, spirits and ordinary human beings are blurred, and ordinary people may acquire the divine estate if they acquire enough Tao.

The principles of Yin and Yang represent the positive and negative elements in the universe. It is believed that all life came into being due to the cause and effect of these elements, and the entire nature is governed by them.

CHAPTER 2

The Ruler on Earth. Mythologically speaking, it was generally understood that the earth was a flat plate, with an inverted bowl over it which contained the sun, moon and stars. There was no other country on earth than the Middle Country (Chung-kuo, or China), and the Middle Country was fringed by Lesser Breeds without the Law. The Ruler on Earth ruled by Divine wish. Needless to say, in Tang Dynasty, when the capital Changan was the cultural centre of the world, the people knew better.

Empress Wu Tse-tien was the only woman to rule China. She reigned in Tang Dynasty from 684 to 704 A.D. She entered the Palace first as a woman attendant – a lady of the sixth rank – and after sharing the bed of Emperor Taitsung, she shared that of his son, Emperor Kao-tsung. When Kao-tsung died, she usurped the throne from her own son, Emperor Chung-tsung, and declared herself 'Female Emperor'. She tried to found a dynasty of her own, and bring her own Wu family to power, and called her reign the Chou Dynasty.

Empress Wu was a woman of great intelligence and many sides, who ruled China with a cruel hand and was responsible for a reign of terror and political purges unprecedented in Chinese history. At the same time, she was admired by her subjects for her great intelligence. She was in her sixties when she became 'Female Emperor', and retained her amazing vigour almost to her death at the age of eighty-three. She was particularly notorious for keeping a harem of young men. In the end, it was the people's hate for two gigolos which prompted the ministers at court to effect a *coup d'état* and force her to abdicate in favour of her son.

The nether world, or the *nine streams,* refer to the place the spirits go when people die.

Fangchow, where Emperor Chung-tsung was banished, is in present-day Hupei province.

Shu Ching-yeh was the grandson of Archduke Li Chi, who presided at the coronation of Empress Wu, and also called himself Li Ching-yeh. When the Rebellion led by scholars met with defeat, Shu tried to escape to the sea coast and flee by boat to Korea. In this novel, Shu's son and niece were found in the waters of the Country of Scholars. It is not known whether Shu's family went there. But while waiting for the boat, Shu himself was assassinated by one of his officers.

Lo Pinwang was the author of the famous Declaration of War, which has become a classic piece of prose. The document caused Empress Wu to say, when she read it, 'It is a shame that such literary talent should have been overlooked. It is the fault of my Ministers,' although its content was devoted to charging the Empress with lack of morals and misrule.

Changan is in the present-day Sian in Shensi Province. In Tang Dynasty, it was known as the Western Capital while Loyang was known as the Eastern Capital. In Tang Dynasty, Changan was the centre of the world, and cultural streams from all directions converged there. Women at this time enjoyed greater liberties than before, and even played polo. Their intellectual activities were encouraged by Empress Wu and Empress Wei, who had a direct hand in the promotion of writing verse among the ladies.

Emperor Chung-tsung was the weakest of Empress Wu's four sons by Emperor Kao-tsung. She had him made Crown Prince after she murdered one son, and banished the other two. Two months after Chung-tsung, at the age of twenty-eight, ascended to the throne, his mother arrested him and had him literally dragged from the throne by palace soldiers. He was forthwith declared Prince of Luling, and deposed. A month later, he was banished to Fangchow. Chung-tsung had already lost his wife at the hands of his mother.

But being weak-willed, he was hesitant even when the rebels had poured troops into the capital, and were going to put him back in power. After he was restored to the throne in 705 A.D., he ruled for only four years.

Princess Taiping had many of the qualities of her mother, Empress Wu. Together, they shared a weakness for members of the opposite sex, as well as for intrigues and cabals. When her husband, Shui Shou, was killed in the Prince's Rebellion, she wanted to marry her cousin Yuchi. Her mother conveniently had Yuchi's wife killed. Princess Taiping and Empress Wu also shared the amenities of the Chang brothers, the notorious gigolos they kept in the male harem.

Shangkuan Waner was the daughter of the poet Shangkuan Yi, who was condemned to die for trying to induce Emperor Kao-tsung to get rid of Empress Wu. The family was turned into slaves to work in official households. Waner grew up in the Palace, and became a lady of rank. She was distinguished for her literary talent, and from the year 696 began to draft Empress Wu's edicts. When Chung-tsung was restored to the throne, she served for a time as Chief Examining Official in the Imperial Examinations. She, however, was also attracted by the gigolo Chang Tsang-tsung. One day, they were found together by Empress Wu, who immediately took a golden pocket-knife and brandished it at the girl, cutting her on the forehead. The gigolo Tsang-tsung went down on his knees to beg for forgiveness on her behalf. Waner never tried to flirt with him again, at least she was not caught by Empress Wu, but later, she shared a lover with Chung-tsung's Empress.

CHAPTER 3

li. One *li* equals one third of a mile.

The Wheel of Karma is based on the Buddhist concept that one's moral conduct and good character determine the form one takes in the next rebirth in the 'ocean of transmigration', or that a person's destiny can turn from 'good' to 'bad' and vice versa according to the cumulative effects of his character and conduct. By building a good 'foundation' of good conduct and character, a person may eventually free himself from the wheel of rebirth, and work toward his ultimate union with 'Tao', or become an Immortal. The Wheel is popularly believed to be divided into six sections, three 'bad' and three 'good'. This is an example of some of the features of Buddhism getting mixed up in Popular Taoism.

CHAPTER 4

The Kingdom on Earth. In this novel China was called *Tien Tsao*, or the Celestial Kingdom. In order to distinguish it from the celestial world of the fairies and spirits, however, I have called it the Kingdom on Earth, since, in the fashion of ancient mythology, the characters in this book do not acknowledge the existence of any other country on earth. The Kingdom on Earth was surrounded by islands on which lived 'uncivilized' breeds.

The Ten Provinces. China was divided during the Tang Dynasty into ten provinces. Lingnan occupied the present Kwangtung and Kwangsi Provinces on the southern coast.

The equal of nine-fold magic properties means that a metal has been transmuted nine times. Popular Taoism emphasized the technique for realizing the effects which flow from Tao, especially long life, and Chang Taoling antedated the West in looking for the philosopher's stone. A metal which has undergone transmutation once is supposed to make the Taoist who swallows it an Immortal in three years. A metal which has been transmuted nine times makes the Taoist who swallows it an Immortal in three days.

CHAPTER 5

Hsiu-tsai is the title which is given to a scholar of the lowest rank who has passed only the county level of the Imperial Civil Service Examinations.

Imperial Examinations. In Imperial China, Civil Service Examinations were held once every three years at the capital. Scholars, who traditionally sought an official career, had to pass the Examinations with high honours to be awarded official posts. Those who passed only the local, or county Examinations were usually the brunt of many jokes, and like Tang Min, resorted to teaching as a career. The scholar who took first place at the Palace Examinations was called *Chuang-yuan,* and as the first scholar of the land, was immediately famous, and awarded high official position, and sometimes even managed to marry a Princess. The man who took second place was called *Pang-yen,* and third place, *Tan-hua,* which is the position Tang Ao wins in this story.

Destiny. The word 'destiny' occurs many times in this novel. When Tang Min tells Little Hill, 'If it isn't in one's destiny to become prominent in life, there is nothing a person can do about it,' it is an illustration of Taoist philosophy in its purer form. In the chapter called 'Destiny and Effort' in *Liehtse,* the difference between the two is defined as follows :

'Your achievements are not equal to mine,' said Effort (to Destiny).

'Please tell me, what do you achieve in the working of things?' asked Destiny, 'that you would compare yourself with me?'

'Why, the length of man's life, his measure of success, rank and wealth, are all things which I have the power to determine,' said Effort.

To this, Destiny replied, 'Peng Tsu's wisdom did not exceed that of Yao and Shun (the 'perfect' Emperors), yet he lived to the age of eight hundred. Yen Yuan's ability was not inferior to that of the average man, yet he died at thirty-two. The virtue of Confucius was not less than that of the feudal princes, yet he was reduced to poverty between Chen and Tsai. The conduct of Chou of Yin Dynasty did not surpass that of the Three Men of Virtue, yet he occupied a kingly throne . . . If these are the results of your efforts, how do you explain that you allow long life to Peng Tsu and give untimely death to Yen Yuan, that you awarded straitened circumstances to the sage, and success to the impious, humiliation to the wise man and high honour to the fool . . .?'

'If you say I have really no control over events, is it not due to *your* management of things that they turn out as they do?' retorted Effort.

Destiny replied, 'The very name Destiny implies that there is no question of management. When the way is straight, I follow it; when it is crooked, I yield to it. Old age and early death, failure and success, high rank and low, riches and poverty . . . all these come naturally of themselves. How can I know anything about them?'

The Dream Spirit was invented by Li Ju-chen to convey the idea of illusion in life. In *Liehtse* in the chapter called 'Dreams', it is said,

Lao Cheng Tsu went to learn magic from the venerable Yin Wen. After three years, having obtained no communication from him, Lao Cheng Tsu humbly asked permission to go home. Yin Wen bowed and led him to the inner apartment. There, having dismissed his attendants, he said, 'Long ago, when Laotse was setting out on his journey to the West, he told me, "All that has the breath of life, all that possesses bodily form, is mere Illusion. The point at which creation begins, the change effected by Yin and Yang, are called life and death. That which underlies the manifold workings of Destiny is called Evolution; that which produces and transforms bodily substance is called Illusion. The ingenuity of the Creative Power is mysterious, and its operations are profound. In truth, it is inexhaustible and eternal. The eye is patent to the ingenuity of that which causes material form, and its operations are superficial. Therefore, it rises anon, and anon it vanishes . . ." Only one who knows that Life is Illusion, and Death is Evolution, can begin to learn magic from me. You and I are both Illusions. What need, then, to make a study of it?'

Lao Cheng Tsu went home and for three months pondered deeply over the words of Yin Wen. Subsequently, he acquired the power of appearing or disappearing at will, and could reverse the order of the four seasons, produce thunder storms in winter and ice in summer, make flying things creep and creeping things fly. But to the end of his days he never told the secret of his heart, so that it is not handed down to us.

From this, it can be seen how Liehtse embroidered on the philosophy of Laotse by inventing parables to elucidate it. But throughout, Liehtse was true to the philosophical treatise of the Master.

Making a foundation for Tao means that before a person may attempt to 'find Tao', he must first make himself worthy by laying a 'moral foundation' from which progress toward the goal may be built. This means that his conduct must be righteous, he must be honest, ethically reputable, charitable, etc. The aim is to destroy the selfish craving in oneself. By righteous speech, conduct and vocation, one pledges one's readiness to order his daily life in a manner consistent with his announced goal.

The seven emotions and six desires. The seven emotions are joy, anger, grief, fear, love, hate, and greed. The six desires are sexual desire, desire for beauty, desire for status, desire for flattery, desire for material comfort, desire for acclaim.

Immortals. In the popular Taoist hierarchy, there are eight hundred divinities and innumerable Immortals. They are divided into three classes, Saints (Shengjen), Spirits (Chenjen) and Immortals (Shienjen). According to the popular belief, a person can become an Immortal after he has prepared a moral foundation, when he usually repairs to the mountains to live as a recluse, and 'contemplate' or 'cultivate' Tao. One who is trying to become an Immortal aims by power of absolute concentration to free the mind from the sudden promptings and unpredictable flittings due to selfish craving. Usually, one cultivates Tao by sitting in one position and meditating. When he achieves his goal, he is no longer subject to rebirth. In Buddhism, he enters Nirvana, which is to be in a state of oneness with reality.

A perfect mortal, or *ti-hsien,* is literally a fairy of the earth, as opposed to *tien-hsien,* a fairy of Heaven.

CHAPTER 6

Cultivating abstention from food is practised during periods of meditation. People may sit for days without moving or eating, 'contemplating Tao'.

CHAPTER 7

One catty is equal to one and a third pounds.

Neglected her parents because of her husband. According to Confucian concepts, it is wrong to be more devoted to one's spouse than to one's parents. In this passage emphasizing filial piety, the author is more Confucian than Taoist.

CHAPTER 8

Birds' nests are a delicacy which are eaten in China much as caviar is eaten in the west – because of its rarity. Actually, only the gelatinous substance, on which the mother-swallow feeds its young, is eaten. This substance is collected from birds' nests, and after much soaking and cleaning, is taken either in chicken broth, or with rock sugar as a 'cooling' tonic. It has no taste in itself.

sea-slugs (stichopus japonicus) are also called bêches-de-mer. Sea-slugs are consumed for the same reason as birds' nests and sharks' fins, because they are a delicacy, although they have no food value of their own. It is not clear what Flowering Maple's mother was suffering from, but in China, they are not as a rule regarded as having medicinal properties. Sea-slugs usually come in dehydrated form, and are as hard as rocks and may be stored indefinitely. When they are wanted, they must be soaked and boiled for days before they are soft enough to eat. Then they are cleaned, and look like small pieces of rubber tyre. They may be cooked in many different ways, and are eaten by gourmets for their consistency, which can be gelatinous, crisp and crunchy, or gooey, depending on the method of preparation.

CHAPTER 9

Keepers of temples. The author here is making fun of the monks and nuns who only show outward piety without true religion. Monks and nuns in China are not accorded the reverence which their counterparts are in the West. When Buddhism was introduced to China, many monks interfered in politics, and nuns became concubines of Princes. Taoist nuns and monks, on the other hand, are known for their poverty and are sometimes treated like beggars. Many who beg on the streets are indeed little more.

CHAPTER 10

Scholars are sour by nature. Li Ju-chen took special delight in making fun of scholars, who, whether in the East or in the West, are very sparing in their praise of each other's work. There is a saying in China : 'The other man's wife is always better-looking than one's own, but one's own writing is always better than the other man's,' which truth may be observed when an author reviews another author's book, especially if they happen to be specialists in the same field !

Basin of wick and incense. This was used to tell the time. People measured a coil of incense as it burned.

The Country of Scholars. In this passage, the author, who was only a scholar of the lowest rank, is speaking up for mass education. In the Imperial Examinations, subject matter was limited to the writing of prose and poetry.

The thrifty scholar Ru. Here again, the author is poking fun at scholars who literally 'give nothing away'.

Exposing one's face to the public was not allowed for unmarried girls of good family in olden times.

CHAPTER 11

Pellets are shot from an arch called the *tiao-kung* which achieve the same kind of effect as shotguns.

CHAPTER 12

Boy's urine as medicine. Startling as this may seem, certain properties in urine are regarded in Chinese medicine to be good for reducing fever. A boy's urine is used because it is 'cleaner' than a girl's, and has not the impurities of a man's. At the time the novel was written, urine was as much used in many parts of Europe as in China for medicinal purposes. Today, its properties are still cherished by some Westerners, who value it for the treatment of chilblains and insect bites, among other things.

Rhyme scheme. This was an attempt to break down the Chinese language phonetically. The lists consist of Chinese characters or combinations of characters to represent a breakdown of consonant sounds in the vertical column, and vowel sounds in the horizontal column. Here, I have used the translation made by the phonetician Chien Hsuen-tung, which appeared in the preface written by Dr Hu Shih in the Yatung Library edition of the book published in Shanghai in 1932. The transliteration into the International Phonetic Alphabet is derived from *Kuo-yin Chu Yin Tse Mu* or the phonetic symbols of Kuo-yu (Mandarin) sponsored by the Chinese Government. The breaking down of the Chinese language into thirty-three consonants was Li Ju-chen's chief contribution to phonetics, although *Who's Who in China* does not give him credit for being an expert in this field. In his preface, however, Dr Hu wrote, 'The author lived in a time when attention to phonetics was paid mostly to classical and ancient pronunciation, and he was the first man to pay attention to current phonetics. He does not deserve the dismissal as a phonetician that *Who's Who in China* gave him.'

It was the idea of the author that if a person memorized these two lists of sounds, by cross-reference, any word may be 'spelled' phonetically. If a number is given to each sound, people may talk to each other in a sort of code, in which case the author notes that a number must be given also to each of the tonal values in the language. Thus, 33–22–1 might 'spell' the word *chuang,* meaning *hamlet.*

Actually, the breaking down of words and trying to spell them phonetically dates back to the 5th century. It is called *fan chieh,* and the system is in current use in Chinese dictionaries, to indicate the pronunciation of characters.

CHAPTER 13

Bound feet. Foot-binding in China went out with the Ching Dynasty. In its heyday, the custom was never universally practised in China, and Empress Wu herself did not have bound feet. To bind a foot, bend all except the big toe under the sole by snapping the bones in the arch. Use yards of foot-binding cloth to bind the foot so that it keeps its shape. After many weeks, the bindings are taken off, and if the foot retains the shape desired, the task is deemed accomplished. Henceforth, the foot must be kept constantly bound, in order to prevent it from growing bigger. Although the process was painful, mothers eagerly bound their daughters' feet when fashion prescribed it. A woman with bound feet was forced to walk in dainty, swaying steps, which emphasized her other physical attributes.

Pan An and *Sung Yu* were famous for their good looks in ancient times.

CHAPTER 14

Astrology and Fortune-telling. Chinese astrology was based on the twenty-eight constellations, which exerted influence over the weather and affairs of mankind.

When a person draws a lot, or sliver of bamboo from a fortune-teller's bamboo container, it bears a number. An oracle with the corresponding number is supplied, which, besides bearing a message, notes whether the man in question's fortune is 'Up', 'Middling', or 'Down'. Each category is subdivided into 'Up and Up', 'Middling Up', and 'Down Up', etc.

A fortune-teller also determines one's future by taking into consideration a man's *five elements,* i.e., gold, wood, water, fire and earth, which guide his destiny, as well as the hour, day, month and year of his birth. The whole is known as *Pa-kua,* or the Eight Trigrams, which looks like this:

360 combinations are possible. In the centre the figure represents the 'limitless circle' of *Yin* and *Yang*.

Propitious Days are determined by taking cognisance of the five seasons, the elements, colours, parts of the body, animals and tastes which control and influence one another.

In navigation, a *lo-pan* or 'reticulated plate' was used. A magnetic compass about an inch in diameter was in the centre. The disc is inscribed with concentric circles, and the Eight Trigrams formed the inner circle. The whole arrangement is the synthesis of the conception of the harmony between the forces of nature, time-relation as indicated by the sun and moon, and the directions in space from any point on earth. As many as sixteen concentric circles may surround the compass, but there are usually fewer. The Eight Trigrams denote the evolution of nature and its cyclic changes. They represent heaven, water as in a lake, fire, thunder, wind, rain-water, hill, and earth. They also stand for eight animals: horse, goat, pheasant, dragon, fowl, swine, dog and ox, and the points of the compass.

In the next circle are the twenty-four hills, which are divided into three parts, from which derive the fortnightly climatic periods of the solar cycle and the twenty-four characters. This is known as Trench Hill over the Land Line. Next come sevent-two lines, each divided into five parts, representing the five elements, making three-hundred and sixty combinations which are called the Over-sky Lines. Outside are the twenty-eight constellations.

Such a plate was made of wood, or baked clay.

CHAPTER 15

Talotien is the uppermost stratosphere where Immortals reside.

The Yellow Emperor is a legendary figure. For a time, Taoism was known as the philosophy of Huang-Lao (Huangti is the Yellow Emperor). In Book III, *Liehtse*, it is said that the Yellow Emperor, after sitting on the throne for fifteen years, grew melancholy although he was careful of his physical well-being, sought pleasures for his ears and eyes, gratified his senses of smell and taste, and the empire held him in high regard. He sighed and said, 'The misery I suffer comes from over-attention to myself and the empire from over-regulation of everything.' Thereupon, he retired to live in seclusion, and for three months abstained from government. He fell asleep, and dreamed that he journeyed to the Kingdom of Hua-hsu, 'which was beyond the reach of sleep, or vehicle, or any mortal foot. Only the soul could travel so far'. There, the people had no head or ruler, and things simply went on by themselves. 'Its people were without desires or cravings; they simply followed their natural instincts. They felt neither joy in life nor abhorrence of death. Thus, they came to no untimely ends. They felt neither attachment to self nor indifference to others, thus they were free from love and hate alike. They knew neither aversion from one course nor inclination to another, and were untouched by the emotions of love and sympathy, jealousy and fear. Water had no power to drown them, or fire to burn . . .' When the Yellow Emperor woke up, he told his ministers that he realized that the 'Perfect Way' was not to be found through the gratification of the senses. 'This Way I know, and hold within me, yet I cannot impart it to you.'

In the time of Prince Huainan in Han Dynasty, Emperor Wen tried to practise the policy of letting people govern themselves, in other words, leaving them alone, and the record of peaceful government during his reign was proof of the effect of Taoism on administration.

Rock Fungus, or *polyporus ludicus*, is a cryptogram of the lichen family which does not have flowers, but roots, stems and fronds.

CHAPTER 16

Decrees for the welfare of women. These express the author's aspirations for women at a time when women had no such social benefits. Empress Wu issued no such decrees.

Imperial Examinations for women. No such examinations were ever held, although Empress Wu did encourage the writing of poetry and prose among women scholars, both at Court in the Forbidden City, and outside. It is known that in Tang Dynasty, a large number of talented women lived in the Forbidden City, and spent their pent-up emotions in writing poetry. An Emperor was entitled to one Queen, four Imperial Concubines, nine Consorts, nine Graces, four Beautifies, five Selects, and twenty-seven of each of three grades of palace maids, all of whom were known as the ladies of the back court. A lady who did not catch the eye of the Emperor was very likely to spend her life in idleness and frustration, cut off as she was from the outside world.

Sheng Li is one of the royal designations of the years of Empress Wu's reign.

The Banquet of Flowers was a ceremonial dinner at which successful candidates gathered in the Palace to celebrate their new-won honours, when two handsome candidates were selected to visit the palatial gardens and parks, and gather specimens of beautiful flowers. The custom started in the Tang Dynasty.

Szema Hsiangju was a renowned scholar and poet of the Han Dynasty.

CHAPTER 17

Clear tinder, or *chih tsao,* is a type of mushroom with the latin name of *fromes ludicus.* In the search for the elixir of life, Taoists wrote many books, some of which are still extant. Most of the recipes for long life stressed the consumption of rare plants such as this one, and pineseeds.

The turning of the head means the 'awakening' of the spirit, which enables the human being to leave behind the realm of unstable, transitory and illusory life.

The Country of Husbands. Li Ju-chen did not elaborate on the travellers' experiences in this country. Li himself was twice married. His first wife died before he was twenty, and he married the sister of a friend at Haichow when he went there to live with his brother. One can only surmise that he bypassed such a fertile ground for satire because the experience left him speechless.

CHAPTER 19

Chuan characters are an ancient style of writing, sometimes also called 'seal' characters.

Blue-purse is by the author's own admission a mythical flower which is based on a pun, while *loru, shui-sheng* and *ying-nien* could not be discovered in any dictionary or encyclopedia.

'Face and Head'. The story goes that in the North-South Dynasty, Princess Shan Yin asked her brother, the Emperor Liu Yi Fu why, although he had so many wives, she had only one husband. The Emperor therefore presented her with thirty handsome men to be her 'Faces and Heads' meaning that they were handsome in the face, and had a full head of hair.

Chapter 21

Protocol soap was made of goose fat. Low-ranking officials or newly appointed ones who were meeting the Emperor for the first time were escorted into the Presence by protocol officials, who wore this soap on their faces to give them lustre.

Burning paper money as well as other earthly material comforts, such as effigies of servants, all kinds of furniture and modes of conveyance, for the dead to use in the nether world, is a custom of Taoists and Buddhists and reflects the Chinese matter-of-fact attitude regarding the supernatural or unknown world. In the same manner, a pudding made of glutinous rice, sweet and sticky, would be offered to seal the lips of the kitchen god at New Year, so that he would not tell *everything* he saw go on in the family kitchen to powers greater than he is.

Chapter 23

Besides those who are listed at the beginning of the book, the cast of characters is as follows :

The ten sons and four daughters of the family of Governor Chang Ken :

Prince's Feather
  his fiancée High Spring
Mushroom
  his fiancée Melting Spring
Asarum
  his fiancée Glorious Spring
Hibiscus
  his fiancée Fragrant Spring
Basil
  his fiancée Brocade Spring
Wildhop
  his fiancée Complaisant
  Spring
Bignonia
  his fiancée Luxurious Spring

Parsley
  his fiancée Graceful Spring
Fragrant Weed
  his fiancée Beautiful Spring
Artemisia
  his fiancée Fair Spring
Fragrant Orchid
  her fiancé Nobel
Fragrant Marsh Orchid
  her fiancé Ultimate
Fragrant Jade
  her fiancé Ocean
Fragrant Moon
  her fiancé Tide

The five sons and two daughters of Governor Wen Yin :

Honeybush
  his fiancée Beautiful Orchid
Sedge
  his fiancée Red Feather
Shepherd's Purse
  his fiancée Red Jade
Cabbage
  his fiancée Fair Heroine
Senega
  his fiancée Noble Jade

Fragrant Book
  her fiancé Brave
Fragrant Ink
  her fiancé Extraordinary

Narrator, son of Governor Shih Yeh

Silver Moonlight and Jade Moonlight, daughters of Governor Tsai Tsung

Fragrant Plant
Completely Virtuous } nieces of Governor Tsai Tsung
Little Canary

Purple Jade
   her brother Courage
Lovely Tower }
Baby Phoenix   her cousins

Jade Clasp, who lost her Examination papers

The ten young ladies who were late for their Imperial Examinations:

Quest-for-Seclusion	Orchid Language
Fragrant Grass	Virtuous Beauty
Profound Fish	Charming Beauty
Literary Brocade	Wide Celebration
Brocade Heart	Good Omen

The offspring of Examining Officials :

The Pien family :

Precious Cloud	Fragrant Cloud
Rainbow Cloud	White Cloud
Brocade Cloud	Green Cloud
Purple Cloud	Badge, the son

The Meng family :

Orchid Mushroom	Lustrous Mushroom
Bright Mushroom	Fairy Mushroom
Fragrant Mushroom	Purple Mushroom
Honeybush Mushroom	Jade Mushroom

The Chang family :

Spring Glory	Moon Glory
Autumn Glory	White Glory
Star Glory	Pretty Glory
Worthy, the son	

The Tung family :

Precious Ornament	Flowery Ornament
Pearl Ornament	Blue Ornament
Jade Ornament	

The Chiang family :

Red Pearl	Black Pearl
Many Pearls	River Pearl

The Lu family :
    Yellow Lily   Propitious Lily
    Fair Lily

The daughters of officials who were posted in Lingnan :
    Clever Prose   Orchid
    Country Smoke   Embroidered Field
    Painted Flower   Fragrance Returns

CHAPTER 24

The Book of Medical Plants or *Pen Tsao* was supposedly written by Shen Nung, the founder of Chinese medicine and Divine Husbandman, who reigned between 2838 and 2698 B.C. He was one of the triumvirate in the Taoist Ministry of Medicine, another of whom was the successor of Fu Hsi, the leader and discoverer of the Eight Trigrams. As the father of agriculture, he taught the cultivation of the five grains, examined a hundred herbs, and wrote the *Pen Tsao* which was the first treatise on the healing art. Today, the book still serves as the encyclopedia of Chinese medical plants. It was the subject of extensive research by Chinese and European scientists in the 1930s.

The Tapestry poem is the pride and joy of Li Ju-chen. It is, unfortunately, impossible to translate. The poem may be read backwards and forwards, up and down, in squares, whorls, diagonally and in a dozen other combinations.

The prose-poem, or *fu*, is a piece of writing which adheres to a set of prerequisites regarding number of words in a sentence, tonal value, rhyming, and contrast. Szema Hsiangju is generally considered to be the master of this form of composition.

CHAPTER 26

The Method of Difference is a form of differential calculus.

CHAPTER 27

The Fairy of Long Fingers is Maku, who had fingers which resembled the claws of a bird.

The flying carriage was one of Li Ju-chen's brain-children. Perhaps he foresaw the present-day helicopter?

CHAPTER 28

Chang Chang-tsung and Chang I-chih were the two gigolos kept by Empress Wu, who led to her downfall. These notorious brothers were in their twenties when they became the Empress's 'mistresses', and she was seventy-five. They were both fair-skinned and remarkably handsome. They were given mansions and huge estates, but practically lived in the palace. As a result of taking aphrodisiacs which I-chih gave her, Empress Wu grew a new set of eyebrows at the age of seventy-six. The story was created by Empress Wu that Chang-tsung had been a Taoist Immortal in his previous incarnation, and he dressed in a feather coat, and rode around the Palace grounds on a wooden stork, playing a flute, to the admiration of all. Privilege went to the heads of the brothers, and when the Empress was in her eighties, they tried to found a dynasty of their own, and interfered with the administration of the countries. When Chang-tsung consulted a fortune-teller about his own chances of becoming emperor, the Ministers charged him with treason, which explained the reason the official Li Tuo-tso said to the Empress during the *coup d'état*, 'I-chih and Chang-tsung are guilty of treason,' which occurs at the end of the book. During the *coup*, both gigolos were beheaded, and their heads were later prominently displayed at the Tientsin Bridge. Their brothers and cousins, who were all hated, were executed in public.

The twelfth pulse. According to Chinese medicine, there are twelve pulses in the body, six in the arms and six in the legs. The twelfth pulse is the one from which the circulation of the liver flows, and therefore, from which liver disease can be diagnosed.

Seven men in Chou Dynasty costumes. These are Chi Kang, Yuan Chi, Shan Tao, Hsiang Hsiu, Liu Ling, Yuan Hieh and Wang Jung, poets and Taoist philosophers of the Chin Dynasty (3rd century) who were 'men without restraint, whose eyes were above all the world', who led unconventional lives and avoided being entangled with the politics and chaos of their time.

The Incomplete Mountain. The mythical Empress Nu Kua had among her vassals one King King, who wanted to extend his power, and fought against Chu Yung, but lost the battle. In his anger, he knocked his head against the Pu Chou mountain and died. The pillars of the sky cracked, and the fibre of the earth was damaged. Nu Kua melted stones of five colours to mend the sky, and cut down the legs of the monstrous tortoise to uphold its four extremities, and spread the ashes of reeds to stop the flood. This story is to be found in *Liehtse*.

Talismans, or charms to ward off evil are a feature of Popular Taoism, and sold by Taoist priests to supplement their income. A talisman may cure a toothache or headache, or protect a person against evil spirits. They are usually made of a piece of yellow paper with writing on it which has been waved over burning incense and prayed upon by a priest.

CHAPTER 29

Streets of flowers and willows, and mulberry groves all mean houses of ill repute.

CHAPTER 31

Descendant of Laotse. When the author says that he is the descendant of Laotse, he means that they both had the surname of Li.

Three thousand universes. According to popular Buddhism, there are three thousand universes, one thousand small, one thousand medium sized, and a thousand large ones, over which there are other universes. All this implies that the creation is boundless and beyond imagination.

'Richly ambivalent and mysterious . . .'
Washington Post

KISS OF THE SPIDER WOMAN
Manuel Puig

'Manuel Puig is one of the most consistently interesting novelists to have emerged anywhere during the past ten years.'   *The New York Times Book Review*

Prisoner 3018, Luis Alberto Molina. Sentenced July 20, 1974. Condemned to eight years' imprisonment for corruption of minors. Transferred on April 4, 1975, to Pavilion D, cell 7. Conduct good.

Detainee 16115, Valentin Arregui Paz. Arrested October 16, 1972. Held under Executive Power of the Federal Government and awaiting judgment. Transferred on April 4, 1975, to Pavilion D, cell 7. Conduct reprehensible.

Sometimes they talk all night long. In the still darkness of their cell, Molina re-weaves the glittering and fragile stories of the films he loves, and the cynical Valentin listens. Each, in his way, is a dreamer. But Valentin believes in the just cause which makes all suffering bearable; and Molina believes in the magic of romantic love which makes all else endurable. Each, in his way, has always been alone, and always — especially now — in danger of betrayal. But in cell 7, as the long days and longer nights move inevitably on, each slowly surrenders to the other something of himself that he has never surrendered before.

'Puig dazzles one with sheer technical ability'
Newsday

ARENA

WINTER'S TALE

Mark Helprin

A haunting rhapsody of imagination –
A white horse that learns to fly
A chase that lasts one hundred years
A beautiful consumptive girl asleep on a mansion roof
A mile-long ship to build a bridge of light to infinity
An apocalyptic fire that heralds the millennium
A dazzling epic of lovers and dreamers, eccentrics and
    beauties, madmen and geniuses . . .

'Massive fantasy-saga . . . this extraordinary work,
defying synopsis, vaults time and space'
Sunday Telegraph

'Utterly extraordinary . . . a piercing sense of the
beautiful . . . funny, thoughtful, passionate'
New York Times

'Prodigiously inventive imagination and dazzling use
of words . . . a cascade of brilliant, sensuous images'
Publishers Weekly

ARENA

KOKORO

Natsume Soseki

When the old values meet the new in Japan

In Tokyo a lonely young student from the provinces is befriended by a sophisticated older man. Yet the man himself is lonely too. For a dark shadow from his past makes him feel like a mummy left in the midst of living beings. Even the man's wife has never penetrated this tragic mystery.

Then one day the student is dramatically taken into his mentor's confidence . . .

In this beautiful, evocative portrait of Japan at the turn of the century, Natsume Soseki explores the tragic conflicts between old and new, love and duty, friendship and self-interest.

Natsume Soseki is regarded as the greatest novelist of the Meiji era, when Japan began to blend Western culture with oriental traditions.

'One of the most important Japanese writers of the modern period'   *The Times Literary Supplement*

'Exquisite. The novel represents the moment at which the limitations and gifts of the native genius triumphed over an alien literature' *New York Times*

THE DREAD AFFAIR
Collected poems

Benjamin Zephaniah

FIGHT DEM
ESS DOUBLE YOU NINE (BRIXTON)
CAN'T KEEP A GOOD DREAD DOWN
NICE ONE HANDSWORTH
THE BOAT IS SINKING
GANJA ROCK
THE DAY DAT I MET LADY DI
DIS POLICEMAN KEEPS ON KICKING ME TO DEATH
etc.

THE DREAD AFFAIR

poems for now

Benjamin Zephaniah has a lot to say. His humour, anger, passion and contentiousness have already established him as one of the most important and popular of Britain's new wave of performing poets. His poems speak for themselves.

AKÉ
Wole Soyinka

'What if V. S. Naipaul was a happy man? . . . What if
Vladimir Nabokov had grown up in a small town in
Western Nigeria and decided that politics were not
unworthy of him? . . . *Aké* locates the lost child in all
of us, underneath language, inside sound and smell,
wide-eyed, brave and flummoxed. What Waugh
made fun of and Proust felt bad about, Mr Soyinka
celebrates . . . Brilliant'   John Leonard,
The Sunday Times

'A superb act of remembrance . . . dazzling reading
. . . *Aké* has an enchanting effect . . . Soyinka's
memoir makes everything seem wondrous'
Village Voice

'Enchanting' *The Observer*

VIRGINIE
Her Two Lives
John Hawkes

She is in her eleventh year and at the eleventh hour of her innocence. She lives in two worlds, two centuries apart; parallel lives in which dream and reality fuse as one, in which purity and decadence, innocence and knowledge, heart and mind must meet.

VIRGINIE

'Hawkes' serene, inviolable prose is so precise, luminous and evocative as to make this novel seem dreamed rather than read . . . troubling, strange, a marvel'
Angela Carter

'This is the stuff of fable and romance . . . a celebration'
New York Times Book Review

'Lyrical and elegant' *The Literary Review*

'A lush, erotic masterpiece' Robert Coover

**Winner of the BBC Bookshelf/Arrow First Novel
Competition**

LORD OF THE DANCE
Robin Lloyd-Jones

'A picaresque novel of astonishing imaginative
brilliance'
The Times

In India, in 1575, Thomas Coryat, English surgeon
and rationalist, searches for a cure for his dying wife.
With him is his boyhood friend, Frog, a lustful priest
seeking to save the souls of those he loathes. Confront-
ing them is an alien world: the exotic, violent India of
the Moghul Empires, a world of peasants and lords,
courts and villages, warriors and travelling players,
warlords and princesses.

Colourful, rich, erotic and mysterious, funny and
tragic, *Lord of the Dance* is a magnificent creation, at
once a brilliant picaresque adventure and a profound
literary achievement.

'A marvellously readable, richly colourful adventure
. . . written with style, character, and deft touches of
philosophy, humour and irony!' *Sunday Express*

'Rollicking, ribald, truly imaginative the way Dickens, for example, is imaginative and real'
The Washington Post Book World

OCTOBER LIGHT
John Gardner

She has a crafty tongue, his sister, Sally Page Abbott, even for an old woman. Might've been a preacher or a Congressman, if the Lord in His infinite wisdom hadn't seen fit to send her down as a female, to minimize the risk. He'd told her that, once. After she'd preached him a sermon off television about the Equal Rights Amendment. 'Why, a woman ain't even completely human,' he'd said to her. 'Look how weak they are! Look how they cry like little children!'

It was because of foolish arguments like that James Page had loaded his shotgun while his sister sat stupidly grinning into the flickering light, and without a word of warning, he'd blown that TV screen to hell, right back where it came from. Then he had chased her into her room with a firewood club, and locked her in. Let her cry. There Sally Page Abbott, eating apples and reading an old paperback about a world of sex, drugs and violence far from the farm, carries on her war with her brother. But she isn't crying at all.

'Marvelous . . . John Gardner's most touching and accessible novel'
The New York Times

'Dazzling . . . Profound . . . Superb . . . As rewarding as it is entertaining'
Los Angeles Times

SADLER'S BIRTHDAY
Rose Tremain

'Deeply felt, intelligent . . . touchingly funny'
Angus Wilson

Sadler had come to the house as the Second World War began. He was thirty-nine then, the perfect butler, a man who knew his place and what his world was all about. Today, on the day that might be his seventy-sixth birthday, Jack Sadler woke in what once had been the Colonel's room, but which, like the rest of the house, was now his. The Colonel and Madge, of course, were long dead. Like everything else. As Sadler himself soon would be. Unless fate tricked him and he managed to live another twenty years in his ghastly old body, in his empty old house. 'But all I can say, God, if you're there,' he said aloud, 'is I hope not.'

From the author of *The Cupboard* and *Letter to Sister Benedicta*, an unforgettable novel of loneliness and loss written with sensitivity, compassion and humour.

'A rather special work, a simple novel that dwells lovingly upon the details of simple lives without condescension or bitterness . . . a *tour de force,*
Joyce Carol Oates, *New York Times Book Review*